To
Tr~ ~J.

CUTTING ties

ANNIE JO HAWNER

Annie Jo Hawner

Cover designed by Annie Jo Hawner
Edited by Iris Peony Editing and Rian Haf Kemp
Formatted by Annie Jo Hawner

For the original 'Annie Jo Hawner'; my Nan.

Thank you for introducing me to Eurotrash.

Annie Jo Hawner

Prologue

s the subtle reflection of my features become visible on the phone screen, I realize I've failed. The words of yet another rejection fade into blackness, taking with it my last shred of hope and leaving me with no choice but to look at myself and accept that it's all over. Tom was victorious. He did exactly what he said he would do.

'... We wish you the best of luck in all your future endeavours.'

Yeah, I bet you do. *Asshole.*

I press the lock button hard and drop my head onto the counter, hitting my forehead a couple of times. I can't avoid the agitation and frustration. I guess it's better than the sadness and anger I used to feel whenever I was rejected. I doubt they even listened to it. Yet another demo I have spent hours on in the studio making sure it was absolutely perfect, utterly wasted. I've convinced myself that every company has a blocked list, with my name sitting right at the top, in bold, highlighted, and underlined, to make sure no one risks signing me. Not me, oh no. Tom's made certain that no label will touch me after his lies.

"Remi," my mom's hand quickly creates a cushion between my head and the countertop, "stop. You're not wearing a hole in this granite."

My sister, Riley, chuckles beside me as I lift my head to look at her, putting an end to my tiny pity party, "Take it, it was another no?"

"Yeah…" I mumble, fed up with the fact that this has happened again.

"Assholes."

"Riley!" mom warns, placing a fresh cup of strong black coffee on the counter she was so determined to protect my head from getting hurt. "Here, drink this." I offer her a timid smile, loving how she always knows how to make something feel better. "Are all the big companies contacted now?"

"Yeah, Ryan is distributing my demos out to some smaller labels and talking to people, but nobody is biting... I might as well just give up now."

My mom raises one eyebrow and says, "absolutely not! You're not thinking like that. It nearly happened before it can happen again. And this time a cheating asshole won't get in the way!"

The good thing about my mom? She doesn't let you wallow.

"Amen to that!" Riley adds, pouting and agreeing like she's starring in her own episode of The View.

I lift my coffee, gripping it tightly with both hands, and slowly take a drink, grateful that I took Ryan's friend Mike up on his offer to work behind his bar. My parents are both practicing lawyers, but unlike them and Riley, I didn't go to college. I've wanted to be a musician and perform since I was a little girl. Though my parents have been my biggest supporters, I don't think that when they agreed to let me attend every dance class, have singing lessons, piano lessons, and guitar lessons, I would still have the same fantasy at twenty-three.

The bar is a stopgap, and not at all what I thought I would be doing at this age, but the extra money helps my parents cover the studio bills, and Mike, the owner, lets me perform new material for the customers from time to time.

"If me and Yasmine come to the bar tonight, will you give us beer?" Riley pulls me from my thoughts, leaning across the island and talking quietly while our mom has her back turned to us, cooking some breakfast for us all. Her optimism is amusing—

as well as stupid—because she has drunk in a bar with her best friend before, but not this one.

"Sure! Soda or root beer." Her enthusiasm diminishes instantly, replaced with the mother of all bitch faces. "You have like two months, Ri!"

"Exactly, so you can sneak me a drink early. What difference does sixty days make?"

"The difference between Mike losing his liquor license, me losing my job, and you ending up in jail." Admitting defeat but still not happy, she stands up and mouths '*Bitch*'. I mouth back '*Hoe*' earning a gasp of feigned horror before she reaches across to smack me playfully across the head. I lean back before she can make contact, retaliating by sticking my tongue out at her. We argue and fight, but I do love the crazy girl— even if she steals my clothes and has an opinion about everything I do.

Once it's all ready, my mom serves up the eggs, bacon, and waffles and sits down beside me at the island. We do this almost daily because, for so long, it has been just the three of us. My parents amicably separated when I was nine and Ri was six, when they realized that they had become more like best friends than spouses. Well, that, and my dad came out as gay. The dynamics of our family unit never changed until he met Terry and moved away, but our dad has always remained such a significant part of our lives.

"What time are your lessons starting today?" mom asks Ri, delicately cutting up her food and stacking up her fork, ready to take a bite.

"They're canceled."

"Again?! How do you ever learn anything?" I say, frowning at her.

"I have studying to do, just because I have no lectures."

"Good girl." mom mumbles, proud of her for staying focused when she could choose to go shopping instead.

As I take another mouthful, my phone starts vibrating on the counter beside me. I glance down and see the last name I expected, but one that makes me sit up in excitement.

"Who is it?"

I ignore my mom, swiping my finger along the bottom of the screen and holding it to my ear. "Lucy? What's going on?"

Her joyful laughter hits my ears, and she squeals down the phone at me. "Hi love! You alright?" Her cockney British tone instantly catapults me back to when we met. She was on vacation early last year with her fiancé Spencer; and I was performing in a local bar. They enjoyed it so much they came to speak to me afterwards, and we ended up spending the rest of the evening together talking as though we had been friends our entire lives. We spent more time together before they flew back home to London, so we haven't seen one another since, but she knows about everything that has happened.

I begin to answer, telling her how I am doing and asking her the same question, only moving away when I get an unimpressed glare from my mother. I step out of the kitchen and into the lounge, relaxing on the sofa. "Why are you calling me so early?"

"Well, I have a position in the bar that I wanted to talk to you about." she states, immediately turning from bubbly-friend Lucy to business Lucy, "I know it will be bloody perfect for you after all the shit with Tom. It will give you a chance to escape for a while. And if you like it, you can stay."

"Stay? Like, as in, stay there permanently?" *I don't know why she thinks I would want to escape.*

"Yeah, if you wanted to. Obviously, the selfish cow in me hopes that's what would happen." She laughs, and I can't help but join her.

"What's the position?"

"Performer, two evenings a week. The rest of the time you can work behind the bar if you want, but it's entirely up to you."

Wow. I mean, I understand why she thought of me, but England! Really? "I don't know Luce. I don't know if I want to be running away from here because of my ex."

"Babe, it's not just to get away from that knob'ead. It's to give yourself a clean slate. See what opportunities there are here for you, new audiences, all that stuff. You said it yourself: things are difficult there." *Sure, but not bad enough to elope!* I don't know if I can be so far away from my family like that. "Can I think about it?"

"Yes, of course, but Owen only promised to give you first refusal for a couple of days, then he's going to fill it." *Ah yes. Owen.* Her older brother, owner of the bar she manages, and according to her, an asshole with a capital A, but a successful asshole irrespectively.

"All right, I'll think about it and call you tomorrow."

"OK, bye, babe."

I say a gentle goodbye and sit there for a couple more minutes in contemplation. She's offered me the chance to move and work in London, but why should I run away when I have done nothing wrong? But will I always regret not going and seeing what happens? Like she said, new places bring new opportunities, and I seem to be running out of those fast in this place.

Maybe Tom hasn't won after all.

One

'*You only have one life, Remi, and a life with regrets is one not lived to its fullest. If it isn't you who succeeds, it will be someone else.*'

My mom's words repeat in my head, just as they have every day for years. She insisted I go and said she would have dragged me here had I not said yes. I have zero regrets, zero concerns, but walking out onto the steps of the plane wearing only my oversized sweats and Nike sneakers with my long dark hair coiled on top of my head, it's clear from the April showers that I'm far from the heat of home. *Welcome to England, Rem.*

The morning after Lucy called, I booked a one-way flight for a month's time, with the full support of my family and friends. If I couldn't work, then it would just be a holiday, and I'd book a return once I got here, but after three long weeks, all the documentation came through. And despite the gray, drizzling weather, I'm so excited!

I hold onto my guitar and backpack tightly running across the tarmac to the waiting buses. After what feels like an eternity, and a lot of walking down long corridors, I get my final bag off the carousel, load it onto the luggage carrier thing, and gently place my guitar on top. If anything happened to this, I would die.

As I turn the last corner of the maze that is Gatwick Airport, I see a small crowd of people waiting. I hear Lucy's voice before I see her. She squeals, jumps, and shrieks like a kid at Christmas, telling the world what my name is as her honey-highlighted hair bounces around her shoulders. As I reach them, she grabs me in a strong hug and says, "I can't believe you're here! I've missed you!"

"I've missed you too!" I release through my laughter and the constriction around my diaphragm. Spencer's soft laughter draws my attention to him standing behind her. "Hey, Spencer."

We share a soft smile, and he says, "sorry about her."

"She's fine."

Lucy finally lets me loose but links her arm through mine as Spencer takes over the reins of my trolley and begins to lead us out of the terminal. The walk to the car is dry now the rain has stopped and is filled with Lucy buzzing from the excitement of not only me being her here but of the impending wedding. Spencer is comfortably silent the entire time, letting us catch up properly. From what I can remember, he is an investor and works with Owen, and from the matte black Range Rover we're getting into, he is earning some good money.

He loads my bags and guitar into the trunk, and as soon as I'm clipped in, Lucy twists back in her seat, smiling widely. "Are you up for going to The Rose on the way home? We can have some lunch while we're there." Would I choose to go right now after flying through the night? Probably not, but I am too hungry to say no. If they provide me with food, I'll go anywhere.

They take me on a tour of the capitol, showing me some of the sights I have only seen in movies and in pictures, and it suddenly hits me that I am in London! My eyes can't absorb everything they show me, but I manage to snap a few images on my phone.

Eventually, we get through the heavy traffic and turn off the main road into a side-street. As the car comes to a stop, I notice there's a tall, olive-skinned gentleman dressed in a smart black suit standing in front of a sweet-looking dark gray Mercedes G Wagon.

Why is he just standing there? Lucy smiles at him softly and Spencer give him a quick, 'alright?' but he only nods as we walk through the back door.

From the outside, the building appears dark and mysterious; its age must predate World War I, with the unusual yellow bricks perfectly contrasting with the slick black modern signage of, "The Rose" telling everyone what they need to know. Lucy guides us past the cellar, kitchen and into the body of the pub. It is much larger than I was expecting. The colors from outside continue inside with soft, muted lemon walls, and intricate cast iron rose decorations. It feels sleek and upmarket whilst also being welcoming and inviting.

I notice a DJ booth positioned opposite the long bar which covers the length of an entire wall. The stock of beers on tap and the masses of bottled spirits staggered in different levels looks a little overwhelming, but I'm sure I will figure it out. Busy working behind the long bar are six members of staff all wearing black t-shirts with the same rose logo on the left breast. A dancefloor fills the floor space between the bar and stage, though there are more dark-stained wooden tables and black seating full of people eating and drinking than dancing right now. The atmosphere is comfortable, and all the patrons look like they're having a great time.

"Wow!" I enthuse. "This is incredible."

"Thanks, babe, I'm glad you like it." Lucy sets off with Spencer by her side and me falling in line behind them. Between saying hello to several people dining, she explains that it's open every day except Mondays, and they serve food from 11am to 11pm. And from the look of the food on the plates, it looks damn good!

Lucy said I'm performing on Wednesdays and Thursdays, and we agreed for me to do two shifts behind the bar, with the potential to do more. Initially, I'm happy to settle in, earn some money, get used to my surroundings and find a studio who is happy to work with me. I'm here to focus on me and my music first and foremost. "Thank you." I twist on my heel, taking in another lap of this space, imagining myself standing on the stage and doing what I love. "I can't get over how amazing this place is, Luce. I love it."

"Thanks, love." She smiles, looking proud of herself, and so she should be. Sure, her brother is the owner, but it is clear this is more than a job for her.

"Wait 'til you see out here." Spencer moves to a set of double doors, opening them to allow a fresh breeze to fill my lungs, reminding me quickly that I'm definitely not in Florida.

"Holy shit!" I step out into a large walled courtyard, taking in the scene in front of me. Gray garden furniture is positioned in small clusters around the edge and taller individual tables litter the center of the space. I notice the crisscross of unlit lights strung up above our heads and the spotlights sunken into the floor along the walls. At night, I bet this place looks incredible.

"We hold small private functions out here, but it's mainly for night use—"

"—when it's not raining," Spencer adds, making us all chuckle.

"Luce, seriously, this is fucking awesome! I can't believe I get to work here!" She stands there smiling, and you can tell she's pleased with what she's created. "What's on those floors?" I nod, looking up to the building above us.

"We have our offices up there—" *Our?* "—and Lewis our DJ lives in the flat that comes with the building. Neither of us wanted to live in it so we always allow staff members to use it. I thought Owen would be here actually; I said you were coming. I wanted to introduce you."

Is it wrong that I'm a little relieved? I know I need to be on my A game when I meet this guy because if he doesn't like me, I could have come all this way for nothing. Lucy might be the manager, but he has the final say, and apparently, he's already pissed that it's taken me a month to get here. "Well, another time."

"Yeah. Alright, I know you're starvin' so let me go and—"

"Lucy?" From the doorway, a petite brunette woman stands there. "There's a problem with the order that came in."

"Again?!" She huffs, shaking her head before looking at me with regret. "I'm gonna have to go and sort this out. I'll be straight back as soon as I've ordered, is that okay?" It's clear she is reluctant to leave as I have just arrived, but I'm a big girl.

"It's fine, honestly, I have Spencer here with me. Go... do what you need to, *boss*." I muse, enjoying watching her squirm.

"Oh, my God! You are not calling me that, ever!"

She disappears into the bustling heart of The Rose. Spencer soon follows after, kindly offering to get me a drink, leaving me alone. Spencer has such a calm personality and is so easy to be around that I can see why they work so well as a couple; she is the powerhouse, and he is a strong, supportive partner. He knows what his role is in their relationship, and I admire what they have so much.

I use the opportunity to message my mom and Riley, letting them know I'm at the bar and how awesome it is. I knew it would be nice from what Lucy had told me, though I never expected this. Even with the sounds of the city reverberating off the tall buildings, it feels intimate and like a little piece of Eden in such a concrete jungle. The sounds of my new home scream out from the silence I find myself in, and I try to separate each one.

"D'you get paid to sit there doin' fuck all?"

I turn, shocked, taking in the guy standing in the doorway. Dressed in a smart suit, he has no tie, and the top buttons of his shirt are undone. His deep brown, freshly cut hair is messy, and pink lipstick marks linger on his neck and collar. "Excuse me?!"

"You're supposed to be cleanin' up out here, not fuckin' chillin'. Do some bloody work or piss off." His voice is slightly higher pitched compared with Spencer's, but even with his deliciously strong London accent, I'm so pissed right now. *Does he think I'm a cleaner?*

I glare back at him, opening my mouth to speak my mind when Spencer nervously comes into view behind him, two drinks in hand. "Owen—" *Wait... Owen?* This is asshole, Owen! I'm glad Spencer came when he did because I would have regretted what I was about to say back to him. "—I see you've met Remi?"

"Who the fuck's Demi?"

I take that back. I should have said what I was going to! "It's Remi. Are you deaf as well as ignorant?"

Spencer looks bemused, and looking the complete opposite to Owen whose eyes narrow at me. "You would do well to shut up, love."

"And you would do well to get my name right, *Odin*!" I glare at him. *Two can play that game.*

Owen's nostrils flare a little before he focuses back on Spencer and says, "this!" He points a finger at me, "This is who I've been waiting for?"

Spencer shifts awkwardly, irritated by his mood, but no way in hell am I letting Owen signal at me like I'm nothing! "Excuse me, who are you pointing at like I'm nothing?"

He lowers his hand, but they both ignore me, with Spencer finally answering, "yes, that's Lucy's mate."

Owen glances back at me for a brief second, his gaze scrolling down my body, forcing me to cross my arms and block him as much as I can. "What a fuckin' let down."

"And yet you're exactly what I expected!" I roll my eyes and laugh dryly because I don't give a fuck what he thinks of my appearance right now.

He takes one last narrowed look at me before leaning into Spencer's ear, talking too low for me to hear, but when Spencer gently nods to him, it pisses me off more. *Who does he think he is? Some kind of Kingpin? Dickwad.* Before I can say anything else, Owen storms back into the building and out of view.

"Well, that didn't go quite to plan." Spencer admits, more to himself than me.

"You think?! Lucy wasn't joking. He really is an asshole!"

Lucy delicately comes into view from the doorway, oblivious to the abysmal atmosphere until she's outside with us. "Oh. What's happened?"

"Your brother happened." I scoff, kindly accepting the eagerly awaited drink from Spencer's hand.

She looks at Spencer. "Owen's here now?" He nods, making her face screw up. "Right, where is he?" She marches off, and he rushes after her.

"Lucy, you're only going to make him worse!"

"Like I give a shit!"

Owen

I storm up to my office, sliding off my suit jacket and taking off the shirt Carmen got all her stupid fucking lipstick over. A month! I've waited a fuckin' month and that's what I get!? A girl who looks like she's just come back from a fuckin' sleepover! It's a load of bollocks.

I'm sliding on a fresh shirt when my door flies open, revealing my darling sister...

"Oi!" Lucy yells.

"Don't come in here with a fuckin' attitude! I told you we didn't need her. She can fuck off back to America, 'cause she ain't gonna pull no one in!"

"Oh, shut up Owen! You haven't even heard her sing yet!"

"No, but I've bloody seen her!"

She scoffs loudly, moving in closer. "Then you're definitely a dickhead!"

I stop buttoning up my shirt and point at her quickly, "watch it!"

She bloody rolls her eyes at me, but she stands defiantly, irritated. "It's about business, and I know she's gonna be great for business! When have I ever been wrong?" She's usually never wrong and if anyone else was shouting at me right now, they'd be dead before they'd even close their lips.

"She's got a month." I mumble, only doing this because it's her that wants it. "She ain't got the punters in by then; she's gone."

"D'you trust me?" She's been doing this since she was a kid, always managing to get me wrapped around her little finger.

"You're one of very few, Luce, but I mean it."

She softens a little and says, "I know." She turns to leave but stops, saying, "Oh, and clean your neck and sort your hair out. You look ridiculous. I knew you were in the car with her when we walked past."

"And? That's why Charlie stood there."

"Doesn't mean you get to walk about like you're a pimp. She's a leech. Be careful."

I nod, and she goes to leave, but I make sure to have the last word. "Does Miss America know anything?" She stands with the door held open and shakes her head.

"Good. Keep it that way."

Two

he lunch at The Rose was delicious, but by the time we got back to Lucy and Spencer's beautiful white Georgian terraced house, I was more than ready for a nap. Their property is on a private crescent with a cobble road and iron fencing around a small communal garden, and honestly, it is nothing like what I expected to see here. The inside is more modern with white walls, natural flooring and classic colors of sage and navy to bring the spaces to life.

"Want a coffee?" If Lucy didn't wake me up early evening, I doubt I would have woken before the morning. She is in the kitchen when I enter, finishing stirring a mug.

"Yes! Strong and black, please. I definitely need it."

"Is that how you like your men?" She muses, following it up with a side glance.

I let out a laugh. "You sound as bad as Riley… and you really need to get a coffee machine." I nod in the direction of the kettle she fills up the mug with that she just put the coffee granules into.

"I drink tea! I've never needed one before, my kettle does the trick. But I will happily get you one."

"No, I insist."

She taps the spoon on the rim of the mug and passes it to me carefully. "That's probably for the best as I know literally nothing about coffee. That's Owen's domain." She instigates us moving to sit at the wooden table and takes a sip of her own hot drink, "I'm sorry about Owen earlier. Spencer told me what happened."

I cock an intrigued eyebrow. "Do you always apologize for him?" I don't know what she was told happened, and she wouldn't know what his initial comment was, but it isn't her place to say those words to me.

"No," she shrugs. "But I don't normally care about the people he upsets, so…"

"Girl, please! He didn't upset me. He pissed me off, but I was definitely not upset."

"Yeah," she grimaces, "he has a habit of doing that an' all."

It's clearly a difficult subject for her, and I am grateful she has acknowledged his behavior. I don't want things to be difficult as soon as I arrive, and I was under no illusion of him being an asshole.

"Look, I'm going to have to get used to him, but I will keep my distance as much as possible. That way I know I will keep my opinions to myself." She smiles softly. "And I love you, Luce, but if he wants to apologize then he can do it. You're not."

She seems to digest what I'm saying. And honestly, I was equally as rude to him. The difference is, I will apologize when I need to. I doubt he ever will.

***

Lucy wanted me to get a feel for the nightlife straight off the bat if I was up for it. Safe to say, I was. I needed a night out even if I had only had a handful of good hours sleep in the past two days.

We pull up into the same spot as we did this afternoon, though the G-Wagon that was here is nowhere to be seen, with a matte black BMW now in its place.

The atmosphere inside is so different from earlier. The dancefloor that had people eating calmly, now has hordes of people dancing, with the surrounding tables an array of laughter, talking and drinking. With it also being a dry night, the doors are open for patrons to flow freely between the garden. I'm absolutely buzzing, standing here in my deep red short leather skirt, and plunging white long-sleeved top. Lucy takes my hand and guides us through the crowd to the other side of the room to where a group of men sit in a row against the far wall. Their table is littered with an array of different drinks.

As I assess them, one guy moves back in his seat revealing Owen sitting in the middle. My eyes lock with his alluring mahogany ones briefly before I break away, rolling mine subtly. *You have got to be kidding me!* I thought I was going to enjoy this night without being under his observation the entire time. Obviously not because being too damn curious for my own good, when I dare to look back at him, our eyes reconnect making him frown. Didn't he know we were coming?

"All right, you lot?" Lucy shouts over the music, forcing me to break away and notice all of them are wearing suits and tieless shirts–which is a little weird considering how casual the rest of the men in this club are. Lucy instigates us sitting on the spare chairs opposite them. Mine is conveniently next to a friendly-looking guy who smiles widely as Lucy begins to introduce me properly. "Rem, this is Freddie and Jack—" Lucy points to the guy sitting opposite me and then to Mr. Tall, Dark and Handsome to my right. *Jack. Well, aren't you cute!* "—you know Owen—" *Unfortunately, yes,* "—that's Charlie, and lastly, that's Chris. Guys, this is Remi: my friend from America."

All of them acknowledge me in some form or another, but not Owen. No. He sits there so stone-faced that I would rather put the highest stilettos on and go for a run than say 'Hi' to him, but I need to make a half-decent impression on the guy. I smile and give them all a gentle wave and watch as his left eyebrow rises momentarily before he looks away to his right. *Deep breaths, Rem.* Cutting my loses, I quickly move onto the others, and I'm sure Charlie is the one who was standing outside earlier. He appears more serious that the other three, giving me only a straight-faced nod while Chris smiles and raises his hand to say 'Hi' but doesn't move to speak, and Freddie stands over the table to lift my hand, bringing it to his lips to place a playful kiss on the back of it.

"Pleased to meet ya. So, you're the new singer?"

"I guess you didn't put two and two together when she said I was the American friend'?" I cock an eyebrow, wondering what else he needed to confirm who I was.

"Maths ain't really my strong point love, especially around beautiful women." He adds a cheeky wink making me smile bemused.

"I hope that's the only thing you're not good at around beautiful women, otherwise I feel sorry for them already."

He takes my playfulness well, sitting back in

his seat. "Sweetheart, I certainly make up for the lack of intelligence in other ways, if you get me?"

I chuckle, appreciating his personality, "Ok, Casanova, I'll take your word for it."

We sit with the guys for a while, getting comfortable with my unfamiliar environment before Lucy gets me up on the floor to dance with her. Having had four bottles of beer as well as a few shots of some awful aniseed flavored stuff and tequila whilst jetlagged, I am definitely on the tipsy side. We dance together like we have no one around us. It has been so long since I've been out, it's amazing to feel so carefree. My body moves with a mind of its own, totally immersed in the layers of lyrics, bass, and melodies.

Lucy stops. "I need a wee!"

"Want me to hold your hand?"

"Nah, I'll be fine. I just didn't want to leave you with all of them by yourself."

We look back at the table and the only one looking at us is Owen. I haven't seen him smile all evening; he's only had hushed conversations with Charlie and Chris who sit to his right. "I'll be fine. Go."

She walks off through the crowd and instead of joining them at the table, I decide to go to the bar It doesn't take me long to get the attention of a male bartender, ordering another beer and two extra shots. When in Rome, as they say.

"Mind if I join you?" I flinch a little as Jack's voice tickles my ear.

"Damn, you made me jump!"

He chuckles lightly, still standing awfully close to me. I do like the heat that radiates from his body, warming my own, and he smells divine. A deep muskiness with some floral undertones that suits him a lot. His kind smile is infectious, and I know I'm smiling just as widely as he apologizes.

We stare off for a second before he looks down and I realize that I'm still standing here with an undrunk shot still in my hand. "Do you want one?" I pick up a small glass and hold it between us so he can take it.

"Sure." He holds eye contact as he takes it from my hand, placing it to his lips. He waits for me to join him with the other shot, and I drag my eyes away from his mouth to drink mine.

"Ugh!" I suck in my face as the taste bursts in my mouth. "God, why do we do these again?"

"Fuck knows!" He musters back with his own screwed-up expression which makes me giggle, "but yet we always end up doing more." We stare at one another again and I quickly move the attention away from me.

"I'm sorry, I kind of took over and you didn't get what you came here for." I don't believe he came here to get a drink, especially since he has had his back to the server since he got here, but I don't want to come across as too eager.

"How do you know I didn't?" His conviction impresses me, and soon he's moved in even closer than before, "D'ya wanna dance?"

I manage a simple 'Yes' before he pulls me back onto the dance floor, holding my body close to his as we begin to dance together. Normally I'm more reserved than this around men, but Jack made me feel at ease at once. He is a sexy guy! There was no way I wasn't going to dance with him when he asked me.

We danced together for a couple of songs. His hands swapping from being linked with my own or on my hips as they swayed. He says it's retro hour and clearly, it's very popular with the crowd as the floor is full of people having a good time.

"You want another drink?" He stills his movement enough to talk to me.

"Yes please. No more shots though!" I blurt out, knowing that I need to have something with a little kick.

"Another beer?"

I nod, "Yes. I'll meet you back at the table though, I need to use the restroom."

***

I join the extremely long queue for the ladies and check my phone for the first time this evening. Smiling, I open a message from Ri.

Riley: Hi, Mom said you arrived
Ring me when you wake up
I wanna know what it's all like x

Remi: I will. Having fun at the bar x

I place it back into my purse and look at the line. It hasn't moved, and I know that I will be wetting my underwear before I get to the front! I shift from one foot to the other when I sense a presence behind me.

"That looked cozy."

What the hell is it with these British guys stalking you? I turn my head to look at him, twisting the rest of my body to follow. Owen. Thankfully, he isn't as close to me as Jack was, but it's still close enough to inhale his woody scent with hints of fruit. It's confident and strong, exactly how I would have expected him to smell. *I just wish it wasn't so good.*

"It was a bit of fun." I scoff, still irritated by his presence from this afternoon to be polite – despite the fact I should be winning him over No matter what I tell myself, he gets under my skin. "Maybe you should try it sometime."

"What?" He asks, dryly, "dirty dancin'?"

I roll my eyes. "No, Odin, I'm having some fun. You might even crack a smile! Imagine that…" The only response I get is him reaching out to grab my hand, which I instantly snatch back, causing the girls queueing around me to turn and look. He looks at them briefly, causing them all to quickly look away as I warn him. "Don't touch me."

His jaw clenches tightly, drawing my attention to his jawline for a moment before he finally offers an explanation to his sudden interest in me. "There are staff toilets. Use them."

I straighten myself up, cocking my head to the side at him. "Do you know how to ask a question, or do people simply do what you demand?"

He glares at me so intensely that I almost wish I'd have kept my mouth closed and followed him, though he takes a breath before speaking, "would you like to use the staff toilets?"

I don't want to go anywhere with him, but my bladder is screaming at me that I have no other option. "Fine. Just don't touch me."

"Don't worry, I won't make that mistake again." He turns and walks off in front of me, leaving me no other option than to trot behind him with my hand still tingling from the shock that hit me when we touched.

Owen

Why am I doing this? She's been gobby since the second I met her, and she still doesn't seem to want to stop it either. But I saw her standing there and couldn't bloody help myself, could I! That damn outfit... those tits and those legs! She's certainly showing me how wrong I was earlier. Who knew she was hiding such perfect curves under all that fabric?

I open the door to my office and walk in, using my hand to signal where the toilet is.

"This is the staff restroom?" She asks, oozing curiosity. *No. It's my own personal one but will I tell her that?*

"Yeah, so be quick."

"Must like your staff..." I hear her mutter to herself as she pushes open the door.

I take a seat at the desk and wait for what seems like ages. God knows what she's doing, but at least I've got the space I wanted. If I must sit here for the rest of the night because she's in here, so be it; I wasn't exactly in the mood to be there tonight anyway, but as I didn't get to interview her, I wanted to see that she takes it seriously. I don't want anyone new coming in here and causing a load of fucking agro. God knows, I've got enough of that shit to last me two lifetimes.

When she slowly pulls open the door, I stop reading the paperwork on my desk and look up at her. Her fucking eyes! Those alluring silver circles greet me every time I dare to look at her, and I hate it. She looks like she's trying to work me out. *Good luck with that one sweetheart.*

"Took you long enough." I state.

She purses her lips, drawing my attention to them for the first time. Their rosiness glistens in the ambient lighting and highlights just how full they are. "Are you always an asshole?" I watch as they move, taking a second to register what she said.

I hold back the desire to smirk at her. *You have no idea.* "Are you always such a straight talker?"

Her gaze doesn't falter as she confidently says, "yes," as I finally rise from behind my desk and begin walking over to her. "In that case, if you get to stay here, I won't have to answer that, love," Her head rises slowly with every step I take until she's looking up into my eyes. The pupils that I thought were simply grey are a unique mix of pale turquoise, muted blues, and a scattering of fine grey lines. They don't blink; they just glare back as I continue, "you'll be lucky enough to find that out by yourself." I'm still watching for signals that she likes it and how close I am, but her breathing stays the same. No colour rushes to her cheeks; she doesn't bite her lip or shift on the spot. No, not this one. Instead, she places her hand on my chest and gently pushes me away, forcing me to take one step back with my skin, remembering the pressure of her fingers even after they've gone.

"I wouldn't say that's lucky, *Odin*." She cocks her head to the side. "And it's something I already know about you. I just wanted to see if you admitted it."

I scowl as she moves away walking to the door before stopping and waiting for me to join her.

"Can you take me back now?"

Can I? I can't fucking wait to.

Three

I have had a few days to settle in at Lucy and Spencer's, unpacking and getting over the jetlag, and today I am going to The Rose to get some training in before my first shift in two days' time. Lucy has been my own personal tour guide when she hasn't been at work, and I must admit it has been just like having Riley with me—obviously without me losing my belongings all the time, but I have felt like I've still had my sister around me whilst we eat out for lunch, do some shopping, travel on the underground, and talk for hours.

"Sorry I can't be there today, I honestly forgot all about this bloody thing. My mum loves having a mother and daughter day." Lucy collects her purse from the kitchen counter. I remain sitting with my coffee in hand as she slips on her jacket.

"Honestly, Luce, it's fine. I'm sure I can survive for a few hours without you."

"I know." She offers me a regretful smile, "I promise, as soon as we're done, I'll come and pick you up."

"Go and have fun with your mom, you are allowed to get pampered."

"I can be around if you need me. Just give me a call." Spencer says, entering in the kitchen behind me. I watch them kiss, gazing into one another's eye. I knew they were perfect for one another before but observing them over the last three days it's clear just how in love they are.

"I can't believe you're getting married in three months! It's so exciting!"

"I know. My dad gets back in a few weeks, so it'll be perfect then." Lucy says, smiling at me then at her beloved holding her in his arms. "My wedding planner is having kittens try'na sort it all out, but I know she'll do it."

"She'd bloody better sort it for how much she costs!" Spencer grunts as she moves away, coming closer to the table.

"Are you looking forward to dress shopping next week?" She asks, smiling softly. I'm still shocked she asked me to be bridesmaid along with her oldest friend, Alice. We are going to look for dresses with her mom.

"Of course, I wouldn't miss it for the world."

She beams widely, "Right, I'd better go before my mum starts moaning that I'm late."

***

"How are you finding it?" My new co-worker, Roberto, hands me the bottle of lime juice I keep misplacing; or someone keeps moving it from where I was shown it was kept.

"It's different, I'm not gonna lie." I admit honestly, earning a chuckle from another colleague Sydney at my expense. What did they expect me to say? The registers are different, almost all of the people who work here are from different parts of the world—Roberto is from Italy, and Sydney is from South Africa—the patrons all ask for drinks I've never heard of, and their money is totally different.

"You'll get the hang of it. It's certainly busy enough this afternoon." Sydney says, offering a highly amused smile in addition to it. He is the shift manager and made me feel at ease straight away, but Roberto swooped me under his wing instantly and hasn't left my side for much since.

The three of us, along with a French red headed girl called Stephanie, who hasn't really spoken to me, spread along the bar, serving customers, and although it only feels like it has been an hour, I know it has been a lot longer.

"Oi, you!" Owen's voice bellows across the bar, causing us all to turn and look at him. I look around wondering who he's summoning when Sydney looks at me.

"Think he wants you, Remi."

"Me? Why does he want me?"

"No idea, but I wouldn't keep him waiting."

"Great..." I say under my breath, slowly leaving the safety of the bar and heading over to him; the heaviness of his gaze grows as I get closer. "Can I help you?"

"Not here." he snipes, almost barking back at me before he rotates on his toes to walk back to the staff stairwell.

"I'm sorry, am I supposed to be following you?" I press, crossing my arms.

He halts, quickly turning back to narrow those enigmatic eyes I'm slowly getting used to. "If I wanted to talk to you down here, I'd have bloody spoke to you there wouldn't I?"

He is such an obnoxious asshole. "So?"

His nostrils flare as I stand my ground, but he eventually asks through gritted teeth. "Can I speak to you upstairs in my office?"

There's not a please at the end, but at least I got him to ask another question.

"Sure." I walk forward. "All you had to do is ask." I make a head start in the direction of the office and start climbing the stairs. "Don't even think of checking out my ass."

I hear him scoff. "Trust me, that won't be an issue. You're not my type."

"You into dudes?" I know he isn't, unless they like wearing pink lipstick, but I just couldn't help myself. He is so serious and grumpy, and the distaste look on his face makes me want to laugh.

"I only sleep with blonds."

With curiosity getting the better of me, I stop on the top step, turning to look down at him. "What do you do with brunettes then?"

He takes the two steps that separated us, replacing me as the taller person. "Nothin' you could handle."

I hold his gaze, raising an eyebrow suggestively, "I'll bear that in mind."

There is a miniscule change to shock in his expression before he moves away first, and just like I had to the other night, I trot behind him and into his office. I take the empty seat opposite him with the dark wooden desk wedged perfectly between us. He leans back casually, placing one elbow on the arm of his office chair. But he says nothing.

"What did you need to speak to me about, Mr. Turner?"

With his face as stern as usual, he holds my attention. "You're talking too much to the punters. Stop with the chit chat shit."

I spontaneously laugh. *He's joking right?* But his face doesn't change. "Wait, you're serious?"

"Deadly."

"Well, okay. Fine. What else was there?"

"That was it."

Okay, now I know he must be joking. "You brought me up here just to tell me I talk too much?" Another chuckle of mine slips free.

"They've gotten used to the service we provide here. You're technically here to sing, although that's still to be determined, so just pour them a bleedin' pint, alright?"

I take a long contemplative breath. "So, I can sing to them but I can't talk to them?" He looks like he would shoot me right now if he had a gun. All I know is, catching him out on his bullshit might just be my new favorite pastime!

"Look, shut your gob more, pour their drinks, take their cash, and get on with serving the next one. Simple. Now, you can go." He retains his uptight frame in the chair, waiting for me to stand and leave. Instead, I stay sitting for a little longer, unable to not say what is in my head. Maybe he has a point about me talking?

"You're far too uptight, Owen. Live a little, maybe call the blond who left the lipstick over your collar from the other day."

"Why? Aren't you curious to find out what I do to brunettes?" he asks, a little mischievously. He might not realize, but it is the opening I needed to know that underneath that granite exterior there is another side to him.

I lift my chin for a second, pursing my lips, making him wait for my answer. "No. I don't sleep with assholes."

———————————

Owen

She leaves my office, slightly slamming the door, giving me the chance to readjust the semi that I've had since she stood her ground downstairs.

I only seemed to get harder the more she mouthed off at me. I nearly hit the bloody table with my dick when she said 'Mr Turner' all fucking sassy. Her words ring in my ears: '*I doesn't sleep with assholes...*' I've fucked a lot of irritating women, but none of them wind me up like she does. Why can't I ever get a break?

Lucy asked me to be here in case her little friend needed help, so I've been here all afternoon making sure she didn't get into any issues. Even though

43

I had loads to do, I kept checking the CCTV when I could be arsed. I wasn't gonna go down; I didn't wanna look too friendly. But every time I looked, she was standing there laughing and flicking her hair, chatting to someone. That's why I went down to get her, but I can't stay here no more.

I gather my shit together and make my way into the bar, immediately wishing I fucking hadn't. "Hi darling!"

Today just couldn't get any better, could it? *No. Course it couldn't.* I walk over slowly and give her a kiss on both cheeks, "Mum." I love her, but right now I just wanna get out of here and get to the warehouse.

"I thought I'd come and surprise you." She holds me at arm's length and scans me down, looking proud as she takes in my black Armani suit. "Lucy said about coming after our spa trip this morning. She's gotta pick up her friend."

"That's fine, you know you can come here whenever." I manage to escape her hold, looking at Lucy who's wrapped up in the arms of Spencer. "Just so you know, Jury is still out on her. I suggest you have a word and make sure she does what I've told her. I can't be here all the time babysittin' her."

"You not goin' to stay and have a drink with me?" mum says as I shift away getting ready to leave.

"You're just his type, sweetie—" Little Miss America's voice interjects, "—I think he will. Just don't expect a smile or polite conversation. Well, any for that matter, but he could use the distraction." My mum's eyes widen before turning around to look at who just said it. I watch in delight as Remi clocks that my mum is significantly older than she thought, and not someone I was about to 'release that tension' with. Though I get why from the back she would think my Mum was younger, she likes to take care of herself with her immaculate long blonde hair, designer clothes and airbrushed makeup.

Lucy opens her mouth to speak but I want to have this moment, "*Demi*, let me introduce you to Paula Turner. Our mum."

Embarrassment washes over her that her cheeks finally glow, and she's soon tripping over her words to form some sort of apology. "Mom? Oh, I am so sorry. It's because you look so young from the back, I didn't think you could possibly be his mother, let alone have a kid his age." My mum's mouth tightens into a very unimpressed line and Remi's eyes widen some more. "Not saying that you were underage when you had him! I'm sure you were the perfect age to have a baby and have just aged really well."

Lucy is sitting there, jaw slack watching the car crash happen. Me? I'm unable to stop the smirk of delight forming on my face as she digs herself a bigger hole.

"Sorry, who are you?" I don't need to see my Mum to know that she's scowling at her. I'm like her in that way.

"Um..." She holds out her hand, "I'm Remi."

"...my friend who we've been waiting for." Lucy completes the introduction.

My mum's hand tentatively clasps hers, shaking it a fraction before letting go. "Do you know how to pour a large white wine, Remi?"

"Yes, ma'am."

"Then I suggest you get one and a coke with ice very quickly!"

Remi scurries off as Lucy smacks my arm, making me glare at her, "What the fuck was that for?"

"Don't you hit him!" My mum quickly comes to my defence. "Owen said nothing wrong!"

As my mum carries on talking, I can't help but look at Remi. She has her head down, focusing on getting the two drinks. She's chewing on her bottom lip anxiously. "We were discussing doing something for when your dad gets home."

"Like a welcome home party?"

"Not quite, but it would be nice to celebrate that he's with us again after so long, wouldn't it?"

I look away feeling my chest tighten. It is going to be weird having him back home. "Yeah, sure, whatever you wanna do." I'm grateful when she returns, placing the two glasses on the bar, breaking up the conversation for a moment before Lucy takes over.

"I'll plan a nice meal with everyone at his favourite restaurant."

"That'd be lovely darling. Your dad will love that."

I stay for ten more minutes, supping my drink quickly so I can get out of here, asking Spencer if he's coming with me.

"Nah, still got stuff to do."

"Fine. See you all later."

I get in my car, heading off to meet up with Charlie and the lads at the warehouse my family own. Charlie sits there with the rest of them doing nothing like they've probably been doing all morning.

"'Bout bleedin' time." Charlie points out, getting my back up instantly.

"Do I need to report to anyone?"

Charlie takes all he needs to from my glare and continues looking at the paperwork in his hands. He has his shit to do, so do I. He monitors the stock going out, makes sure the guys do what I've told them, and then Spencer makes sure all the monies right that we collect.

When Freddie's little revelation of where I've been slips out, Jack's ears prick up straight away. "On a Monday?"

"Checking to make sure the staff are behaving."

"One in particular, though, 'ey?" Freddie laughs, nudging a bemused Chris.

"Who?"

Like I need to ask?

"Come on, O, the new girl. She is fit as fuck!" Freddie informs me. *Little cunt.*

"She's crap at the job and annoyin' as hell. Can't wait 'til she fucks off back home."

"You're so full of shit, Owen." Jack pipes up, "You're telling me, if she let ya you wouldn't wanna be balls deep in her?"

I don't even bother to look up from the document I picked up off my desk, "Not a chance. I wouldn't touch her if you paid me." Especially after the last time I did, and she screamed at me not to.

Jack smirks, turning away to carry on looking at his phone.

"Bullshit!" Freddie unknowingly calls me out.

Happy to change the subject, I turn the attention back to the bundles of stock that's packed and ready to go out to be distributed.

They might wanna act like they have fuck all to do, but they do, and I'm gonna make sure they get it done.

Four

ow that I know how much traffic we sit in daily and how freaking crazy the drivers can be, I've changed my mind about getting a car of my own. Spencer offered to bring me in again, which I was grateful for, but I didn't want him to disrupt his day simply to transport me across the city, so I took an Uber. Not having a car of my own felt a little restrictive at first, but I'm getting my bearings with things slowly.

As soon as I arrive at The Rose, I go straight to the bar, standing my guitar case against the wooden panelling, and order a soda. I've chosen to sing a few covers and throw in one or two of my own songs that were hits back home. I didn't want to put the audience off by playing only mine, and I really love adding my own spin to well-known tracks.

It's been a nice couple of days working here, possibly because Owen the asshole hasn't been in. Lucy said he doesn't come in often, and I was damn grateful after the episode on Monday. I literally wanted the ground to open and swallow me when he said she was his mom! I tried a few more times after he left to make amends, but she shut me down every time. Even Lucy tried to help me out, but it's clear to see where Owen gets his personality from. I hope their dad is where Lucy gets hers from.

Lewis, the resident DJ who lives upstairs occasionally finds me in the bustling bar, taking a seat beside me. "Looking forward to your first performance?" I finally met him yesterday and he has been a huge help already, putting me at ease and answering all my questions about their PA system. He offered me a sound check last night after we closed, and I almost snapped his hand off.

I nod excitedly. "Yeah! I'm excited, and a little nervous." He frowns softly in confusion. "You know, what if the audience don't like it?"

"Pfft, from what Lucy said last night, Rem, you ain't got nothing to worry about." Lewis instantly reassures me. I have confidence in myself, but I need to make this work. If they don't like me then I might not be able to continue performing.

"Thanks." I take a sip of my drink, when his next words catch me off guard.

"You ever thought of recording some stuff?"

I turn back with a twinkle in my eye. "What made you ask that?"

"My mate Dom owns a studio. He doesn't usually have artists like yourself but I'm sure he'd help you out if you wanted to."

"That would be amazing if you don't think he would mind. I recorded some songs back home and nearly got signed, but it just didn't work out." I shrug trying to play it down. I'm not ready to spill the drama of my past right now, but I have no idea what Lucy has told him about me.

"That's shit. Tell you what, give me your number and I'll arrange something with him. He owes me a favor."

"And you want to cash in that favor for me?" I chuckle and hold out my hand. He smiles, unlocking his phone and handing it to me.

"I have a feelin' about you, and usually my feelin's are never wrong."

"Getting her digits already, mate?" Freddie's voice calls out as he walks up to us. "You work even quicker than I do!"

Lewis says some stupid guy thing back while I copy the new UK number from mine, saving it before handing it back to Lewis.

"Thanks. I'll message you so you will have mine. Can I give this straight to Dom?"

"Of course. I have to say, Freddie, I wasn't expecting to see you here tonight. Lucy is always saying how much you and the other guys are working."

"I'm just doin' what Luce told us all to. We all have to be here, or she'll kick our arses." Freddie explains, and I struggle not to believe him. Lucy is far more authoritative than I realized. She bosses them all around, it's quite entertaining seeing these grown men bow down to her. He looks around taking in the number of patrons in here. "She's done well getting everyone in here."

"Luce might have got them in here, but Remi will keep them coming back." Lewis says, smiling at me, "dunno what Owen's moaning about."

My ears prick up immediately, "Owen's moaning?"

Freddie looks a bit unsure whether to continue or not but does. "Yeah, but he moans about everything mate so don't worry about it."

"Why doesn't that surprise me!" I finish off my drink, collecting my bags and my guitar case. "I'm going to go and get ready."

"Okay. I have everything ready to go, so just bring yourself." I smile, thanking Lewis. I appreciate their support, even if Freddie had no other choice.

I walk into the office that Owen took me to the other night, leaning my guitar against the desk, and lock the door behind me. I slide off my everyday clothes, pulling free my stage clothes. I'm just pulling the black long-sleeve body suit over my feet when the door shakes. I freeze, then breathe out a sigh of relief as it stops, continuing to pull the suit up higher.

Suddenly the door flies open. I scream losing my balance and fall back into the stall door.

"What the hell?! Why you in here?" Owen stands in the wide-open door. His brown eyes scrolling the entire length of my near naked body.

"Oh my God! Get out!" I squeal, trying desperately to cover my exposed breasts with one arm and hold up the suit with my other hand. He instinctively takes a step closer; his arms open to show he wants to help.

"Are yo—" His wide eyes show me he doesn't know what to do, but I know exactly what I want him to do!

"I SAID GET OUT, OWEN!"

"Alright… fuckin' hell." He leaves quickly, closing the door with a bang.

Still stunned and still barely covering myself, it sinks in. How did he even get in here because I know I locked it! *Jackass.*

I brave a glance at my hip that collided badly with the frame, seeing the large red mark that now sits there. It's going to leave a big bruise. "That's just wonderful. Thanks asshole!" I holla out, but there is an abrupt knock on the door. "Can I help you?" I snipe back, pissed off that he hasn't gone.

"What are you doin' in my toilet?"

I frown as Owen's voice echoes through the door. "*Your* toilet?!"

"Well yeah, it's in my bloody office!"

I stomp to the door, opening it enough to peek through the crack. "You told me it was the staff one!"

He keeps his eyes firmly on my face as a vein protrudes from his temple. I don't know how much older he is to Lucy, but I can tell he is a lot older than I am. "This is the only time! Tomorrow, you need to get ready downstairs." The clenched words squeeze from his mouth before he quickly turns and walks away.

"FINE BY ME!" I shout after him. I hope he continues to walk until he is out of the building, but I know that is wishful thinking... he will be there tonight, front and centre, making sure I can do everything Lucy says I can.

***

"There she is!" Lucy hollas out over the music as I walk confidently over to the same table that we all sat at last time. The same five guys sit there with Spencer and Lucy, with Owen poised in the centre. "Where did you get ready? I came up to show you where to go but Justin and Fred said you had already gone?"

Owen hasn't looked in my direction, leant in to listen to Chris talk but I look to him smiling sweetly, sitting down next to Lucy. I see him raise his glass to his lips. *Perfect.* "Owen over here let me use his personal bathroom." He chokes on the liquid, spraying it finely over the table and himself.

"Aww bro, that was nice of you." Lucy muses, as he wipes his mouth with a napkin.

"Yeah, fuckin' gent me." He glances at me briefly before looking back at his sister. "It was only a one off 'cause you didn't show her where to go."

"Why didn't you show her where to go?" Spencer calls him out making me smile openly.

"My office was closer." He stares at me, a glint forming in his eye, "Plus, it was nice to see more of you even for a few seconds."

I hold the smile on my face, determined to not show him how mortified I am he caught me half naked and at his mercy. But he knows what I'm doing and clearly isn't letting me play solo. "A few seconds? Sweetheart, I could barely get rid of you. If you want to spend time with me, all you have to do is ask."

He lets out a bemused breath, "If I can ever fit you in darlin', I'll know where to find you."

"Hmm... in that case, if I ever want to be bossed about and told what to do, I know just where to find you!" I wink and his eyes widen almost enough for others to notice.

Yes, two really can play this game, asshole.

Owen

I hate her. I really fucking hate her.

I hate her attitude.

I hate that my body reacts unnaturally to her. And right now, I hate my sister for bringing her here.

We stare off until she breaks away. Only then do I realise everyone around us has stopped to take notice of our little exchange. Remi turns in her seat and begins talking to my sister, but my attention doesn't leave her until Charlie leans in to talk to me.

"Think you've met your match mate."

I pick up my glass again. "Quite possibly."

"So, what ya gonna do?"

"What d'ya mean, 'what am I gonna do?'" Charlie is my guy. Always cool, calm, and collected, but not right now. Right now, he's looking at me like I've just turned down fifty grand. "What?"

"Mate, come on..."

"Don't care what you have to say Charlie-boy, I'm not interested." She's here to prove to me that she should stay. I couldn't even consider what he's insinuating.

"Yeah, alright! Just don't go all caveman when she's taken by another guy." He nods in her direction. I look back quickly to see Jack hovering, loitering, and hanging off every word like he has been since that first night.

"Like I said, mate, I ain't gonna do shit."

And I don't, sitting exactly where I am, ready for the moment I find out if Little Miss Gobby can actually use that mouth for anything other than pissing me off.

"Okay... duty calls!" Remi says loud enough to grab our attention, with Lucy squealing with excitement.

"Break a leg, babe!"

I'm not alone in my gaze, following Remi across the floor and onto the waiting stage. Lewis is there to accept her with the guitar she dropped off after our little altercation in my office. She looks confident but I can tell from the way she's nibbling the inside of her bottom lip, she's a little nervous.

"Good evening, everyone." As Remi's smooth American voice rolls through the sound system, I glance around and most of the punters draw their attention to her immediately. "I'm Remi, and I'm going to be performing here for a while. I like to do covers as well as my own songs, so I hope you enjoy it!" She strums the first chord on her guitar, closing her eyes. When they reopen, all her nerves have disappeared, and the strong confident woman who mouths off at me stands holding everyone's attention.

She begins to play the intro, opening her mouth to sing the first line from a song I have never heard before.

Shit. Fucking. Bollocks.

Her voice travels through my body like an electric current. Every hair stands to attention across my body and my heart does some funny shit. *What the fuck!?* She's sang like three lines of a song she must have written because I don't recognise it, and I'm stuck to my seat, unable to fucking move!

I watch as she flows through the bridge and into the chorus; her whole body infused with the song and the feeling within it. My glass sits in my hand untouched by my mouth the entire length of the song and it's only once the impressed applause starts up from every single person in the room, I blink for the first time.

"Bloody hell, Luce," Jack gushes, "she's amazing!"

"I told you!" Lucy's excited, no doubt to have proved me wrong but Jack looks at Remi with a look I recognise. Because it's probably the same one on my own stupid face.

This is not good.

"Alright there, mate?" The smirk on Charlie's lips is evident in his words. Little prick.

"Fuck off." I stand and leave the table, glancing to the stage to lock eyes with her as she begins to sing the next song. Her brow furrows a little, but she doesn't falter.

For once, Luce got it wrong, because this was a bad idea.

Five

It's been a crazy couple of days I've worked every day, including yesterday when I didn't need but chose to. Today I spent the day exploring the city, managing to navigate my way through alone to get where I wanted to. I brought a great outfit for tonight. I'm ready to let my hair down again, and maybe get to know Jack a little more. It has been easy as he comes to the bar often, always sitting at the bar to talk to me the entire time. Lucy said he doesn't usually come in this much, so it shows there's a reason... and I'm quite happy to be that reason.

When I get back to Lucy and Spencer's house, I get a relaxing bath before calling Riley.

"You would love it here, Ri."

"I don't know if I could cope being cold."

I scoff, rolling my eyes. "You don't have to wear t-shirts and shorts all year you know that, right?"

"Well, obviously! But I'd still want to..."

"You're crazy."

"How was the shift last night? Any drama?"

"No, it was fine. I went exploring by myself this afternoon. Found this amazing boutique, you want to see this dress I brought. Hang on, let me Facetime you." I pull my phone away and switch the call to Facetime. Instantly her face pops onto the screen. *God, I've missed her.*

I flip the camera and reveal myself to her from the reflection in the mirror. The dress I found is white with beautiful soft pink flowers on it. It has thin straps and hugs my body, with the skirt split from the knee length up to my thigh on one side. I knew as soon as I saw it that it was perfect for tonight. Paired with my heels, I know I may catch the eye of a guy...

"Girl, you're gonna be cold." Riley declares, making me groan. "But the dress is amazing! Why do you buy nice things when I can't steal them from you?"

"Because you can get your own damn clothes!" I see Lucy's head poke through the door in the reflection. "Hey, Ri, there's someone I want to meet."

"Oooh! Is it the hot asshole, or the cute one who smells nice?" Riley excitedly questions, earning curiously raised eyebrows form Lucy. I wish she had a damn filter at times! I have lost count of how many times I have wanted to smother her, just like I want to right now.

"Neither actually, especially the asshole!" *Thank God.*

"You didn't deny he was hot though..." She laughs through the phone as Lucy stands beside me.

I ignore Riley, regretting being honest with her. "I want to introduce you to Lucy."

"Hi!" Lucy shrieks as excited as she was when I arrived here.

"Hey! It's so good to finally meet you!"

"An' you! God, you're bloody gorgeous as well. Your mum and dad must have good genes!" Me and Riley laugh. My parents are just my parents. I know my mom looks great for her age and my dad takes care of himself, but I don't see it.

"Well, mom gave me all of her best ones so, you know..." I gasp as she shrugs playfully. She tells everyone the same thing when they comment on how alike we are to one another and our mom. We share the same skin tone and hair color. The only difference is she shares our mom's green eyes and our dad's smile.

"Are you gonna come over and visit us?" Lucy asks, snatching the phone out of my hand.

"I have school, so I won't be able to come over for a while. But I definitely want to."

"You're welcome anytime."

"Jeez! Don't tell her that!" I exclaim, trying to collect the phone back from Lucy.

"Hey! I'm here all alone, you know. You at least have a substitute sister over there."

"You have mom!"

"Pfft, it's totally different!"

I glance at the time, *21:48.* "I know, you love me, you miss me... but we have to go. I'll call you tomorrow."

"Ok, have a great time. Love you."

I end the call after I tell her I love her too.

"Owen's hot huh?" Lucy asks, laced with amusement.

"I don't know why she said that. I have never described him as hot, ever!" *I'm sure I haven't...* But I'm also not blind. Just because I can't stand the guy doesn't mean I'm immune to the fact that he is attractive.

"Who was the other one she said about?"

"Jack..."

She gasps excitedly, linking her arm with mine. "Well, he's gonna be over you like a rash. And I can't wait to see it."

***

"Yes! Beat that loser!" I yell, throwing my hands up in the sky before me and Lucy high five. Jack and Chris laugh, but Freddie doesn't.

"That's a fuckin' fix, bruv! You can't drink five shots that bloody quick!"

I playfully pout, feigning sympathy for the poor guy. "Aww, poor Freddie. He can't handle being beaten by a woman."

He glares at me as Chris laughs, bumping his shoulder. "Mate, she told you she could beat ya! It's your fault for taking her on."

"I challenge you again!" Freddie tries to flag down someone at the bar, "right now!"

"Nice try Fred, not happening." I clutch my stomach, knowing if I have one more soon, I might barf over the table. "I've had those five as well as the rest. I want to enjoy the rest of the evening." An arm snakes around my hips. I feel Jacks body move closer to me on the seat.

"That was pretty impressive." His breath tickles my neck as he talks into my ear.

I glance back at him. His blue eyes are darker and hooded, and I know he has been desperately trying to get closer to me all evening. "Oh, yeah?"

"Mm-hmm." he murmurs, nodding slowly but never breaking the connection of our eyes. "You look really nice tonight."

"Thank you. It's new." *Like that makes a difference Rem!*

"Well, I like it." He leans in closer still. "How about I take you out for dinner tomorrow? Give you an excuse to buy another new dress as beautiful as this one."

I hold my confident smirk, but internally I'm jumping with excitement. "I'd like that."

"All right then. I'll look forward to it." As Jack pulls away, I notice Lucy looking at the two of us, a knowing smile on her face. She was right, the dress was a hit.

***

"Oh my God... I don't think I've been this wasted for a long time!"

"So?" Lucy mumbles, applying a fresh coat of her lipstick, "live a little!"

We have danced and drank all night. My bladder was as full as Lucy's so we both came to the bathroom together, though I think she was helping me to walk more than anything.

"D'you know, Tom used to limit my drink intake? He would tell me how many I was allowed at events. He didn't want me to 'embarrass myself' in front of possible record execs."

Lucy moves closer, closing her clutch. "What an arsehol—"

"And then *he's* the one that's unfaithful!"

"He's a knobhead babe, you're better off without him. Can—" She reaches her hand down to help me up, but I wave it away.

"I know right!" I exclaim, cutting her up once more, "fucking prick. He took away the only chance of a record deal I've ever had, Luce! He has everyone under the illusion that he is this amazing guy. He had me on a pedestal, pushing me in front of all the producers and managers; he wanted to make me a star. Pfft, yeah. If I obeyed him and let him fuck whoever he wanted." Brief memories of catching him and her flash through my mind, making me shudder. "He wasn't even that good in bed."

"I know, it's really unfair but Rem, you need to get up off the floor. Other people need to use this toilet too."

"Huh-what?" I finally look around, remembering I'm sitting slumped against the door of the bathroom. "Oh shit, help me up."

She pulls me to stand but I stumble even more than before, causing us to both laugh hysterically. "You're gonna break your bloody neck! Take your shoes off!"

"No…! They finish off the look, Luce." I know I should take then off, but now I have been sitting still for so long, being upright just makes my head spin.

"Oh my God, stand up!" she demands as I slump back to the floor. "Dammit, Rem! I can't carry you! Shit! Wait there..."

I close my eyes as she leans me against the wall. I have no idea how long I've been here when I hear her mumbling to herself. "What are you saying?"

"I can't get hold of the others! Please help me with her. Then I'll owe you again. Come on. Please?...Thank you!"

The music vibrates the walls and floor, and the room spins around me. I just need a little longer and I will be okay.

But I don't get a little longer because I'm swept up into someone's arms, making me shriek from the motion. And as I chance a glance at who is carrying me, I suddenly feel a lot more sober Owen. With a face like thunder, and not giving me any attention as he carries me out of the bathroom.

"Put me down!" I fight against his hold instantly.

"Suits me. Didn't wanna help you anyway." Owen stops and near on drops me to my feet, causing me to stumble. Instinctively, he pulls me to his body to stop me from falling. *Why did he do that? Why didn't he let me fall if he didn't want to help?*

"Sure you wanna walk?" he mumbles, still holding onto my naked arms.

I wish I wasn't, but I definitely am enjoying the feeling of my body igniting under his touch. The way he looks into my eyes, feeling his body this close to mine is doing things I wish it wasn't. Every nerve ending is tingling, covering my body this time, not just my hand. *It's just the drink! That's all it is.*

"What?" I finally whisper, buckling under the weight of his lack of patience.

"Can. You. Walk?" He asks like I have no ability to understand English. Believe me, I do. It's just that my brain is being smothered by my nervous system. My legs feel like jello, and I'm starting to realize that it might not be just the toxins running through my bloodstream as I muster a mere whisper, "no."

"What?" He demands, losing the last ounce of patience I doubt he had in the first place.

"No, I can't walk."

He huffs loudly, reaching down to once again raise me effortlessly into his arms. I tentatively place mine around his neck, trying not to be distracted by how perfect his aftershave is.

"Where are you taking me?" I dare to ask, though he only grunts in return.

"To get some air." He keeps walking and although I can't wait for him to put me down, I pay too much attention to everything. Things like how my body fits in his arms perfectly. How he has a day or two's growth to his beard. And how he looks tired, and not just because it's the early hours.

I take in tiny details about him that I never thought I would before I'm placed down on a leather sofa. I slowly take in my surroundings, oblivious to the fact that he brought me to his office I was banished from until this moment.

"Here." He hands me a crystal glass of water.

I take it politely, placing it slowly to my lips. "I thought I was getting some air?"

"It's raining outside. This is the best I could do." He grunts and sits back at his desk that is littered with papers.

"Have you been here all night?"

He doesn't look up, picking up with his work that he must have left off to come and handle me. "Yeah."

"Why didn't you come down to join us?"

"'cause I didn't."

"Do you like being on your own?" With each question, I can see him tense further. The reluctance to answer me becomes more evident.

"Sometimes."

"Why don't you drink?"

He looks at me quizzically. *Does he not think I've noticed?* He hasn't touched a drop of alcohol since I've been here, and he owns a pub!

From the quick glare I receive from his brief piece of attention, I know I've asked one too many, but to my surprise he does answer.

"'cause I don't."

My curiosity peaks. "Is that why you're an asshole?"

"What?" he asks, looking all the way up from the paper he has been idly looking at, "because I don't drink?"

I nod.

"No. I don't drink 'cause I don't want to." He looks back down at the papers on the desk. Though it was small, I'm grateful he answered.

"I don't think I should drink anymore..."

"...And yet, you probably will."

"Ugh!" I moan, "Can you not be a dick every time we speak?!"

"Drink your water, then you can go."

I take another sip before placing it down onto the small round table beside the sofa. I slip off my shoes, savoring the relief from my feet with a moan. I knew Lucy was right, I should have taken them off a long time ago.

"Seriously?!"

I look up and he's glaring at me rubbing my feet. "What did I do now?!"

"You're so bloody annoyin'."

I don't understand him. He clearly doesn't want me here, so why did he agree to help. "Well, that makes two of us then doesn't it!"

I sit quietly taking sip after sip until I've drank it all and feel a little more sober. The atmosphere is peculiar, not quite uncomfortable but not inviting. I know he doesn't want me here, but he also isn't ushering me out—despite what he's said.

I rise from the sofa and walk slowly toward him; curiosity getting the better of me. "Why did you leave after one song on Wednesday?"

"Why d'you have to ask so many questions?"

I walk around to where he sits, perching on the edge of the black wooden desk that matches the dark bookcases behind his head, complimenting the dark blue walls and feeling very *him*. "You're not exactly giving me much conversation."

He sits back in the chair, rolling away to put some distance between us. "Maybe that's because I don't want to talk to you."

"Would you rather just keep staring at me instead?" I raise an eyebrow, knowingly. *Yes, I've seen you, Odin.* He says nothing, and his face equally gives nothing away. "If I'm such a disappointment, why am I still here?"

He slowly pushes himself out of the chair, moving towards me with questioning eyes. He towers over me until he is mere inches away from my face, and my inebriated body celebrates his proximity, even without a single touch of our skin.

"Who says I'm disappointed?" He leans in closer, allowing me to take another intoxicating draw of his woody aftershave. "I think you just need showing how to behave while you're here." His deep voice reverberates through my body. I swallow hard causing his eyes to follow the motion down to my throat and to my breasts. He watches my chest rise and fall, looking back up at my face with eyes a darker shade of brown than they were before, holding me under his spell. "I just don't know if Jack has it in him to do it."

I snap out of my trance and push him away quickly. "You've been watching me and him?!"

He looks on with a taunting smile. "I see everythin', love, and I know your body don't react the same as it did just then."

I glare at him. "Oh, get over yourself, *Odin*. I'm drunk, it doesn't mean anything."

A smirk morphs from his smile, and the nerves in my stomach only grow further. "Whatever you say, *Demi.*"

Six

My fucking neck.
I slowly sit up from my awkward bloody position in the chair, rubbing my hand over my face. Even though I feel like I need to go back to fucking sleep, I need to wake up.

My phone starts ringing on the desk, so I grab it quickly, clocking Charlie's name on the screen. "What?"

"You alright?"

"Mmm-been better..."

"She still with you?"

"Who?"

"That sweet slice of *American Pie?*" He sings while I glance up, seeing her sleeping soundly on the couch. "I'll take that as a yes. She's making you lose your head."

"No, she ain't." I lie because she is. And I don't like it.

"You are so in denial mate."

"Was there a reason why you're calling?"

"Yeah, Marky asked to see you at 10am."

I look at the time, 8:12. "I'll get there when I get there. I'm not doing anything that little prick demands. He can fuckin' wait."

I hear the smile on his face. "Alright. I'll let him know."

I end the call and walk over to her. She looks so beautiful right now, sound asleep. And what's even better? She's silent. No sarcy words leaving her plump lips; no sexy innuendos that make me hard in a split second. Just, silence. But I've gotta wake her and deal with whatever shit she's gonna say now. "Oi." I gently shake her shoulder. She murmurs but doesn't wake so I shake a little harder. "You need to get up." She moans again, but louder this time. *Dear God. Her moans! She's killing me!* "Oi! You need to wake up, now."

She yawns, sitting up, slowly rubbing her eyes. Tiny, black flakes of mascara fall on to her cheeks, as well as an eyelash. She notices me looking at her, worry flooding her tired face. "What?"

I just can't fucking help myself, can I? "You've..." I slowly raise my hand to her cheek, waiting for her to let me know it's ok with a single nod before I gently touch her. "You've got an eyelash." My skin tingles as it barely touches her face, using my index finger to lift the lash from her cheek. I hold it out on my finger in front of her lips. "Make a wish and blow it away."

Her tired eyes softly sparkle as a delicate smile plays on her lips. She closes her eyes for a second, then as she opens them puckering up her lips, moving closer to blow the tiny hair away. Shivers trickle down my spine, making me instantly wish I hadn't done it but liking it all the same.

"Thanks." She timidly pulls up a strap from the dress that slipped off in her sleep. Just the simple action makes my eyes glued to her. "What is the time?"

"Quarter past eight."

"I'm sorry I fell asleep—" she halts, looking alert instantly, realising something. "Wait, where did you sleep?"

I glance over my shoulder to my desk. "In the chair." She looks surprised, but I've gotta get my shit together. "Look, I need to get going, I'll drop you off at Lucy's."

She reaches down to pick her shoes and bag up, "It's fine. I'll make my own way."

Can she just do what I say? "I promised Lucy you'd get home alright, so I'm kinda obligated."

"Oh..." She raises an eyebrow, "then, thanks."

She stands, shifting nervously and not looking at me. "Can I use the bathroom? Please?"

"Yeah." The corner of her mouth raises a little. "But this is the last time." And it drops again. *What?* I meant what I said. I don't want her in here, especially without my consent.

She doesn't answer back, which surprises me, as she turns away and disappears behind the door. I stand here like a twat, confused. This is not the mouthy woman I know.

After she pushed me away last night, she sat back down with her arms crossed. But even then, she couldn't resist asking me some more questions. I held her off as much as I could and was grateful when she fell silent, but then all I did was sit and watch her sleep, remembering how it was holding her, feeling her arms around my neck, and looking into her eyes until mine grew heavy. I don't know why I didn't get up and leave the second her eyes closed. I probably would have for any other stupid girl. But Charlie and Spence are right; however much I deny it, she's under my skin and in my fucking head.

"I'm ready." Her soft voice draws me away from my thoughts, making me look back to her. She must have run her fingers through her hair and wiped some water on her face as she looks fresher and smoother haired, but shit, still equally as beautiful. *I should have left last night.*

"Come on."

She quietly follows me down to my car. Sliding into the small space, the subtle remains of her vanilla-musk perfume fills my car. I start the engine and pull away, glancing over to see she's staring out of the window. "You're quiet?"

She looks to me. "And you're awfully talkative." My muscles involuntary pull on my mouth. "Wait, was that a smile?!" The excitement in her voice is hilarious, so I keep my eyes on the road to stop it from happening again.

"No. It was a smirk. There's a difference."

"Mhmm... whatever helps you sleep at night, *Odin*."

We drive a bit longer in silence, until it seems she's woken up enough to start asking yet more questions. "Were you stiff this morning?"

A surprised laugh leaves me. "Well yeah, kinda happens most mornin's."

"I didn't mean that—" I internally smile listening to her trip over her words again like she did in front of my mum. "—I meant like your back or neck, you know, from sleeping in the chair."

"Yeah, I knew what you meant. Just thought it would he funny to watch you blush again." I glance and yeah, her cheeks have a flush of pink to them, but her features soften.

"You should smile more often. You have a nice smile."

My face drops as I roll my shoulders and neck, uncomfortable with the compliment. "Thanks."

"You're welcome."

As I pull up outside, she gathers up her stuff, getting out still barefoot onto the damp cobbles. I make it to the door first, standing under the porch to try the collection of keys I have, trying to find Lucy's. After the third key, we're in, and I turn to look where she is to find her close—really fucking close to me—shivering a little in the cold air. I want to wrap my arms around her, and although I won't do it, I can't help myself but gaze into her beautiful grey eyes.

She looks back into mine, and after what feels too long, I finally say something. "There you go." I step aside, opening access to the unlocked door, making my way back to my car.

"Owen?" her soft shout stops me just as I'm about to get in.

"What? No *Odin*?"

"Thank you." She smiles, genuinely at me for the first time, and I feel like someone needs to slap me. I thought she was beautiful before but now? *Fuck me...*

"You're welcome."

***

"'Bout time." Charlie calls me out as soon as I step into the warehouse. "Thought you'd got lost in America?"

I wanna smack the smirk off this cunts face.

I walk past him, going into my office where Marky, one of my 'associates' sits waiting with Fred. I sit behind my desk and get ready to listen to his bullshit, "What d'you want, Marky?"

"I was just telling Freddie over here how well that new products going down with everyone. People are blowin' up my phone day 'n night to get it, word's definitely gettin' out." he says confidently, but I ain't stupid. He ain't due more stock for a while.

"If you've come for another delivery then you wasted your time, you've gotta wait. You know, like you made me fuckin' wait for my money."

"Owen," he shifts, using his arms, to help him raise his skinny arse off the chair, "I've got to keep my guys happy, mate."

"Marky, Marky, Marky..." I lean forward, resting my arms on the desk, "I think you forget I know about you skimming a bit off the top of each ounce for yourself." He begins to protest, but I ain't fucking stupid. "Stop sniffing it up your own nose, and you'd have enough for your '*guys*'. Now, get gone. You ain't getting' shit." I get up out of my chair. I need a fucking coffee that I still haven't had the chance to have because of Little Miss America.

"Oi! I need—" He rises to his feet, but Fred has my back and blocks him instantly. Freddie might be the joker of the group, but he can be a fucking psycho when pissed off. He'll have my back for life.

"Sit your lanky arse back down, right now." Fred instructs him, but he's an idiot, so I know he won't listen.

"No! I need the gear!" He tries to follow me but can't, so shouts out instead, "OI! You're nothing like Jimmy! If he was 'ere, he'd have give me i—"

I don't even give him chance to finish his sentence before my hand is gripped around his throat, pushing him back violently until I ram his back so fucking hard against the wall, he struggles for his next breath. He could have said anyone, but not Jimmy. Not my old man.

"DONT! DONT YOU FUCKIN' DARE SAY HIS NAME!" I warn, snarling at him.

"He... would be disappointed... in you." Marky manages to choke out. I pull my knife from inside my jacket, pushing it between his lips. He gargles against the blade, steaming up the silver with his breath.

"Say that again, then. Go on! I DARE YA!" His eyes widen in fear as I press deeper, "SAY IT AGAIN!" I scream in his face; my spit spraying over him. From the state of this cunt, even with his gold chains and designer gear, it looks like this is the closest thing to a shower he's had in days, but no one bad mouths me, or brings my old man into it. I'd slit his fucking throat if he didn't distribute the most out of all our associates.

"I—" I relax my grip allowing him the chance to say whatever he dares to, "I'm sorry." It's gargled as the blade sits in his gob. But he won't take this as his lesson.

"Not good enough." I whip my hand out to the side, slicing right through the corners of his mouth. As he falls to the ground hands to his mouth yelping in pain, I look down at him. "Let that be a lesson to ya, Marky, I ain't someone you come dictating to." I kick him hard in his stomach for good measure, "And *never* mention my old man again."

Remi

I close the door and lean against it, dropping my head back with a gentle thud.

Fuck.

Why did I get so drunk? Why did I let him carry me to his office? And why the hell did I let him get that close to me?

The way he made me feel as he looked down my body, stopping at the part he caught a peak of earlier, made me ache for his touch again. And fortunately—or unfortunately depending on how you look at it—my mind created exactly what he could have done to me when I was asleep whilst he sat only a few metres away at his desk. My mind imagined the way he could have slowly moved his lips to mine but then kissed me hard and aggressively, running his hands up into my hair, pulling it hard to make me moan. How he could have ripped my dress from where it sat between my breasts to expose my body before stepping back to take me in. The feeling of his tongue as he could have taken my nipple into his mouth, biting and lapping whilst kneading the other with his hand. How he might have torn off my tiny G-string before pushing me back to lay across his desk before he slides a hand into—

"Rem?"

I open my eyes as Spencer catches me out, and I immediately blush, delicately panting from my memory. "Oh! Erm, hey Spencer. I wasn't sure if you would be up."

He stands just inside the hallway, no shirt, messy hair and a steaming mug in hand. "How'd you get back?"

I push myself away to stand upright, walking toward him. He gratefully moves to allow me space into the kitchen, still holding my shoes and purse in my arms.

"I got a ride with Owen."

"Owen?!" The surprise in his voice tells me things will get out of hand if I don't change the topic of conversation.

With everything I just reimagined, I want to forget all about Owen freakin' Turner.

"Why did you leave me asleep in the office?"

"Lucy came to find you when you didn't come back, and you were out for the count apparently. Owen said he'd make sure someone got you home. I just didn't expect him to do it."

"Well, I'm sorry if I woke you when I came in, but I really must get a shower."

"Alright. See ya later."

I quickly get myself out of there and upstairs to my room, slipping out of the dress and into my robe. Taking a very long soak in the bathtub, easing my aching body. *'Don't think of him'* I repeat to myself, but it's pointless. He's infected my mind. I could barely talk to him this morning because of how awkward I felt after everything; waking up to see him staring back at me.

Once the water is cold, I make my way back to my room where a message awaits.

> *Jack: Hi beautiful. What time would*
> *you like to go tonight? J*

Shit. I'd forgotten about this. I'm confused by how I feel but this is exactly what I need. Jack is exactly who I should be dating.

> *Remi: Good morning, sorry I*
> *disappeared before the night was over.*
> *Is 8 too late? x*

> *Jack: 8 is perfect. See you tonight.*

Seven

"*I* can't believe you dreamt of him. How hot is this guy?" Riley's voice declares through my ear pods.

"Seriously!? I knew I shouldn't have told you."

"What!? I'm sorry, I just can't believe you got all hot and wet for *Mr. Asshole*."

"I'm not talking about it anymore. You're supposed to be helping to choose a dress!" I filter through the rails, sliding selection after selection from right to left, hoping something will catch my eye.

"Then find one to try on, and I'll help you."

I pull a second option to go with the other one and make my way to the fitting rooms. I stay talking to her the entire time until I have the first one on and make the switch to Facetime.

"Option one." I show the full length of the red, spaghetti-strapped dress, which is more revealing than I was expecting, and barely covering my ass.

"That is too short, no. You might as well sit there showing him his dessert straight away."

I gasp a little within my laugh. "Okay, not a fan." I put the phone camera down as I get out of the first one and slip into option two, picking up my phone once again. "Well?"

"Yes..." She starts off positive, then ruins it, "if you were mom at a funeral."

"Yeah... goodbye."

"No!! Wai—" I hang up on her and smile holding my phone in my hand, waiting for her to call back. And on cue, it starts chiming. "That was a bit dramatic."

"You're supposed be helping me."

"That was helping you, Rem. You couldn't go on a date wearing any of them. Do they not have any other places to shop in London? It's supposed to be big."

"Of course, they do. I just haven't found them yet, clearly. I got the other dress from here and it was perfect."

"Then go and see what else is around. I've got to go now anyway, but I hope you find something. Send me a picture."

After saying goodbye to one another, I admit defeat, redress, and leave the store, disappointed that I'm leaving empty handed. Walking down the sidewalk and around the corner, I find another store that has the perfect dress in the storefront, I rush in and purchase it.

After picking up a takeout coffee, I'm walking back to the Underground when a car slowly pulls up beside me. Nervously, I look over my shoulder, until I recognize who it is that's hanging out of the open window, and instantly burst with excitement.

"Fancy seein' you 'ere!" My smile widens to match his.

"I brought myself a nice dress for our date tonight."

"Mm... can't wait to see you in it." His words laced with want, it's an abrupt clearing of a gentleman's throat that forces me to look away. For the first time, I notice Charlie in the passenger seat and Owen in the backseat with Freddie.

"Oh, er, hi guys."

Owen doesn't respond to me verbally, instead choosing to nod before quickly turning to look to the left out of his window.

"You wan' a lift? They can squeeze up in the back?" I look into the car. There would be space in the huge, black Range Rover, but the atmosphere doesn't seem so inviting.

"No, it's ok."

"Great!" Owen pipes up from the back, "Then d'you think we could fuckin' go?! I ain't got all fucking day." His voice is harsh and a little sarcastic.

"Okay, well, if you're sure... I'll see you later." Jack winks, making me smile again.

"I can't wait." Jack smiles for the last time before indicating and pulling away, but not before I notice Owen's eyes glaring angrily. *What is his damn problem!?*

***

There's a happy knock on my bedroom door, as I finish applying a final layer of mascara. Lucy informs me that my date has arrived like my mom used to with Tom.

I walk down behind her, and into the kitchen. The sound of two male voices gets louder the closer we get.

"Woah!" Jack gushes, taking in the appearance of my ruched, figure-hugging white dress. Though I'm covered, thanks to the knee length skirt and long sleeves, it shows just the right amount of cleavage to make me feel sexy.

"She looks amazing, don't she?" Lucy adds to the Remi-appreciation party.

"Incredible... are you ready?"

Nodding that I am, Spencer and Jack clasp hands before we say our goodbyes and leave the house, getting into his BMW. Jack holds the door open for me, the sign of a perfect gentleman. The conversation is light and easy, relaxing my nerves at long last. He is easy to be around, and it feels natural.

We aren't travelling for more than twenty minutes, when he pulls up outside a very fancy looking restaurant, slotting the car into a space immediately outside the door. He smiles before getting out and walking around to collect me from my side, letting me link my arm through his before we walk into the busy atmosphere where we're greeted by a polite looking gentleman.

"Bonsoir Mr. Stevens et Mademoiselle." The Maître D' fusses around Jack, like he is some celebrity. His French accent is thick when he continues. "Please, let me show you to your table."

We follow behind him, walking through the tables to one reserved for us. It has crisp white tablecloth and black velvet high backed chairs that the Maître D' pulls out for me to sit on. Once I'm tucked in, he flutters out the napkin, placing it perfectly across my lap.

"Merci beaucoup." He smiles as I thank him, before politely bowing and leaving us alone.

While we begin looking through the menu and placing our order, the conversation flows easily. He tells me about his sister, Alice and his mom. His mom has her struggles, but I can tell he loves her a lot, and he is equally as close to his sister. I tell him about Riley and my family. He had the same reaction as everyone does when I tell them my father is gay – the initial surprise followed with the usual questions of when did he know, was my mom upset, and do I still see him? Like that would stop anything; he's my dad.

"That's cool. So, you all, like, get along?"

"Yeah. My mom gets on well with Terry, his fiancé. They're like her protective brothers, who just happen to be my dad and future stepdad."

"That's mad."

I shrug. "Not really, it's just how it is. It might not work for everyone, but for us it does. Would you want to see your dad if he was around?"

"Not particularly. My mum said he was a twat who preferred beer over everything else, so I'm glad he disappeared when we were little. Done us all a favor." I can see that he is saddened by the situation even if he wouldn't admit it.

"I'm sorry."

"It don't bother me. It upset Alice more when we were kids, but we have a good relationship with Jim, so he made up for it. He's like a crazy uncle who looks out for us."

"Jim?" I say, frowning. Am I supposed to know who that is?

"Jimmy Turner, Owen and Luce's dad."

I smile, liking that he had a father figure even though it wasn't his own. "That's nice."

"Yeah, it is. I can't wait 'til he gets out."

"Gets out?" I furrow my brows, confused once more. I thought he was away working?

Jack suddenly looks nervous, "I mean back."

"Oh, where is he?"

He shifts uncomfortably in his seat, mumbling a little, "he's dining at His Majesty's pleasure."

"What does that mean?" I ask as the creases develop between my eyebrows.

"Don't worry 'bout it... I can't tell you anyway."

"What? Why not?" I exclaim. Why did he say anything if he isn't allowed to tell me?

"I just can't." he says assertively, almost biting back.

"Oh, well I'm sorry for prying." I'm a little annoyed he snapped at me, so I pick up my glass and take a couple of small sips of my white wine, wishing I hadn't asked the damn question.

"Remi, I'm sorry. It's just one of those things, it's not my business to say."

"It's fine. Don't worry about it."

"You sure?"

I muster a reassuring smile and murmur, offering pacification, but the atmosphere has gone from comfortable to awkward quickly and I don't think either of us know how to bring it back.

We both eat the rest of our meal, asking questions to try to fill the time until I excuse myself to use the restroom. He smiles softly back at me, promising to settle the bill.

I stand at the wash basin, looking at my disappointed face in the mirror. I was convinced we had good chemistry, but even before the Jimmy-related nosedive, I realized I didn't feel like I thought I did. Jack is an attractive and really nice guy, and I do like being around him, but I don't feel how I expected too tonight. But I didn't have instant chemistry with Tom either. Maybe the '*zing*' is a myth?

Then why do I keep thinking of last night?

I walk out of the restroom and collide with a body as they rush toward the door. A super slim woman with platinum hair and over-plumped pink lips slams into my shoulder before glaring at me.

"Watch where you're going!" Her polite, posh accent contradicts the attitude she oozes.

"Excuse me, you ran into me!" Despite my retaliation, she still looks back in disgust.

"Er, no I didn't darling!" I clench my jaw at her condescending tone, but she enters a stall before I can shout back at her.

I glance up ahead to the tables to see if Jack is ready to go, when a figure to my right catches my eye. *You have got to be kidding me!*

"What are you doing here?!"

Owen's face is as deadpan as usual. "Having dinner." He gestures with his head in the direction of the restroom door behind me.

"Ha! Now, why doesn't that surprise me?" I laugh out, not at all surprised he is with her. Go figure! She is one hundred percent his type, after all. "Good luck with that one." I attempt to walk past him, but he lifts his arm out to stop me. He doesn't touch me but even the presence of his hand so close to my stomach makes my breath stall. When he moves closer as if to talk in my ear, the breath from his nose against my skin sends shivers down my spine. *What is he doing?* My eyes momentarily close, eagerly and strangely waiting to hear his deep, commanding voice.

"Hmm. Just as I thought."

My eyes instantly reopen as I turn my head to glare at him. "And what's that, asshole?"

He moves away from me with an obnoxious grin on his face, but I turn my body to square up to him, determined to get to the bottom of his little game, or whatever the hell he's doing right now.

"It wasn't the drink that made your body respond to me."

Oh, I get it now! I smile smugly. "Sweetie, I've been drinking and flirting with a hot guy all evening. Your little experiment is void."

But when his face turns devilish, he steps forward, somehow pushing my body back against the wall. He never touches me yet gets me exactly where he wants me. "Is that why you've looked uncomfortable for the last half hour?"

I wish I could say this surprised me, but it doesn't. Of course, he's seen us! He *"see's everything"*.

"So? It's not like you're any more comfortable to be around, is it?" His lips pinch into a line, as he soaks in my words. But he says nothing. "Now, I have to get back to my date. Please move."

He allows me space to leave, letting me walk back to the table. I take long, deep breaths putting a smile on my face, putting all of that out of my mind, leaving all the feelings he ignited back behind that wall. Jack sits there patiently, looking a little relieved when I sit back in front of him. "I thought you'd jumped out the window." He laughs, nervously.

"No. I'm not like that. I ran into someone by the bathroom who wouldn't stop talking, sorry." *I'm not lying... just missing out the part where his boss confronted me.*

"That's okay. You ready to go?"

The conversation is less strained on the journey home, which I welcomed. I think the bathroom break was the space we needed to reset the evening, I know it certainly made me appreciate being here with him. When he walks me back to the door, the porch light is on, lighting up his handsome face, and I mean what I say. "I had a lovely evening."

"Me too." We stand for a second under the canopy above the door, gazing at one another. "Would it be inappropriate to kiss you?"

"No."

He returns my smile, leaning down to connect his lips with mine. They're as soft as I thought they would be, and after a second, his tongue asks to be granted permission. I allow it, feeling his tongue tickle against mine while his hands snake around my back. I hold his forearms, feeling the muscles under my touch, when I hear him moan softly in appreciation. It's what I hoped would happen in this moment, though the only thing I feel is guilt. I can try and deny it, but all I can think of is Owen. He didn't even touch me, and the world around us disappeared for that moment. I break away naturally, ending it where his eyes slowly open to meet mine, only doubling the guilt. "Thank you for a lovely evening, Jack."

"Can I take you out again?"

"I, er…" I know I need to try again; I know I need to push Owen out of my mind and give Jack my full attention, "I'd like that."

He nods happily, smiling like the cat that got the cream, before stepping back slowly to his car. "Until next time."

Eight

The past week has been amazing. I went dress shopping with Lucy, Alice and her mom, Paula to get the bridesmaid dresses. I tried my hardest to build the bridge with Paula, though I didn't get far. It's easy to see where Owen got his personality from!

Alice on the other hand was lovely and made me feel instantly comfortable. She even knew her brother and I had been on a date, but thankfully didn't pry. She looks like Jack with long, soft brown hair and matching eyes, and while they both are friendly, their personalities understandable differ.

Jack and I have slipped back into the talking and flirting we were doing before our date and I'm glad that I agreed to go out again next week. I really want to give him a chance to prove that last time was just a really bad first date. And hopefully Owen freakin' Turner will be nowhere in sight. I have enjoyed having no interaction with him this week, and long may it continue.

On another note, the people who come to the bar to watch me sing are loving it. I get so many coming to speak to me afterwards, wanting to know a little bit more about me, and can't wait to return the following week to hear me again. Lucy said that they haven't had as many patrons staying for the performers as they do now, so that must be a good sign? Surely Owen can't complain about that? Roberto is buzzing, eagerly waiting to hear my set this week. We have gotten closer with every shift worked together and he is a real breath of fresh air. He's as camp as they come, and I absolutely love being around him.

"Babe, with the stuff you're posting online and what you've been singing here, you're gonna be signing a deal in no time! I can feel it." I love his enthusiasm, but pessimism outweighs mine. Like it has for the last year.

"It's not that easy, but I appreciate you."

"Of course it is! That's how that stuff all works doesn't it?"

I laugh lightly, making the most of our relaxed afternoon in The Rose. "No. I nearly got signed before and it's a lot of meetings discussing terms and what they expect you to do and what you can provide, if you want to tour and how many albums they'll agree to sign you for."

"Woah, can't you just go on the X Factor?"

I laugh louder, "Oh... no, no… that's not for me."

"So, what happened? Why didn't you get signed?" He is full of sincerity. I haven't told anyone since I have been here why I am here, but I trust him enough to tell him.

"I was in a relationship with a sound engineer, and he helped put me in the right places, speak to the right people. He wanted me to have the perfect image that all the label execs wouldn't have to touch. I was a ready-made artist - especially with everything I had done since I was little. Then I found out he had cheated on me, so I broke up with him." Roberto tuts, knowing all too well how it feels to have a cheating ex, but lets me continue. "I soon discovered it wasn't a one off and he had also slept with a lot of girls, but to save himself from embarrassment, he turned everyone against me. He said I was aggressive; I was blackmailing him into being my manager and I was forcing him to get me a record deal otherwise I would fake injuries that he physically assaulted me."

He looks at with me shock on his face, "Jesus! You're feisty, but certainly not aggressive! So, he made all that up because you dumped him?"

"Yes. Apparently, I'm a crazy, mean girlfriend who pushed her adoring boyfriend into making me a star. He made everyone believe I was ready to fight dirty and stop at nothing to get it. No one wanted any connection with me then. My parents tried to fight it, but I didn't really have anything to back or support my case, the same way he didn't have anything to back his. They believed his word, and here I am in a different country talking to you."

"Babe, that's a load of bullshit." Roberto says, giving me a big hug. "But if it's any consolation, I'm glad you're here. I know you will get what you want, Remi. I feel it in my bones."

We both laugh out, sharing another hug when I hear Lucy asking. "Is everything alright?"

Both turning to look at her, I see a small blonde-haired boy holding her hand. He must be around four, maybe five, and he's super cute. "Hey! Who's this cutie-pie?"

"This is my nephew, Bradley."

I'm momentarily stunned. I didn't know she had a nephew? "Hi Bradley, I'm Remi, pleased to meet you."

Bradley gazes up gingerly, hugging onto her leg. "Say hello, she won't hurt you." Lucy encourages earning a small wave from him. "Sorry, he's a little shy with new people, but trust me, it doesn't last long."

"You're alright Brad," Roberto scoops in, putting him at ease. "Rem is super cool. She can play the guitar and will give you sweets."

His little eyes light up. "Can I have some sweeties please, Auntie Lucy?"

"Only one small bag."

"Shall we go out to the storeroom and see what you want?" He is hesitant at my question but then let's go of Lucy's hand, walking up to me. I instinctively hold out my hand, which he takes. His small hand fits into mine with room to spare as I guide him through, looking down at his excited face.

"Why do you talk funny?"

I giggle. "Do I talk funny?"

"Yeah, like the people on YouTube."

I release a humoured breath, smiling at him. "I'm from America. Your Aunt Lucy asked if I wanted to come over here and work with her, so I did."

"Did you have to come over on an airplane?"

I smile at the way he says the word. The innocence of a babe... "Yes. It was a big airplane; the biggest one I've ever been on!"

"Wow! I haven't been on an airplane. Mummy says when I'm bigger she will take me on holiday."

"That's exciting! Where would you like to go?"

"Disneyland!" He bursts with excitement, and I can't help mirroring it.

"I have been there, it is AMAZING!" He beams back at me, eyes full of awe. "Who's your favorite Disney character?"

He thinks long and hard, "Buzz, or Mr Incredible! He's super strong, like me. I have big muscles like he does, look." He lifts his free arm and flexes it. His tiny little arm doesn't change but my heart swells at something so simple but important to him.

"Oh wow! I think you have even bigger muscles than even he does." He giggles happily. "So, what candy would you like?"

We talk about other things he likes. He loves Spiderman and all the superheroes, which is cool because I am a big Marvel and DC fan. I could talk all day about them with him, but with his sweets in hand, we make our way back to the bar. Lucy sits at the usual table checking her phone until she sees him running toward her.

"I hope you were a good boy?"

"I was."

Lucy looks at me to confirm this as he sits beside her. "He was an angel."

Now I know she's lying." she jokes, pulling him into her side to place a kiss on his hair, "You're definitely not an angel."

He begins to giggle infectiously making the two of us laugh with him.

But the happiness is sucked out of the air in a split second when Owen's voice sounds off behind me. "What's so funny?"

Hearing his voice causes me to stop laughing instantly. I haven't seen him since that night in the restaurant. Okay, I haven't physically seen him since then, but he hijacks my dreams from time to time.

"Daddy!" I watch Brad shout out in excitement and run into Owens arms, answering my unasked question from earlier. *Bradley is Owen's son.*

As he gathers Bradley up and wraps him in a big hug, you can see how much he loves him. The way he closes his eyes, savoring the moment with his child like it has been a long time since he last held him. Eventually he pulls away but keeps him in his arms. "Sorry I couldn't get you today. Have you been good for Auntie Lucy?" Bradley nods, adding another piece of candy into his mouth. "Any issues?" Owen asks, looking to Lucy who shakes her head. He nods once, receiving the silent information she shared with her own simple gesture. I've noticed that they do this from time to time, like there is a silent understanding between them that no one can know about, but it's subtle, and could easily be overlooked.

"Why you eatin' sweets? You haven't had your dinner yet?" He looks annoyed as Bradley takes yet another piece out of the packet. *Great...*

"She gave me them." He points to me, which is instantly followed by a pair of glaring eyes.

"Of course, she did." Owen says, laced with irritancy.

"Hey! I didn't just give them to him. Lucy said he could have them." I don't want him thinking I just took it upon myself to give them to Bradley.

Owen quickly glances to her, needing confirmation. *Is my word not good enough?*

"I said it was okay. He'll be alright, calm down." Lucy graciously confirms.

"Whatever." Owen mumbles before his voice and demeanor lightens when he looks back to his son. "Where d'you wanna go for dinner tonight?"

"You know where I want to go, daddy!" Bradley wraps his arms loosely around Owens neck giggling playfully, earning a genuine smile from Owen. Then again, I have never seen him smile like this before. But then I have never seen him with his child.

"Again?" I watch him ask, completely transfixed. Though I knew Owen had more to him, I'm still confused by the softer man standing here interacting with his child. I didn't think he had the ability to be this gentle, or playful. It's clear he has the capacity to be a nice guy—I saw it the morning he took me back home, and I certainly see it now, so why does he insist on acting like an asshole?

"Yes! It's my favorite! Can Remi come with us?" Bradley asks out of the blue, pressing the emergency stop button in my brain instantly. *Say what now?*

"Oh, um—" I try to dissolve his interest in me, but Bradley continues.

"Did you know she went on a big airplane from America?"

"Yeah, it's cool ain't it? But no, dude, she can't come with us." Owen explains to Bradley, giving him all of his attention.

"I'm working sweetie. You will have much more fun with Daddy anyway." I offer too, trying to keep my eyes focused on Bradley and not the two inches to the right where Owens eyes bore into my soul.

"Well technically, Rem, you shouldn't be working today. Why don't you go?" *Why did she have to say that?*

We both turn to look at Lucy, no doubt pleading with the same expressions for her to shut the hell up. Believe me, the last thing I want to do is go out with him—in any capacity!

"I really should stay." I begin to insist as Owen talks over me.

"She should finish her shift."

"Look," Lucy says, rolling her eyes, "it's hardly bloody busy, is it? It's just dinner for God's sake. Go."

I know it's just dinner, but can it ever be just dinner with Owen? Nothing is *just* anything when it comes to him! I barely know the guy, but the more time I spend with him, the more of an enigma he becomes. The way he switches from the asshole to someone who I know has a caring side, the way he can control my body with nothing but close proximity, and finally, this man right here: the loving father, and the way I can't work out how I feel about him.

"Are you coming, Remi?" Bradley's softly sweet voice asks. I dare to look at Owen, his face is as unreadable as always, so I ask with a look if he is okay with this.

"If he's happy, I'm happy. But if you're coming, I'm leaving now." he confirms, making me immediately nervous.

"I'll grab my bag then."

Please God, help me get through this.

Nine

$\mathcal{I}$ am sat in a dinosaur themed bloody restaurant with my son, who I'm desperate to spend some time with, and someone I don't want to spend any more time with than I have to, but when have I ever been able to catch a fucking break?

Me and Remi have ignored one another as much as humanly possible since she got her bag and joined me in the front of my car. I think that's so we don't argue, or I lose my shit in front of my kid. I don't want any crap, just a nice couple of days with him.

"Daddy, have you been on an airplane?" I smile softly. *God, I have missed this boy.* He has grown so much, it's scary.

"Yeah. I'd love to take you on one too. Maybe one day..." My voice drifts off as the realisation that it might never happen rolls through my mind.

"Mummy said she's going to take me to Disneyland when I'm bigger. Can you come with us?"

I let out a big sigh. *What the hell do I say?* "I think we should go on our own, dude. That way we can both go on the rides together, otherwise me or your mum will have to miss out enjoying the ride with you."

"It's okay, you can come on with me and mummy can wait." he says, completely unaware – just as he should – that me and his mum will never, ever go on a holiday together. Hell will fucking freeze over, then thaw and refreeze before that happens. I close my eyes for a second, trying to think of something to say.

"But then your mommy won't get to see you enjoy it. I think that'll make her sad." Remi's voice delicately speaks out. I glance at her, and she gives me a soft understanding smile. I appreciate her saying that because she said it in a way I never could.

"Yeah," he states, satisfied, "mummy doesn't like to be sad."

"Exactly. And you can have twice the fun by going two times!" I internally smile at her enthusiasm which seems to seep into Brad, because his little eyes light up. If I had my way, he would have already been there as well as a million other places in the world. But I don't have my way.

When our food arrives, we watch Brad begin eating his food in comfortable silence whilst tucking into our own.

"How old is he?" Remi's tone is quiet and shy. I knew she'd have to ask something eventually because if I've learned anything about her, it's that she *must* ask a question!

"Four. He'll be five in October."

"He's a fantastic kid." She smiles, but not at me; her gaze is drawn to my son. I swallow nervously as I see how they sparkle as she watches him eat in fascination. I don't surround him with many people, but I can see now that I shouldn't have been concerned about her. I've never seen anyone look at him like that.

"Thanks."

We eat a few more bites before she speaks again. It reminds me a little of her asking six thousand questions in my office the night she was drunk, and one I've relived a few times.

"Do you get to see him often?"

"No, not as much as I'd like."

"That must be hard." *You have absolutely no idea.*

"Yeah. Me and his mum... it's complicated."

She nods in understanding and continues to eat, never asking anything else. She must get that I don't want to talk about it. I doubt she would understand anyway.

Once Brad has finished his chicken and chips, with a rather large dollop of ketchup, he fidgets in his seat, "Daddy, did you know Remi loves Spider-Man too!" His happy little face is amazing to see. It's been a long time since I was last allowed to see him, and it's been fucking hard. He's growing and changing so much each time, that I'm scared one day, I won't recognise him.

"She does?" I cast my eyes upon her, she wipes her mouth politely on a napkin. Her carefree giggle that comes next is euphoric.

"You love Spider-man, I love Thor."

"Of course you do."

"Hey, I'm not even sorry. That man is literally a God." She smiles at me becoming animated. I genuinely think this is the most normal conversation we have ever had, and I've gotta admit, I like it. "And like you wouldn't turn down Black Widow if you had the chance?" she continues, suddenly realising something. "Oh wait, no, she's not blonde... you'd probably prefer Pepper Potts." She winks mischievously and my dick bucks in my boxers. *Jesus Christ...*

I play along and smirk a little back at her, "Natasha has blonde hair at one point, you know... but I wouldn't say no to either of them." The irony of how she makes me feel when talking about the blondes I usually go for, is completely lost on her.

Her eyes light up. "Ha, I knew it!"

"So, what's your favourite film?" While we have common ground, I'm gonna take all the opportunities to find out more about her.

"Oh my God, I love them for all for different reasons, but Ragnarok is up there as one of my favourites." I fight the urge to do a big smile, agreeing with her. "How about you?"

"Black Panther."

"Yes!" she enthuses, "See! They're all so good."

We lock eyes with one another for a second, her genuine smile gripping my chest like a vice, before she nervously breaks it to look down at her food. I contemplate whether to say what I was thinking to compliment her on her smile as she did mine—but gratefully Brad interrupts.

"Daddy, can I have ice cream, please?"

He could have anything he wants, so he orders a big ol' bowl of vanilla ice cream chocolate sauce and sprinkles, and Remi has a small bowl too.

Watching her mouth expertly suck the sauce and mould the ice cream on her spoon is driving me insane. I shouldn't be imagining it as anything else. I know it's disgusting but my God, if she can do that to ice cream, how would she take a dick in her mouth?

We finish up the meal and though she insists on paying for hers, I'm not that much of a twat to take it. I'm enjoying that she's a lot more relaxed than when we arrived—like I am. Maybe Lucy wasn't so stupid in insisting that she comes.

"Are you coming back to daddy's house too?" Brad asks innocently. *What is it with him and forcing us to be together?*

Her soft, kind eyes looking at him. "No, I have to go home to my house now."

"Do you live with your mummy and daddy?"

"No, I live with your Aunt Lucy and Spencer. But when I'm home in America, I live with my mom and sister." she explains, making sure it's innocently enough that he understands it. Can't lie, I'm enjoying the little pieces of information he's extracting from her. I focus on driving, quietly listening and mentally making notes of it.

"Do you have a daddy?"

"I do. I'm lucky like you because he lives in a different house, like yours does."

I swear, I don't know how she's doing it but even interacting with Brad like this is making me hard. I love it and hate it all at the same time. She's a beautiful woman but I shouldn't be feeling this way; I can't give her what she would want.

When curiosity gets the better of me, I ask my own question. "How long have they been separated?"

"Since I was nine."

"Do they get on?"

"Yes, they make it work, for me and Riley."

"That's nice. You're lucky." I wish Portia and I had a better relationship, simply for Brad, but I would happily rip her head off if he wasn't here. He has the right to have a mum, and I won't take that away from him – no matter how much I can't stand the air she breathes.

We pull up outside Lucy's and she says a sweet goodbye to Brad before getting out, standing in the open door, almost unsure what to do next.

"So, erm, thanks again for dinner."

"That's alright, it made him happy."

Her smile this time makes my heart race.

"He's amazing, it isn't hard to be with him. Have a fun sleep over at daddy's house."

She gives Brad a soft wave and shuts the door. I wait until she's gone in before pulling away.

"I like her, daddy."

"Yeah..." *It's getting harder not to.*

Remi

From the second I stepped outside of the restaurant, I knew. The journey gave me time to digest it because it really happened: Owen and I have a common interest. And more significant is that he isn't an asshole twenty-four seven! Neither of these things were expected, and dare I say it was nice, almost comfortable by the end.

Lewis is picking me up to take me to his friend's music studio, and to say I'm excited would be an understatement. I didn't expect this to happen so soon, I haven't been in the studio for around four weeks due to getting everything sorted for my move here.

Lewis and I walk through the plain black door and down some corridors. Nothing highlights what this building is from the outside, and if I was alone, I don't know if I would believe there is anything here other than doors leading off from this one long corridor.

He stops outside one and I can hear the soft, melodic base pulsing from inside. He enters first gaining the attention of the four gentleman working behind the desk.

"Alright fam?" Lewis says, gripping the hands and bumping shoulders of a guy wearing dark glasses and designer clothes.

"S'up man?" When they break apart, the man in glasses, and the only one Lewis acknowledged in this manner asks me. "You must be Remi P?" I giggle as he uses the name Lewis now calls me.

"Remi is fine."

He smiles a perfectly white smile, enhanced by the depth of his natural skin. "Well, 'just Remi' I'm Dom, nice to meet ya." His deep, bassy voice has an air of authority. He is a man comfortable in his surroundings and the guys working with him appear to know their place as they don't stop working he gives me and Lewis all his attention.

"Thank you for agreeing to meet me."

"No need to thank me, I knew if Lewis asked, you were worth my time." *Is that a compliment?*

"Thanks?"

Sensing my confusion, Lewis explains. "I've only asked Dom to see one other artist, they're selling shit loads of records now."

"Then thanks to both of you."

They match my wide smile before Dom stands up and walks over to me, encouraging me with a soft nod of his head to follow him. "So, you wanting to sing tonight or just get a feel for the place?"

Are all British men straight talkers? "I didn't bring my guitar as I wasn't expecting you to be free, I'm sorry, I just assumed we would be meeting and then I'd book to come again. He guides me down a couple of doors, stopping at the end of the corridor to another plain black door that identifies as 'Available' on the slide board in the wall beside it.

"Nah, man, you have my time anytime I can give it. You can come use the rooms anytime you like." He opens it and walks inside. I gasp taking in the grand piano, microphones, acoustic guitars, electric guitars, keyboards, drumkits and other handheld percussion instruments perfectly placed in the soundproof room.

"Not all have recording equipment, as you can see from this one, but you can practice and write, or whatever. You only pay for when we're recording." It feels like all my Christmases and birthdays have arrived together because this is perfect. The studio back home was small, if you were there, you were writing or recording together. The only space I had just for myself, and my instruments were at home.

"This is incredible, thank you so much." I look behind me to Lewis thanking him too. I cannot wait to get in here. Especially this one with that piano!

The two of them continue to show me around the place. There is a stocked kitchen and bathrooms, complete with showers should you need them. We settle back into the room where we started and Dom sits back at the mixing table, making some selections on the large screens and playing an instrumental reggae-vibe dance track. Just as Lewis said, dance music is not my genre, but I can still appreciate it.

"Wow. Did you mix this?"

"This is one, a group I work with put together one night, but didn't think it would come too much. I still think it's good. Has the beginnings of somethin' I know that much."

The longer it rolls over, some lyrics I had written before seeming to fit effortlessly. I play around with the melody and key in my head, and naturally start humming along. They both notice, with Dom stopping the playback.

"What's that you've got going there?" he asks, eyes narrowing a little but holding their sparkle.

"It's nothing." I brush it off, feeling stupid for adding words to a song about Tom over something so uplifting.

"It's never nothin', Rem. The best songs in the world start from somewhere." Lewis expresses, putting me at ease.

"I was just playing around with some melodies to flow over the top. Maybe a verse and chorus?"

"If I play it again, wanna hum it?"

"I can play it on the keyboard if you like?"

He looks excited. "Yeah! The Yamaha one over there."

I head into the booth and stand, quickly warming up my fingers and playing a few chords to get the feel.

"Ready?" he asks over the speakers.

"Yeah."

He plays it from the beginning, and I play too, pausing between the separate parts of the song. It isn't a lot, but he nods his head, screwing his mouth up in appreciation. By the third time, I begin to sing, adding in the words. Memories of the headspace I was in fill my mind: hating Tom so much, discovering him cheating on me, and wishing I had never met him. I could never live my life how I wanted to while he was in it. I was never free then, but I feel freer now. Being here without the fear that someone will know him and have heard his lies This is my second chance, and I will not waste it on another man.

He stops the playback after we have heard my voice singing over the backing.

"I like it!"

"Me too." Lewis declares, nudging my shoulder playfully.

"You do?"

"Yeah. I'll send it on to them."

"Stop! It is just playing around; the lyrics weren't written for this. They won't want them."

"And? What if they do?"

He's right; *what if they do?*

Ten

J slept like a baby last night, feeling more settled here than I have the whole two weeks. Moments from the studio and many moments from dinner replayed throughout my dreams. Some making me smile, some making me confused. My smile grew from meeting and spending time with Bradley, and I hope to see him again one day, and of course going to the studio for the first time. I still can't quite believe how insane that is. I know nothing will come out of Dom sending off the sample to the artists, but I still appreciate it enormously. He didn't have to do that for someone he just met.

The confusion comes, of course, from the enigma that is Owen freakin' Turner.

Why can I not get him out of my head?

After a playful tap on my door, it opens quickly and in walks Lucy, holding my lifeline in her hands.

"Coffee?" she beams, passing it to me gently, holding on to her own cup of tea.

"I could kiss you right now."

We giggle as she slides into my bed beside me. I have gotten used to our little bedroom chats, where she talks about her wedding, The Rose and moans about the silly things Spencer still does. It's nice to see that even though they look perfect, they're as normal as any other couple I know. She asks me with a burning desire how it was yesterday. I tell her all about what happened at the studio, enjoying her excitement as it grew to match mine. Then the conversation turns to the one person I don't want to think about any more than I am.

"Was it really bad?" She screws up her face, expecting the worse, just as I was when we left together.

"Surprisingly, no."

"Piss off! Really?" she exclaims in astonishment, making me giggle nervously.

"Yes. It was so awkward to begin with, but it turns out we have a mutual liking of the Marvel Cinematic Universe."

She laughs, relaxing back and taking a soft sip of her drink. "Oh yeah, he's a big comic nerd. He's loved them since he was a kid. He would never even let me near them when I was little, threatened to kill me if I did."

She says it so blasé, like it's nothing, but I could actually believe him doing that. The glare he has given me on multiple occasions, I'm sure if I pushed, he could snap. I just don't know if she means it metaphorically or literally.

"What happened to make him such an asshole?" I dare to ask with the edge of nervousness. As much as she dishes the dirt about a lot of things, one thing I've known from the beginning is she is guarded about her family. Protective, almost.

"Are you really asking me about Owen?" She drops her mug from her face, side smirking at me.

"You made me go out for dinner with the damn man!"

"Technically, I encouraged you to go out for dinner with my nephew..."

"You get how wrong that sounds don't you?"

She chuckles to herself before looking lost in thought. I take a tentative sip, unsure if she will talk or not.

"Owen's just Owen." There's that word again, *just.* "I know he's a proper arsehole but underneath it all, he is a good guy, he just doesn't trust people easily. I think he gets it from my dad, he's very much like him. When Owen lets you in though, he can be very transparent."

The way she says *'you'* I automatically assume she means me, but I know she said it in general terms. Truth be told, she said more than I thought she would. So, I am right; there is more to him. Why doesn't he trust easily? He's been hurt in the past... is that what the situation is with him and Bradley's mom? The worst bit about her declaration is the resemblance to their dad. Knowing what Paula is like, I was sure Owen was like her, but if he is like Jimmy, his dad, what is it going to be like when he is home?

***

I've done my shift behind the bar and now getting ready for my performance, and as I expected, I am really enjoying playing here. Each time I perform, the crowd gets a little bigger, the applause gets a little louder. Lewis is buzzed from it all and Lucy said that if we keep going the way we are, in a few weeks, we'll be filling every table.

Lucy eventually showed me the small room near the cellar that has been set up with a vanity mirror and changing room, and some lockers to keep my belongings in. She keeps apologizing for not showing me this the first day, but like Spencer said, Owen could have.

I'm applying a final layer of gloss to my lips when my phone rings. *'Unknown'*.

I frown before answering dubiously. "Hello?"

"Hey, Rem."

"Tom!?" Stunned would be an understatement. Dumbfounded is more like it. "How did you get this number?" Shock turns to annoyance.

"You know I have my ways."

"What do you want?" I don't know why I am entertaining him, but there must be a reason he has gone to this length to call. He isn't the type of ex to call bragging. That is one positive I can say, one of very few.

"I just wanted to let you know that some of the songs you wrote and recorded with me were released as potential records for other artists." My eyes widen in surprise. *He sold them?*

"My songs?"

"The songs we recorded together. I'm legally obligated to inform you that we have sold them on, and they will be released on two artists EP's."

My songs are being released?! I don't care that they're not by me; nothing I wrote when we were together is as meaningful to me as it would be now. *This is so exciting!* "Okay, so, what do you need? Bank details—"

"No, I don't need anything. You're not getting paid."

Maybe I have forgotten how to understand English because I'm sure he just told me I am not getting paid. "I'm sorry, what did you just say?!"

"I own them."

"What?! HOW?"

"You really should read the things you sign, baby."

My nostrils flare in rage. I can't stand it when he calls me 'baby'. I used to love it, now it makes me feel physically sick. "YOU FUCKING BASTARD! They're mine! I wrote them!"

"Doesn't mean shit when you sign them away." I signed something before the label decided to end all connection to me. I thought it was protecting my work, not giving them away. He tricked me.

"You're a lying, scheming asshole! I wouldn't have had to do anything if you hadn't made up lies about me to save yourself! I lost everything because you couldn't keep your dick in your fucking pants." I don't like that my emotions are growing thick in my throat. I really hate him. I didn't think he could get any lower, but he has. He's twisting the knife he stabbed me with four months ago.

"It's a dog-eat-dog world, Rem."

"Yeah, well, I can't wait for a bitch to come and fuck you up!" I screamed down the phone before hanging up. I groan out loudly in frustration, fisting my hands and pressing them hard into my temples. I hate him! I hate him with every fibre of my body.

Fucking asshole!

Cheating bastard!

I scream the words over and over, calling him everything I can spit out, hitting my fisted hands against the wall, and wishing it was him.

"Hey!" I feel hands grip my arms, pulling me away from hitting the wall anymore. I know who it is, my chest has tightened and the tingling from his touch trickles down my wrists to my elbows. I don't stop though, I keep punching out, trying to get away from Owen's touch, but he pushes my back gently against the wall.

"Get off me!" I seethe. *I don't want him here.*

"No." He scolds, unrelenting his hold.

"Owen, I am *really* not in the fucking mood to play your games right now! Let. Me. GO!" I push with everything I have in attempt to get him away from me.

"No." he holds me tighter, looking deep into my eyes. *Those eyes.* We have a silent stand-off; me wanting him to leave and him not letting go. "Just... calm down, okay?"

Just. Why can I never *just* do anything when it relates to him?

I close my eyes to take a few long, deep breaths, gazing back into his eyes. My heart is still racing, but his proximity is dowsing the fire engulfing me slowly, like he's my own personal conductor, drawing my anger away until I'm calm enough to ask him what he's doing here.

"I was walking past and heard you shoutin'."

I can't believe in just a few seconds he has been able to calm me so much. I shift uncomfortably making us both realize he still has my wrists in his grasp.

He drops them like they're hot potatoes. Only then I feel the tears trickling down my face. I quickly wipe them away, hoping that my makeup is salvageable.

"You still look beautiful."

What did he just say?

My eyes widen in shock. but he looks just as calm and collected as he always does.

"Thanks." My gratitude comes out shy and pathetic, I'm not happy about it. I'm not happy that he has seen me like this, and I'm not happy that I feel like this in the first place.

Our eyes stay locked, both unwilling to acknowledge just how close we are. *Why is he still here? Why haven't I moved? Do I want to?* My chest pants softly, and his presence is heating multiple areas of my body. He goes to lift his hand to my cheek then stops dropping it again.

"Owen." The weakness of which his name escapes finally reveals to us both how much he affects me.

"I'm sorry…"

I open my lips to ask why he is apologizing when I remember the night when he grabbed my hand. The night I felt the electricity hit me for the first time, and the night I told him never to touch me again. Right in this second, I wish I hadn't. "Touch me." It's a mere whisper but I mean it.

Looking conflicted, he slowly brings his hand up to my left cheek. The second his flesh touches mine, my body reacts like I haven't been functioning completely my entire life, and this is what one hundred percent feels like: the clarity to see clearer, the ability to feel every woven fibre of my clothes against my skin. I take long shaky breaths, watching him mesmerized by his hand. It leaves my face, brushes down my neck, and travels along the edge of my shirt. I squeeze my thighs together as his fingers creep slowly closer to my right breast. I can feel how wet he's making me as it leaves my body and coats my underwear.

Owen edges forward, pushing his body against mine. I feel everything beneath the material of his pants; he's as aroused as I am. His eyes flick to my mouth before he moves towards me. I close my eyes ready to feel his lips against mine, but they never connect. His beard rubs against my cheek, and instinctively turn my head, enjoying the sensation of it against my skin. "I'd love to touch every inch of you, but you should stay away from me." His raspy voice and breath against my neck sends those shocks straight between my legs. My eyes stay closed enjoying it too much, my voice a wanting whisper.

"What if I don't want to?" I want him to know that I'm okay with this. I know that what I feel when I'm with him is something I want more of. But although he is close, he is still so damn far away from giving what I'm now craving.

"Then you're gonna get hurt." There is pain in his statement.

"I'm already hurt."

His lips dangerously tease the lobe of my ear, making me want to grab his head and kiss him passionately, but his words stop me. "Not in the way I can hurt you."

He pulls back enough to graze his lips across mine, but he doesn't kiss me; he leaves me and walks out of the room.

Eleven

Looking in the rear-view mirror to see my son sitting in his car seat, a soft smile on his innocent little face still makes me smile even though he left that seat an hour ago.

Brad will never know what he gives to me when I see him, but I hold on to every memory as though it's my last. His big smile as he lay in my bed was infectious and his giggle was intoxicating. He always stays in my bed because I just want to be close to him. We ate popcorn and watched films until he drifted off to sleep. I watched him, taking mental notes of how his hair is longer, his features have matured, and his cheeks aren't as innocently chubby as they were. I sat in silence watching him sleep until my eyes couldn't stay open any longer. He is the only person I am truly myself with because to him, I'm just dad. That's his only expectation, and the one job I will put above everything else.

If only Portia could see how much he needs me in his life.

The sadness in his little eyes as I strapped him into his seat, broke my fucking heart. He loves his mum; it was clear by how he ran into her arms, but she won't change. No matter how much she says she loves him, she won't ever put him above herself. I finally realised when I took him home to the house I paid for...

"Did daddy brush your hair today?"

I scowl at her, taking a steadying breath. "If his hair wasn't so long, it wouldn't look such a mess when he's playing would it?"

"It never gets in a mess when he's playing at home." Portia says, smirking. *'Course it fucking doesn't!*

"Daddy made me a den with sofa pillows and cushions and blankets. It was so cool!" I smile, but her sour words cause it to drop.

"Did he now? Was that so he could work?"

"He's had my undivided attention the whole time."

"Nice to see you *do* have the ability to stop working for at least one minute of your life." I grit my teeth together, desperately wanting to rip her a fucking new one but knowing if I wanna see my son again, I have to play by her fucking rules.

"Here." I thrust his bag into her long manicure-nailed hands.

I ignore her comment about just having them done because I don't give a shit. I bend down to lift Brad into my arms, holding him tightly. "I'll see you very soon, okay? And maybe then we can start looking at one of those Spider-Man films, yeah?"

His little eyes light up at that but what he says surprises me. "Can we see Remi again?"

"Who's Remi?"

I don't owe Portia an explanation, but I feel obligated to protect Remi. I turn my attention quickly back to answering Brad. "I'll talk with your mum so you can come stay again."

"It'll have to be when daddy isn't working. He's very busy remember." If I had my gun, I'd shoot her because his disappointment nearly breaks me.

"Dude, I will never, *ever* be too busy to have you sleep over, okay? I promise."

She mutters something under her breath as I put him down and encourage him to go into the house, telling him I love him. "When?"

"I'll let you know." She begins to turn away from me, but I grab her by the arm.

"I want to know now! I'm not waiting three months again, Portia!"

She twists her shocked face into a sick smile, revealing the dragon she is. "Owen, we both know you're not going to do anything to me." She pulls her arm free from my grip, holding her head high. "I'll let you know exactly when you can see him again. Now, I suggest you move so I can go and get *my* son ready for bed."

I wouldn't spit on her if she was on fire I'd happily stand and watch her burn. I wanted to squeeze the life out her with my bare hands. I want to grip her so tight and watch her eyes bulge as she gasp for air, and God, do I want to watch her eyes glaze over as she slips away from this world. No matter how much I fucking hate Portia, I can't touch her because of my son.

When I pull up at The Rose, I don't even remember the journey. I have one thing on my mind, and even though I know it has the biggest of consequences, it's the one thing I crave whenever I see Portia: drink.

I'm on the way to the cellar when I hear Remi scream out. Her anguish immediately resonates with me, and when I see her smashing her fists against the wall, I have to stop her from hurting herself and from doing something she would regret; just like I was about to.

I don't care how pissed off she is with me, to see her vulnerability and angry tears, I can't stop myself. It doesn't matter how she got here; I want to make sure she's okay. I want to help her, but I get sucked in with her beauty, her perfume, and the way my body feels when I am with her. The world becomes wobbly except for her. She is the only straight thing I see when I'm around her.

The desire to touch her is harder to reject than my need to down a bottle of Jack, and when she gives me the approval to touch her, I almost can't breathe as my hand explores her face and skin and neck. I want to see her breasts again, this time without the chaos and without her hands covering them like last time. I want to kiss every fucking inch of her exquisite body; take us both away from the bad place we're at.

But when she says she's already hurt, I know I can't.

No matter what I want, if I wanted her, I can't have her. Portia will always be there, and my life will always be the same. I can't do this again. Remi doesn't deserve to be involved in this.

I voice my warnings, and just like I've done with the booze a hundred times over, I turn and walk away, pulling out my phone to call the one person who can help right now.

"Hello?"

"You home?"

"Yes, but..."

"I don't really care right now, Alice. I just need to not be here."

She hesitates, but she is the only one who knows and understands me. "Okay."

————————————

Remi

I rush after Owen, but he got away faster than I thought. I stop, confused to what happened and slowly go to the dressing room and drop into the chair facing the mirror. My mascara's smudged but my face is salvageable. Seeing myself, my eyes flood once more. I won't waste tears on Tom anymore, but these are for Owen and the humiliation I feel. Why did I let myself get that out of control? No one has ever had so much control over me before, and I hate it. Tom was controlling but I never lost my mind to him like I do around Owen. I was able to fight him the first time he got close, but every time since, I find myself unable to. He can hurt me? Maybe I should heed his warning because the last thing I need is another man ruining my life.

I pick up my phone to call Ri, but when she fails to pick up, followed by my mom, I dial the man who has always had my back, my dad. *I miss him.* I haven't spoken to him since I moved here, and hearing his voice is the safety I need to let a single tear drop. After the usual pleasantries, he knows I'm not calling to check in with him. Telling him what Tom said to me has all that anger bubbling up again. My entire body is restless and full of pent-up energy.

"That little fucker. Has he not done enough?! There must be something else that you haven't shown us, otherwise we would have seen it. He can't tell you he was legally obliged to inform you they had been sold but you don't own any rights. It contradicts itself. If you had no rights, then you wouldn't be informed."

"So, there might be some hope after all?"

"I will need to dig deeper, but I don't believe what he told you. I'll get this son of a bitch for something I swear!"

"Thanks, dad."

"He's messed with the wrong family, Rem. You gotta stay strong, okay? Don't let him beat you down."

"I won't."

***

"That's all for tonight ladies and gentlemen. Thank you for coming and I look forward to seeing you again."

The applause lasts until I'm off the stage before quickly dying down, and I wish I was able to enjoy the buzz as much as should, but I can't. If I wasn't obligated then believe me, I would have gone home after talking to my dad. Tom was bad enough but adding Owen into it all just tipped it over the edge. I must stop being a player in his game.

I see some of the usual crew sitting at the same table as they always do, all but Owen. I make my way through the full tables, smiling and thanking the patrons as I encounter them. Suddenly, a blond gentleman blocks my path.

"Excuse me, Remi?"

"That's me. Can I help you?"

He puts out a hand to me, waiting for me to clasp my own around his. "Jamie Cooper. Pleased to meet ya." He holds my hand politely as I try to figure out his accent. He doesn't sound anything like anyone I have spoken to so far. It's harsher but his presence is warm.

"Pleased to meet you, too. Did you enjoy your evening?"

"Yes, I did. That's why I've come to talk to you. I really liked your vibe, and your voice is electric! I'm from WB Records and saw the posts on social media that you were playing. I came last week and wasn't disappointed. I thought I would just touch base with you really and see what your plan was for the future?"

Is this really happening?

"I wouldn't be singing publicly if I didn't want to get noticed."

His friendly smile widens, "that's very true. So, you're looking to make this a profession?"

"Absolutely... if the offer is right." Call me stupid, but after last time, I will not accept anything simply because it is being offered.

"That's good to hear. I will report back, and you never know, you might just see me again. For now, just keep doing what you're doing."

"I will. Thanks for taking the time to come and watch me. Have a good rest of your evening."

I complete what I set out for and arrive at the table of my friends. Spencer hands me a welcomed chilled beer, immediately asking who I was talking to like a protective big brother.

"Some guy from a label, who is interested in my sound."

"Shut up! Babe! That's so exciting!" Lucy jumps up from her seat to hug me excitedly Whilst I don't disagree with her, I'm trying not to get my hopes up, but of course this is what I wanted. This is why I came here.

"It's something for sure. He must have known I needed some good news today, but after last time, I'm not going to get too excited, there is still a long way to go before I can get truly excited."

"Why, what happened last time?" Jack asks, moving in closer. I haven't seen him the past couple of days, and I feel bad as I haven't missed him. Since my lunch out with Bradley yesterday, I think it is fine to say no one has been on my mind more than Owen freakin' Turner.

"I'm gonna need more of this beer first."

They patiently wait until I have four more mouthfuls of the numbing golden nectar down my throat. Maybe it's because of my mood in general tonight, I know I haven't drank enough to not give a fuck, but I put it all out on the table; taking a deep breath readying to relive it all once again. The way Tom sold me a lie, the way he moulded me into what he could sell me as, how he controlled my life without me even realizing, and how when I found out about his infidelities, I kicked him to the curb only for it to backfire on me astronomically. And how this was all followed with the shock, the devastation, the humiliation, and final this evening's latest piece of shit to add to the mounting pile. They all listen without saying a word until I am done.

"There must be something you can do?" Lucy spits out. She was grinding her teeth the entire time I spoke. I've told her before, but it was clear she didn't enjoy hearing it.

"I called my dad to see what he can do. He's going to look into it."

"Is he gonna sort him out? Shame we don't live closer, I think I'd quite like making the little prick squeal like a pig as I beat the shit out of him." Freddie jokes, but the way he cracks his knuckles, I can believe it. Still, I laugh.

"No, he's a lawyer like my mom. He thinks he's lying."

"I hope he's bullshitting because that's a piss take! They're yours." Jack voices and I appreciate that he is irritated for me, but I can't change what's happened, only find a solution. The people who truly know me knows the truth and that is all I can ask for right now.

"Thanks, Jack."

He wraps his arm low around my waist, his hand sitting on my hip, pulling me into his body. I look at him and stupidly lean into give him a gentle kiss on the cheek. As soon as my lips connect with his skin, I instantly realize it's a dumb move. One, because we're not alone, and two, because I know I don't feel for him the way I think he does for me.

I pull away and immediately move back to my original place hoping I look nervous and not like the idiot I feel. But it's too late. Freddie hollas out loud enough that I'm sure everyone hears him.

"Shit! When did this happen? Thought O— Oi!"

I frown when he looks like someone kicked him. *What was he gonna say?* "You thought what?"

"I... er, thought... o—nly younger, hot guys like me stood a chance. Not old farts like Jacky boy." We laugh at Jacks expense, but I know that's not what Freddie was going to say. Question is, what would he have said had someone not stopped him?

"Oi! I'm only five years older than you, you little cunt! And if you must know, we're just getting to know one another."

He follows it up with a nervous smile, but I'm glad he isn't thinking this is more than it is. I really shouldn't have kissed him knowing how I feel. I can't lead him on. The next time we're alone, I will talk to him about it. It's not fair.

Twelve

"I think he's well and truly got the message, O."

I ignore Charlie and hit the twat again with a hammer, for good measure. I can't even remember why I started hitting this piece of shit in the first place. One minute he was talking and the next, I was hitting him. The sound of the metal smashing against his bone is all that repeats when I think back. I dunno if he's alive and I can't say I care. If he's in this warehouse then it's because he deserves it.

I see all the splatters of blood on my shirt and hands. Another shirt ruined. I walk into my office at the factory, ripping my shirt apart instead of undoing the buttons. Charlie follows me in, shutting the door and it's when he does this, I know it's my mate about to speak, not my employee.

"You been drinkin'?" he asks, making my nostrils flare and my mouth screw up angrily. He isn't the first to ask me this the past week. "Why the fuck does everyone think I've been fuckin' drinkin'?!"

"Cause you're fuckin' angry!"

"No, I ain't." I lie. *I am.* I haven't hidden my rage and frustration because I don't give a shit. I'm not here to be everyone's fucking God. I'm here to do a job and I'm making sure it gets done. Freddie is the only one who loves me when I'm *this* Owen, he's the one beside me kicking the fuckers with me.

"No? Last week, I couldn't find you all evening when you'd dropped Brad home, so fuck knows what you were doing! You squared up to Fred 'cause he said Remi was getting close to Jack, and you almost killed someone when Chris said she kissed him on their date. Saturday, I saw you looking for her at The Rose, and then mysteriously fucked off to God knows where when Luce said she was at Dom's studio the other night. Spencer sees it too Owen."

"I haven't had a drink." I manage a simple declaration and take my shirt off, chucking it in the bin. I'm washing my hands when Charlie just can't shut his fucking mouth.

"Then it's her."

I don't stop what I'm doing, because I'm not having this conversation. "It don't matter if it is or it ain't. Nothin's gonna happen."

"You keep saying that to me O, but history ain't gonna repeat itself! You can't keep avoiding women."

"I don't avoid women, I avoid relationships." I admit, pushing past him to get a fresh shirt.

"You're chattin' shit mate. And don't include this weird as fuck arrangement you have with that fuckin' Barbie doll, Carmen, as you not avoiding women. She's using you as much as you are her." I ignore him because I really mean it when I said I wasn't having this conversation. I slip on my jacket and leave the office. "Where ya goin'? We have rounds to do!"

"Then you fuckin' do it, that's what you're paid for! Don't need me holdin' your hand every pissin' time."

***

I drive to The Rose to do the shit I need to do there. Luce told me on Saturday that some paperwork had been delivered that needed completing. But I didn't hang about once I knew Remi weren't there, though finding her at Dom's studio like Lucy said she was, I left her alone. I'm happy to admit to myself that I was very, very wrong about her talent and her impact on the place. The punters rave about her, and so they should.

I enter through the kitchen entrance and slip up to my office that way. Opening all the letters, I see an important looking one, and it requires a signature from a certain *Miss America.* I spend about ten minutes checking the CCTV to figure out where she is, but continually coming up empty handed. I call Lucy, asking where Remi is before she can even say 'Hello'.

"She wasn't feeling too good, so I let her have the day off." *Fuck's sake.* "Why, what's up?"

"She needs to sign somethin."

"Ok, put it on my desk and I'll take it home."

"It's fine. I'll drop it at yours. Needs doin' straight away."

"Alright, whatever, but don't be havin' a go at her like you have everyone else recently." *Spencer has loose lips around her.* "She's going through some stuff at the minute and don't need you being more of a dickhead."

I'm aware she's going through some stuff; I stopped her from injuring herself. "I'll be in and out. Simple."

Pulling up outside Lucy and Spencer's, I don't knock but I do shut the door hard to show someone's come in. "'Ello?" I call out, looking around downstairs but no-one's here. I walk up the stairs to make sure she hasn't gone out and can hear soft singing, looping over the same line as Remi plays some chords on her guitar. I knock loudly causing her to stop, almost instantly the door creaks open enough for me to see her beautiful face. The second she sees it's me, the smile drops and her whole body deflates.

"Oh God, what are you doing here?" From the small window of vision, I see that she crosses her arms as she rolls her eyes.

"I need you to sign somethin.'"

"Sign what?" Those steel eyes narrow at me, but I can still see the swirls of colour in them.

"Some legal shit for workin' here."

"Fine." She huffs, walking out of her bedroom and finally revealing her shorts and vest sleepwear combo. *Fucking hell!* I try, and fail miserably, not to check her out as we walk down the stairs, but my dick tries to reach for her pussy from within my trousers. I'm left with no choice but to look up to the heavens for help 'cause damn she looks fucking amazing. Nothing, and I mean nothing prepared me for seeing her like this. Even semi-naked in my bathroom didn't affect me like this is.

"Huh?" I think she said something, but I weren't listening.

I can almost hear her second eye roll in the space of a minute, "I said, couldn't Lucy have brought it home?"

"Nah, needs sendin' off today." She turns at the bottom of the stairs and goes straight into the kitchen, to get a pen, walking over to the table. With an unamused look on her face, she waits impatiently as I slip out the paper from the envelope and put it on the table pointing to the two places she needs to sign. She bends over the table letting me see down her top a little.

She has no bra on which does sweet fuck all to help me go soft. She reads it, thoroughly, giving me the chance to ogle her for longer, imagining those tits against my skin. It's only the slam of the pen on the table that pulls me from my wet dream.

"You can go now." she calls out over her shoulder, moving across the kitchen to a coffee machine I don't remember Lucy having before.

"Don't worry, I'm goin'."

"Mhmm, yeah you do that." She mutters. Her attitude is both welcomed and hated in equal measure. It was banter before, but this arsey Remi ain't fun. She's really pissed off and the only positive is it's keeps me away from her. She needs to get over what happened.

"You're bein' a bitch anyway." I mutter, sliding the paperwork back into my jacket pocket.

The spoon clatters onto the worktop, and she turns, staring daggers at me. "Excuse me?! I'm being a bitch? And what, you're the friendliest man on the planet all of a sudden?"

"Just callin' a spade a spade."

"Get out!" Remi moves away from making her coffee and guides me out of the room, but I voluntarily walk ahead of her into the hallway and toward the front door.

"I'll send Jack over; he can help cheer you up."

If I thought she was pissed off before, she really ain't fucking happy now. "What did you just say?!" she says through gritted teeth, so I stop to turn around, taking one last glance at her in that outfit. Her fired up like this is sexy, even if it is directed at me..

"I said, I'll send Jack over—" My reactions are normally spot on but of course round her they're shit. I don't realise she's slapped me until my face tingles and I'm looking to the right, not at her face.

"Fuck you, you asshole!"

She fucking slapped me! Reactively, my hand grips her neck as the red mist descends. I don't want to and wouldn't hurt her, but I'll be damned if she thinks she's gonna do that to me and get away with it!

Remi

Owen's dark eyes stare into mine as his hand sits loosely around my throat. My back is pushed against the hallway wall, and I know I should be scared. He says he can hurt me, right? But I'm not, not in the slightest. I only wish I could slap him again.

"That was a very stupid thing to do." His voice is menacing and not like anything I have ever heard from him.

"What are you gonna do? Huh? Slap me back?" I taunt, matching his attitude.

"Be careful what you say, love!"

"Oh yeah, that's right! You can *really* hurt me, can't you."

He squeezes just slightly, proving that I am at his mercy, and he could probably end my life right here if he wanted to. But all it does is heighten the unexpected throb between my legs.

"I weren't lyin', Remi."

"Why don't you get Jack over here to help me believe you."

His nostrils flare at the mention of Jack and his eyes glance away from mine for a second, "stop it."

"Stop what, Owen? You brought him up! Jack doesn't act like he wants me then walks away; he kisses me when he wants to!" I taunt, knowing I'm seriously playing with fire, and totally over selling mine and Jacks connection, but I don't give a fuck. Seeing him again reignited the anger and embarrassment of how he walked away from me that day back with a bang, and I'm not prepared to forget about it.

Owen's eyes match the anger his clenched teeth voice, "I said stop!"

I lean into his hand further choking myself, uttering the last two words I ever expected to say to him. "Make me."

He presses his lips to mine so abruptly, it knocks the air out of my lungs. This was not what I had in mind but my eyes close savoring the feeling of the

Owen-shaped itch finally being scratched. I needed to push him away, not draw him in but God, I feel like I'm floating, and I think I would be if his hand wasn't still gripped around my throat adding to the pooling between my legs.

Owen is kissing me.

And I'm letting him.

I involuntary moan as he grips my hair in his other hand, fisting a handful of my hair and making me moan. My hands slide up his back, stopping to grip his neck and pull his mouth closer to mine hungrily. Our tongues swirl and dance around one another like they have been confined in our bodies and for the first time they have been allowed to explore. His taste, his beard, his smell, makes time stand still.

I'm kissing Owen.

His hand finally leaves my neck and slides down my body, brushing over my nipple which causes my body to surge with want. And God, do I want him. My dreams have failed miserably to prepare me for what reality is actually like.

This is insane.

His hand stops at my ass, taking a big handful of it and squeezing hard. The pain makes me moan again and he pushes his body against mine. I can feel his hard and wanting dick down the leg of his pants against my bare thigh, the feeling alone is another small step to losing my mind to this man-shaped enigma.

Owen's mouth moves from mine across my jaw and to my neck, stopping just below my ear, "is this what you wanted?" His deep voice and hot breath against my skin, combined with the roughness of his beard, gives me goosebumps all over. I manage to mutter a hushed 'yes' before his mouth kisses and sucks on my neck to replace his hand, which slips inside the front of my shorts. When he discovers I'm not wearing panties, he moans in delight. I never imagined it would work in my favor. His fingers perfectly press against my clit, causing my head to drop back. There are no more steps in this climb to lose my mind, he's won this game.

I wobble, opening my legs wider, grinding against him, panting and moaning to seek my high. And, as if he already knows how I like it, he rubs me with his thumb as he slides his fingers between my folds and enters me. His digits satisfy my desire, as he pumps in and out powerfully, teasing and caressing my neck with his mouth. I whimper, knowing I am almost there.

"Come for me." Hearing him command me as he pushes deeper and faster into me, drives me crazy! He curls his fingers and hits a sweet spot at just the right time, making me shudder and scream into his neck. I know I'm soaking him as I pulsate around him.

We don't move for a minute, allowing me to catch my breath a little, but eventually he pulls his fingers free from my confines at the same time as stepping back.

I'm stunned; this is not how today was supposed to go, but I'm rendered speechless as he places his moist fingers in his mouth. He sucks my release from them before opening his palm and licking the rest that collected in his fist. "Mmmm, just like I imagined." I smile seductively, but it only lasts a second until he speaks again, "but this can't happen again."

Is he serious?!

"Owen..." I don't know if I can take another rejection from him. Not now, not after that.

"I mean it," he scolds like I'm a child who won't take no for an answer, "it was a one off."

"Are you being fucking serious right now!" That came out a lot more aggressive than I intended, but its warranted. Orgasm or not. "Why did you kiss me? Why did you do *that*?!"

"'Cause for some crazy reason, I can't seem to control myself around you."

Why does he need to be in control?

I try the softer approach, lifting my hand to touch his left cheek, hoping to soothe the area of his skin that took the blow. "Then stop trying. I know you feel this as much as I do."

He pulls my hand away. "It's not that simple."

"I'm not a toy for you to pick up and drop when you like, Owen!" He ignores me, stepping away further and letting my hand fall to my side. He grips the door handle, twisting it. This is it, the last time I could see him.

"Please stop running out on me." My confident voice wobbles, but true to Lucy's description, he stays the emotionless asshole he proudly presents to the world.

"It's better this way."

"Then go. Run away again, but don't you *dare* think you get to do this to me again if you do. I'm done. Whatever the hell this is—" I point back and forth between him and myself, "—is over. Your choice, Owen."

Thirteen

'*J*'ve given him an ultimatum, but from the way he hesitates, looking down at his hand on the handle of the open door, I can't watch him contemplating any more. I walk away because I'm not waiting for an answer I may not like.

I walk back into the kitchen feeling the weight stack on my shoulders with every step, then I hear the door close with an undeniable click as the latch slots into place. I close my eyes in disappointment, accepting his answer, my answer.

He left.

I throw away the cool coffee out of the mug, and as I pour myself a hot one, I shake my head annoyed. *What the hell was I expecting?! That he would really stay?* He's been playing this game with me for weeks and now he's proved his point, had his fun, why would he stay for more?

"God! I'm so fucking stupid!" I mutter to myself picking up the spoon I dropped.

"No, you're not."

I gasp, turning slowly to discover Owen standing in the doorway, leant against the frame.

He didn't go?

I stand frozen feeling my breathing pick up and my heart rate increase, watching him stalk towards me. *What the hell is going to happen now?* He stops only a couple of inches in front of me, looking down with a calm face.

"... I am." he states, bringing his hand up to my face, running his thumb across my lips. I move my hand to swipe it away, but he reacts just as quickly to grip it, stopping me from connecting with him. "I don't think so."

I'm battling with wanting to melt from his touch and wanting to knee him in the balls. If this is just another tease, I don't want it. I *can't* want this.

I try with my other hand, making him stop my other wrist equally as fast as he did the first time. The undeniable tingles trickle down my arms as he holds them crossed in front of my body, as I stare defiantly into his eyes I know; I know I am not going to stop him anymore. His pull is too strong. He's captured the King and called 'Checkmate'.

"So, what now, huh?" I ask, needing to know but he manoeuvres me so fast, twisting my body in a way I've only seen on Dancing with the Stars until both of our arms cage me to him, my back pressed hard against his chest. His nose nuzzles into my hair, taking a deep breath. I roll my head into it, loving what he is doing despite the risks that could come from it.

One of his hands releases my wrist before I feel my hair move. I take a shaky breath, loving the feel of his lips meet on the base of my neck offering peppered kisses between his words. "Just don't say I didn't warn ya."

My eyes close, consumed from his warm, wet tongue licking as his soft powerful lips hungrily make out with my skin. His hand leaves my draping hair to trail down my body, brushing over the small mounds of my breasts where the lack of bra becomes immediately evident from my body's reaction. Sparks feel like they fly as he pinches and delicately rolls my nipple between his fore finger and thumb, and I moan out.

"D'ya like that?" he commands like he always does.

"Yes..."

He stops what he's doing, turning me to face him so quickly, it takes a split second for my brain to catch up. He stares deep into my eyes, "D'you still mean what you said?"

About us, and being done with the games? "Every word."

"Want me to stop? To go?"

"No." I drag one hand through his tamed hair as I answer his questions, gripping a handful gently. I can see from the pulse of a raised eyebrow he likes it. "But I don't give out second chances, Owen. If you really want me, take me, make me yours, just stop playing games."

"Ok."

Normally, those two meaningless letters would mean nothing, but from the way he assures me that he will follow my instructions, they might as well have said "Go" with a green light because the instant my body recognised the signal, it leaps into his arms. He catches me, holding me tight to his body putting his hands on my exposed ass, and I wrap my limbs around him like I'm a Koala Bear. His kiss is hungry and desperate, matching my own intensity. Feeling his tongue roll around with mine again is still as mind blowing as before in the hallway; the light-headedness; the fireworks; the racing heart; all of it is like nothing else.

It's clear from the hard lump in his pants that he is as affected by this as I am, but when he attempts to sit me on the counter, "No," I mumble within the kiss, "your sister... Spencer... upstairs."

He groans but takes my weight once more, heading out of the kitchen but not before he hits my back a little on the frame in his haste. It doesn't bother me in the slightest, he could drag me anywhere and do anything to me and I'd let him. I move to kiss his neck as he begins the ascent up the staircase, letting him see but not losing that connection. I can't help it, rotating my hips against him, longing to play with it even though I've never reacted this way to any man I've been with. Sex has always been cool and calculated, getting hot through foreplay. Not with Owen though, I am more than prepared for this.

He kicks open my bedroom door and I'm soon dropped onto the bed when he immediately begins removing his suit jacket, leaning over to kiss me. My hands raise to help push it off his shoulders, sliding it down his arms and begin on the buttons of his shirt, but he holds my wrists to stop me, but before I can argue, he rips it clean open, leaving the buttons to scatter around the room.

When his mouth leaves mine to stand up straight, my hands wander across his toned skin. I desperately want to stay close to him, so I follow him around like a negative pole to a positive. He stands taller than me, taking deep breaths while gazing down at me with captivating dark eyes. It's a chance to acknowledge who we are and what we both want. Is this the earliest I've ever slept with someone? Yes. However, I have never felt this chemistry with anyone before. Owen may be the grade A asshole I was told he was, but this man has more sides to him than that, and that man is the one gazing down at me like I'm the most beautiful thing he has ever seen.

I slide my bottom lip between my teeth as I take charge to start undoing his expensive looking belt, keeping my eyes locked with his as I do. When his pants are undone, he pushes them down along with his boxershorts. I take a sharp intake of breath as his hardened cock springs into my face. I'm transfixed on it, wanting nothing more than to make it my own personal popsicle. Though I edge forward only for his hands to stop me by my shoulders.

"Not today." he commands, and I listen, feeling his strong hands slide down my arms, taking the material from the bottom of my vest and lifting it slowly up my body. My arms naturally follow in the direction so he can remove it entirely, leaving my hair to fall naturally around my shoulders and tickling against my now exposed chest.

"Fuck me." His words are quiet, gentle, like he's talking to himself rather than me. "Touch yourself." From the change in volume, I listen, nervously lifting my hands to caress my breasts, gripping and tugging on them, using my palm to stimulate my nipples like I want him to do.

I feel my diaphragm taking shallow pants, barely letting me speak. "Like this?"

"Mhmm." he murmurs, nibbling on his plump bottom lip. Enjoying watching him, watching me, I close my eyes letting out an appreciative moan.

"Stop." he begins, "stand up." I gingerly raise, not trusting my legs to support me but trusting him to catch me like he has before. "Take them off." He glances down to my shorts. My pussy flutters at the thought of freedom, and relinquishing it from the fabric prison, I watch in awe as his eyes scan my entire naked body. "Holy shit..."

He closes the small gap, gripping my head in a vice like way, kissing me with a new level of rawness. I've never felt so wanted by a man or wanted a man like I do him. His hands move under my thighs to raise me. I wrap myself around him once again as he crawls on to the bed, lowering my head on the pillows.

"You protected? I didn't exactly come prepared..."

"Yes." I confirm desperately, holding my hands around his neck, unwilling to acknowledge that he could stop. If I wasn't protected, he would still have a difficult time getting away from me.

"Thank fuck for that."

I giggle but then moan out loudly as I finally feel his tip at my entrance, sliding my lips apart to slide inside me perfectly.

"Fuck... you're so tight!" He fills every millimetre of me in a way I've never experienced before, but then again, no one I've been with before has been as well-endowed as him. When he begins moving, I let him immediately know how incredible it feels, digging my nails gently into his ass cheeks, hooking my feet around his legs. He thrusts deep leaving nothing of all that length untouched by my walls.

Wanting to taste him again, I lift my head up to kiss him open mouthed. His tongue licks and teases against mine before entering my mouth to fight for dominance. The fight between us still there regardless of our connection. Every single nerve ending is on fire right now, my body celebrating his strong and fierce movements. I love feeling his ass muscles contracting under my touch and I rock my hips in a perfect rhythm to co-ordinate. Though this is our first time, our synchronicity is undeniable.

My moans become too strong to maintain kissing him, and I have to break away. The sounds leaving me are a mix of screams and grunts. "Shit... oh my God... Owen! This feels so good!"

He unexpectedly flips us so I'm now on top. I bend my legs beside him to support myself, placing my hands on his abs. He has the perfect amount of body hair on his chest, as well as a teasing trail down from his belly to what is usually hidden in his pants. The only defect I notice is a scar below his right rib.

"You look so fuckin' sexy ridin' me." His hands come up to caress my breasts, making my head fall back in appreciation. I feel sexy riding him, but all sense and logic has gone. I suck in a breath as he squeezes them roughly. "These fuckin' tits have haunted my dreams. You like that, don't ya?"

I move my head to look at him, his face has a devilish smile. One I haven't seen many times but one I've grown to like – a lot!

"Yes."

He sits up, holding my gaze until he can't any longer, and takes my right bud into his mouth. I involuntarily whimper, increasing my movements, rocking harder against him, and making sure all areas are stimulated. His hands grip my ass cheeks roughly, spreading them wide, helping me to get him deeper. All the while his tongue laps roughly, dividing his attention between each of my nipples. I can feel his teeth dangerously grazing around the edge. I know I'm being loud, but fuck, he is driving me insane! He bites down, making me scream out louder; it hurts for a second until his tongue licks making it all the better.

"Oh my God!" *Do it again!*

I'm close, and as much as I want to reach a climax, I don't want this to end. He's helping me from below, grunting from the energy he's using. No, I definitely do not want this to end. No one, and I mean no one, has ever taken me this good...

"Owen, I'm gonna come!"

"Then come, come with me." He moans out among his grunts.

I feel my eyes roll to the back of my head, and I'm gone, hearing him find his own release, groaning out my name loudly into my neck whilst his dick pulsates with his release. We both stay as we are until our breathing calms enough to speak. I can't believe I just had sex with Owen. *Mind-fucking-blowing sex!*

He lifts his head to look at me. We stare at one another for a second before he bends down quickly to place a soft kiss on my lips. "I've never wanted to kiss lips as much as I have these."

I chuckle softly at his revelation. "It took you long enough."

He smiles back genuinely. *Damn, he is gorgeous!*

"Yeah, but you know you loved the tease."

"Please! You were teasing yourself more, honey."

"You're not fuckin' wrong!" He pecks my lips again before continuing his taunting gaze. There is only one thing I need to know.

"What happens now?" I ask, hoping he doesn't do what he did before and pull away at the last minute.

"We can work that out along the way." He brushes his knuckles down my cheek, "you're the last thing I ever expected, but all I know is I can't walk away from you again. Not after that."

Fourteen

Owen freakin' Turner, what are you doing to me?

I stand in the bathroom, looking at the subtle love bites across my chest, remembering the bite of his teeth on my nipple again, the roughness of his beard against my skin… fuck, it was mind blowing.

Every.

Single.

Second.

Am I worried about what will happen next? I guess. He still confuses me. This gorgeous enigma slowly seems to be revealing tiny pieces of himself, even if it's on his terms. Do I regret what happened? Not in the slightest. I think I'd have regretted not giving in more if I'd have stopped. I just need to let whatever this is play out and hope it's worth it.

Lucy's voice echoes through the house, informing me that they're home, so I leave the confines of my room and make my way down to the kitchen.

"Hey."

"How are you feelin'?" Lucy asks, looking at me with sympathetic eyes.

"Wonderful." Her eyebrows rise, probably wondering if I'm being sarcastic or not, "Well, better than I was for sure."

"Oh, that's good then. Have you eaten?"

"Um, no." *I was consumed reliving getting fucked by your brother all day that I forgot to eat.*

"Then it's a good job, I brought a Chinese then!"

"Did Owen come over?" Spencer asks, making me notice him sitting at the table for the first time.

"Yeah, briefly." I look away to hide my blush. There is no way I am prepared to talk to them about what happened. It's her brother. I have no idea how she'll react to that, so I quickly change the subject. "Was The Rose busy today?"

Lucy begins to serve up an array of food on three plates, "Usual lunchtime rush then it was calm for the rest of the day. Beginning of the week's generally quiet so I've been busy planning a meal for when my dad gets home."

My ears prick up because this is the first time she has brought her dad up since me and Jack went on our date.

"I bet you can't wait to see him. How long has it been?"

She goes quiet for a moment, before tucking her hair behind her ear, "Since the last time? Three months. But he hasn't been home in over four years."

I let out a garbled noise at her revelation, looking quickly between Spencer and her, unsure of what that means. Spencer gives me a taught smile, telling me it's a sore subject.

Lucy finally turns her attention to me, "He ain't working away, Rem. He's in prison."

My eyes widen in surprise. "What? I mean, why? Is that what Jack meant by 'dining at His Majesty's pleasure' or whatever it was?"

Her nervous face morphs into a frown. "Jack? What did he say?"

"Not much, honestly, and he got quite annoyed when I asked more. I'm sorry, Lucy, I don't want to cause any issues. Jack was saying how good Jim has been to him and Alice."

She looks really irritated but is quiet. I soften, reaching out to put my hand on hers. This must be hard to talk about, and I understand why she didn't tell me the truth. I can't even imagine being in her shoes, and whatever Jim did to get put in jail is his consequence, not his entire families, even if they carry the burden too.

"I'm sorry Luce. Thank you for telling me."

"It's ok, it's just not something we talk about outside of the family. Jack should know better. I feel like I can trust you Rem. I haven't always had friendships like that."

"Me too." I open my arms to give her a hug, feeling like a real bitch for not telling her about Owen after she has just been so honest with me, but I do genuinely feel the same. I wouldn't have moved my entire life to live with someone I didn't trust, and I also don't want to cause any issues between us, especially without knowing what will happen with Owen.

"Right, let's eat this before it gets cold." Lucy says, and I take the hint that this subject is over, taking the plate she offers and sitting with the two of them at the table.

I have to admit, I didn't realize quite how hungry I was until I finish my food long before they do and begin cleaning up.

"Remi, you don't need to do that." Lucy says, insisting but I will always clean up after myself.

"You brought the food, it's only fair."

"Okay, well thank you. I'm gonna go and get a quick shower." She hugs into Spencer, "I'm tired so I'm going straight to bed."

"Alright, babe. I won't be long." Spencer acknowledges, giving her another quick kiss before she disappears.

I busy myself with loading the dishwasher when Spencer's words stop me instantly. "Was it who I think it was earlier?" Anxiety explodes in my body, knowing instantly what he means but also hoping I'm wrong. But I'm not. "It was Owen in your room, weren't it?"

I raise my head and shake my hair out of my face gently, pinching my lips between my teeth before looking at him as I stand up straight and lean against the countertop, crossing my arms. "Yeah."

"Jesus Rem!" he says, sighing and shaking his head in disappointment. *But why?* "When the fuck did it start?"

"Spencer, please... it's a little confusing right now."

"Didn't sound very bloody confusin' to me!"

I cover my face with my hands "Oh God, you heard us?"

"Yep. Does Lucy know?"

"No!" I almost shout. If he's reacted like this, how will she take it? "And I want it to stay that way." I plead with my eyes, and he instantly gets it.

"Oh no! No way! I'm not lyin' to her, Remi. She's my fiancé."

"I know, and I never asked you to. All I'm asking is for a bit of time to figure out what this is. Today was the first time."

"Remi..."

"Please, Spencer. I promise, I wouldn't ever want you to lie for me. It's just keeping quiet for a couple of days, that's all, just until I can talk to Owen."

He lets out a big sigh, running his hand through his hair. "I don't like it. Owen, he's..." he pauses, so I finish for him.

"Complicated? Confusing? Arrogant? Obnoxious? An asshole?"

He breathes out a laugh. "You have no idea."

"Look, I'm under no illusion, Spencer. But it happened; it's happening. I just don't know what '*it*' is yet."

His face keeps strong. "Fine. I won't say anythin' but I won't deny it either. If anyone asks, I'm gonna say you two were fuckin'."

"Good Lord, kill me now..."

"It sounded like he was." His wide smile tells me how much he's enjoying watching me squirm, and after one last chuckle, he turns serious, "Just... be careful, Rem."

"I will."

Owen

I'm fucked.

I hear her moans of pleasure remembering her body on top of me, riding me so fucking well every time I close my eyes—so I've had them closed or daydreamed a lot since I left there yesterday. I still can't believe it happened. I know I tried to keep my distance, but I couldn't. Not anymore. This game weren't gonna make any of us happy without both of us being the winners.

"Wo-ooo, 'ello? Earth to O?" Freddie says, dancing around in front of me like some court jester on speed.

"Get your fuckin' hand out my face, you dickhead." I slap his waving hand away, "How many times have I told you to stop taking a line when you're checking on things?"

He shrugs his shoulders dramatically, making me shake my head at him.

"Sit down." He does as I command, letting me focus my attention on them. "Did everything get done yesterday?"

"Yeah" Jack says. They had the usual tasks to do, people to go see, deposits to drop; the same ol' shit.

I inform them of what meetings I have today and who we're paying a visit to, then send them out of my office so I can run through some paperwork before we go. I notice a figure in my peripherals, and when I look up, Spencer's closing the door.

"Mornin', thought you were out today?"

"Yeah, I was but I thought I'd let ya know I got home a little earlier yesterday." he says, raising an eyebrow at me.

"Okay, good for you." I move my attention back to the papers in my hand when he takes a seat opposite me and speaks again.

"I heard you."

I pause writing, looking back up at him. *He heard who? Me and Remi?* "Okay?"

"I'll tell ya the same thing I told Rem. I ain't lying for ya—"

"Why would you need to lie?" I ask, sitting back in my chair.

"She didn't seem too keen on telling Lucy yet, so I won't say anything but I ain't lying."

I know we didn't exactly discuss specifics but if she doesn't wanna tell Lucy yet, then so be it. "I figured she hadn't. I've been expecting Luce to turn up all morning. Whatever Remi wants to do, is fine with me."

"Just like that?" he asks, cocking his eyebrow.

"Just like that." He takes in my words and stands, but it's clear there is more he wants to say. "What is it?"

Mine and Spencer's relationship is different than with the others. He hasn't been involved in this

his whole life like me, Jack, Charlie, and Freddie have; he fell into it like Chris did. Spencer was always cooking books and moving money around, that's why he's good with figures but he just slotted in when my dad went inside. Then he caught the eye of my sister and there was no getting rid of him. He has a better moral compass than the rest of us which is why he don't get involved outside of the businesses, but I respect that he tells me how it is.

"With everything you said, why drag her in to this?"

I let out a sigh, grinding my teeth. I could have anyone, sure, but no woman has ever made me so fucking agitated and hard at the same time as Remi has. But aside from that, she came from nowhere and made me feel a level of calmness that I've only ever experienced from an empty bottle of Jack or my son. Stuff like that doesn't happen for no reason. I don't know if it's going anywhere, but I do know that Charlie and him were right; she's made me lose my head, and I don't think in a bad way.

"I tried, alright?" I say, holding his gaze confidently but lacking all the bravado I normally do.

"Tried what?"

He's gonna make me say it.

"I can't stay away from her."

He smiles like a Cheshire cat. "I fuckin' knew it."

Fifteen

"Someone's smiley!" Riley's voice sounds out through my phone, loud enough for both me and Lucy to hear. "Tom didn't upset you that much then?"

"He made me miserable for long enough, am I not allowed to smile?"

Riley's eyes widen in realization. "You had sex!"

"Oh my God, when?!" Lucy takes her attention off the road for a second to eye me up with the same enthusiasm as my sister.

I must look like a deer caught in the headlights, talking to both of them. "What? No, I didn't!"

"Please! You hardly got laid with Tom—" *I'm going to kill her!* "—it was always easy to know when you had! Was it—"

"I did not sleep with anyone." I cut her off, glaring down the camera at her hoping she takes the hint. I need her to drop it, especially with Lucy sitting next to me. "I'm simply having a good day; until now anyway!"

"Hmm... yeah, maybe my sex-dar is on the whack today," she says, winking at me.

"Definitely! I had that music scout stop me last week didn't I, I'm hoping to see him there again tonight." *Though that is true, I'm hoping to see someone else here tonight...*

"He would be crazy not to be shouting about you to his boss, Rem." Lucy adds.

"I hope so..."

By the time we arrive at The Rose all the talk of my sex life with Tom is forgotten because even though I'm working my shift today the only thing I can think about is whether Owen is here. He doesn't come by that often, so I don't hold out much hope. I wish I had his number, something to have been able to make contact with him. I couldn't exactly ask Lucy for it.

Roberto's smiling face welcomes me when I step in behind the bar. "Hi babe!"

"Missed me?"

"Always. Are you feeling better?"

"Yes. I didn't know but it was exactly what I needed."

The shift goes smoothly with the midweek rush coming in and out, and I'm gathering empties from the tables when my phone vibrates in my back pocket.

Unknown: Looking good Ghost

Ghost?

Remi: Who is this?

Unknown: Come on, Demi. It isn't that hard

Owen.

I smile, chuckling to myself before looking around for him. He isn't at the bar, and he isn't sitting at their usual table. *Where is he?*

Remi: Where are you?

Unknown: Upstairs

Remi: Then how can you see me?

Unknown: How do you normally see everything without being there?

I look around again, none of the guys are here either, but then I notice the cameras on the ceiling.

Remi: Spying on me is a little weird don't you think? Sitting all alone in your office, watching me on a screen.

Unknown: Why don't you come up here so I'm not weird. Or alone.

Hurrying to place another load of glasses to be washed, I make my way over to Sydney. "I know I don't have long left of my shift, but do you mind if I just go upstairs to take a call?" I can't say that Owen has summoned me upstairs, especially when he didn't come down and holla across the bar like last time.

"Yeah, sure."

The adrenaline pumps through my veins with every step up the stairs, and when I reach the door, I knock and wait. Owen's voice invites me inside, so I slide inside the room, purposely leaving the door open behind me.

"You asked to see me, Mr. Turner?"

There he sits behind that desk, authoritative and brooding as always; and fucking sexy.

"Shut the door." he says, his voice deep and commanding, but I raise an eyebrow expectantly, "... please?" Pleased with myself, and hiding my smirk, I turn and close it feeling the excitement bubbling up inside me. "Come 'ere." He slides the chair out from his desk as I walk over to him, positioning myself into the space between him and the wooden piece of furniture. I thought it would be weird or awkward to see him again, but it isn't.

He takes me in, just as I take him in; the depth of his eyes, the pout of his lips, remembering how soft they are and how he tastes. I swallow, my gaze unrelenting until he opens those lips to speak again. "You didn't tell Luce?"

"Nor did you?"

He gently shakes his head. "It's none of her business." He stands, placing his hands either side of my hips and caging me in place, allowing me the opportunity to run my hands up his strong forearms. Even through his shirt, I can feel the structure of his muscles that have held my body so tightly.

"She will have to know one day." I manage to say as his face hovers teasingly close to me, the pull irrefutable.

"When and how is up to you."

"You sure?" Our lips get closer and closer.

"Mhmm..." I can't work out who makes the move first, but our lips meet abruptly like we can't fight the magnetism any longer; the tease, the tension, the memories pulling us together.

I grip my hands in his hair as we kiss one another roughly, opening my legs wider to invite his body closer to mine. I want him close to me, and I internally melt from the feeling of his arms wrapped around my waist. His tongue fights for dominance showing me that he knows what he wants and takes it. There's no second guessing anymore, no playing games.

He wants me. And I want him.

I break the kiss, moving down to the base of his neck. When his fingers grip into my back alongside a soft moan, I know he likes it. I unhook my hands from his hair, moving them to his belt buckle. I have wanted this since I saw it.

"Rem..." He is trying to warn me but failing miserably.

"Shh, keep quiet and enjoy it." I feel his body relax, resigned to what I'm going to do I pull away, tugging his pants and boxers down enough before pushing him back to fall into his seat. Seeing him sitting there, hard and ready for me is electrifying.

"You got me ready, what ya gonna do now?" he asks, his eyes glistening with excitement as I take control of him.

I sink down to my knees, taking him in my hand and stroking him gently. He throbs as the tip begins to glisten from the bead that flows out.

"See what ya do to me?"

"Mhmm," I lap my tongue across his head, licking him clean, "I love it." I wink at him as I move forward placing my lips around his tip, rolling my tongue around it.

"Fuckin' hell..." he hisses through gritted teeth.

I allow the saliva to build in my mouth as I bring my head up and down his long, thick shaft, sucking as I get to the tip. To make sure nothing is left untouched I use my hand to help pleasure what my mouth can't take down, using my spit to lubricate my movements.

I like that he's not seeking permission to do what he wants to me, because his hand slides through my hair, collecting a fist of it. There's some pain as he tugs on it, with pieces of hair snapping, but I don't feel annoyed or hurt. I feel sexy, strong and turned on even more. His breaths are laced with a low hum making me glance up to meet his eyes watching me. *Fuck!* They're so intense, I feel close to coming just from the friction of my panties on my clit.

"Take me deeper." Wanting to please him, I take him further, making myself gag a little. "Keep going." I feel his hand push me down deeper making me hold him in my throat, choking me for a beat before letting me move up. *It's exhilarating.*

I thought I would hate this: being told what to do, being pushed out of the comfortable vanilla life, I don't. In fact, when he does it again, I moan in satisfaction as tears slip from my eyes. His breathing increases, and on the fourth time, he pushes me the deepest yet shooting his load down my throat moaning out in satisfaction.

I swallow down every drop he releases until there's nothing left, and he sits softer between my lips. His grip loosens to reach for the tissues on his desk offering me one.

I wipe my mouth and eyes, feeling his gaze on me. "You're rather good at that ain't ya?"

I'm about to answer him when a knock on the door interrupts me.

"For fucks sake!" He stands quickly, making himself appropriate again. But sits down, bringing the chair forward, caging me in the space between his legs.

"Owen! I am not staying here!"

"Stay there and be quiet." I huff as he tells me what to do, folding myself in smaller, hoping it isn't Lucy, as he invites in whoever it is.

"O, I've just had a call from Lemar."

Oh my God! I sink down lower, desperate to make myself as small as possible as Jacks voice cuts through the silence. *Are you kidding me?*

"Why'd he not call me?" Owen asks back, pulling his seat in a little closer.

"He did. You didn't fuckin' pick up! What ya been doing in here?"

"Nothing you need to worry about. I'll call him back."

"He told me they've moved the delivery forward. It's gonna be here on Sunday now instead of Wednesday."

"Fine. Why you 'ere already?"

"Came to see Remi before she performs. Syd said she was up 'ere."

"Oh right, well I ain't seen her, so I can't help ya there."

"Okay... well, see ya later then."

It's only when I hear the door close that I let out the breath I'd been holding in, peaking up from my hiding space waiting for him to look down at me. Owen rolls back, giving me a hand to help me stand.

"Should've come out and said 'Hi'." There's a hint of enjoyment in that sentence and I don't like it.

"What?"

"It was Jack." He doesn't hide the smile this time.

"I'm well aware, Owen. You don't need to be a dick though."

"Hey..." He pulls me onto his lap, sensing my annoyance. "I'm sorry."

I raise my eyebrows. "What was that?"

His face is stoic and standard Owen. "Don't get used to it. I don't say it often."

"Oh! I know!" I say, smiling and wrapping my arms around his neck comfortably. *Why does this feel so natural?* "I will talk to Jack. I'm going out to dinner with him on Saturday."

He recoils back instantly, changing the atmosphere. "Sorry, what?"

"We made plans, Owen."

"Why would you still go?"

"Why would I not?"

"Because..." I wait for him to complete it, "would you go with me?"

"I only went to dinner with you last time because your son asked me." I don't hide the smirk on my face as he looks back playfully.

"Oh, I see how it is, pickin' my kid over me. Well *Demi*, we've fucked, so I'd say you have no choice."

"You know that only means we've fucked, not that we're dating and going out for dinner. You get that right?"

He pulls me tighter to his body. "Oh yeah, but I think you're forgettin' that I don't ask."

Sixteen

Remi didn't hang around long after Jacks untimely appearance, and I surprisingly didn't want her to go.

Do I want to go down and pretend everything is normal? Not really. Me and Remi haven't been around one another with everyone else for a while so it'll be a bit random rocking up, touching and kissing her like I fucking want to. But do I want to sit there watching Jack all over her? *Yeah, I'm going...*

Making my way to the table, Lucy and all the guys are there.

"Alright stranger? I didn't know you were already here?" Lucy says, standing to greet me with a polite kiss.

"You saw me three days ago."

"Did I? Seems like it's been ages..."

I sit my arse down in the middle of everyone as usual, pouring a bottle of coke into a glass. "Yeah, it's been a while. Wanna see if she's improved, or not. She doesn't have long left of her trial period, you know."

"Mate!" Freddie speaks up. Glad to see he isn't off his face this evening. "She's fuckin' sick!"

"She had a music guy chat to her last week." Jack explains. *This is new information.*

"Oh right?" I try to sound uninterested, but I am.

"Yeah, you've missed quite a bit." Spencer adds, cocking an eyebrow for a split second.

"So it seems." My eyes look out to the crowd who are slowly filtering in filling all the seats, ready to watch her when she emerges from the far end, walking towards us. My eyes roam down her body, taking in the tight black leather trousers and co-ordinating black cropped long sleeve, revealing her stomach. She's worn this on purpose, and I've got no choice but to sit here and not touch.

Have I said that I fucking hate her?

"Fuckin' hell..." I say to myself, but I know Charlie hears me when he looks in the same direction as I am and laughs.

"Well, this should be fun!" I glance at him quickly before looking back to her. I see her smile as she makes eye contact with me. *God, she's fucking beautiful.* "Hey, you got somethin'..." Charlie dabs my mouth with a napkin, pretending that I'm drooling, but I smack his hand away quickly.

"You're a prick."

He laughs at me without drawing any attention to himself just as she arrives at the table, saying a friendly hello to everyone but me. Charlie narrows his eyes; I know he's not buying it. She sits in the same seat as she always does; the perfect filling in a Lucy and Jack sandwich, and just as I expected, he closes in talking with a big smile on his face. She's being polite and "friendly" back but it's irritating me.

By the time I've drank my drink, coupled with the guys chattin' to me, it's time for her to go and perform. I hate sitting here, watching Jack gush over her to Luce as she goes through each song because Fred's right, she is incredible. Just like the first time I watched her, the crowd are completely taken in by her and I'm unable to keep my eyes off her, with my body responding just the same. She deserves to be noticed; I can't believe she's had to come over here for it to happen though.

I see her looking out to the crowd in our direction a lot, and I'm not blind to the small smiles that she does when I sneak a cheeky wink at her.

"Okay everyone, this last song is called 'God is a woman' by Ariana Grande. It's not one I do often but it feels right tonight." Remi says putting the guitar in a stand and nods to Lewis who starts the backing track. I listen to her soft, seductive voice, totally consumed in it. Then she sings the second verse, and I get it. The song is about a strong and confident woman getting what she wants - even if it's slow to begin with, and even if the guy doesn't deserve it, she'll show him how she wants it. *Shit...* It's not lost on me. She's singing this to me, about us. Our little game and if only I'd have not played for too long, I could have had her sooner.

Her eyes close as she sings her heart out hitting high notes effortlessly. I don't care if it's written on my face, my jaw's dropped in amazement. This exceptional, stunningly beautiful woman wants me and fuck do I want her!

The crowd applaud and holla as the song ends, and I am there with them, clapping making Charlie and Spencer look at me. Yes, Spencer knows, and smirks, but Charlie don't.

"Got somethin' to say?" I ask, feeling the weight of Charlie's eyes on me.

"That depends, is there somethin' to know?"

"Nope." *It's our business, not his.*

He murmurs, but doesn't push it. He knows I won't say something I don't want to. When I look back, taking to my seat again, she's almost jogging over to us with the biggest smile on her face. I'm struggling not to match her, which is difficult until I see Jack wrap her in a big hug. My lips rise like a snarling animal and my body instinctively wants to jump up, but I watch as she friendly and naturally pulls away, thanking him before giving her attention to Lucy, Freddie, and Spencer.

I wait until she's sat in her seat before speaking to her. "Good job."

She smiles deliciously at me. "Yeah? You still want me to stick around?"

"Mhmm, I think I will keep hold of ya for a while. Wouldn't want anyone else snapping you up now, would I?"

"You've got your work cut out, Owen, I'm hot property you know." She follows it up with a taunting smirk. *Jesus Christ, this woman is something else!*

"I think I can handle it." I wink at her before she looks away as she smiles.

"We doin' shots?" Lucy asks us all causing a mass *'yes'* to roll around the table. It's gonna be that type of night then. I find it hilarious sitting around people drinking. It bothered me to begin with but now it doesn't. I drank for my own reasons, not as a social thing. I used to watch them being so over dramatic in their reactions, losing themselves in their intoxication, but tonight I watch only her as she laughs and jokes around with Jack and Freddie.

"Oh my God!" Lucy squeals, flailing her arms around before pointing at Remi. "You slept with Jack!"

Remi chokes on the saliva in her mouth, coughing, at my sister's ridiculous outburst. At least I hope it's ridiculous...

"What?" Jack asks, frowning in confusion, as Remi manages to croak out Lucy's name.

"Er, we hav—" Jack tries to explain but Lucy is on one and isn't going to stop. And I'm all for it; I wanna know if they have slept together.

"You two are flirting, you've been on that date and all that, and you are like next level happy. You've so had sex! Even Riley said it."

"I have not slept with Jack, Luce."

I look at Remi's irritated and Jack's confused faces when Spencer pipes up. "Luce, just leave it yeah?" Is he saying that because they have and I'm here, or because it's me and Remi that she's talking about? He said he wouldn't lie about us, so is this how it's going to happen?

"I'm not having this discussion." Remi says, trying to move on by taking a small sip of her drink.

"You've not denied it, though." Jack states, an edge to his inebriated words. She looks surprised, but this is him. He wears his heart on his sleeve, and Lucy has just highlighted something to him.

"Excuse me?"

"You just said you ain't slept with me, not that you hadn't slept with anyone at all?"

Remi's whole demeanour changes as she turns in her seat to face him. "I have a vast collection of toys, if I was smiling because I got off, sweetie, believe me when I say I'd be smiling *all* the time."

His eyebrows shoot so far up his forehead, and everyone bites their lips trying not to laugh in surprise, but I don't hide my laughter. I knew she'd say something good but that was bloody brilliant.

And very good to know...

Remi

Last night didn't quite end how I thought.

Jack made some excuse and left not long after our conversation, but I know I need to speak to him today. One, because of course he needs to know the truth and two, I cannot sit there another evening pretending like my whole body isn't desperate to be in Owens arms.

I roll over in bed to check my phone, smiling when I see I have a message from him.

Owen: Morning

Remi: Good morning, Odin.

Owen: Still going with Thor's dad?

Remi: You know how much I love me some Thor...

Owen: And here I was going to ask if you wanted to go for dinner. Just with me this time?

Remi: What? No Bradley to ask and entertain me?

*Owen: I can ask Freddie if you want a little
person to come too?*

I laugh to myself.

*Remi: In that case, I'm there 😊 .
I'm going to talk to Lucy and Jack today.*

Owen: OK. Do you want me with you?

I never expected that response. I didn't think he would be openly available for me. Tom was only free on his terms and rarely emotionally available. It's probably why he cheated so easily.

Remi: I will let you know if I do. Thank you x

I haul myself out of bed, making my way down to the kitchen to get my morning coffee. Spencer stands at the stove, cooking something that smells divine!

"Yesterday was interesting." He says smirking.

"Yeah, no kidding!"

"You should come with a warning sign, I swear." We both laugh softly.

"It shut him up though."

He goes to speak when Lucy comes in walking straight up to Spencer, giving him a kiss, saying good morning to us both.

He looks to me. "We were just talkin' 'bout last night."

She turns in his arms, still looking remorseful, "I'm honestly so sorry for just blurtin' that out like that. I need to keep my mouth shut." She kept apologizing yesterday, I said it was okay because it was but now I need to explain why.

"It's fine, really. I kind of have a confession to make."

"Okay?" She asks turning her head to the side cautiously.

"I did sleep with someone."

"What?!" She calls out louder than my delicate ears can handle this early. "Why did you say you didn't?"

"Because I wasn't ready to talk about it."

She frowns. "But you are now?"

"Yeah," I sit down at the table, looking at my coffee mug in my hands. *Here goes.* "because I slept with Owen."

Silence.

When I look back, her jaw is on the floor, gaping open until she shakes her head, snapping out of her shock.

"You. And Owen? But you hate one another?"

I laugh nervously. "They say it's a fine line between love and hate."

She leaves Spencer's arms' and sits down opposite me. "But what about Jack? I thought you were datin'?"

"I don't feel like that for him."

"But you do for Owen?"

I nod.

"Fuckin' hell, babe, I'm in shock! For how long?"

"When he came around on Tuesday."

She gasps, a knowing smile on her face, "Is that why you pretended to be ill?"

"No! God no. I hated him when he turned up..." I trail off, remembering it all too well.

"Then how the hell did you sleep with him?"

"I was angry he walked out on me last week when we nearly kissed—"

"What?" We look to Spencer, who's standing there with a cooking spoon in his hand.

"Why does that surprise you? You didn't bat an eyelid when she said they'd sl—YOU KNEW!"

"Babe..." he says rolling his eyes respectfully.

"Don't babe me! Why didn't you tell me?" Lucy demands.

"Because I asked him not to."

"Thanks, Rem!"

"Look, I asked him not to say anything until I knew what was happening. He came home early and heard us, there was no secret disclosure. I thought you would be angry."

"Why would I be angry?"

"Because its Owen!"

"I'm shocked, *believe* me, but I think you two are actually good for one another. He's a grumpy arsehole, and you're a stubborn, hot-headed babe. You don't take his shit, so I think you're perfect together."

I guess time will tell...

Seventeen

I'm meeting Jack at the coffee shop he saw me near the day of our date—mutual ground. I just hope he will understand and not be too disappointed. He can't be blind to the fact there isn't that connection between us, surely?

When I see him sitting at a table with two coffees and the biggest grin on his face, my optimism is smashed to pieces. He stands, giving me a kiss on the cheek before letting us both sit down.

"Thanks for meeting me." I say, smiling tentatively.

"That's alright. I wanted to say sorry about yesterday anyway."

"It's fine, honestly. It's actually why I'm here."

His smiling face drops a little. "Oh?"

I take a sip of the coffee in front of me, plucking some courage to bite the bullet. "You know we have a great time when we're together and you really do make me laugh..."

His body slumps as he realizes what's coming, "Why does this feel like a break-up?"

"I'm sorry, Jack."

"It's alright." He looks so defeated, I feel awful.

"I really do enjoy talking and spending time with you, but I can't pretend to feel something I'm not."

"Don't worry, I get it. Can't blame a guy for tryin'!" We smile at one another before I take another bigger gulp of coffee. *It's like a Band Aid: rip it off quickly.* "But about last night, Lucy didn't know when she said it, but she wasn't wrong," His demeanor changes with the narrowing of his eyes. "Even though I don't have those feelings for you, it doesn't mean I want to affect our friendship, but I have started seeing someone."

He purses his lips before rolling them through his teeth, "Were you datin' us at the same time?"

"No. But I think it's important you know that it's Owen..." I admit, only watching his face contort into anger and disgust.

"Tell me you're jokin'?!"

"No actually, I'm not!"

He laughs out nastily, sitting back in his chair with a smirk on his lips, "What'd he do? Slap you about a bit and you came runnin'?"

Did he, what?! "Excuse me?!"

"Look yeah, it's none of my fuckin business what ya' do, but I know you could do better. Much better."

"Yeah... I'm sure you do, and I'm sorry it's not you but you don't have to be a jerk about it."

"My heart ain't broken, Rem, I'll get over it. You might not be so lucky."

What is that supposed to mean?

"I'll take my chances, thanks all the same." I say, mimicking his scowl while we sit there awkwardly looking at one another. "I think I should go." Standing up, I look down at him, "I just want you to know that I did have the best intentions when we went out. I truly am sorry that I don't feel the same."

Why would Owen slap me? I've seen his anger; he's held his hand around my throat, but I don't believe he would hurt a woman. I knew in that moment as he stared into my eyes that he was not *that* man.

I call Riley the second I get outside. I didn't divulge what he did, but I finally admitted that I slept with Owen. She was stunned to say the least. I've done nothing but moan about the guy every time we had spoken, and even though I was sure he was going to kiss me the time before, never did I think we would end up in bed together.

But from my revelation came her own surprise.

She's coming over to visit me for her birthday in a couple of weeks, and I'm not trying to hide my excitement, squealing in the street as she tells me.

"Are you serious?!"

She laughs. "Yes! Why would I lie?"

"I don't know, that was not what I was expecting you to say. Ever."

"Well, I haven't booked my flights yet, but I have checked with school and they're letting me take a vacation. I can't wait to meet everyone... especially Owen... "

Dread sets in as she has verbal diarrhoea the best of times, Lord only knows what she will say to him. "Yeah... I can't wait."

Owen

I've been listening to Freddie and Chris chatting about some coked up idiot who jumped off the roof of a building, breaking both his arms and legs, but not contributing to it.

All I wanna do is get this latest order sorted and done so I can go to The Rose tonight.

"How's he gonna wank now?" Freddie finally asks because in his narrow mind, that is all that is important.

"Could you two sound any more like two gossiping old biddies havin' their hair done? No-one gives a shit!" They pay no attention to me and continue with their mind-numbing conversation until the door to my office flies open, and a knife goes flying past my head. I look to my left, seeing it embedded into the head support of my chair. Looking back at the door, I don't even need to guess that Remi's told Jack.

"You've got some fuckin' balls, ain't ya?" I say, narrowing my eyes at him before glancing to look at Fred and Chris. They sit poised, ready to act but not sure why Jack is nearly foaming at the mouth furious and I'm sitting calm in my seat with a knife a centimetre from my head.

"You just couldn't let me have her, could ya?!" Jack's nostrils flare on his reddened face, but I keep my composure.

"I strongly suggest you watch your fuckin' mouth. Don't forget who you're talking to!" I grit my teeth together, suffocating the anger.

"Why? You could have anyone! Why her?" He steps closer to me, leaning over the desk to intimidate me. I rise from my seat, walking around my desk, making myself equal to him. If he wants to go for it, I'll happily knock him out.

"If she really wanted you, she wouldn't have even looked at me." I shrug.

"You didn't even give me a chance! I bet you've been tryin' it on for ages, ain't ya? I bet that's why she's been distant because you've been filling her head with all your bullshit!"

I screw my face up, dismissing him with a hand. He's a fucking idiot who clearly doesn't know her because she wouldn't be blindsided by anyone. "You don't know what the hell you're chattin' about!"

"Don't worry though, I won't be goin' nowhere." he snarls, closing the gap between us. "And when you hurt her, I'm gonna be right there—"

That's it!

I punch him so fucking hard he's thrown to the floor. "I ain't gonna do shit to her!"

"Yeah?" He says from his position below me—just where he should be—both of us glaring at one another, "say that to Alice and Portia!"

I launch myself at him, pinning him to the floor punching him anywhere I can, but mainly his pretty boy face. I've seen red that I don't even feel him get me back in the jaw. He's pushed me too far now he's gonna die. He's a vindictive motherfucker bringing them up. It doesn't matter how many times he is told the truth, he won't believe it.

I can feel blood on my knuckles, not knowing if it's his, mine or both, when a pair of hands begin to pull me away.

"Help me get him off him!" Charlie says, tugging me back from under my arms.

"We already tried! He pushed us back!" Freddie adds, before I'm dragged away. I have one of them holding each arm, and Charlie in front of me, blocking any chance of carrying on.

"Get the fuck off me!" I shake them off, straightening up my bloody and damaged clothes before pointing at the cunt laying groaning on the ground, "YOU JUST MADE A BIG FUCKIN' MISTAKE!" Jack doesn't move, he simply looks back at me with a mixture of emotions on his face. "You're on your last warning'! Family or not, I will fuckin' kill you!"

I attempt to get through to kick him, just because I want to, but Charlie grabs me again quickly, pushing me back hard as he looks over his shoulder at Freddie and Chris. "You two, get him outta here... and maybe to the hospital."

Charlie keeps me caged while they lift Jack from the floor and out of my office, only letting me be free when he is happy that I am too far away to finish him. I slide my tie apart and start undoing my shirt, waiting for the Spanish Inquisition to begin.

"What the fuckin' hell was that?!" Charlie asks, looking bewildered. I've smashed the shit out of enough people in my life, but never my guys. This is a first.

"He knows about me and Remi."

"Is he fuckin' blind? You've been close to humpin' her like a little puppy every time you speak!"

I turn to look at him sliding the shirt down my arms. "We're together."

It feels weird to say that. I haven't said it since I got with Portia. His eyes widen. "Like, legit?"

I nod, throwing the ripped shirt in the bin. He collapses onto the sofa, a gobsmacked smile on his face, "Shit me! I didn't think you'd be able to pull it off. She really hated you!"

"Clearly she fell for my charm."

He laughs loudly causing me to frown at him. "You bloody wish."

I grab a fresh shirt and begin putting it on, looking down at my damaged knuckles. They're a mess, and I know when the adrenaline eases off, I'm going to be regretting not killing him after the pain. *What the hell am I going to say to Remi?*

"When?" He asks, grabbing my attention back.

"...did we get together?"

"No, lost your virginity! Obviously, I mean when did you got together! You shagged her?"

I give him a look, revealing the answer. He can know that much, but I'm not going to discuss it with him. It's between me and Remi.

———————————————

Remi

I make my way to the table after my set, really needing a drink—especially since Owen didn't show. I don't know why I got my hopes up, he has only been to a couple of my performances, it would be silly of me to think that anything would change just because we have taken things further.

"You look like you've dropped a tenner and found a penny." Lucy says, drawing me out of my mind.

I chuckle, amused by her little saying. "No, I'm good. It was another good turnout wasn't it?"

"Except for two." she replies, giving me a sympathetic smile.

I shrug nonchalantly. I am not going to become one of those women who become infatuated with a man the instant they take that next step. I've been controlled by Tom, and I wouldn't want to repeat that or do the same to someone.

"I wasn't expecting Jack to come tonight."

"Jack got into a bit of trouble earlier, he's taking some time away." Charlie says, drawing mine and Lucy's attention away from one another. Lucy doesn't look as surprised as I feel though.

"Oh? Is he okay?"

"He'll be alright," Charlie says, to reassure me.

Taking a drink, I inform Lucy that my sister is coming to visit before my phone vibrates in my pocket. Looking at it, I smile instantly.

Owen: *Sorry I couldn't make it tonight.*

"From that smile, there's no guesses for who that is." Lucy says, leaning in to talk. She is smiling happily when I glance up at her.

"He's saying sorry he couldn't make it."

The smile shifts to shock in a blink. "He said 'sorry'? Bloody hell, I think you broke him."

"Oh shush." I dismiss her playfully, focusing on my reply. I know what she means though. This is the second apology I've had from him in as many days.

Remi: *It's fine. I can survive without you, you know.*

**Owen: *Wanna survive tonight without me or
do you wanna come to mine?***

His?

Remi: *What's on offer to entice me?*

Owen: *My tongue finally tasting that pussy of yours.*

I involuntarily bite my bottom lip and squeeze my thighs together. I want him. Too much.

Remi: That sounds tempting, Odin, but it's such a shame you're not here.

Owen: I'm outside.

I pick up my drink, tossing it back and finishing it in one before collecting my bag, knowing that I can think what I want when I'm away from him because the second I am near Owen, all sense and logic turn to horseshit. I am already infatuated with him; even before this started, he was inside my head.

"Where you goin'?" Spencer asks softly.

"I might not be home tonight." I say, hearing Lucy chuckle.

"And so, it begins."

I give Lucy a quick hug and rush off to find him standing leaning against his car waiting for me. It's dark but I can feel his eyes as he takes in my tight black jeans and plunging red top. I rush to him, kissing him hard. How have I craved his taste? I have only had a taste of him on two occasions, but the addiction is there, coursing through my bloodstream desperate for a hit.

His arms wrap around my waist, and I snake mine around his neck entangling my tongue around his. His kisses alone drive me crazy but knowing what he can do to my body has me clawing at his skin and fisting his suit jacket. I want him so badly.

He begrudgingly pulls away and takes my hand, pulling me to the car. The journey is torture. He holds my hand the entire time, rubbing the back of it with his thumb, teasing and coaxing me, unable to disconnect from me entirely while we both sit in sexually charged silence.

Finally, he pulls up and parks in a private underground lot underneath a modern looking high-rise with an old style laced in new windows and paint work. Owen guides us to the elevator and has me pinned against the side the second the door closes, kissing my neck and running his hands all over my body. I moan openly, knowing I have an effect on him. I can tell by the way his breathing deepens and the surge of passion that forces itself out of him from his grip. He grabs handfuls of my ass, pulling me painfully close to him.

As it dings our arrival, he slowly releases me, taking my hand and pulling me out of the sweatbox. There are only two matte black doors leading off from a generous hallway; the simplicity only faltered by a small spyhole. He rapidly unlocks one of the doors and lets me enter quietly behind him to take in my surroundings.

From the small entrance hallway, there is a bedroom, office and bathroom to the right, and an open plan kitchen and living area to the left. I let go of his hand and walk around, taking it in. The soft gray walls and wooden floors cause the white kitchen cabinets that line the far wall to pop, and a huge island made from metal radiators and a concrete worktop doesn't look out of place in the room. A large silver vent is still exposed on the ceiling, running the length of the room. Opposite the kitchen is a large wraparound sofa in a co-ordinating gray to match the island, and a television is poised across the room so everyone can enjoy it, no matter where they are.

"This is incredible. It's so different."

"Yeah," he admits. "It was a factory before we converted it into a load of flats."

"You did all this?" I ask, cocking an eyebrow impressed.

"It's one of my businesses, yeah. This was mine and Spencer's project. He has the other one up here but obviously lives with Luce now."

I run my hand along the cold gray concrete, "I love it."

"You wanna drink?" He moves towards the refrigerator, but I don't want a drink and when I tell him, he looks back at me with a hint of a smile of his lips. I'm not even going to prolong this. I walk straight over to him and take his hand pulling him back toward the bedroom I saw. But he doesn't move, causing me to stop.

"Not that one." he says, pulling me to another door beside the kitchen units. When he opens it, there's a small laundry room and a black metal staircase leading up. He bends down and picks me up bridal style, making me giggle.

He climbs the steps unveiling another two doors. He opens the first door easily even with me in his arms, and steps into the master bedroom.

"Very manly." I joke, taking in the same color palette as downstairs but a beige color bed with white bedding sits in front of me. The same silver vent is the only reminder of what the space once was.

"Bathroom and dressing room's through there." he gestures with his head to the open doorway beside the bed, sliding me down his body and pulling me into his arms. I swallow nervously feeling suddenly vulnerable. After that first time I met him, standing in his bedroom, in his arms with my body wanting him more than I have ever wanted anyone is the last place I ever expected to be, but there is nowhere else I would choose to be in this second. His hand reaches up to caress the side of my face, looking into my eyes with the softness I saw when he was with Bradley; the gentleman over taking the asshole, "I'm glad you're here."

"Me too."

Eighteen

Owen doesn't need to be told to kiss me. He grips the base of my neck like a vice, forcing his lips against mine. We remove our clothes on the way to his bed, falling onto it still connected by limbs and lips, until his mouth moves down my body, giving special attention to my breasts. His delicious nibbling on my nipples causes me to grip the sheets below me.

I moan as the memories of him biting them last time swarm my mind and what it led to. He lifts his head, giving me a panty dropping smile. "You like me doing that don't ya?"

"God, yes."

"Not God, that's all me making you moan." He continues his tantalizing descent down my stomach to my mound. His tongue laps straight through my folds, taking his sweet time to reach my bud before his lips cocoon it, sucking and lapping, pleasuring me in a way no other man has done to me before. Whether that is because they were genuinely bad at it or I react to Owen like no man before him, I will never know, but right now, I am loving his head between my thighs.

My hips rock gently against his face, wanting more pressure which he gives willingly. "That feels so good!"

His eyes smile back at me as he begins to move down, pushing his hands under my ass to lift my pussy higher, hooking his tongue to collect the juices pooling in my opening. I use my hands to play with my breasts craving extra stimulation as his tongue begins to work me inside.

I don't notice that he's looked up until he stops, leaving me desperately panting. "Why did you stop?"

Two of his digits take over from where his mouth was, sliding in and out of me painstakingly slow, "I wanna watch you." His fingers beautifully increase in speed as his trademark commanding tone makes each nerve ending more sensitive. "I wanna watch you scream out like you did the first time I fucked you."

I can't keep my eyes open, arching my back from the pleasure. "Oh... fuck!"

"Look at me."

It's hard to obey his demands, overtaken by the pleasure he is composing, but the second our eyes lock, his smouldering eyes glowing with lust and satisfaction, drives me closer to my peak. All it takes is for him to lean down and blow on my clit to catapult me to come powerfully and scream out his name just as he wanted. I didn't know something so gentle could make my body convulse so intensely. But I want to experience whatever he will do to me.

The instance I stop seeing stars, I sit up enough to meet him, needing his lips on mine and his body against me, "I want you so bad."

He smirks at me with a naughty glint in his eye. "Turn over."

I bite my lip, rolling onto my hands and knees. He places his hands on my hips, guiding me closer to him with my ass gloriously staring him in the face.

"I can see your sweet cum all over that fuckin' pussy." My centre flutters from his words, which isn't then helped by the feel of his hand gliding back and forth across my behind, teasingly brushing across my opening with every swipe. "And your arse is so fuckin' lush." His hand leaves only to return with a sting as his hand claps against my ass cheek. I look over my shoulder in shock. He's towering over me raised up on his knees with his cock thick and standing to attention. I whimper fixating on it, forgetting all about the subtle stinging on my ass.

"You want this?" His left hand slides up and down his shaft, taunting and teasing me while I can't remove my gaze away.

"Yes." I whimper, watching as he spanks me again, slightly harder than before, before massages it.

"You like that too?"

"Yes." I say desperately. If he had asked me beforehand, I would have said no. I never wanted a man to spank my ass, but good Lord is this a next level turn on.

"Do you want my dick?" he asks, unrelenting his tease of my backside, swiping... taunting... pleasuring....

"Yes..."

"D'you want me to leave you drippin' for me?"

"No!" *Absolutely not!* "I want you to make me scream out your name so the whole building knows you're here with me."

I watch him move into position, holding himself in his hand. Seeing him looking down as he slides into me is so sexy. Feeling it and seeing him savor that sensation of me hugging his length is something I've never appreciated before.

"God, your pussy is so fuckin' perfect!"

"Not God... that's all me taking every inch of you." I manage to pant out before the sensation overwhelms me. His fingers grip my hips tightly as he groans out in pleasure, making sure to hold my body exactly where he wants me. He speeds up, pounding so hard he leaves no depth untouched.

"Fuck…" he hisses, revealing how close he is, but it doesn't matter because I can't hold it. I come quickly, crying out his name loudly like I promised I would as my head catapults back. He fucks me through it, not letting me recover, *oh no,* he's close and not slowing down.

"Fuck! Owen! I'm coming again!"

"Good." he growls, "now come with me!"

My scream is silenced as the intensity of my second climax knocks the air out of my lungs and his hands grip my skin painfully tight as he releases into me.

When we've got more control of our bodies, he pulls away. With the breaking of our connection, I feel our mixture of our release slowly trickle out of me. I shift off of the bed, needing to freshen myself up. I never believed it was possible to connect with someone on this level, yet he's proven it to me repeatedly during the past few weeks.

"Wait." he says, standing too but pulling my body flush with his. I don't care that it has now started to roll down the inside of my thigh, I couldn't move if the place was on fire.

"I didn't hurt you, did I?" His words hold an undertone of concern, but I smile back, sliding my hands around his neck. Everything he did hurt but only in the best way possible.

"No, everything you did was amazing."

His thumb runs across my bottom lip, as his other hand presses on my lower back to keep him as close as he can get me. "I still don't know how you ended up here, but I'm hoping this ain't an illusion."

I smile gently. "It's no illusion. I'm right here, and I'm not going anywhere."

He offers me a pleased smile before bending down to lift me from under my thighs, letting me wrap my body around his.

"Where are you taking me?"

"I've shown you my bedroom, now I'm gonna show you my shower…"

Owen

It's been a bloody long time since I've woken up next to a naked woman but looking down at Remi's perfect body, her legs still entwined with mine, I could get used to her in my arms. In fact, I want to get used to it. I want her to stay here again.

Leaving her to sleep in, I chuck on some joggers and quietly head down to get a coffee. As per usual loads of stuff has come through my phone overnight. It's incessant, and there's always an endless amount of shit that needs sorting. Doesn't matter how organised you are, there is always some fucking idiot being a twat somewhere and messing it up.

Sitting on a stool, my coffee adding a delicious fragrance to the room, I feel the energy change when she enters. All my nerve endings ignite at her presence, but when she touches me, wrapping her arms over my shoulders, kissing my neck, I have to close my eyes to calm myself. The softness of her lips make me melt in one way and go rock hard in another.

"Good morning." Remi's raspy, just woken up voice might just be my new favourite sound.

"Mmm-mornin'." I reach around and pull her onto my lap. *Fucking hell.* She's wearing one of my shirts that I doubt covers her arse, but she looks fucking delicious in it. I weren't sure if she would be awkward when she woke up, yet when she looks up to my face, her eyes widen in shock. Her soft, gentle hand reaches up and touches my bruised jaw. It hurts under her touch, but I don't wince away.

"What happened to your face?" she asks, smothered with concern.

"Don't worry about it, I've had worse."

She frowns. "When did this happen? I didn't see this last night."

"You didn't have your eyes open that much…" I attempt to lighten things, but when I pull her hand away, she immediately notices my battered knuckles, jumping off my lap to grab a hold of it to study it closer.

"Oh my God, Owen!" She gathers up my other hand, assessing that too. "What the hell happened? Why are you so hurt?"

I try to move them away, but she doesn't budge. "*Demi...*" I warn.

"*Odin!*" She responds immediately, eyes glaring at me.

"You're not gonna drop it, are you?"

"Nope!"

I look away, muttering to myself when her hand pulls me back to look at her, her eyes softly pleading, "Just because you're an asshole sometimes, it doesn't mean I can't be worried about you." *She's what?* No-one is ever worried about me. Maybe 'cause they know what shit we deal in but even though I've been stabbed twice and battered more times than I can remember, I like that she cares.

"I had to show him that I don't care how pissed off and disappointed he is 'cause you're with me."

Confusion swarms her features as a frown furrows her forehead. "Wait, Jack did this? Because of us?"

"I don't take kindly to people throwing their weight around. Especially over somethin' I want."

"You fought for me?" Her eyes sparkle while she nibbles on her bottom lip.

"I didn't need to 'cause you chose me, but yeah."

She brings her hands to either side of my face, mindful not to hurt me. "I can't believe you did that." Her voice is barely audible, "No one has ever done that before."

I put my hands on her sides and pull her to stand between my legs, looking into her captivating eyes. I still don't understand why my reactions to her are so intense, but I would fight every man on the planet to stay right here with her. "Then they're fuckin' stupid to let you go."

She dips down to place a feather light kiss on my bruise before meeting my lips. This isn't the hot, face-eating kiss we usually share. Nah, this is a type of kiss I ain't had for a long time; it's tender, sensual. And for a guy who usually don't give a shit about kissing, I want to kiss her like this forever. It's like being injected with a drug, and she's my addiction.

I wrap my arms around her body and pull her tight to me, feeling her tits against my skin through the shirt. Having her arms wrapped around my neck feels right. This whole thing feels right.

Before I'm ready to, she pulls away. "Thank you."

"I don't think I got that from the kiss. I think you need to do it again."

She giggles before kissing me again. My arms unravel and my hands slide down to sneak beneath the shirt, cupping her arse I feel the shift in her, hearing the moan of pleasure from her. There is no way she ain't wet under that shirt, and that's all I need to lift her to sit her on the concrete worktop continuing to kiss her. I push the front of my joggers down, holding myself and with having no barrier to pass, I slide straight into her.

Her moans make all the hairs on my body stand to attention. From the second she released that first one taking off her shoes in my office, I've enjoyed what they do to my body.

I begin to move slowly, feeling her cushioned wetness wrapping itself around me, and she's right, it isn't God. It's all fucking her, and I love it.

I lower her down to the table, standing up to rip open the buttons she'd bothered to do up. "You're so beautiful." *She is*. Her body is perfect. She's slim and toned, but not skin and bones. She has the perfect handful of tits, with nipples she loves me to bite and suck. Smiling back at me, her face shows me just how much she's enjoying herself. I lean over her, watching as her eyes close, surrendering to her pleasure. Her fingers grip into my back, spurring me on to draw my hips back further before bucking them forward until my thighs slam against the concrete. I love how it doesn't matter how deep I go, she can take me. She moans in pleasure rather than whimpering in pain like some have before.

Her legs lift and wrap around my waist, keeping me exactly where I want to be. "Owen..." She's encouraging me to go faster, using her heels to push me forward sooner than I want to. I'm enjoying my speed though, feeling her muscles pinching me gently as she gets slicker. "Harder... please."

Teasing her, I thrust in hard and fast; holding still while I ask, "Want me to fuck you like this?" She whimpers out a *yes*. I don't want to disappoint her, so I speed up, slamming into her just like she wants me to.

"Ohhhh… yessss! Just like that. Fuck... Owen!"

Each time with her feels better and better, I can't believe I have her all to myself. I wanna make her feel this good every time I have her.

"I-I'm coming!"

I pound with every piece of energy I have until she clamps down on me, gripping my dick so tight I'm surprised I can even shoot my load.

"Shit!" I hiss, feeling my cum pulsate out. When I've finished, I look down to meet her glazed eyes. The flush of her cheeks and dewy glow that covers her tanned skin is an imagine I wish I could capture and keep forever. She is the most beautiful thing I've ever seen.

"I could definitely get used to this in the mornings." she says, smirking deliciously.

"Good. Cause you just became my favourite kind of breakfast."

Remi

I've never been the type of girl to do the walk of shame in the mornings, yet here I am being driven home in yesterday's clothes.

But I'm not embarrassed. I had the best night of my life; I feel on top of the world! I couldn't believe Owen and Jack fought over me. Did it take me by surprise? Yes. Jack can't be that disappointed, can he? But when I pressed Owen on it later, he was just as dismissive as before. He was curious about Jack's reaction, and I told him the truth. When I told Owen what he said to me, he was painfully quiet before distracting me with a teasing touch of the face, followed by another deep throated kiss.

Owen respectfully said goodbye to me with yet more kissing at the door of Lucy and Spencer's home, and I stood and watched as he entered his G Wagon and drove off before I opened the door and went inside. I have had three showers in the last twelve hours, but I want nothing more than to sink to a bubble-filled bath right now. Though my body is still on a high, it's tender and tired.

"Bloody hell. Thought he was never gonna let ya go." Spencer says with an amused smile on his lips as I enter the kitchen.

"I wasn't expecting you to still be here."

"Yeah, I have some things to check out later, so I won't be here for long. You can chill on your own for a bit."

"It's fine, Spencer, it's your house. I don't want to kick you out." I tell him, busying myself with getting a coffee cup. "Owen told me about your business, about what you do. No wonder you're always so busy."

When he stays silent, I glance over my shoulder to see him looking back with raised eyebrows. "He told you?"

"Yes."

"What we *do?*" He asks again, lingering at the end.

"Yes." I reiterate, bemused.

"And you're okay with it?"

"Why wouldn't I not be okay with it? From the look of the cars you drive and the clothes you wear, clearly the businesses are doing well. I know Owen works hard and I will have to accept that he won't always be available to me, but I understand and respect it."

"Yeah, he never stops." Spencer mutters, dumbfounded. "There's always somethin' that needs doin'. Jimmy ran a tight ship, you know, and Owen's gotta keep it tickin' over. When Jimmy comes out, if things ain't working as good, he'll beat the shit out of Owen, just like he did to Jack."

Wait, what?

I frown. "Hang on, why would Jimmy beat up his son?"

"'Cause that's how things are, Rem. It's not all business meetings and dinners, ya know. Stuff needs to be done and if Jimmy comes out and Owen's let everything be taken over by the guys on the South of the river, Jimmy will have to fight a war to get it back."

My head is swirling right now. I have no idea what he is talking about, and I can't ignore the unsettling feeling in the pit of my stomach.

"How does real estate development come into this? What are they fighting for?"

Spencer's face freezes, his eyes bulging out of his head. "Rem, did Owen tell you anything other than the property stuff?"

I shake my head. *No, he didn't, but evidently there is more to know!*

"You don't know." he states to himself, looking away. "Fuck!" He turns away entirely, putting his hands up to his head. "She still don't know!"

"Spencer, what don't I know?!"

Nineteen

Spencer is turned away from me, but the way he is freaking out has me really concerned.

"Know what?!" I ask more desperately a second time. He continues to mumble to himself, so I rush closer to him, turning him around to face me with my hands on his biceps. "What is going on? What am I missing here?"

"I told them to tell you. I said you should know, but nope! No one listens to me!"

He's pissing me off now, talking in riddles. "You aren't making any sense! Tell me, please…"

Finally, he collapses in defeat, looking at me with regret in his eyes, "The pub, the businesses… it's all a way to launder the money."

I know my ears heard it, but my brain won't accept it. I stand there, trying to take it in. Replaying it over and over to process Spencer's words. *Launder the money.*

"Where does the money come from?" I ask, anxiety gripping my chest.

"Remi, you don't need to know the full ins and outs..."

My eyes dart to his, "I am not leaving this room until you have told me! What am I involved in here?!"

He runs his hand through his hair, "I'm so gonna die for this."

Even with that, I plead. I need to know who I am living with, and who I am sleeping with. I have opened myself up in the most intimate and vulnerable way to Owen, and now I don't feel like I know him at all.

"It comes from all sorts of things. Dealin' and sellin' on stolen stuff, tradin' land and shit, gettin' rid of people, providin' security, transportation of stuff, property and leasin' out premises to businesses. But mainly drugs."

I stand there with my jaw slack, completely and utterly shocked. *Stolen. Removal of people. Drugs!* Lucy brought me here into this world of crime, for what? To perform in an illegally run pub! Are they fucking serious right now?! My parents are lawyers! *This is wrong; I shouldn't be here.*

Does Owen not think I should know? That I *deserved* to know before getting caught up with him too? He's the boss. He is the orchestrator of this entire thing, and I have just begun a relationship with him.

"Rem?" He asks cautiously, but it's too little too late.

"I need to get out of here" I state, edging back to the door, unable to look at Spencer but I feel him getting closer to me. "This was a mistake."

"No! Wait..." He pleads, trying to hold me like I held him, forcing me to listen but I shake free from his grasp. "I know it sounds crazy—"

"Crazy?!" I bite back, "You think it sounds crazy?! Spencer, this is so far from crazy, it doesn't even recognize it! Why did Lucy bring me here?"

His face floods with remorse. "To give you a chance."

A chance sold on a lie.

"I can't be here right now." I shake my arms free from his grasp and move to collect the bag I placed down when I arrived and run out of the house. He calls after me, but I don't stop. Even though I have nowhere to go, I can't stop.

Owen

I never smile but I can't get this damn smirk off my face.

And Charlie points this out as soon I walk into the office. "Guys look, I think hell just froze over."

Even though he is messing with me, the smirk still sits there unrelenting as I retaliate "You're a fuckin' bell-end."

"Bloody hell, what's up with you?" Freddie asks, just as curious as Chris is.

"He's getting himself some sweet, *American Pie*, ain't he?"

Fred's brows furrow but Chris's rise, "So that's why Jack went nuts!" he says, "You and Remi?"

"Really?" Freddie adds, his eyes sparkling like a teenage girl hearing some gossip for the first time.

"Even if I was going to, I don't have time to chat about this. I've gotta get over to Chelsea to see Daniel Hughes." Just then, my phone rings, and I wasn't going to answer it until I see who it is. *I was expecting this.* "Fuck off while I take this. I will be out in a minute, and we'll go." They scarper quickly while I hit 'accept' putting my phone to my ear. "Alright?"

"Why is my brother black and blue and I'm only finding out now?!" Alice seethes.

"Because he weren't happy with me so dragged up the past. What did he think throwing a knife at my head was going to get him? Be lucky he ain't dead." I inform her, hearing her sigh, knowing she'll be rolling her bottom lip between her fingers like she does when she's conflicted.

"It doesn't matter what I say, he won't ever believe me."

"I know, but Portia helped to keep those thoughts there, didn't she."

"Yeah…" She takes another deep breath. "Why did he go off on one?"

"A woman."

"Which woman?" I hear the curiosity peak, and as much I talk to her about everything, I'm not telling her about Remi. Other than Portia, relationships are the one thing we don't discuss.

"A woman, that's all you need to know."

"Whatever. Look, I'm sorry he brought it up again. I'll keep him away from you for a bit."

"Good. I've gotta go, talk to you later."

***

It takes us fucking ages to get there, but the second I step out of the car, the Maître d' greets us quickly like he always does when I come here.

"Good afternoon, Monsieur Turner. Monsieur Hughes is waiting for you." I just nod, following him to their table. Daniel isn't looking too pleased to be waiting for us, sitting with his daughter, Carmen. He better change his sour face, or I won't be shaking hands on any deals; even with all the work I've put into it behind the scenes already.

Carmen's eyes sparkle as I grow closer. "Owen. Nice to see you again." She says smiling politely at me. Her dad has no idea about our little 'meet ups'. He wants her to marry a fake moron like her, so I doubt he will be thrilled to know she's been sucking my dick in the back of my car.

"Nice of you to join us." Daniels adds, sitting up straighter in his chair.

"You know how it is. I got here when I could."

I had hoped this meeting would happen sooner, but alas, it didn't. Carmen put the last piece in play the other week when I came here for dinner. That was so I could finally see what I was going to be investing in. Not that I care about the business other than it staying open. She thinks I'm here to help her, but I'm only here to help myself.

"We know a burst of fresh money can really excel here. Then we can open the second location that you will have a larger share in." Daniel explains over a plate of fancy food I didn't order or ask for.

"I've joined you for dinner once, Carmen, that don't show me it's worth three quarters of a million investment. We aren't on Dragons Den where you have five minutes to impress me."

"I understand what you're saying." Daniel speaks up again, not letting her add anything. "I'm sorry I couldn't join you that evening, we could have gone over things in more detail then."

"So, what percentage are you offerin' me here? And then in the Knightsbridge one when it's open?"

"You'll get ten percent here and an equal fifty percent share of the other."

I raise an eyebrow, running my finger across my lip. My phone starts to go off, but I take it out, only to silence it.

"Do you need to get that?" Daniels asks, nodding at the phone as I slip it back into my pocket.

"No, it can wait. With that percentage, the only issue I have is people asking questions. That would be a no deal for me."

Carmen pipes up quickly. "It will not be a problem, no one will know the share of the business other than us." I know she wants me to take the deal, that's why she's been buttering me up, telling me all her dads plans, how much he is desperate for an investor. All she cares about is her future inheritance and all it took was for me to fuck her a few times and she spilled it all. He's that desperate, as long as his nose is kept clean, he'll let me filter as much money through the books on the new place as I need to.

"Alright. Send Spencer the contract and we can go from there."

He stands up, reaching out his right hand to shake mine. "Pleasure doing business with you."

"Yeah." I quickly reciprocate, then turn to leave.

"Are you not staying? You haven't touched your food." Carmen asks, trying to mask her desperation with the fact I have not paid any attention to my plate—or her. But I've got all I needed from her.

"Nah, you know I'm a busy man."

"We'll be in touch soon, Owen." Daniel confirms, while Carmen sits there with a big smile on her face. She thinks I've done her a favour, but I don't do anything unless I'm getting the best deal. I'll amend their contract; she won't be getting as big of a slice of daddy's money when he carks it as she thinks. All I can say, is she better marry a rich man.

I finally have a look at my phone to discover an array of missed calls and messages from Spencer and Lucy.

Spencer: Ring me back right now!

Lucy: Are you still with Remi? She hasn't turned up for work and her phone is off. Call me x

Spencer: What the hell are you doing?! Call me NOW!

Lucy: I just spoke to Spencer. You need to call him right now!

My heartrate is going mad. "What the fuck?"

"What?" Charlie asks, looking at me through the rear-view mirror.

"Remi's not turned up from work." I hit dial and cut Spencer up as soon as he answers. "What's goin' on?"

"O... I fucked up," he rushes out. "I thought you'd told her! I thought she knew! This is why I told you to tell her!"

What is he on about? Her better not be Remi... "What did you do?!"

"She knows about the Firm." he admits, barely audible.

I bite my teeth together so hard I don't know how they don't break, squeezing my fist so tight I feel my nails digging into my palm, managing to get out the words. "Where is she now?"

"I dunno. She ran out."

Feeling the rage bubble free, I pummel my fist into the head rest in front of me like it's a punching bag, dropping my phone in the process. *What the fucking hell is he doing?!* She wasn't meant to know about this! I made this absolutely clear! The less she knew, the less she could be implicated. If she ever got pulled in for questioning, she would be fine. Now he's not only risked fucking this up for her, but for us.

I reach down to pick up my phone, still raging, I spit out my words. "Be grateful you're fuckin' marryin' my sister or you'd be in a morgue by tonight!"

I end the call and try her phone. Of course, it's off. "FUCK!"

What can I do? I can get people out looking for her, but she could literally be anywhere. On a plane, still in London, I don't know. *Think...*

"What's goin' on?" Charlie finally asks.

"Spencer lost his fucking mind and told Rem about the Firm. She's done a runner."

"To where?"

"I don't fuckin' know! Probably back America if she's got any sense."

"Well, she ain't been many places has she, try those first."

He's right. "Go to Dom's place."

We speed through the city as much as we can and pull up outside the studio she's been going to. I hope I'm right. I rush through the door, ignoring everyone who talks to me, going from door to door, opening them to see if she's inside.

As I throw open one of them, Dom spins round in shock. "What the fuck?" Only for his demeanour to change when he realises it's me. "Shit, Owen, what ya doin' here, fam?" He stands, coming up to grip my hand and pulling me into a respectful embrace.

"I'm lookin' for Remi? She's been here, right?"

"She has but I ain't seen her today." He sees the anguish on my face and sympathises with me. "Gimme a minute, I'll check the other rooms."

"Sixty seconds," I warn him, "I won't be waiting any longer."

He flicks a few buttons and dismisses the person in the booth, before initiating the search, going straight to the last door in the corridor. He opens it quietly, causing the nerves to build, until he reveals her sitting there, playing on a piano with her back to us. Dom goes to speak but I put my hand up to stop him, giving him a look. He knows to fuck off now.

I quietly close the door, standing in front of it so she can't run out, before clearing my throat.

She glances behind her, and instantly pauses though she doesn't look surprised to see me. "What do you want, Owen?" We've gone backwards to the attitude she had in Lucy's house the day we first slept together. The only difference is the chemistry between us is MIA.

"I've been lookin' for ya." I say cautiously.

"You didn't need to." she says, turning back to look at the piano keys.

"I think I did." *I don't know how to do this. I don't know how to fix this.* I never thought I would be in this situation.

"I don't want to be around you right now."

"Well, I ain't goin' anywhere until you've listened to me."

She stands and slams her hands on the keys loudly. The wall of sound that hits me feels like the first of many punches to come my way. Her captivating eyes glare at me. "I have to listen to you? Are you serious?! By the looks of things, you weren't going to even tell me! And now Spencer has, I must listen to you?!"

"Now you know, yeah, you do."

Here we go; both of us butting heads once more, but she crosses her arms and pops her hip. "You have two minutes and then I'm leaving. But I don't want any more lies."

Feeling more confident that she won't just disappear out of the room immediately, I move to sit on a sofa next to the wall. I hold out my hand for her to join me, but she stays rooted to the spot.

"Alright, then." I take a quick breath, "there's a reason we keep people out the loop. You can't be connected if you don't know about it. We were tryna protect you."

Her face remains glaring at me, unmoved from when I sat down. "You are so fucking stupid."

I recoil. "Excuse me?!"

"Are you actually serious?" She finally becomes animated, walking out the space between the piano seat and the instrument, but keeping a distance from me. "Every one of your employees are involved in this through no fault of their own. You use those places to launder illegal money—"

"Keep your voice down!" I stop her, but all she does is roll her bloody eyes. As always, she has a comeback.

"It's a soundproof room asshole!"

I take a deep breath and continue. "It's dangerous, Rem. I was tryna protect you. And the more I liked ya, the more I knew I had to keep you out of it even though I couldn't keep away from you."

She looks to the floor, leaving me hanging before looking back at me. The anger is tainted with regret. "My parents are lawyers, Owen. I can't be involved with a criminal."

Well shit. If this isn't a sign that the universe won't ever give me a break, then I don't know what is?

"I can't change what I do, it's who I am." I finally admit with defeat. *If I could though, believe me, I would.*

We both look at one another, with neither of us knowing what to do. Well, she might but I got nothing! Is this it? Us, over and done with before we even know what *it* is?

"I need time to take this in."

"What about your performance?"

"I'll be there, but I need to think about what I want to do."

"... about us?" I add, knowing that's what she meant.

She has regret in her eyes. "Yes. As well as staying here."

I fight every muscle in my body not to rush toward her, wrap her in my arms and kiss her. I want to, so badly, but I need her to want it, and right now she don't look like she even wants to be in this room with me. I don't know how I'd feel if she goes back to Florida, because any normal guy could follow her; I don't have that luxury. If she goes, I'm going to have no choice but to let her and pray that this thing I have for her travels away with her.

"Okay," I state, getting up and walking to the door.

"Owen," she says drawing me to look back at her. I hope it won't be for the last time, but maybe this is a sign? Maybe this is how it should be because I know the risks of getting her involved in this. "Don't be angry at Spencer for telling me the truth. He is the only one I trust here right now."

Twenty

Owen came to find me. He stopped whatever the hell he was doing to come and find me though I wish he hadn't. All it has done is confuse my feelings for him even more. If he hadn't, I would know I'm not important to him, and what he was saying about protecting me was a lie. But he did, and now I am left with a swarm of thoughts and feelings to decipher and arrange in my mind.

It just won't be happening tonight. True to my word, I am here, getting ready for my performance even with my brain fog.

The door to the dressing room knocks, and I brace myself for them to enter.

"Hi." Lucy says, timidly, slowly making her way into the dressing room. I notice her in the reflection of the mirror, choosing to keep applying the powder to my eyelid. "I didn't think you'd turn up?"

"I almost didn't. But I have a job to do." I answer flatly, noticing her standing there looking at me. She wants to talk, I want answers to my questions, but now is not the right time. "Whatever you have to say, I don't want to hear it tonight. I'm going to do the set and leave."

"Okay, we can talk when you get home." she says, with a hint of optimism I don't share.

"I'm going to stay at a hotel tonight."

"What?! Why?"

I twist around to face her finally. "Because I don't know you, Lucy! We've been friends for a year, and I got that you never opened up about certain things. I understood because it's none of my business, but this impacts my life too. What did you think I was going to say, thank you?! You know my parents are lawyers!"

Her chestnut eyes mimic Owen's when I told him I might not stay, but hers glisten with the beginning of tears. "I'm sorry, Remi."

"I left my whole life to come here, to live in your house." My eyes blur, losing the perfect image of her sympathetic gaze. I'm hurt and disappointed. I never thought Lucy would be someone I would add to that list. "You should have told me something."

"I would have if I could, it's just somethin' we don't—"

"—talk about to others. Yeah, everyone keeps telling me that much." I say, resigning myself to that becoming their go-to response to everything I ask.

Lucy comes closer, bending down to look up at me and cautiously taking my hand, "I mean it, and I can't tell you how sorry I am. I will tell you everythin' if that's what you want? I just don't want you to go because of it."

"I don't want to know everything, believe me." I slide my hand free from her manicured one, not wanting her to think it's that easy, "I can't know about it all without being implicated, like Owen said. I need some time, and then we can talk. But I'm not making any promises. The way I feel right now, I wish I had never come here."

She nods, sadness etched across her perfectly applied face. "I'll be here whenever you wanna talk."

I watch in silence as she gives me a sympathetic smile and leaves me alone. The fact they didn't tell me bothers me more than what they do—which surprises me because I have always lived with such law-abiding values. I can't even comprehend it, and honestly, I don't think I want to. It isn't me. This is not what I want. *Then why can't I stop thinking of Owen?*

Being as professional as I can, I finish getting ready and make my way out to the bar, but I decide not to join Lucy and Spencer for a drink at the table like every night I have since I came here. Instead, I take a seat at the bar with a glass of water. Lost in thought, I feel a hand on my back, causing me to jump.

"Woah, hey, it's only me." Spencer says reassuring me with his hands up in surrender.

"Please, Spencer…" I plead, letting out a deep breath.

"I know. Lucy said you want some space, but I just wanted to come over and say that I'm sorry."

"Why should you be sorry? You had the balls to tell me."

"Look," he begins, glancing over his shoulder to Lucy quickly before continuing, "I've been where you are. It's a lot to get your head around, I know, but remember who they are to you. It don't define them, it's just what they do."

I listen, think, and understand. It isn't who they are; I recognize that, but they still hid the truth from me. I didn't have the choice to make; that's the part that hurts the most. They made it for me.. "You work with them, Spencer. I'm not going to do that."

"No-ones askin' you to! If you wanna quit, then quit and go home, but if you wanna be with Owen, then be with him knowing the truth. You still have the freedom to make the decision of being involved; Owen and Luce never had that." His words are soft and caring. He's trying to give me some perspective and I appreciate that, moving off my stool to hug him. I'm grateful to have someone who understands a little but most importantly, someone who is being honest with me.

***

The set went well but I know it wasn't my best performance. My head was everywhere but on the stage with me.

Roberto knew something was wrong and cornered me before I left to ask what was wrong. I told him I needed some space, and he kindly offered me his sofa for the night, but I couldn't take him up on it. I need to be alone. So instead, he settled on helping me book a room at a nearby hotel for tonight.

I want to call Riley—like I have with everything else—but how can I? *'Oh, hey Ri, so you know that guy I'm seeing? It turns out he's some kind of criminal drug-dealer whose dad is in prison for God only knows what! Please get mom and dad ready to fight my case if I get arrested!'* Not possible, is it?

Having only some clean items of clothing I took from the dressing room, I hail a black cab and arrive at the hotel, collect my key card and head up in the elevator to the fifth floor. As I open the door my phone chimes. Even electronically, I know it's Owen.

I drop my bag and perch on the edge of the king-sized bed pulling my phone free ro confirm I was right.

> **Owen: I just wanna know you're safe.**
> **I'll leave you alone, I promise.**

I can't with this guy.

I throw the phone on the bed and decide to run myself a bath. The popping of a billion tiny bubbles soundtrack the memory of Owen's pained face when I said I need to think about us. *Us.* I don't want to be emotionally attached already but I am. I wanted to run into his arms so badly and kiss his face to make him smile but my body wouldn't listen to my heart. It is protecting me, and I am glad that it did. We need to talk, and I can't truly make my decision until I know more.

Wrapping my hair in a towel, I sit on the bed wearing the robe that came with the room, and finally figure out what to respond to him with.

Remi: I'm fine

I wait and watch as it records him read it before the dots reappear to show he's typing back.

Owen: Thank you

More dots appear.

Owen: I'm sorry

I drop my hands into my lap, looking ahead at nothing. He's pulling at my heart strings, and I don't know how to feel about it.

Remi: I don't know what to say Owen
Owen: Me neither

Remi: I have so many questions

Owen: I will answer anything you
wanna know that won't get you in trouble

Remi: Are you free tomorrow

Owen: I am now

A soft smile tugs on my lips, appreciating that he will clear time for me, to give me what I need from him.

Remi: I'll send you the address in the morning.
Come and get me 9am

Owen: I'll be there. Goodnight

***

Unsurprisingly, I barely slept last night.

I had to call Riley. Of course, I couldn't tell her much, only that I'd learned something out about Owen and didn't know if I could move passed it. She told me to follow my gut and not to act quickly without knowing the whole story. So, I'm stood here, watching Owen's G Wagon roll up by the curb side. Butterflies immediately erupt in my stomach and getting in beside him does zero to calm them.

"Hi."

His face gives me nothing. "You good?"

Good Lord. His voice is deep and sexy—this is not the time or place for me to feel this way. "Yes."

The drive to his apartment is not the usual '*rip your clothes off in a second*' kind of tension, it's the '*get me out of here*' tension that the second he pulls up, I'm out of that car before he can cut the engine, "let's just get this over with."

"Fair enough." he mumbles, leading the way in the same painful silence until we're both stood in his kitchen, where I decline the offer of a drink and take a seat on a stool watching him making a coffee on the opposite side of the island. He's not wearing his usual suit and tie, choosing navy blue sweatpants and a white t-shirt, and looking far too sexy for me not to stare in secret. His shirt is tight enough that I can see every muscle moving in his back. I reminisce of running my hands down them, feeling him between legs...

"So," he says, interrupting my memory by turning to look at me. "Where d'you wanna start?"

I blink, coming back to reality. "Is there a beginning?"

"It ain't a fuckin' storybook, Rem." I cock an eyebrow watching him take the seat opposite me, ready to be interrogated, "Like I said to ya, I'll answer your questions, but there are gonna be some things I'm not gonna tell you. That's just the way it is."

"I understand. All I ask is that you don't lie to me."

"I'm not a liar."

"Okay." I straighten up my back and begin. "Am I here illegally?"

"No. The premises, contracts, wages and shit are all done by the book."

I nod, appreciating that even with this all of this, I can trust that part. "Did you really want to protect me?"

"Yeah." he says without hesitation. "You're strong, but I knew you wouldn't choose to be a part of this. No one would."

"And what is *this*?" I know Spencer told me, but I want to hear it from him. This is his business, his legacy, and his secret after all.

"It's a Firm."

I can tell from the soft purse of his lips he wanted his answer to be enough, but it wasn't. The name of something doesn't help me. "What is that?"

"We control some things and distribute some things to make money which we put through the books of the businesses."

"Like drugs?"

His jaw tenses as his teeth clench tightly together. "Lemme guess? Spencer?" I offer a curt nod. "Yeah. Wanna delve into that?"

"Absolutely not!"

"Good, 'cause we weren't."

I take a second as he takes a sip of coffee. "Why is your dad in jail?"

His eyes pierce into me with a ferocity I haven't felt from him before, "you're really goin' there?"

"You said you would tell me what I needed to know."

"Yeah, well why my dad's in the nick don't have anythin' to do with this."

"How doesn't it?" I cock an eyebrow.

"'Cause it don't."

My eyes narrow at him, but I know that line of inquiry is done. "Fine. Then tell me what the truth is about you and Jack. I know this isn't just about me."

The white coffee mug clatters against the concrete worktop loudly, spots of dark coffee splattering around it, before he stands up abruptly and walks towards the sofa and away from me. "I'm gonna fuckin' kill Spencer!"

"Don't blame him, Owen; I am not stupid!"

He looks back at me, clearly struggling to keep his anger and frustration at bay but failing. *He's not going to tell me.* Even though I knew areas would be off limits, even with the promise that he would tell me what I could know, I knew it was going to be a long shot to get the answers I need. Regardless of how I'm beginning to feel for Owen, I can't do this again.

"I appreciate you trying, Owen, but I've been with someone who was never honest with me. I can't go into this knowing that I will never truly know you." I lift my bag from the floor and calmly make for the door when he rushes to me, gripping my arm tightly and forcing me to stop.

"Rem." His hand slides down my arm and teases against my hand; his eyes, his face that usually gives nothing away softly plead for me to stay. "Please?"

I let him link his fingers around mine and pull me to sit on the sofa beside him. *I hope I don't live to regret this.* He runs his free hand over his face, taking a deep breath and a moment to prepare himself before looking down at where our bodies connect. "Me, Jack, and Alice all grew up together because our dads were mates, but their dad's a twat. He would batter their mum all the time, but eventually shacked up with some other woman and left 'em. It didn't matter to us though, were always still together, and while me and Jack grew beards and started drinkin', Alice and I started a different type of relationship." He chances a quick glance in my direction to gauge my reaction. I don't know what he's expecting? Everyone has a past; I can't be jealous that they were together but I'm uncomfortable. Alice is still heavily involved with the family. Is their past still that? "After a couple of years of messin' around together, one night our experimentin' went a bit too far and she had some bruises. Jack assumed I was like his dad and went nuts."

I don't like what he's insinuating, but I need to ask. "Did you hurt her?"

"D'you think I'd hit a woman?"

"No," I insist, "but how did she get bruises?"

"You know how I like to fuck, but she's worse; nothing is off limits." His statement is confident, and I shift in my seat, because even though we have only slept together twice, I already have a pretty good idea. If he likes that in a woman, will I be enough for him? "We told Jack the truth, which I don't think he's ever believed, but the more time I spent with my old man and the less time me and Alice spent together, he finally seemed to get over it. And, well… then Portia kind of came along…"

"And Portia would be…?" My curiosity is not always my best friend because I really don't want to know more about his exes, and the instant that he sighs, looking at me with regret, I know I should have stopped before those four words fell from my lips.

"She's my wife."

Twenty One

I'm trying to get my lungs to reinflate to speak, but the tightening of my chest makes it incredibly difficult.

He's married?!

This web of secrets is getting bigger, wrapping me tighter within the stickiness and I'm that tiny trembling fly fighting against reality and he is my spider; I'm at his mercy. Even though I can get up and walk out, call this thing between us a day right now, I can't. I'm frozen, *stuck.* "You're—You're married?!"

"I'm tryna divorce her but she won't sign the papers."

I try to take my hand away from his, to move; to leave. *I don't know if I can do this.* "I—Owen, I can't."

"You wanted the truth, so I'm tellin' ya. Would you rather me leave it out?" His eyes weigh heavy on me though I can't look back at him.

"No." I do want the truth—absolutely. It doesn't mean I have to like it. "How long have you been separated?" I finally ask.

"Just after Brad was born."

"She is his mom?"

"Unfortunately." He clearly has a disliking for her from the sour twist of his mouth and the furrow of his brow. "She's a bitch from hell, always finding something to fuckin' moan about. No one in my family likes her but after two years together, I thought I should settle down and do all that shit." His words are venomous, but I listen patiently. "She never fell pregnant the entire time we were together; unless she was secretly using somethin', I don't know, but after we'd been married a year, she fell with Brad." He takes a moment, and I know it's a moment to reflect on that time in his life. He clearly loves his son very much so it must have been something special. "I just had no idea she was seein' anyone else." I gasp softly, shocked and saddened by his demeanor and how it changed from angry to deflated as the breath left his lungs. "Brad was three weeks old when I walked in on her tryna do a DNA swab on him. She tried to tell me I was overreacting and chased after me but as I swung my arm away from her, she fell down the stairs."

My hand goes to my mouth in shock. "Did she…?"

"Nah. She didn't go down the whole thing but she got hurt. That's when all the shit with Alice started again as Jack thought I'd done it intentionally. He brings it up anytime he can."

That's why he said Owen had slapped me about. He thinks this is what Owen does?

"I didn't care, though. My drinkin' got worse, and so did I—my anger, my patience, everything. I've done some bad shit, Rem." His eyes search mine for understanding, and I understand completely. This is so much more than I ever thought he'd say. Everything is being laid out on the table, unweaving the tightness of the web. Is that a good thing, though?

"Owen..."

He squeezes my hand that was never released, making me know he's okay with continuing. "I went on a witch hunt for the bastard I thought was an old mate who'd been shaggin' my wife. And when I found him, I beat the shit out of him." He smiles wickedly. "Luckily for him though, I didn't have anythin' on me to do some real damage, but I was fuckin' wasted so I just kept hittin' and hittin'."

I don't want to ask but I need to know. "Did you kill him?"

"No. My old man jumped on him when I paused but that's when a witness saw him. He took the flack for it all."

"Your dad said that he was the one that beat him up?"

He nods slowly, "got four and a half years for GBH."

"Why did he do it?"

"I'm his son." he declares, shrugging a single shoulder and screwing up his mouth for a second, "I had my own kid to look after, so he told me to sort myself out. Brad is definitely mine, and I haven't touched a drop since. Portia said if I touch a drink or lay a finger on her again, she'll stop me seein' him. She won't divorce me 'cause she knows I'm goin' for custody."

He runs his free hand through his hair releasing a strong breath. A web is intricate and difficult to navigate, just like he is, but when you look closely, it's a simple design once you know how it's been crafted. Owen isn't the way he is for no reason. Each one of those faint frown lines that adorn his skin was out of his control. In life, things happen that you can control, and things happen that you can't. He can't control what life he was born into, the same way I can't. It's sheer coincidence that our lives collided.

"Thank you." I say barely a whisper.

"Now you know everythin'."

I do. I know he is loyal; he fights for people like he fought Jack for me. I know that this man beside me stopped everything to look for me last night and cleared his morning to pick me up and reveal everything.

Owen's hand finally leaves mine as he stands up leaving me feeling so empty that my heart calls out to him before my body can forbid it. "Stop."

He turns to watch me rise to my feet, moving to stand before him. "Do you promise to protect me? To always be honest?"

"Always."

Owen

I never thought I'd ever have to say all of that out loud, but I knew I couldn't let her walk out of that door. I had to open up *for* her.

Remi's not like the others. She listens but tells me straight, and without a doubt she's the best woman I've ever met because of it. She reminds me a bit of my mum, but even she don't stand up to my dad like Rem does to me. If Remi still wants to leave now that I've spilled it all then I'll have to accept it. *I just fucking hope she doesn't.*

As I stand, she stops me looking into my eyes with her voice soft and cautious. "You promise to protect me? To be honest?"

I will; "Always."

She closes her eyes for a split second before opening them and placing her hand on my face. "Please don't keep anything from me that I can know about."

I turn my head to kiss her naked wrist, desperate to touch her since I let her hand go, "I won't."

She steps up closer and slowly brings her mouth to mine. My arms instinctively wrap around her waist just how I like them, realising that yesterday could have been the last time I held her. She fits so perfectly that it's hard to believe I've held anyone in them before. She grips onto my neck tightly, it pinches a little, but I like it, shows she passionate and as hungry for me as I am her.

I tug on the hem of her top, but she pulls away. "Not so fast Mister."

"What?" I pant while my dick strains against my joggers. She smiles bemused, like I should already know.

"I need some coffee and food. I haven't eaten since..." She looks up in thought. "It's been a while."

"Let me cook somethin'." I don't have a lot because I'm hardly here to eat, but I grab some stuff from the fridge and begin cooking a quick version of a cooked breakfast – a couple of sausages, eggs, few bits of bacon, some mushrooms and a fried tomato. She chats a little bit to me but sits content with the cup of coffee she longed for, watching me.

"I never thought you could cook, let alone that you would cook for me one day."

I raise an eyebrow at her, sliding on the last piece of food onto the plates positioned between us.

"Be honoured, not many women have eaten anythin' made by these hands."

I push the plate to her as she lifts up a fork. "Let's hope it's not the only time." She winks playfully before looking down at the contents of steaming food, instantly returning her gaze at me. "Uhm, what is this?"

"That babe, is a traditional English brekkie!" Her eyes glint in the brightening light from outside "Well, minus the toast 'cause I ain't got no bread. Here. You'll want some brown sauce on it, especially the bacon." I pass the sauce, but she hasn't stopped staring at me. "Have I got somethin' on my face?"

"You called me 'babe'."

"Did I?" It slipped out if I did but I don't care. If she thinks it's a big thing then whatever.

She cracks and smiles wider, reaching over to give me a kiss. "Yes. I liked it."

I lean in for one soft kiss as she gives her attention back to the food in front of her. "Come out to dinner with me tonight."

"Are you asking me, Mr Turner?" she says, with a curious eyebrow.

"You know I am."

"Hmmm." she muses, prolonging it. *She's gonna make me ask.*

"Remi, would you like to go out to dinner with me?"

"Yes, Owen. I would love to."

Remi

The atmosphere in the car is a stark contrast to the one Owen brought me to his in. Our linked fingers add to my comfort and reassurance, though my mind is still processing everything. It's going to be happening for a while, I think.

It's only once we park up outside Lucy and Spencer's terraced house that nausea washes over me again. Me and Owen may have cleared the air, but there is still a lot to be discussed with Lucy.

"You okay?" Owen asks gently, squeezing my palm for extra reassurance.

"I haven't spoken to her properly yet."

His lips pull into a tight sympathetic smile but doesn't open to say anything, letting me take the lead to exit the car and make my way into the house. Spencer and Lucy's voices bounce off the walls of the corridor until they hit our ears only to stop when we walk through the kitchen door.

Lucy shifts from one foot to the other looking back and forth between me and her brother. "Is this a good sign?"

I look to my right, meeting his waiting eyes as he mutters. "It's alright, yeah," he leaves me to glare at Spencer, "but I'll still be talking to you another time."

I thought I'd be alone in arguing back with him, but Lucy jumps down his throat quicker than I can.

"Owen, don't you bloody dare!"

"Luce, it's fine." Spencer tries to reason with her. He knows what truly happens in this world. More than I do.

"No, it's not! I'm not lettin' you get all the shit when it was his fault in the first place."

"How is it my fault?!" Owen bites back making me glare at him, "You knew the risks of bringin' her here!"

I don't like that they're talking about the situation around me but it gives me the perfect opening to ask Lucy why she asked me to come here. I still had opportunities back home, though it didn't feel it at the time, over time it would have blown over.

"Every time I'd speak to you, the spark you had when we met was slowly going. It was hard bein' so far away and bein' unable to be there for you. When we needed a performer, it was too obvious to ignore it, but yeah, I guess I wanted my friend here too." Lucy walks closer, wrapping her arms around herself protectively, "Spencer said we should tell you, and I'm so sorry I didn't say somethin' because you were right what you said last night; I was selfish." I bite the inside of my lip, and instantly feel Owens hand on the small of my back as she continues. "I promise, I was always honest about that. I didn't tell you everything, obviously, but I never lied to you. I just wanted you to be happy again." A small smile rises and falls as her eyes shimmer in the light, "I've loved having you here, and everyone loves you, plus you wouldn't have met Owen…"

"Don't guilt trip me, Lucy."

"I'm not! I'm not... I mean it, and if you move out or go back to America, then I get it." she hangs her head looking to the floor as I let out a sigh, reaching my hand to brush her shoulder.

"I'm not going back home, Luce. Owen knows I don't want to be involved at all, I can't, but you shouldn't have taken that choice away from me."

"I know, and I'm really sorry babe." Lucy says with her eyes brimming.

I pull her into a hug, and though it will take some time, I know she didn't do anything on purpose. This is '*how they do things*' and I must accept that.

"So, where's that leave you two?" Spencer cautiously asks triggering everyone to look at me.

Owen's silence gaze affirms my own feelings to answer confidently.

"Together."

***

"I did what you said last night. I heard what he had to say." I inform Riley. The second Owen left I ran straight up to call her.

"And?"

"There's a lot to get my head around but I want to do this, Ri, I really like him."

"Well, duh!" She mocks me in the way only she can. "I could have told you that."

"He has a son." I blurt out because I hadn't told her that before. It wasn't significant when he wasn't anything to me, but he is. We're dating. I am dating Owen freakin' Turner.

That sound's crazy.

"Oh jeez!" I hear her perfected eyeroll. "How old is he?"

"Four. He is the cutest little boy, Ri, I swear."

"Do you really wanna be someone's stepmom?"

"Oh, come on! I'm not about to become someone's stepmom! I'm dating the guy, not marrying him."

"It's a lot to take on though, isn't it? How does that work for you if he's seeing his kid at the weekends."

Riley thinks Bradley is a lot to deal with; if only. We will still get a lot of time together because from what Owen said to me, he doesn't see Bradley often. And when he does, I can give them the space to let him be with his son. I know how important it is to spend time with your parents separately that I won't ever be selfish. Bradley needs his daddy and Owen needs his son.

"It's complicated, Owen's still married to Bradley's mom. Nothing is going to be happening quickly. She sounds like a bit of a bitch though because she's refusing to divorce him. But I won't ever stand in the way of him seeing his son. Terry never did that to dad."

"But Remi, come on?! Why do you want to get involved in all this? He sounds like he comes with suitcases of baggage." *You have no idea.*

"Because it's my choice!" I snap back, "And I'm going to see where this goes."

"I know it is... and I know you really like him, it's just because I love you, I don't want to see you get hurt again."

I feel guilty for snapping at her, but I know her worries are justified. She was the one I talked to the most when the rug was pulled from my feet thanks to Tom. I not only lost my boyfriend but my dream. "I know and I love you too, but it's early days. We don't know what will happen, but I need to find out."

"I know you do. And I'll finally get to meet this Owen whose got you going cuckoo for myself on Monday."

I chuckle as the nerves erupt in my stomach. Her meeting Owen is going to go one way or another and I hope to God everything I've said makes it go the best way. I need her to be supportive of him because she hated Tom and it proved to be the truth. If she hates Owen too, I fear that history could repeat itself.

Twenty Two

*O*wen said he would pick me up at 7.30pm and I hear the door knock before I realize that he's here on the dot. I manage one last glance at myself, readjusting my boobs with my hands in the figure-hugging red dress I can't wear a bra with, making sure my cleavage looks good regardless. Spencer and Lucy are both out at the bar, so I quickly make my way down the stairs without tripping on my black strappy heels.

Owen is looking away as I open the door but when he looks at me, his jaw drops as his eyes scan the length of my body. A delighted smile grows on my glossed lips noting the huge bouquet of gorgeous red roses in his hands that match my dress so well, it's like we planned it.

"Jesus fuckin' Christ!" he mumbles at last, captivated still by my body.

"Do you like it?"

He nods slowly, "I thought I liked you in that white dress, but this. Red's my favorite color."

I raise an eyebrow. "You remember the white dress?" *The one I went on a date with Jack in?*

"You have no idea how hard my dick was in that restaurant, seeing you in that." I swallow deeply, remembering all too well how he pinned me against the wall and blurred my mind just with his proximity. "Shame you'll have to burn it."

I chuckle. "Why? Because I wore it on a date with another man?"

"I'm glad we're on the same wavelength."

I roll my eyes, turning back to go into the house. "You're so ridiculous. Let me put these in some water and get my purse, then we can go." I don't realize he's followed me into the kitchen until I feel his arms snake around my waist. He nuzzles his face into my softly curled hair igniting tingles down my spine. This man makes me feel like nothing I've ever felt before. My body becomes his to do with whatever he wishes in a second. And he has been able to see it from the second I sat on his desk weeks ago.

"Sure you wanna go out?" he pulls my hair to expose my neck, peppering soft kisses along it.

"Yes." I say breathlessly. His lips graze against my skin, making me moan again.

"Are you sure about that?" When he speaks like this, I will quite literally do anything he tells me to. No questions, pleases, or thank-yous are required. I turn my hand to the side, desperate to feel his lips on mine. "You didn't answer me... do you want to go still?" He teases me with his lips, making me chase around for them until I put a halt to his tease with a single word.

"Yes. So, suck it up, Mr. Turner."

***

With the bouquet he arrived with and how smart he is dressed—more so than normal—I'm not surprised by how posh the restaurant is that he pulls up in front of. The large, white-framed windows and the sleek, silver words informing me of the name are nothing short of what I would expect from him. He is all for grand gestures, and I'm glad I wore this fancy dress.

We're greeted before I have even walked through the door completely, with my coat politely asked for before we're guided between the precise lines of white tables and chairs. It's strange to see people glancing around at him. The way the staff act like he's very important has me assuming this place is one of his. Is this what I'm going to be like? Constantly thinking if something is or it isn't related to them? Is it all a façade for the illegal money they're washing through the books to look legitimate? Should I ask if it is, or would he not be able to tell me?

"You alright over there?" His words shock me out of my quandary, his head angled to match the curiosity on his handsome face.

"Sorry, I was just thinking of some stuff." I admit, nibbling on the inside of my bottom lip and readjusting my position again in my seat.

"You can ask me anythin' you want, you know."

A smile pulls on my face for a second. "No, it's fine honestly. I don't want tonight to be more conversations about *that*."

He nods in agreement as we're handed a menu. I say menu, it is one piece of extremely expensive paper, with gold inlays listing six equally elaborate plates of food. The options are not what I would normally eat or enjoy, but I respect that he's brought me here and order, and once we have, he sits there looking at me silently; my body warming under his gaze. My bemused smile extends to a giggle, making him smile wide enough to reveal a glimpse of his teeth. This smile doesn't appear often, but Lord knows, it affects me.

"What's so funny?"

"It's so formal. We've never been alone for anything other than talking or—"

"Fuckin'?" He cocks an eyebrow, pursing his lips. *Hm-hmm, all that talking we do…* "We're talkin' now, it's not any different just 'cause we're out havin' dinner."

I lift my wine glass from the mirrored place his water sits, resting my elbows on the table, taking a sip. "Do you miss drinking?"

"No." He insists with a soft shake of his head. "Even without the reasons for givin' it up, I don't like who I become with it."

"Have you never been tempted this whole time?"

"Ironically, it's only Portia that makes me wanna drink. But I know I can't. Brad means too much to me."

"She shouldn't stop you from seeing him though if you're doing what she said."

He looks down at the glass of water, I can't even imagine having a child who I love more than anything, but not able to be with every day. "Like I said, she's the bitch from hell." He lifts the glass and takes a slow sip before placing it back and looking at me. "So, what's your deal? Why did Lucy wanna bring you over here so bad?"

"She never told you?"

"Nothin' other than a dickhead ex you needed to get away from."

I raise an eyebrow. "Tom was not the reason I came here; I could stay living where I was."

"What did he do, then?"

"How do you know he did anything?"

"Well, if you broke up with him, you wouldn't have been gettin' worse. Same if it was mutual. So he did somethin' or broke up with you."

I smirk at him. "You're good."

"I'm the best, babe."

I smirk, shaking my head before taking a deep breath. "He cheated on me. I don't actually know with how many, but he was having a full-blown affair with another singer he was recording with when I caught them on Christmas Eve."

"Broke your heart at Christmas. What a twat."

I nearly laugh at that statement. "We were together for a year but I realize now I didn't love him, at least not like I should have or I thought I did. I was just about to sign a record deal that he had spent months manufacturing me for, then he turned them all against me. He made them believe I was crazy, and I'd been manipulating him into getting me a deal. And if I didn't get one, I'd get violent."

"It was probably the other way around, weren't it? That's what these guys are usually like."

"No. Manipulating, absolutely, but he was never violent. He's pathetic, he wouldn't do that. My parents tried to fight it in court, but I had no evidence and neither did he, so it got thrown out."

"I'm sorry."

"It's okay. He won't be going anywhere anytime soon, so I have to let my parents deal with it."

"Are they still tryin' to get it through court?"

"Not that, no. He has some of my songs and he's sold them, but I don't have any rights as the writer of them. That's why I was so angry that day, he'd just called me."

Owen's nostrils flare. "It's a good job he lives in the States!"

"I'm glad he is." I cock my head to the side, "I dread to think how you'd handle it."

"That's who I am, Rem. People deserve what they get when they hurt people I care about." I blink in surprise. '... *I care about.*' I like how real he's being with me. The enigma gone; I feel able to really get to know him now. He asks another question as our plates get put in front of us. The perfectly stacked food and colorful swish of pea puree looks delicious. "Your parents aren't together are they?"

"They had been together for years and always been so happy, but they fell out of that type of love for one another. We never saw them fight though; they were like best friends who were our parents. We didn't know until years later when we were older, but my dad confided in my mom that was gay."

"For real?"

"Yeah, they stayed living together until he knew it was time to move on and then they separated."

When he purses his lips, I know what is coming next. *It's always the same.*

"Wow, that's cool." *Wait, what?* "Your mum's awesome for being there for him. It must have been really hard for her, but shows she has a kind heart."

I don't know what to say, with the next mouthful of food poised on my fork waiting for me to envelop it with my lips. I wasn't expecting that. When I tell people they all react with shock and assume my mom was angry. And yes, it wasn't easy for them both, but no one has ever commended her for her support and strength.

"Yes, she is an amazing woman."

"Shame you're nothin' like her then." He winks, taking another bite of his own as I gasp, laughing a little at his cheekiness.

"Be grateful I am very much like her, or I wouldn't be here." I calm the chewing of my food, looking up when he doesn't say anything back. He isn't looking at me and I know already it was a low blow—even if I meant it light-heartedly. "I'm sorry."

"It's right though. I'm glad you are being open to this and open to being with me." *Open? I guess. Consumed by you so much I can't walk away? Definitely.* "What's your sister like? Is she as understanding as your parents?"

I laugh openly, receiving a nervous look in return from him. "Riley is a law onto herself. I think you'll love her."

"Yeah?"

"Mm-hmm, she is even more stubborn, sarcastic, and outspoken than I am. And she's arriving Monday afternoon."

"Here?!" His eyebrows raise.

"No, Armenia… yes, here!"

"Two of you... well, that should be fun…"

I wink, leaning forward to tease him with a deeper look down my cleavage. "Sweetie, you have no idea."

———————————————

Owen

Having Remi's hand in mine as we walk out of the restaurant back to my car, I feel like I can achieve anything. I'm thanking my lucky stars that she's as amazing as she is, otherwise, I'd be somewhere else smashing someone's face in just for the sake of it.

Although it was fucking hard not to get distracted looking at her in that dress, I could have listened to her talking all night. I was the one asking a hundred and one questions, desperate to know everything I can about her because she really is something special.

"Are you sure you want to go to The Rose?" she asks, smirking at me. If she thinks she's going to continue this sexy fucking tease she has been doing since we were at Lucy's when we leave here, she's got another thing coming.

"Yeah, because I can touch you at The Rose. Sitting opposite you for the last two hours and not being able to do this—" I push her gently against the passenger door, pressing myself up against her gripping and the base of her neck with one hand, forcing her to look at me "—has been harder than I thought."

She confidently moves her mouth closer to mine. "Do you not like the tease, Mr Turner?"

My lips roll between my teeth enjoying how good it feels as the blood rushes to my dick. "You can tease me all you like, but I will always get what I want." I lap my tongue through her parted lips, before taking her mouth under my control. She grips my jacket like her legs will fail to support her. *Don't worry, I won't let you fall darling.*

The moans she releases when she succumbs to me still gives me goosebumps, but even though I could stay here kissing her until the sun comes up, I can't.

"Come on. We've got somewhere we need to be." I wink, leaving her standing there panting softly as I walk around to my side and opening the door to slide inside.

***

Arriving at The Rose, it's heaving, this is what it's always like on a Saturday night, but since Remi's been here, the mid-week footfall has never been better.

I continue to hold her hand the entire way through the bar, wanting everyone to know this gorgeous fucking woman in *this* dress is off limits. I don't want anyone questioning if she is or she isn't because she is mine. I'll shout it from the damn rooftops if that's what it takes.

Seeing Lucy's eyes sparkle as she clocks us walking over is a nice treat. Like I said, my family couldn't stand Portia and never wanted to spend time with us as a couple, so this is a new thing for me and Luce.

"Look at you two looking all loved up and cute." Me and Rem look at one another bemused. *We look cute?* I was thinking sexy and powerful.

"How was your date?" Spencer asks, trying to be chill but I can tell from his lack of eye contact he knows I won't have dropped it—despite what Lucy said. I'm still pissed off with him because he's clearly told her a lot more than he should have and I need to know what she knows.

"I'm still here, so that has to be a good thing, right?" My hand leaves hers and pinches her arse. "Hey!" She leans in to talk in my ear, purposely pressing her tits into my chest. "I wouldn't do that if I were you. If you get me any wetter than I am already, it will show up on my dress."

"What about your knickers?"

"I'm not wearing any." She winks, walking off to sit down on my usual seat, leaving me stood there like a twat whilst the blood runs below my belt yet again. "Are you coming?" Remi teases once more. She has no fucking idea how much I want to be... inside that delicious pussy of hers.

We should've gone straight back to mine.

We grab a drink from the usual selection that's always on our tables, and soon Remi's tipsy, giggling and being carefree with Lucy. She has great banter with Freddie and Chris, even Charlie chats a lot to her because she's so easy to be around, it feels like she's been here for ages.

"Rem!" Lucy shrieks over the music, "come and dance with me."

I laugh to myself, shaking my head watching them holding hands walking into the middle of the dancefloor.

"She took it better than you thought then?" Charlie asks, placing his drink back on the table.

"I weren't sure for a second, but I couldn't let her go without knowing everything."

"She knows?!"

"Not all about this shit, no. I didn't spill all that stuff, but I told her about Portia and Alice."

Charlie's eyebrows raise, gaining three deep lines on his forehead. "All *that* shit?"

"She knows why my old man's in the nick too."

"Fuckin' hell... you do like her!"

You know have no idea.

I sit up straighter, searching the crowd for her needing to lay my eyes upon her, but I can only discover Lucy walking back to the bar. "Where the hell's she gone?" Rising to my feet, I begin my search, finding her laughing and smiling at two guys I've not seen in here before.

"Here you are." I say loud enough for them to hear, slipping my hand around her waist expecting her to be surprised by my arrival, but she isn't. She beams up at me, placing her hand on my chest.

"I'm sorry, Jamie here pulled me aside to talk." She looks to the blonde dickhead in jeans, white t-shirt and black leather jacket, but it's the other cunt in the navy pinstripe suit whose eyeing her up that I lock onto. "Jamie, Wayne, this is Owen. Owen, they are from WB Records."

My mind swirls for a second while she bubbles with excitement. *WB Records? Great...*

Wannabe-Bruce Wayne stretches his hand out to me "I've heard a lot of good things about Remi here. I had to come and meet her for myself.". I wanna ignore his lingering, out-stretched hand waiting for me, but it's not about me, it's about Remi. I pull her tighter filling his hand with mine and showing him again that she's mine.

"You wantin' to sign her or somethin'?"

"Owen!" Remi hollas, raising an eyebrow at me but bogus Batman laughs like a pompous knobhead.

"Well, I'm certainly interested in having a meeting with Miss Prentice here."

Yeah mate, I bet you fucking are the way you're looking at her.

"Then you better make an appointment, hadn't ya."

He stares right at her as he speaks. "Absolutely. I'm not going to leave it for her to get snapped up by anyone else."

Try it on motherfucker...

Twenty Three

"Keep rubbin' your arse against me and I'm gonn slide straight in."

I smile to myself at his tired voice croaks out, feeling his arm pulling me tighter to him, my back flush with his chest. "Just seeing if you're awake."

His body moves, his breath blowing against my skin as he talks in my ear. "Even in my sleep, I'll react to you. My body's under your spell."

I roll onto my back to look him in the eye as he hovers over me. It's officially the longest date I've been on; two nights and a day to be precise. And I wouldn't change a second of it.

"I'm sorry I can't stay again tonight."

"I think I'll manage."

I cock an eyebrow. "Oh really?" Teasingly, I draw my hand across my chest, running it along my naked sternum and down my stomach to between my legs. His eyes follow as I start to caress myself. "I think I can manage too, Mr. Turner."

He snatches my hand away, holding it beside my head on the pillow. "I don't think so. Not unless I tell you to." He shifts his body between my legs, nudging them further apart as he begins to kiss my exposed neck. I move my hips to give him the exact angle to push into me, but he teases me—just as I had him—by hovering at my entrance before sliding in, causing us both to release a satisfied moan. His fingers entwine with mine, pulling both hands above my head. He grows hungry, devouring me until he meets my waiting lips. The movements between my thighs are more controlled but still as powerful, his dick barging into me before moving back slowly. With every jerk forward, my climax draws closer. The fact I can't touch his back or grip his ass is painfully tantalizing, though I like him having control of my entire body— it's exhilarating, and he has it down to a T. He wants to be in control, no matter what, and the only situation in which I won't fight him is when he ends up between my legs.

"Owen... I'm gonna..."

"Come for me." His deep, commanding voice is, as always, the switch to reach my climax.

"Fuck!" He stills on top of me, pulsing away and filling me for yet another time this weekend.

I've never experienced anything like this before. Being physically unable to keep away from a man. My body being instantly ready to accept him from just a look or brush of a finger. The chemistry is unfathomable.

"You sure you don't wanna stay tonight?" His eyes sparkle, hopeful that I will scrap the fact that my sister's flight is landing in just a couple of hours and continue to find new places in his apartment to fuck.

"I wish I could, but Riley is coming remember." He hesitantly leaves my body but not his position.

"I ain't gonna see you much, am I?"

I match his disappointment, but I'm also excited to see Riley. We've never been apart for this long, and with everything that has happened, I can't wait to tell her it all and introduce them. "You'll be busy, I'm sure. You won't have time to miss me."

"It's fine, I'll just spend my time watching you from the office at The Rose." he says confidently, pecking a kiss on my lips and leaving the space in my arms.

"I'm not working this week, Owen."

"At all?" He asks, sitting at the edge of the bed.

I lean onto one elbow, pulling the sheets further up my body, "I'm performing but that's all." He drops back to the bed beside me, defeated.

"Fucks sake." I find his disappointment cute, sliding across to kiss him softly on the lips.

"I'll make it worth your while when we can be together, I promise."

His hand slides down my back to my ass. "You'd better."

***

Riley's plane landed almost an hour ago, and I'm grateful to have Spencer and Lucy here with me to collect her. I can't wait for them to meet.

I can't keep still, the excitement bubbling up too much as her arrival draws. Then I see her walking through the gateway and begin waving just as Lucy did when it was me. "There she is! RILEY!" And as Spencer asks me who she's with, I lose it! "Oh my God!"

I run to them and jump into my father's arms. "What are you doing here?!"

"Am I not allowed to see my baby girl?" I've always been a daddy's girl, so having him here is just perfect right now.

"Yes! I'm just so shocked." I leave his arms and move to Riley. "Why didn't you tell me?"

She grips me as tightly as I do her. "You only asked if mom was coming, not if dad was."

I roll my eyes playfully at her. She never changes. "You know what I meant. But thank you. I love he's here with you."

I hold Riley's hand as dad pushes the baggage cart, walking back to where Lucy and Spencer wait patiently. Riley leans in closer. "Who's that?" Curiosity thick in her voice, I put her out of her misery.

"It's not him."

"Mmm, he's cute."

"... and engaged to her!"

Getting to them, Lucy stands there excitedly waiting to envelop Riley. "Ah! I'm so glad you're here!"

Riley chuckles looking at me bemused over Lucy's shoulder, but I giggle softly making the introductions, "Lucy, Spencer, obviously this is Riley and my dad, Zander."

Exchanging friendly hugs and pleasantries, my dad holds his arms around my shoulders as we walk to the car. "Who's 'him' then?"

She's been here five minutes, and I already want to kill her. I giggle nervously, feeling my cheeks heat up. "I, erm, might be seeing someone."

"And he just sounds fantastic, dad! I think you'll love him." Riley says painfully sarcastic from beside him.

"He is, thank you!" I narrow my eyes at her momentarily. "His name is Owen, and he's Lucy's brother. He's working today, but I hope you will be able to meet him whilst you're here."

My dad murmurs, making me nervous. "I'll look forward to meeting him."

Oh God... the butterflies in my stomach that were anticipating Riley and Owen's meeting have long since disappeared, and all that is left is the tightness in my chest after how she has spoken of him since his arrival and my dad's quiet interest.

We bundle them and their luggage into the car and take them on a similar tour of the city as the one they took me on. Their hotel is beautiful. Unlike the ultra-modern building I stayed in the night I learned the truth about Owen, the exterior is exquisite. Carved stone, arched windows and pillars at the huge entrance doors. Inside is the perfect blend of new and old, with cream marble flooring and chandeliers, but modern furniture.

Once they have checked in, the three of us go to the adjoining restaurant for lunch, to spend some time together.

"How's Terry?" I ask my dad, once we've ordered.

"Working, you know what he's like. But he's good, he's sorry he couldn't make it. His latest build must get its sign off in a couple of days as the owners want to move in. He sends his love, though."

Terry and my dad have been together for ten years, and he's an amazing man. If we had to pick someone for either of my parents, Terry would have been it. My dad proposed a couple of years ago but they've yet to tie the knot. They're both career minded and always super busy, so while my dad is working on cases, Terry owns a successful real estate building company.

"I haven't seen Terry for so long, I'll come to visit you both next time I fly home."

"You know you're welcome any time, baby girl." The waitress places our drinks order in front of us, and after we have all taken a quenching sip, I feel another band go around my chest when my dad asks. "What have you been doing since you got here?"

"Remi's been so busy, dad, you'd be proud of her." Riley says with a playful glint in her eye. "She's always working, sometimes in the bar and sometimes doing overtime with her boss."

My jaw slackens and my eyes widen. *She did not just say that!* I'm beginning to wish I'd not told her so much about Owen and me!

"Thank you, Ri, I have been busy, *working,*" I smile through gritted teeth, "so why don't we go sightseeing together?" I manage to throw out, hoping to turn the attention away from me.

"That sounds good to me." my dad says, pushing his chair out, "I'm just going to use the bathroom before the food arrives."

The second he is out of earshot, I glare at Riley until she stops picking at her nails for a second, looking innocently at me.

"What?"

"What are you doing? And don't play the dumb blond routine 'cause you're never getting that dark hair lighter."

She gasps. "Hey! I pay good money for this color, thank you very much!"

I lean one arm on the table, propping my chin on my palm, "Riley, please... give Owen a chance. I know he has baggage, but I really like him."

She leaves me hanging until a deep breath accompanies her moving forward in the seat. "Ugh, fine."

"Thank you, that's all I want." I pause, still amused by what she said before. "You... paying good money... we all know mom pays for your hair." We both titter together, our laughter in key with one another. It feels so good to have her here, even if she could be dead and buried twice over already; I've missed her.

"I use my own card."

"That's she pays for."

Our food is not far behind my dad's return to the table, and as if no time has passed since we last did this, the conversation flows freely. Riley's not loving school, and I smile internally as my dad scolds her yet again for her indecisiveness. I tell them all about The Rose and how the audience is growing week on week, but the part I'm too excited about is soon rolling out of my mouth.

"A guy who works from WB Records came to see my shows, and on Saturday he brought the boss, Wayne who wanted me to send him my demo's. He said if his team likes them, he's going to call me to arrange a meeting."

"Shut up!" Riley calls out. "Oh my Gosh, that's so exciting."

"Yeah, well done! I knew it wouldn't take long for someone to recognise you and your talents, darling."

"Thanks guys. Dad, will you come with me?"

"You don't even have to ask, I will be there even if I have to stay here longer." My heart swells, knowing as always, he will move heaven and Earth to make us happy.

"Thank you."

My phone chimes in my purse and I know it's rude to look at it, but I sense it's him and my compulsion gets the better of me.

Owen: Did she make it OK?

Knowing I have been on his mind makes me nibble on my bottom lip.

Remi: Yes, she arrived safely. I'm just having an early dinner with them. My dad's here too.

I watch as he starts then stops and starts typing again, indicated by three wobbling. dots, before a message comes through.

Owen: Can I pretend to be excited about meeting your old man?

I laugh out loud, gaining the attention of my dad.

"What's funny?

"I've just told Owen you're here. He's excited to meet you."

Remi: He's harmless sweetie. But if you want him to like you, don't forget he's gay so if all else fails, just take your top off and twerk a little 😊

Owen: Aren't you hilarious

Remi: I'm the best

When I use his words from our date to reply, I smile as the butterflies begin to rise, only to burst into life when he responds quickly.

Owen: Yes, you are

"Someone's melting over there." Dad calls me out, smirking happily.

"Maybe a little..."

"Just don't go melting too fast, sis." Riley warns, cocking an eyebrow, which is followed up further by my dad.

"She won't. Remi's got a good head on her shoulders."

I wish I had your optimism, Dad. Owen is as hot as the sun, so it wouldn't matter if I was the North Pole, I'm melting faster than I expected for this man.

———————————————

Owen

Just when I thought I had enough to navigate around, Remi tells me her dad is here. Do I really need a lawyer sniffing around the place? Definitely fucking not! But the bonus is, ironically, that Remi knows, and I will truly see how she handles it around her family.

When I hear the office door open, I glance up and see Spencer enter, moving closer to take a seat opposite me. I make him wait until I've finished writing the message I had started and I send it before giving him my full attention. I've made him wait all weekend to talk, a few more minutes won't hurt

I place my phone on the desk and sit back in my chair looking at him. "So?"

"O." He pushes his weight up with both arms to reposition his arse in the chair. They're used to impulsive and reactive Owen. Quiet and calculated Owen makes them all nervous.

"I'm in a bit of a predicament here Spence, because normally I wouldn't let you explain yourself. You know where you'd be right now, and my little sister would be at home crying." He opens his mouth to speak, but I glare at him shutting him up quickly. "But luckily for you, Remi told me not to be angry at you." Spencer's eyebrows rise. "Believe me, that is the *only* reason you are sat there unharmed. But I need to know what she knows."

"I didn't tell her much."

"DON'T bullshit me! She knew a lot fuckin' more than she should have!"

"Alright..." he resides, taking a steadying breath. "Remi said you'd told her what we did. How the fuck did I know she was on about the bloody flats we'd done! I just tunnel visioned and said too much to take it back. It just kinda came out about how your dad would beat ya, and how you have to make sure it's all still running."

"So, you just spilled everything just because she said one comment?!"

"No! You know she's like! She wouldn't stop until she knew everything. You know it yourself, O, she's as strong headed as Lucy."

Spencer sighs before letting go of what he really wants to. I know what he's gonna say, because he has already said it. It doesn't mean I wanna hear it again. Not now. "O, I told you and Lucy to be honest with her, to a degree. I knew she wasn't the sort of woman to 'shut up and put up', but you didn't wanna hear it. I know I went too far. I told her about the drugs, the money, what pressure is on you from your old man, but she didn't do a runner back home did she?"

My elbow resting on the arm of my chair allows for my index finger to move along my lips, trying and failing to mimic the sensation I feel from the lightest of Remi's kisses. I agree with him, both outwardly and internally. She could have been on the first flight home but chose to stay, but if she had have known before, she wouldn't have come and then I wouldn't have met her. And that's the part I'm glad I listened to him for.

"She's still here mate. You've just gotta make sure you don't fuck it up."

My eyes once staring off in thought fly to his in a blink. "Watch it."

"I'll take whatever you give me if I hurt Lucy, you know that, but Rem don't have a brother or anything. I'd take the same for her if it needed."

My jaw clenches as my teeth bite together. Galant Spencer, always being the level-headed one even on this a rollercoaster, but I can't deny hearing this reiterates everything I feel. *She's something special.*

"Would you be willing to wave her goodbye if she got implicated on her Visa and had to leave?" I ask genuinely curious to see where he had thought of this.

"She's not getting involved."

I raise an eyebrow at the lack of conviction in what he said. "As she's so rightly told me, every employee could be seen to be involved through no fault of their own. She might not have the choice."

He looks down, lost in thought until he returns as the Spencer, I know with his shoulders back and his head held high. "Then we make sure she does. We include her enough to keep her safe from anyone but far out that she is squeaky clean for the Old Bill."

It's gonna be one of those things we'll have to cross if and when we get to it, because just being with me now means she's caught up in this—whether I like it or not.

"Go on, get out of here. We've both got stuff to do." I say, bringing my chair forward so I can lean on the desk. He stands, without looking back at me. "But I mean it though, pull any-fucking-thing like that again, you won't be walking anywhere."

"There won't be a next time."

Twenty Four

Remi: I miss you x

It's been 24 hours since I woke up in his bed and yes, I miss him. Is it too much though?
Ugh. I'm being ridiculous.
I delete and type again.

Remi: Good morning, hope you have
a good day x

I hit send, happier with my less obvious statement and finally look to my left feeling Riley moving beside me.

"Why are you up so early?" she croaks out, rubbing her eyes.

"I'm planning our day." I say, smiling happy I have at least booked us tickets to do some things today.

"Mm-hmm..." she mumbles, "I believe you." My phone chimes quietly in my hand, getting her to raise her hand up just enough to look at me through one sleepy eye. "And from that smile, I was correct. You're texting lover boy."

I laugh from my chest. "Trust me Ri, he is no boy!"

She finally rises from the covers, sitting up against the headboard beside me. "You know, I was kind of wanting to know before but now I'm gonna meet him… not so interested in knowing how big he is."

"Good! Because I wasn't going to tell you." I say chuckling aloud at her as I open the message.

Owen: Am I gonna see you today?

Remi: So needy Mr. Turner... 😊

Owen: I am extremely needy but very generous in return

Remi: Oh I know and I'm not complaining

Owen: I'm as impatient as I am needy…

Remi: No, you won't see me. We have a full day of sightseeing planned

Owen: When are they going home?

I giggle like a little schoolgirl, already feeling the muscles straining from my smile.

Remi: Monday. They're only here for one week

Owen: Please tell me I'll see you tomorrow?

Remi: Riley's birthday is tomorrow so yes, if you join us for dinner?

The dots linger, taunting me; I hadn't arranged with him how they'd meet. I just hope this isn't more than what he was expecting. Finally, they stop, and a tinkle rings out.

Owen: Let me know when and where I need to be, and I'll be there

Remi: Thank you baby x

Only once it is sent and instantly read do I register that I called him *'baby'*. He calls me 'babe', but it doesn't feel a term of endearment from his lips, more as cute pet name. How I said it, it had feelings. I mean, we're dating, but we haven't labelled this. I couldn't even imagine Owen being okay being called a 'boyfriend'! *Ugh... this isn't me!* I don't second guess everything that I do, but he makes my body submit and my mind a muddle.

"I can literally see your brain working from here. What is it?"

"Nothing, don't worry. It's not important."
Especially as I know he's read it and is still yet to reply.

She throws back the comforter and flicks her hair as she walks off to the bathroom, "Fine, then while you sit there lying to yourself, I'm getting in the shower first."

***

Note to self: Don't try to visit too many places in one day.

I got us tickets for a bus tour that Riley was desperate to go on, and we passed over Tower Bridge and the Tower of London. Saw and rode the London Eye, stood outside of Buckingham Palace and watched the changing of the guards and shopped in Hamleys and Harrods where Riley got herself a mass of birthday presents. It has been the best day, and now, after a late dinner, I'm starfished across the bed, exhausted.

"You do know this is actually my bed, right? You're sharing *my* bed." I reluctantly roll over a little to give Riley the space she's bitching about now she has finished unbagging all of her goods.

"I'm so tired. But it's so nice spending it with you and dad."

She smiles softly at me, showing off her single dimple for a second, "Yeah, it was fun exploring together and pulling dad wherever we wanted to go, just like when we were kids in Disneyland."

I release a single chuckle, gazing up at the ceiling. "Do you remember our last day there and we both wanted to stay late but mom wanted to go back to the hotel to start packing so dad stayed with us. We rode Winnie the Pooh ride again and again until we got bored—"

"And dad farted sitting down on the boat in It's a Small World?" She adds making us both giggle as we reminisce that holiday.

"Do you remember mom wearing a long dress and getting her leg caught in the tail of the horse on the carousel by the castle?"

She laughs in surprise. "No!? I don't remember that!"

I turn my head to look at her. "How do you not remember that?! She was showing all the people in view her underwear until someone came to help her! I was on the horse in front of her, but I couldn't help for laughing."

"Yeah, I remember now. She was mortified!" We lay chuckling to ourselves for a minute before my mind wanders straight back to Owen... as it has done every time I've let it today. "You're thinking of him again aren't you?"

Resigned to the fact she knows me so well. "Yes."

"What's his son like?" Her question catches me off guard, and I force my broken body to sit up with my legs crossed.

"Bradley… He is the cutest little boy, who loves superheroes, really wants to go to Disneyland and loves "manilla" ice cream with chocolate sauce and sprinkles."

"Manilla?" She piques an eyebrow, "Now, that's my kind of flavor, especially with sauce…" She licks her lips with a wink making me roll my eyes chuckling.

She asks me further questions about when they broke up and if he shares custody. I revealed as much as I feel is acceptable because it isn't my story to tell.

"She must still love him if she won't divorce him."

I don't believe what Riley just said, but there's a reason why they're not together and if he's the one wanting a divorce then it shows me, he's moved on. That's all I care about.

Leaving me with my thoughts, she disappears in the bathroom to get ready for bed, when a light double tap on the door forces me to rise. Expecting it to be my dad, my jaw drops open as wide as my eyes when Owen appears in the opening.

I quickly open the door, taking him in fully.

"You're a very difficult person to find, ya know."

Once my brain engages, I stutter, "w-what are you doing here?!"

"I couldn't wait another day to see ya." He steps closer to me, and my body forgets instantly about how tired and aching it is and begins exploding with excitement that he's here.

"How did you find me?" I ask, getting lost in his eyes.

He smirks creating a little crease in the corner of each eye. "Probably best not to ask love."

I'm trying to hold the door closed as much as I can to avoid Riley coming out, and true to form, he notices that I pull it closed behind me. "D'you want me to go?"

"No! No... my sister is in here."

His hand links into mine, "let's go then."

"Go where?"

"I got a room."

"Wait here." I don't even question it, I rush back inside, grab my shoes, purse and phone, shouting through the door as the water runs inside, "Riley, I have to go back home. Something important came up. I promise I'll be back before you wake up."

Stepping through the door, Owen stands there leant against the wall looking so suave and sophisticated, but damn sexy. *He is all mine!*

I link my arm through his, hugging myself into his side. "Ready?"

The desire in his face as he smiles sets off the fireworks, and he says nothing as he leads me to the elevator and up to some fancy looking doors.

"Penthouse Suite? Little fancy for a booty call, isn't it?" I tease, but he freezes holding the key card in his hand.

"You aren't a booty call, babe… trust me."

The second the green lights flash, he has me inside in a flash. Like the rest of the interior, it's the perfect hybrid of ultra-modern and exceptional architecture. The tall ornate balcony doors in the living area frame the twinkling lights across the city skyline. windows everywhere.

My body tingles as he closes behind me, moving my flowing hair over my shoulder. The lightness of his kiss at the base of my neck makes my eyes close and my breathing increase. He places another slightly higher up and slightly harder. Each one gaining in strength until he's nibbling on my ear lobe. "You won't ever be a booty call." He whispers making my head drop back. "And I wanna feel you in my arms—" I gasp softly as he pulls me tight against his chest, "—as I hear that word fall from those perfect lips."

"W-what word?" I manage only a stuttered reply.

Dragging his moist lips back in the direction in which he started, I pant as he bites down on my collar bone. "The one I've been re-reading all day…"

I rotate in his arms to wrap mine around his neck, "I never thought you'd be one for pet names?"

"I ain't, but from your mouth and with that sexy accent, I can make an exception."

I lean right into his ear, squeezing my breasts against his chest using the most seductive tone I can think of. *"Thank you, baby…"*

His lips find mine in a flash and we're soon naked, with me in his arms again. I have no idea where I'm going, and I only stop to pay attention when I feel us drop and stop with me straddled over his lap. Lust burns in his eyes as his chin tilts upwards with the drop of his head against the back of the sofa. His hands gently hold my hips while his solid cock sits waiting between my leg, so I take him in my hands and begin pumping slowly. Rotating my palm around the head, I feel the precum coat my skin. Stealing a glance, I see his eyes close from the pleasure. Having him melt under my touch is exhilarating and I've never felt so powerful, sexy, and feminine.

Desperate and unable to resist him any longer, I rise on my knees positioning him in just the right place, rubbing his tip along my wet slit before sinking down onto him. A fulfilled moans escape us both, as I stretch and fit around him like a glove made to measure. It felt like we'd been apart for so much longer than we had, but in this moment, it doesn't; it feels like we never separated.

I ride Owen slowly, expecting him to dominate in turn, but he doesn't. He sits back on the sofa, letting me have complete control of how fast I go and how deep I take him. Knowing he likes to watch me; my hands roam along body.

"You like that, baby?"

He moans out as his eyes turn from soft caramel to steaming hot chocolate. "I could watch you ride me all day."

The force of his eyes match his grip as his fists my ass in his hands. He spreads them and encourages me to go deeper still, rocking myself against his groin as the delicious pain detonates throughout my body. He creates feelings in me I've never discovered before, hits places I've never felt touched before, and fills me with a width I've never had before; he is unlike any other man I've known before.

The moans of pleasure leaving me spurs him to begin rocking beneath me.

"I'm nearly there..." I pant out, resting my palms against his clammy skin.

He lets me ride over the waterfall and into the dizzying drop of my climax before he scoops me up like I weigh nothing, holding me in place over his dick as he rises and walks over to the large window. The feeling of the iciness against my back makes me gasp but he swallows it with a hungry kiss. All restraint he had on the sofa has been left there because this Owen is the one I am learning about quickly. This is the man who takes what he wants and, as always, I'm glad to be the one he wants.

He slams into me over and over from below, tasting my skin wherever he can take a bite. Each brush of his lips is like fuel to this fire between us, but I'm still surprised when his hand slides over my mouth. My stifled moans vibrate against his palm, making my lips tingle. His other fingers dig deep into my shoulder, holding me in place as our bodies bang together.

I have no warning of my orgasm until it hits me so powerfully I'm grateful he's holding me up or else my legs would have given way.

"Rem!" Owen almost pleads as I milk every drop from him. "Shit...!"

He stills inside me, pulsing away, letting our pants replace the moans in an instance. Once I've caught my breath, I finally raise my head from the crook of his neck. "That was… amazing…"

One of his callous hands pushes the locks of hair that has fallen over my face. "You're amazing, babe."

There is no question of the sincerity and meaning behind this '*babe*'. The look from his eyes tell more than I could handle verbally.

I think the last piece of me just melted away... "Thank you for coming to find me."

"I'll always find you."

Twenty Five

Eyes still closed, I smooth my palm across the sheet, needing Remi's skin against mine and unusually she isn't linked with my body like she normally is. The smell of her vanilla musk perfume is still there, but the cashmere softness of her skin and the buttermilk smell of her body lotion is missing.

Coming up empty, I peak one lid open to discover I am indeed alone in bed. I quickly lift my head off the pillow to look around the room. Nothing.

"Rem?" I call out, sliding out from under the sheets to walk through into the living room where our night began. My clothes that were discarded around the room now lay neatly folded in a pile on the sofa with my phone poised next to it. "Remi?!"

Nothing!

I check in the bathroom, even though I know it's empty, before grabbing my phone. *Why the hell did she just leave? She could have woken me up.* Unlocking it, I'm greeted by endless notifications and messages that have come through during the night but all that can wait because I see one message from her sent at 5am.

> *Remi: Baby, I'm sorry I had to leave, it was hard not to stay believe me! I promised Riley I'd be there when she woke up. We have a full day planned but I will find us somewhere for an early dinner before my set. I'll let you know where to come. Don't miss me too much*
>
> 😊 *xx*

This bloody woman, I swear! So sweet and so goddamn cheeky, but yeah, I will miss her. That's all I've done since I dropped her off at Lucy and Spencer's two days ago. If she wants us all to meet and go out for dinner tonight then I know exactly what to do, and after a quick phone call to a mate, it's sorted.

> *Owen: Glad I don't need to send out the search party again. Be ready for 5pm. I'll send a car for you all. Have a good day*

***

Walking into The Rose to complete some work that needs doing, I clock my mum and Lucy sitting at the bar, long stem glasses in front of them. Making my way over to them before they call me, I place my hand on mum's back to let her know I'm here.

"Didn't expect you two to be here this early?"

"Hello darlin'." I give her a kiss on the cheek, like I always do before I sit down beside her.

"I have my first dress fittin' so we came for a quick drink before we go." Lucy tells me with sparkling eyes.

"Nice." I don't care but I do care about her being happy, and this wedding makes her happy.

"Is that girl coming again today?" Mum asks out before taking a sip of her wine.

Lucy frowns for a moment. "What girl?"

"Ya know, the delightful American girl."

"Remi?" Lucy answers, knowing full well that's who she means. "No, I told you it's just me and you for this."

"Thank God." She sounds relieved and it grates on me instantly. I know they had a dodgy introduction, but shit, I didn't help that. And I certainly don't agree with this negativity continuing.

"Why d'ya say that?" I avoid giving into my instinct to narrow my eyes at her.

"Well, she's just..." Mum starts, shrugging a shoulder and twisting her face up like she smelt something disgusting.

"*'She's just'* what!? Cocky? Opinionated? Not afraid to speak her mind?" I reel off getting more passionate as I go. "Intelligent? Beautiful?! What is she, mum?"

"Owen..." Lucy sympathises quickly, knowing I'm pissed off.

Mum looks between us quickly. "What's goin' on?"

"That '*girl*' you don't like? I'm seein' her."

"Owen James Turner!" she hollas, eyes widening. "What the hell are you thinkin'?!"

I could have told her that me and Portia were back together, and she wouldn't have been this bothered. I'm not ashamed of being with Remi and though I know she is coming into something she still doesn't truly understand, she is the one I want to be with. "I'm thinkin' she's comin' next week as my plus one."

"You can't bring her!"

"I can do whatever I like, mum."

She blinks in astonishment before looking to Lucy with her thumb extended and pointed in my direction. "Is he for real?"

They continue to ignore me as Lucy supports us by confirming that we are together. "They seem really happy, mum, honestly. She's good for him, and Brad loves her—"

That gets my mum looking back at me in utter shock. "She's met Bradley?!"

"Yes."

My family know how protective I am of him and who he spends time with, so her surprise isn't a shock to me. Remi and Brad's instant friendship was a shock to me. She sits awkwardly before Lucy breaks the silence asking if she's ready to go. They quickly finish off their drinks and stand to leave.

"I hope you will reconsider your guest." My mum says with a sour look on her face.

"There is nothing to reconsider. She is comin' with me."

She lets out a lung-emptying sigh, holding her head high as she leans in to give me a meek kiss on my cheek. "I'll see you soon."

I murmur a quick response, giving Lucy a more comfortable farewell. She pulls away giving me a sympathetic smile.

Overtaken with the work still to complete, I make a quick dash up to my office. Sitting at my desk my phone chimes. Finally seeing Remi's name on the screen makes me smile like a little kid at Christmas. *What the hell is she doing to me?*

Remi: You didn't have to do that Owen x
Owen: I know I didn't, I wanted to. Might even save m from twerking

Remi: It might... Bring the oil just in case 😊
See you this evening x

Owen: The oil will be for you if I do.
See you later

I'm stopped before I can start by a knock on my door. Inviting them in, I raise an eyebrow as the person enters, taking a seat opposite me.

"The fuck d'you want?"

Jack clears his throat quickly. "I wanna clear the air."

I put my pen down and fall back into my chair. "Heard that before… more than fuckin' once." This is his go to routine every time we come to blow. It's wearing thin though, and I don't know that I can be arsed to go through it all again.

"I wanna come back to work."

"Why?"

"Because it's my life. I thought it was better I stayed away for a bit, let things settle, but I'm ready now. Alice has spoken to me. I shouldn't have behaved how I did."

"So what? Ya needed to hear it a hundred more times before you believe I didn't hurt her?"

"She's my sister, you know what my mum went through!"

"Yeah, I do! I saw what she looked like when he'd beat the shit out of her. I ain't like that and you fuckin' know it!"

"I know," he begins quietly, fidgeting in his seat before looking me dead in the eye. "I fucked up, and I'm sorry."

"And I know all about what you said to Remi, so unless you're willin' to throw that in to that apology too, then don't waste ya breath. I meant what I said."

His jaw tenses as he looks away. "Are you two a proper thing now?"

"What you gonna do if I say yes?" He slowly brings his eyes back to connect with mine with a look I know well. His jealousy rears its head from time to time and unfortunately, he wears his heart on his sleeve.

"I'd say I'm happy for you." I can hear the strain in his voice to sound genuine, but he's here and I know that he wants to carry on as normal.

"Then you better mean it. You've used your last chance wi' me, Jack."

Remi

Sitting in the back of the car Owen so generously provided for us, I text him to inform him that we're on our way—at last. Riley took her sweet time to get ready, arguing why we have to eat so early in the evening but she's happy enough to be sitting behind the black-tinted windows of the expensive Mercedes now. My dad wass impressed too, as he slid inside. Not because of the car, he has money to buy this luxury, but because it was done by Owen for us. *For me.*

The journey isn't as long as I expected, and soon the car pulls to a stop outside a sleek-looking restaurant. The beautifully glass-fronted Italian may be narrow in width, but it's not lacking in stature and design. A scattering of tables sits along one wall as we enter, but as I inform them of who we are here to meet, we are quickly requested to follow a smartly dressed woman up a glass staircase at the far end of the premises.

As I reach the ability to peer over the top step, I see him sitting by the window at the front of the building. He hasn't seen us yet, but it doesn't stop my heart from beating harder just at the sight of him. My palms begin to dampen, and even if I weren't being led to him, my feet would be walking without any instruction from my brain. The gravitational pull towards him is stronger than the sun, and his smile when he turns to look at me is just as blinding.

He stands up to greet us looking so calm and collected; the complete opposite to how I feel. The butterflies swirl and multiply with every step. He moves away from the table to meet me halfway, revealing an exquisite red rose in full bloom in his hand. The second he is close enough he gives me the softest of kisses on my cheek, placing his hand respectfully on the bottom of my back and in turn calming all of my nerves.

"Hi." I say, smiling widely.

"This is for you." He patiently lets me accept the thornless rose from his grasp, earning another smile from me before I take a quick inhalation of it.

"Thank you."

I turn to do the introductions but have trouble focusing on what I'm saying because he's still touching me.

"Owen, this is Zander, my dad." Owen stretches out a steady hand to shake my dad's. "And dad, this is Owen—"

"—her boyfriend."

I stutter, not wanting to correct him, but trying not to choke on the saliva that tidal waved into my mouth. *Boyfriend? Just like that? No discussion. No hesitation. He's my boyfriend.*

"It's very nice to meet you, Owen."

"And you, sir."

My dad corrects him with a reassuring smile on his face that it's fine to call him by his name. There is no need to stand on ceremony here.

"And this is my baby sister, Riley."

He rotates his open gesture to shake her hand. but Riley doesn't reciprocate. She looks at his lingering hand, "Do you normally shake a woman's hand?"

Mine and my dad's eyes widen in embarrassment. *She has to be joking?!* But it's clear from the jut of her hip that she is serious.

"Not normally," he says unfazed, which I'm grateful for, "but you didn't look like you wanted a hug…"

"I'm good, thanks." She initiates sitting down at the table he rose from, leaving Owen's hand unmet and my jaw on the floor. I quickly look at my dad who shakes his head in annoyance.

"I'm sorry." I muster an apology on her behalf, while my dad sits there quietly muttering something under her breath. I'm relieved when Owen looks unfazed, even keeping a hint of amusement on his face.

"Don't worry 'bout it."

Ever the gentleman, he pulls out my chair before a single glance triggers the waiting staff to promptly take our drinks order. As they both order wine, I join Owen in having only water. He smiles knowingly at me before looking at my dad, who—unlike my sister—sits open to receive the attention.

"Have you enjoyed your tour of London over the last couple of days?"

"I have. I came here years ago, long before these two came along, so it's been amazing seeing how much it has changed since then."

"Yeah, it changes from year to year in places. What did you do today?" Owen asks, this time looking to Riley to see if she will engage with him. But she doesn't.

"We did Madam Tussauds..." I say filling the gap, and I start to giggle unable to stop. And knowing what I'm giggling about, dad joins me.

"It wasn't that funny, Rem." Riley retorts, pausing her intense interest in the menu for a moment.

"What wasn't?" Owen asks, bemused.

"Riley was standing waiting to get a picture of one of the waxworks, but there was a lady standing in the perfect position taking a picture..." I giggle once more as Riley rolls her eyes, "Only she wasn't taking a picture. She was another waxwork." All three of us chuckle, as Riley fidgets in her seat.

"How did I know she wasn't a real person!"

"Maybe the fact that she hadn't moved for five minutes?!"

She scoffs loudly. "It was not five minutes…"

"It was funny, Ri," Dad adds.

"Yeah, funny like this place. Italian? Really? Isn't there anything more authentically British you could have taken us to?"

What the hell is up her ass?! I could handle the attitude she had before she met him, even though none of it was justified, but now she is here, with the chance to get to know him better, I can't help but think she's being a bitch.

I'm about to call her out when Owen's calm voice answers. "Yeah, of course I could." But I know

Remi's favourite meal is lasagna, from when she was a kid. I took a chance that you would like it too as a family, and well, this place makes the best one I've ever had." I can see the Ice Queen develop a hairline crack, but that's not enough. I don't know why she's being so hostile. It's not like I'm making her date the guy. I've asked her to give him a chance, but this is anything but.

"Yes, we all love lasagna. Thank you, Owen, that's a nice thought."

"Yes, thank you, baby."

"We serve food at the pub so you can have that if you go there another day."

Again, she doesn't answer, allowing my dad to ask the next question. "You own the pub Remi performs at, is that right?"

"Yes," Owen says, sitting back in his chair and resting an arm along the back of mine. "I own the business, but my sister, Lucy, manages it. We do property development, which we lease out to businesses or convert into apartments, and I also have shares in a number of other places. "I'm just in the process of buying into a successful Michelin-starred restaurant that is looking to open a sister one in Knightsbridge."

I'm so proud of him from the way he talks about it, and although I can't think too much about how it is all funded, he is equally proud of his family's success.

"Wow." my dad says, raising an impressed eyebrow, "It sounds like you're a busy man."

"It can be full on sometimes, but I wanna do the best for myself and my family."

"Do you have your own family, Owen?" Riley finally directs her attention to him, but I call her name in disgust, wanting to kill her even though Owen chuckles.

"Yeah, I have a little boy called Bradley." I take his hand under the table at the soft sadness in his voice.

"You don't get to see him much?" My dad sympathizes.

"Unfortunately, no."

"Why? Don't you and his mom get along?"

"Riley, stop right now. What's with the third degree?!"

"Nothing. I'm just getting to know the guy! Like you wanted me to."

"No, you're not." Owen tries to play it down, but she's gone too far. "You've just met him and you're delving into the relationship with his sons mom. What the hell?"

"Alright… fine! I'm sorry for prying, Owen. It is none of my business."

"Honestly it's fine. It's complicated with me and his mum, but we do what we can, even if it's difficult."

"That's all you can do, be there when he needs you." my dad says, able to relate to his situation.

Owen nods in agreement, and the conversation thankfully ends there.

The rest of the meal has a less murder-inducing atmosphere—thanks to Riley holding her tongue—that and I finally feel able to let myself relax when all four plates are empty. The ease of conversation between my dad and Owen has been more than I could have wished for. If he was worried about meeting him, you would never have known, but then he must be used to talking to all kinds of people.

The waitress offers us the dessert menu as she clears our plates, and just as before, I follow Owen who declines, while my dad and Riley choose Tiramisu. Conversation tries to ensue but stops quickly when a chorus of, "Happy Birthday to you…" draws closer toward us.

Riley's furrowed brows soon rise along with her smile as she realizes it is indeed for her. I look to Owen, who sits there stone-faced as always. "What?"

"Did you do this?"

"Well, you clearly didn't..." His wink is the only thing that gives him away. *This man… I swear.* I thought I had read Tom wrong, but boy! I couldn't have been more wrong with Owen.

As they place the beautifully decorated cake and gift bag in front of her, she looks the epitome of a little girl at her birthday party, eyes sparkling as they

307

finish up the song, signalling for her blow out the candles.

"Make a wish!" my dad instructs as he does every year.

Riley blows them out with her eyes closed then claps her hands together in delight, "You guys... thank you!" She picks up the gift bag, opening it to unveil a smaller, instantly identifiable duck egg blue bag. "Shut up! Tiffany! You got me something from Tiffany's?"

I look to Owen with wide eyes, but he watches her without letting anyone know he did this. I never would have thought he'd be like this, especially when he was stood in that doorway with lipstick on his collar, and it worryingly makes my heart swoon for him. The ice is thawing, and it's thawing quick.

She squeals with delight as she opens the velvet rectangular box and lifts out a delicate silver pendant made up of two interlinked rings on a chain. "That's so beautiful, thank you!" Leaning over to give my dad a thankful kiss on the cheek, he reveals to Riley what I already know, and that it was not him that brought her this. She had our gifts this morning.

"What? Was it mom?" she says picking up the bag to read the card, "*'Happy 21st birthday from London... Owen'*. Wait, you did this?"

He offers her a simple nod. "Just a little token to remember bein' here. Your 21st is pretty important."

I see that hairline defect split wider as she softens, looking at him with a gentle smile on her lips, "Thank you Owen... That's really thoughtful."

"No problem."

She examines the jewellery more closely, holding it out to show my dad, while I become lost in the richness of Owen's eyes, which match the cocoa that covered our desserts. Thanking him doesn't feel enough, though that along with a kiss is all I can give him right now.

Twenty Six

We all traveled back together with Owen; me riding shotgun, his hand in mine, and Riley's new silver addition hanging beautifully around her neck. Driving through London at night is like being in yet another city. Though the stores are closed, they don't look like they are. They're all still lit up like it's Christmas, with hordes of people pounding the pavement no matter the time of day.

Owen pulls into his space at the back of The Rose but takes us in through the entrance from the sidewalk. My dad and Riley look how I must have, taking in all the details with impressed lop-sided eyebrows and they nod in appreciation. I lead the way with introducing them to my friends and colleagues behind the bar and Justin who is playing some ambient music in the build up to my set.

With a cold pint of beer in hand, my dad takes a seat at the table with Owen, Lucy, and Spencer, while I hook my arm around my sisters, giving her no choice but to come with me, and the second I have her contained in the dressing room, I turn on her.

"What the *hell* was that?!"

"What?" she pleads ignorance, sitting in the chair I do my make up in.

"You know exactly what I'm talking about." I know her far too well. She is old beyond her years—despite what she has shown Owen tonight—and she knows exactly what she is doing.

"It's my job to give him a hard time. He's my big sister's *boyfriend*!" She raises an eyebrow at the title he introduced himself as. "Which, by the way, surprised me, given you never said you were that serious."

"Okay... One, You don't need to do anything. I have told you to give him a chance and get to know him! All you did was act like a bitch. It was embarrassing. You went too far, even for you." She pouts her lips, waiting for me to continue. "And two, well, that... That was a surprise to me."

"Why? Don't you want to be his girlfriend?"

"How can you even ask me that? I got him wrong at first; he's not that man, Ri; surely you can see that." I plead, feeling ridiculous that I want her acceptance—especially since she was the one I vented to about him—but I need to know my family at least respects him and my choice to be with him. The man I spoke about is not the one I see now.

"Okay! Fine! I get it, he's your *boyfriend*, I'll stop being the bitch..." Her hand rises to play with the entwined rings of silver metal resting on her chest. "Plus, it was really nice that he did that at dinner."

"I know. He didn't have to do that for you."

She laughs out quickly. "Puh-lease! Remi, he *so* did that for you!"

I cock an eyebrow, crossing my arms. "Mm-hmm, because I'm the one wearing a Tiffany necklace right now, am I?"

"Whether you are or not is irrelevant. He definitely cares about you as much as you do about him. He wants to make you happy, and based on tonight, I don't doubt he'll go to any length to do so."

***

With my make-up on point, and my silk red shirtdress on, me and Riley walk back to the table hand in hand. I'm waiting for Owen to notice me—which doesn't take him long. It's almost as though there is an invisible force between us, and I watch in delight as his eyes scan my body, appreciation written all over his ruggedly handsome face as he discreetly licks his lips. *That tongue…*

He extends his hand out to help me to sit beside him, while Riley sits next to our dad. Just as Lucy did with me, I introduce her to the guys who have joined the group in our absence. Freddie's eyes bug out of his damn skull, unapologetically ogling her until Chris slaps him round the back of the head for me. The last person I was expecting to see here waits patiently for me to get him. *Jack.* It's the first time I've seen him since the day I told him about Owen.

Is he here because he wants to, or has he been made to? He returns my smile with a soft, friendly one, putting me at ease and allowing me to properly introduce them. "It's her 21st birthday today, so we're going to give her a good night, right guys?"

"You have no idea what you're letting yourself in for, love." Freddie shouts out over the bustling around us.

"Is that right?" Riley asks, cocking her head to the side. Freddie is a player. He may as well have a flashing neon light saying so above his head, but he has a sincerity about him that makes you look past it. His heart is in the right place—even if he is an idiot at times.

I feel Owen's arm wrap around my lower back, distracting me from Freddie and Riley's conversation, pulling me close to his body. He leans in to talk to my ear. "You've done this on purpose, ain't ya?"

Holding my gaze forward, I tease. "Done what, Mr. Turner?"

I hear him suck in a breath before he breathes out slowly over my neck, making me shudder as the goosebumps erupt across my body. "You know I can't have you tonight, yet you wear that?"

I rotate to moan into his ear, "Mmm... who says you can't have me tonight?"

"Don't tease me Rem..."

"I would never tease you, *Odin...*" I discreetly slide one finger up the inside of his thigh, stopping only when I'm close enough to his dick that he shifts in his seat. "That wouldn't be very nice."

His fingertips deliciously press into my hip, eliciting feelings not suitable for here. "Your dad's sittin' just there. Keep doin' that, and I'll show him how well you can come as well as sing..." He winks as I move away, keeping my hands to myself but knowing my cheeks are flushed. My dad hasn't noticed at all; he's too engaged with talking to Spencer about something, but I can muster a guess it's about money. I take one small drink from my bottle of water and leave the haven of being in Owen's arms to take my position on the stage, my guitar as always in my hands.

"Good evening, everyone. It's an extra special day today because it's my sister's 21st birthday. Stand up, Riley!" Springing from her seat like a jack in the box, she stands and does a little twirl as people applaud. "So, as a treat, she's going to come up on stage with me!" I watch on as her beaming face falls and her eyes widen in shock. She subtly shakes her head, only to grow in strength. The full table of my friends encouraging her does nothing to draw her closer, and I'm forced to leave her alone. "Aww, she's a little shy, everybody." Soft chuckles titter throughout the room, only doubling when I tell Fred to get her a stronger drink.

"Don't worry, I'll sort her out..." His words are laced with want and his eye roam the length of her body.

"And you can keep your hands to yourself! Dad... watch him!"

"Oh, I am!" The crowd laughs louder as Freddie shifts away from Riley nervously and my dad glares at him; though I know my dad wouldn't do anything. He just likes to make them sweat.

As the ruckus settles down, I strike the first chord and begin my first song, watching my dad look on proudly. It has been such a long time since I performed with him in the audience. Who would have thought we would have had to travel across the ocean for it to happen? Owen's eyes return to me as I cast another glance toward their table, making me immediately feel like I'm performing exclusively for him. This connection has always been there; from the beginning, I could feel his eyes fixated on me when I sang that very first song whilst standing in this exact spot. I find it tougher to sing now because of this new, tightening feeling in my chest, but I also feel like I could fly. He's a contradiction, but he's mine, and the sparkle and adoration gazing upon me ensures I do the best show for them.

Thanking the audience for a final time, I move away from behind the keyboard and make my way back to the table. My dad's arms immediately wrap around me with Riley beaming from over his shoulder.

"That was incredible, baby girl! I'm so proud of you." I chuckle as he releases me but still holds an arm around my waist. "Are you staying here now?"

"Yes, we usually stay for a little while after. Why? Are you going?"

"Yeah, it's been a long couple of days and you haven't had time on your own with Ri. I'll get a cab back to the hotel."

"No." Owen's voice takes over before I can argue, feeling him close behind me but keeping a respectable distance so me and my dad can have this moment. "I'll get Charlie to take you back."

"You don't have to do that. Let him stay, enjoy himself. I can manage."

Owen quickly looks to Charlie who is up on his feet without a second of hesitation. "It's no trouble."

"Honestly, dad, let him take you. It will be nicer than a cab or an Uber." I give my dad one last hug as he resides and lets them do this. "Thank you for coming to watch me."

"I'm sorry it took so long, and I'm sorry all that happened with Tom. You could have been selling out concerts by now..."

"I know." It makes me sad to think of how things could have been, but equally and perhaps a little scarily, I can't help but feel grateful for what happened. I wouldn't be here with Owen otherwise. "I'll see you tomorrow."

"Have a good time, and don't let your sister drink too much. She's not used to it."

"I'll look after her, don't worry."

Dad says a quick farewell to the group and Riley before leaving with Charlie through the back, and I immediately go to sit with Owen. He gathers me in his arms before I can sit down, guiding me to sit across his lap. I link my hands behind his head and cross my legs as his hand sits gloriously on my naked thigh keeping me in place.

"I've been wanting to do this all evening." I press my lips to his, showing him just how grateful I am for him and how tonight has gone. I don't care if we're in a group or a room full of people, I need this. I need him.

"Jeez! Way to switch the gear now dad's gone, Rem!" I chuckle into the kiss as I hear Riley and the others laughing around us. "Are they like this all the time?"

"Not so PDA as that but it's definitely getting more of a thing, yeah." Lucy confirms, giggling along with Riley.

"Ugh, you're so Bella and Edward." The taunt in Riley's words makes me break the kiss to belly laugh. I was obsessed with Twilight and their chemistry. I always said I wanted what they had; that unrelenting desire and need for one another. Though I knew it would never be with a Vampire, I didn't expect it to be with a Firm boss.

"Excuse me, don't diss Bella and Edward! You're just jealous." I tease, knowing she was always Team Jacob anyway.

"Oh, am I?" Riley cocks an eyebrow. "Fred, do you think I'm jealous of them right now?"

"Erm... No?" he says nervously, his eyes jumping between Riley and me. "...Yeah? Fuck, I don't bloody know!"

She slides her hand onto his thigh causing his eyebrows to raise the higher her hand gets to his crotch, "No, Freddie, I'm not."

I pinch my lips between my teeth to stop myself from giggling. He looks so intimidated by her, it's hard not to find it funny seeing this cheeky, flirtatious guy completely blindsided by a tiny twenty-one year old.

"Do you wanna get some drinks, Fred?" Owen disturbs her fun, and just at the right time. Freddie was either about to fall off the seat away from her or jump onto her. I couldn't guess which.

"Are you trying to get me drunk, baby?" He raises an eyebrow at me. *Yes, I know how that word affects you.*

"Maybe I am... maybe I ain't. You do what ya want." He leans in to talk in my ear, "Just know you're gonna be screaming that word again tonight."

Consumed by the physical trigger, my eyes close. Owen's lips linger painfully close to my neck, and my skin sizzles as I wait for them to touch me, but instead, he pulls away. As my lids begrudgingly open, I unexpectedly lock eyes with Jack across the table. His face is flat and looks uncomfortable with being here and watching us. I should feel bad for rubbing our relationship in his face like this; it can't be easy, but what he said to me that day rolls back through my mind, making me look away first. It's going to take some getting used to having him around again.

Two large trays of drinks are placed on the tables, with Riley eagerly plucking up a shot in each hand.

"Ri, told me to make sure you don't drink too much."

She bursts into laughter, taking one quickly as though to defy him without him knowing.

"I'd be careful, Riley; she's whipped my arse doin' shots," Freddie says, lifting his own duo of shots from those on offer.

"I don't doubt it." She cocks her head and asks, "Who do you think she practised with?" Her subsequent wink at him causes everyone to laugh.

I reach across to collect my own, waiting until everyone has something to toast with. "Hey," I begin, calling out across the group to gain their attention, "I just want to say, Riley, thank you for coming all the way over here leaving mom and all your friends behind to celebrate your birthday with us. I hope you had a wonderful day, and let's have a fantastic night! To Riley!" I raise my glass, which is quickly mirrored by everyone, including Owen with his soda.

"To Riley!"

***

Owen let Lewis play some music through the system once the bar had emptied so me, Lucy and Riley could dance like our bodies were desperate too. I was alive with the happiness of having my man, my sister, and my friends all together at last, and even though Jack maintained his silence, even after the shots flowed, it didn't hinder the celebrations.

"I love this song!" I scream, throwing my hands in the air pointing to Lewis who sits at the table with his phone in hand manually playing the songs wirelessly. My body starts moving slow and sexy, putting on a little show with Riley as we gyrate our bodies together to Rihanna's Rude Boy. I sneak a glance across to Owen. Sitting between his friends means nothing because we may as well be alone. Just like when I'm performing on the stage, it's just me and him; two entities with a connection.

Owen's jaw stays tight, but I don't stop for the entire song, and by the time I'm at the last chorus, he looks ready to blow. I lean in to talk to Riley. "I think I need to get my man home."

She looks back at him, pouting her lips, "He looks like he's gonna do some freaky shit to you tonight."

"Ri, you have no idea." I wink, and she slaps my ass as I walk back to him and into his arms, which receive me and place me back on my seat for the night: his lap.

"You alright?"

"My feet are hurting; can we go now?"

"What about your sister?"

"We'll make sure she gets back." Spencer openly volunteers, looking back at Lucy and Riley still dancing together. "It looks like we're gonna be here for a while anyway."

Thanking him, I stand and hold my hand out for Owen to take, "Coming?" A soft smirk forms on his face and he doesn't reply, just stands to take my hand.

The journey home is charged, too fucking charged. The hungriness of my core screaming at me, the closer we get to his apartment. The simple touch of his hand in mine causes nothing but longing and need to have more of him touching me. "Pull over."

"What? I ain't exactly a convenient place to pull over, Rem," he blinks at me, looking back and forth between me and the road ahead.

"I need you..." I unashamedly whine, dropping my head against the seat rest and sliding my free hand along my thigh.

"Five minutes." He glances repeatedly at me watching in quick bursts as I slowly spread my legs to let my hand slip inside my underwear. "Remi..." he warns but I disobey, not recognizing myself as I start stimulating my body.

His hand, still locked in mine, grips it tight as a soft moan of pleasure escapes. Never having played with myself in front of someone else in my life, I lose all inhibitions around him. The absence of judgement from this man gives me more confidence than I could ever imagine.

I close my eyes, sliding my ass forward to allow the opportunity to slip my fingers inside myself. "Mmm... yeah..."

"Fucking hell..." he almost whispers, breathless.

"Do you like watching me, Owen? Knowing that thinking of you inside me is going to make me come? " My motions are unrelenting, and I can feel myself building. His hand could slip in to help, but it doesn't. I know he's loving the show, even if he won't admit it.

"You want me to fuck you hard?"

"Oh my God... yes…"

"Wanna feel my dick ram inside your wet little pussy?"

"Yes!"

"Want me to bite on your tits and choke you with my hand?" His dominating words and rough stimulation bring me to my climax fast, and I pant out a moaned "*yes!*" within my orgasm as I ride the high.

"Gimme your hand." he orders. Breathlessly, I remove my hand from between my thighs, giving it to him. I watch in awe as he takes my wrist and places my glistening fingers in his mouth, cleaning off my cum to bring about a secondary pulsation from my vagina from the feeling of his tongue, leaving no millimetre untouched. "That was a very naughty thing to do, Remi."

"Didn't you once tell me I needed showing how to behave?"

A moan reverberates from deep within his throat, "yes, I did."

Twenty Seven

e said we were five minutes from his place. It felt longer... much longer.

Getting out of his car, he pulls me by the hand into the lobby and quickly into the elevator. Regardless of how hot the journey was, irrespective of my orgasm in the car, the need and desire still has my heart racing. I expected to be ravished, pinned by his body the instant the door closed but nope. We stand here, not saying a word, the only thing connecting us is our hands. I sneak glances. I know he can hear my breaths, feel the heat escaping from every inch of my body. *How is he so calm?*

He continues to ignore me, pulling me easily from the metal cocoon to his door. Once unlocked, an authoritative nod tells me I am to enter before him. It's making me nervous because this quiet and collected Owen gives me nothing—no hints to what he is thinking or what he is about to happen next. His poker face is something quite exceptional.

"Where d'ya think you're goin'?" His voice snaps at me, stopping me from getting closer to the doorway leading to his bedroom.

I glance over my shoulder, discovering him in the kitchen doorway, leant against the doorframe. "I was going to bed."

"You're not goin' anywhere."

I turn completely, raising an eyebrow. His dominance is sexy as hell, but I love to push it, seeing just how much I get under his skin in the best way. "Oh, aren't I?"

He confidently strides over to me, stopping just shy of touching toes, "You don't move unless I tell you to." He holds my gaze as his hands undo the belt around my waist. Slowly, he slides it from the loops holding it in place and hangs it around his neck. "It's a shame to ruin such a delicious dress…" In an instant, he tears the silk dress open, leaving it hanging loosely around my body, exposing my black lace bra and thong. "Take it off." I shrug the now ruined dress free, letting it slip down my arms and pool around my feet, awaiting my next instruction. "Everythin'." he commands, continuing to hold my gaze inches from touching me. Excitement bubbles through every nerve ending in my body. I want him to run his hand along my skin and press his cupid's bow lips to my neck, but he doesn't move a millimetre; even his breathing is stable while mine only increases.

I look at him as his eyes focus on my body, watching as I unclasp my bra, and trace my sensitized skin with the thin straps, dropping it to the ground beside me. I shimmy the damp underwear down my thighs. "Is that better, Mr. Turner?"

"No. Hold your hands out." With a hint of a small smile, I comply. He loops the strap of my dress around my wrists, bonding them tightly together before beginning to back me up slowly to the island. Only once my ass hits it, he lifts me onto the cold surface. "Lay down and spread your legs." I bite my lip as I lower myself. The cold concrete makes my body shudder, but I do as he says, gaining the best reward as he murmurs in appreciation as I open my legs wide to show him just how alive he makes me.

"Do you like what you see?"

"Very much. I knew you could behave when you want to. Now, keep your arms above your head. Move and I'll stop." I lift my hands up quickly but, in my haste, my thighs squeeze together. He tuts loudly, shaking his head and pulling them open abruptly. "Naughty."

"What can I say, I like being naughty for you."

"I know," he moans deeply. dipping down to lap his tongue right through the wetness of my centre and up to my clit in one torturously slow movement. "Such a shame…"

He steps back, smirking with a depth to his eyes that makes me unsure whether he is about to fuck me or kill me. My curiosity is soon answered, though. With one swift flip of his wrist, he slaps my pussy making my back propel off the countertop.

"What was that for?!" I gasp out, catching the breath that escaped.

"Tease me like that again and you'll regret it. I don't take well to people disobeying me, Rem."

I didn't have the intention to finger-fuck myself in the car, though right now, I would do it again in a heartbeat to have him gazing down at me in the manner that he is. The awe and sheer fascination of my body laid out as his own personal banquet; I have never felt more like a Queen, *his* Queen to do with as he wishes.

"Okay, I'll try and be better…"

"Then we'll see won't we." He says nothing more, reversing the step back that he took, licking his lips before disappearing out of view to envelop my clit with his mouth.

My vocal announcement ricochets off of the bare walls as the beautiful assault on my pussy begins, lapping and sucking on me. It feels amazing, consuming me completely that I don't realize I've moved my hands to grip his head, pushing him deeper into my body, riding his face until he stops.

Shaking his head, he wipes the evidence of where he has been from his mouth, "I wasn't fuckin' jokin'!" He may be scolding me with his mouth now, but his fingers begin teasingly rolling around the opening of my walls, buttering my skin with my own liquid gold. "Do you want me to let you come?"

"You know I do!" My mind can't process it— the scolding, the attitude, the teasing. My body can't keep still as oxytocin builds within my bloodstream.

"Then do as you're fuckin' told!"

My hands return above my head, and his fingers slide effortlessly into my wetness soon followed up with his mouth to make sure all areas are given attention. He pumps into me, curling his fingers up a little to hit the right spot, and my hips rock against his face.

My fingertips grip around the edge of the table, making sure I do absolutely nothing to make him stop. I'm so close, I physically couldn't cope if he did.

"Fuck... oh my God! Owen... I'm gonna... shit, don't stop!" I close my eyes and enjoy the rapid build-up of my climax, until I can't prolong it any further. I finish by pulsing around his fingers and heavily dren ching his lips in my cum.

Blinking open my eyes, the thin layer of perspiration makes me shudder softly from the rapid change of temperature. He notices, because of course he does. He sees everything. His right eye twitches innocently, softening for only a microsecond before my hot, demanding boyfriend leans forward to grab my tied hands.

"Stand up and turn around." I squeeze my thighs together as I slide forward and onto my feet. I purposely take my time turning and the second I'm all the way around, he presses his body flush against mine, moving my flowing hair away from my neck and pressing his lips teasingly over my skin. "You gonna pull that stunt again?"

"Maybe." *Absolutely, if it means I get this.* "Don't tell me you didn't love it as much as I did."

"Bend over and I'll show you how much I loved it." he murmurs, running his nose behind my head and down to the base of my neck, taking a gentle bite of my skin.

I breathlessly get three little words out. "Yes, Mr. Turner."

An undeniable growl comes from him as I lean over, spreading my entwined hands out in front of me. The moment I'm in position, he slaps my ass making me scream out in surprise.

"Say that again."

"Yes, Mr. Turner!" A second sting burns but feels so good along with my hardened nipples brushing against the cold surface below me.

"What do you want, Rem?"

"You."

He spanks me for a third time. "Tell me what you fuckin' want."

Pressing my entire chest and stomach to the concrete, I push myself into his crotch, feeling the bulge against my ass. "I want you to fuck me, Owen. Like you never have before."

I expect another whipping against my skin but instead I'm rewarded by the sound of his pants undoing and the tip of his dick rubbing against my opening. "That weren't so difficult now, was it?"

He doesn't give me a chance to reply before he slams into me. There's no allowance for expansion, no deliciously slow teasing. Mr. Turner is a hungry bastard, and I'm all in favor of his feast on my body. His hands hold onto my hips as he pounds into me, driving me to oblivion, grunting loudly and clearly loving his cock sliding against my walls as much as I am. I press my teeth into my arm to stifle my screams, but I feel him tangle his hand within my hair, pulling it back tightly.

"I wanna hear your fuckin' screams. Don't you dare hide them from me." He holds my head exactly where he wants it, but there's no pain. It just heightens what he's doing to my insides.

"Oh my fucking God!"

"You wanna come?"

"YES!" He tugs once on my hair harder than before, "Ahh! Yes, Mr. Turner!"

"Go."

I grip him with my muscles, causing him to release and crying out my name before our satiated panting soon replaces the sound of our bodies slapping each other. I don't care how big the bruises will be around my wrists; I don't care that my ass is going to sting for a day or two. I couldn't give a fuck if it was supposed to be my punishment; I was made for him.

Owen

I don't need to feel around the bed for Remi this morning; she's tangled up in my body like she's spent most of the night, with the only exception that my dick's not inside her. She's doing shit to me that I've never experienced before because I've fucked women, but I ain't fucked anyone like I do her. Nothing is too much, and hearing her moan and scream sends me into a frenzy.

I keep my eyes closed, even if it is only to snooze because I'm happy to stay here with her like this for as long as I can instead of going to get a coffee the second my eyes open. For years, I haven't shared a bed, but everything she does makes me feel more at home than ever—
even with Brad here, it feels right.

She stirs, and when I look down at my chest, her misty eyes flutter open to meet with mine. "Good morning." Her voice makes my body sink further into the springs of this mattress beneath us.

"You sleep alright?"

"Mm, I always do when I'm with you." She smiles softly and even with the remnants of mascara under her eyes, she is captivating. I want to tell her to stay here forever, but I don't. The purple-red marks around her wrists from the strap are clear to see. And I don't feel good about it.

"I'm sorry. I didn't think I'd done it that tight."

"It doesn't hurt." Her eye's follow her arm as she lifts it off my chest, getting a better look. "My pussy and ass... now they definitely hurt. You certainly proved your point, Mr Turner."

Her smile widens, and I copy with a lopsided smirk of my own. I wouldn't ever hurt her in any other way than this. She's the only one I've allowed my guard to drop with since Alice. I just don't want history to repeat itself in the way I have feared.

We lay talking, her fingers playing with the scar on my ribs which she's never asked me about nor have I volunteered the information. It's easy, comfortable. She sits on the stool, and begin to brew two strong, black coffees.

Her phone begins to vibrate in the bag she discarded last night on the worktop beside her. She pulls it free and frowns at the screen then answers with a hint of curiosity. "Hello? … Yes, this is she ... Oh hey, I've been waiting for you to call. Yes, what time?

Fantastic…" She motions for a pen and piece of paper. I slide them over quickly, watching as she scribbles down some address on the other side of the river. "That's great, I'll see him then. Thank you so much!" She ends the call and squeals in delight running around to jump into my arms.

"Who was that?" *I have an idea... It's one I've been waiting to happen.*

"Wayne's assistant finally calling to make an appointment! He loved the demo's I sent over and wants to see me tomorrow afternoon!" She's bubbling with excitement, but I hold her in my arms with her limbs wrapped around me.

"I'm glad he finally rang ya.."

"I have to ring my dad!" She plants an excited kiss on my mouth, before wriggling free and back to the phone, tapping away before holding it to her ear.

So, the dipshit who was eyeing her up like a tasty meal is legit? I watch the earthy liquid begin to fill her cup, listening to her making plans with her dad to go to the meeting. I'm glad she isn't going to be going alone, and if he wasn't going with her, then I would have. She ain't being in a room alone with that cunt. No chance.

I place her coffee on the edge of the worktop and begin drinking mine when my own phone chimes with a message.

Portia: Can you have Bradley next weekend?

I put my mug down, typing out the reply quickly. I don't know if I am, but I bloody will be.

Owen: All weekend?

Portia: From Friday afternoon until Sunday lunchtime, if you can manage that? I wouldn't want to take up too much of your precious time

Breathe.

Owen: I'll be there at 3

Portia: Don't be late

"Oh, shut up you stupid fuckin' bitch!"

"Excuse me?!" Remi calls out behind me, getting closer.

"Not you babe. Portia just messaged to ask if I'm free to have Brad."

Her whole demeanour softens, standing beside me. "Really? Baby, that's wonderful. "When?"

"Next weekend." I take her hand and pull her to stand between my legs, cupping her arse with my hands as hers naturally wrap around my neck. "I'll still see you, right?"

"If you want to, of course, but I know time with him is precious, I don't want to spoil it for you."

"You won't spoil anythin'. He already asked to see you again."

"He did?!" She says, smiling with wide eyes. I nod, earning a light chuckle. *How did I get this? How did I get so lucky to have her?* "He is just the cutest. I'd love to see him again."

"Stay with us the whole weekend."

She narrows her eyes, pulling back a little with a mischievous smirk. "Is that you asking me without asking me again, *Odin?*"

"Yep."

"Okay, *boyfriend.*" She cups my face in her hands. "I'll stay."

Twenty Eight

itting in the minimalistic, overly gray waiting area with my dad, the nerves are buzzing. I have been here before, yes, but that makes it even more daunting. I've had these conversations; I've spoken to managers and discussed deals; and had my hopes up only to crash and burn.

Before I can get inside my head, the tall, strikingly beautiful receptionist collects us and takes us into a meeting room that is yet more shades of gray, with a striking white oval table in the centre of the room. It's a stark contrast and not at all what I was expecting. Neither were the three other guys here, though seeing Jamie sitting between the two older gentlemen makes me feel a little more confident. Without him, I wouldn't even be here.

"Remi," Wayne stands quickly, coming to greet me with a kiss of both cheeks whilst holding my shoulders. "Lovely to see you again."

"Thank you, and you," I say, watching him greet my dad beside me who meets Wayne's eager hand confidently before shaking it. "This is my dad, Zander. I hope you don't mind that I brought him with me."

"Not at all. You remember Jamie, Remi?" I nod, smiling and waving timidly. "Please take a seat." Confidently, he gestures for us to sit in the square, white leather chairs that are much more comfortable than I expected. He returns to his opposite us, looking like the captain of a spaceship with the vast empty desk between us that holds nothing bar a couple of perfectly poised pens and the three additional men to his right. "Let me introduce you. This is Aanil, he is the best songwriter we have here right now."

Songwriter?

"I have to tell you," Aanil begins, sitting forward to rest his elbows comfortably on the desk, "the demo's you sent really were something special. I love the vulnerability that you put into your lyrics and how it comes across in your voice as you sing."

Okay, maybe I jumped the gun... we may be able to work together here.

"Thank you, I do try to connect on the same level with those who hear my songs."

"And it definitely shows." the third and final man jumps in, his voice demanding to be heard by the volume in which he speaks, his thick Irish accent immediately recognizable. "Sorry, I'm Connor. I'm one of the manager's here. Jamie and Wayne insisted I keep a space free to represent you."

"I did indeed," Wayne finally gets a word back in. "I made sure that you had the best of my team available to you, Remi."

I blink excessively, trying to put the correct words together in my brain ready to speak, under the glare of four pairs of expectant eyes.

"Um-wow, that's amazing, thank you." I nervously look back at my dad who, as always, sits and listens, taking in and observing it all. He gives me a reassuring nod, encouraging me to take the lead again. "I guess we should discuss what it is you're thinking of and what you have to offer."

Connor and Wayne share a quick glance before Wayne clasps his hands, resting them ahead of him, leaning the weight on his elbows. "You don't like to mess around, do you?"

"This… well, it's not exactly my first rodeo." I take a deep breath and put it all out on the table. Not the craziness of what really happened with Tom, but that I got to these discussions before and how, at the last minute, the label decided to retract their offer.

"Then their loss is our gain." Wayne says confidently, earning a nod in agreement from each of them sitting opposite us.

"With that, what would you be looking at providing for Remi? On the basis that she does indeed sign with your company, of course." my dad speaks up for the first-time getting things back on track.

"Of course," Wayne begins, "initially, it would be a two-album deal working with Aanil and doing appropriate promotional performances around the country to get as much exposure as we can whilst you're recording. You have some amazing songs already that we can easily get a band together to play with you. They'll learn your songs and your arrangements."

"Yeah, exactly." Connor interjects. It's hard to tell who the Executive is—whether it's him or Wayne. "I would like to see you moving into daytime TV performances, you know, Breakfast TV or chat shows. Anything that we feel the audiences will resonate with your music the best."

My head swims as they continue to mention festivals and eventually crossing over into Europe and America, seeing as I am native to there. It would be considerably harder to get a British artist the same airtime, but they seem to believe it would be easier for me. It was fucking hard enough when I lived there, let alone trying to break it from another country, but they are very optimistic, and I'm sucked in completely.

This is what I wanted. This is what I have imagined my entire life. And it is within arm's reach once more.

"What do you think, Remi, does that all sound good?"

I swallow, taking a steadying breath. "Yes. I think it sounds pretty amazing." They all beam with more confidence—if that was even possible— but there are a couple of things that instantly play on my mind. "No disrespect at all, Aanil, but I sing songs that I write. I can't tell you how much of an outlet writing is and has always been for me. I don't think I could sing someone else's songs."

"You wouldn't be, not unless you wanted to," Aanil reassures me quickly. "We would work together. I work with many artists, so the creativity will always be yours, I would only be adding my experience into the mix."

I can cope with that. These dynamics I can get used to; the other part may be the hardest.

"Will I have any time off? You know, to see my friends and family some time?"

They talk over one another assuring me that I will have time to do that, even after my dad informs them that all my family are still back in the States, and I will need a couple of weeks off at a time to do it.

"We have incredible producers all over the world. If it would work out better, we can arrange for you to record out there for a couple of months and visit your family. Kill two birds with one stone."

They're saying all the right things that it would be hard to find a reason why I wouldn't bite their hands off for this opportunity. But there is one reason that I never had before. *Owen.*

When would we be able to see one another if I'm doing this and he is running everything he does? I know it is still very early in our relationship but we're a couple now and I want to include him in this.

***

Despite my inner predicament, by the time we leave, I'm buzzing with excitement, immediately throwing my hands around my dad's shoulders the second we are outside the building.

"I can't believe it, dad!"

His beaming smile celebrates with me, but his parental advice is never far away. "Just remember to think long and hard about it. It might all sound perfect in there but check through the contract and then make the decision."

"I know, I will."

He hails a black cab and once inside we begin to dissect everything they had to say on our way back to Lucy's. When we walk in, Lucy and Riley are sitting in the kitchen talking amongst themselves before bouncing excitedly in their chairs.

"How did it go?" Riley asks as I join them at the table, and Dad leans against the counter next to Spencer.

"They're offering me a two-album deal." They both squeal excitedly, with Riley wrapping me in a tight hug, as I continue to tell them everything on offer.

"But she has to think about it," Dad quickly adds, causing Riley to slowly release me from her grasp.

"Why?" Riley asks, before Lucy adds to it with a matching look of confusion.

"It's what you dreamed of, Rem! Why do you have to think about it?"

"They're going to give me a week to think it over and go back with any questions I might have. I want to talk it through with mom, and dad wants to see the contract before I sign anything."

"What's Owen said?" Lucy interjects.

"I haven't spoken to him yet." And I don't know how he is going to take it.

"I'm sure he'll be thrilled for you, babe." Lucy smiles, but Riley is in tune with me as always.

"Will he be alright with you being so busy? You're barely going to see one another once the first record gets released and you're doing all the promotional stuff. He doesn't exactly look the type of guy who is going to stop working for you."

Me and Lucy share a quick look because he can't stop working, that is obvious, but hearing Riley openly verbalize what I've been thinking doesn't help at all. If anything, it only adds to that unsettling feeling I don't want to acknowledge. "Like I said, I haven't spoken to him."

Quickly realizing that I have some thinking to do, dad and Riley leave to go back to their hotel so Riley can get some dinner and fresh clothes before joining us at The Rose this evening. I, on the other hand, need to call my mom.

Sitting with my legs crossed, I stand up the iPad and dial her, listening to the dial tone before her smiling face appears in large on the screen. "Hello darling. I've been waiting for you to call."

"Yeah, I'm sorry, I didn't want to call you too early. How are you?"

"I'm good, tired because this case I'm working on right now is taking a lot from me, but otherwise I'm fine. Missing you and Riley. It's too quiet!" We share a light laugh together. "Go on then, tell me how it went today."

I take a deep breath, feeling the butterflies spring to life as I inform her just as I did Lucy, Riley, and Spencer the opportunity presented to me. It's surreal, exciting, and goddamn terrifying.

"That sounds perfect, Remi, even with working with the songwriter. Me and you both know once you're in that studio, all those creative juices will just be squeezed out of you, and working with different producers will be a great experience for you, especially if it means you coming back here for a while."

"Yes, that was certainly a bonus. I'm excited, mom. I didn't think I would get this chance again."

"I'm so proud of you, darling. I knew someone would see what an amazing, talented, beautiful, creative, and wonderful person you are. You were meant to go there because you were meant to have this chance."

I know she's talking about the record deal but why is my heart fluttering like she's talking about Owen? It feels like I came here for the chance at love too.

"Thanks mom."

"What has this boyfriend of yours said?" A surge of new nerves fills my body. I hadn't told her, but clearly Riley or my dad has. "Is he excited?"

"So far he is, but I haven't seen or spoken to him since this morning. I will see him later."

"What is his name?"

"Owen."

She nods, taking it in. "What is he like?"

"Honestly? When I first met him, I hated him."

She giggles at my honesty. "Well, if you hated him and now you're together, there must be something about him that won you over?"

"He's gorgeous, which obviously helps," I smile, blushing a little, "but I don't know what it was. My body gravitated toward him no matter how much of an asshole he was. He would show small pieces of who he is underneath his hard exterior, I just couldn't help it, I couldn't stay away from him. And luckily he couldn't stay away from me either."

I look down at my hands twisting together in my lap, only blinking up when my mom speaks again, her words soft and gentle. "You really like him, don't you?"

I tuck a strand of hair behind my ear, nodding confidently. "Yes, which is crazy! It's only been a few weeks; I shouldn't like him as much as I do."

"Darling, the right man doesn't come with a sign above his head. You just know when you meet him that he's the right one. It just happens."

"Is that how you felt with dad?"

She smiles sadly and says, "at the time, of course. Neither of us knew what would happen down the line, but absolutely. I thought I'd found my happily ever after. I'm glad that he found it again with Terry."

"You'll find someone one day too, like you just said to me, they don't have a sign above their heads."

"We'll have to see." She raises her chin confidently, moving on from the sadness she never lets us see. "How old is Owen?"

"He's thirty-one."

"Oh?" she says, raising both her eyebrows in surprise.

"Yeah… he was married and has a little boy with her." I grimace, waiting for the onslaught of judgement like Riley but hoping she will be understanding like dad.

"Have you met this son?" she asks, cautiously.

"Yes, once, but I could see he's a great dad…"

"Then that's all that matters. Just know though, Remi, I want to meet him ASAP!"

"Yes, okay. I'll call you another day when we're together."

"You'd better or I'll get Riley to!"

***

Getting ready for the show tonight, the nerves usually build for when I'm on stage but this time it is about telling Owen.

I take a lift with Lucy and Spencer as always, saying a quick hello to the guys behind the bar on my way up to his office. I knock and let myself in, finding him sitting behind his desk jacketless and with the top two buttons of his pale blue shirt undone. The quickly growing smile on his handsome face ignites the fire in my body like it always does.

"Bloody hell. I thought you'd signed up and gone on tour already!"

I laugh at his intrigued face. "I'm sorry, baby, I've had a lot to think about and I had to call my mom."

He slides out from behind the gap in his desk and gestures for me to sit on his lap, "How did it go, then?"

I straddle him in his seat linking my hands behind his neck. I need to judge his reaction as I tell him. I want to know he's excited for me too, because I don't know how I would feel if he wasn't. "I've got an amazing offer," I begin, "but I want to speak to you about it."

"Why? It's nothin' to do with me, babe. This is your dream."

"Because it affects us. I will be gone for days, sometimes weeks at a time. They even said about me going back home for a couple of months to record and visit my family."

"So?"

"Will you be okay with that? You can barely cope without seeing for a couple of days now."

He deliberates, leaving me on tenterhooks for a moment.

"Tell me somethin', are there married singers and actors?"

"You know there are."

"So why do you think this will have an impact on us? Just 'cause you're away don't mean I can't see you, that we still can't be a couple?"

"Could you do that, you know visit me, with everything you have to do?"

"Course I can." He smiles widely, "My dad is back next week which it won't be all down to me. I will have time to myself again, and I wanna spend that time with you." His confidence gives me the reassurance I needed and eliminates the only reason I questioned taking the chance on this. "Look, don't stress thinkin' about all the 'what ifs' alright, we'll still see one another, no matter where the hell you are and no matter what you're doin'. And if it means we spend a few weeks apart here and there, then we'll make the most of our time together when we can."

I match his enthusiastic smile. "Thank you for being so understanding."

He lifts one hand to gently run his coarse knuckles down my cheek and says, "I've never been so happy to be proven wrong because you're incredible, Rem. You deserve this."

Twenty Nine

Almost like the universe wanted to test us after our conversation, I haven't seen Remi in two days. She went home that night and then to a spa with Luce and her sister the next day. I tried to get to The Rose to see her last night, but I just couldn't with everything I had to do, and she went back to the hotel with Riley to see her dad after.

I'll be grateful when my old man is back so I can dedicate my free time to her. I wanna go away with her, wherever in the world she wants, and somewhere with Brad too. Anywhere as long as it's just me and her. For the past four years, I haven't been able to put my life first, and in all honesty, I didn't have a life *to* put first. I couldn't see Brad, and I had no desire to be anywhere near a woman. That's all changed.

I get myself sorted and head over to the warehouse to meet the others, and walking in, it's clear something's going on.

"Is that who I think it is?" I ask Charlie, nodding to Daniel Hughes whose sitting in my office waiting for me.

"Yeah. Said he needed to speak to you." he confirms as I walk past and into the room, feeling the tension from Chris and Freddie glaring at Daniel in my absence.

"Daniel... what brings you here?" I ask, knowing precisely why he's here.

"You're a sneaky cunt!" Coming from a private educated, silver-spooned knobhead, that word carries no weight behind it. It's almost comical. "I've just received *my* contract back, signed and dated by you." He slams the document down on the table, a few pages from the front folded over with a big yellow post-it note slapped above one highlighted paragraph. "What the bloody hell is this?!"

I sit forward in my chair to glance at it, faking my curiosity. "From here it looks like a good deal?"

His face screws up in disgust. "*That* is *not* a good deal, Owen!"

I shrug nonchalantly. "For you, Dan... maybe not."

"It's Daniel!"

"Same difference."

"We agreed on a fifty percent share of the new restaurant. According to this, I will have twenty-five percent."

"Correct."

"How!?" he shrieks, gesturing at it, "I've even signed the damn thing!"

I rest my elbow on the arm of the chair, brushing my index finger along my beard. "I'm gonna be putting all the money I want into it. On paper, mate, that place is gonna be a fuckin' gold mine. You think I'm gonna let you have fifty-fuckin'-percent of what's that's worth? You're havin' a laugh, Dan."

"You're leaving me with nothing."

"Na, I gave you a quarter. It did feel generous though, I ain't gonna lie..." I tease, watching his face redden further. "You'll still have the seventy-five percent of your current place—unless you want me to invest more into that."

"No, I bloody don't! This is not what we agreed, *this* is not what I signed, and this is NOT what is happening!" He grabs the contract from in front of me and holds it taught between both hands ready to tear it in half.

"Do that, Danny-boy, and I'll sue you for failing to keep a legally binding contract." He freezes, though each muscle in his arms and hands is poised and ready to move in a blink. "You'd have to pay me all of the projected earnings for the first three years if

351

you did that, plus my initial investment." His eyes widen as I confirm that Spencer made the change to. "Which we all know you ain't got, mate—even if you gave me the other restaurant. The choice is yours. Take the contract as it is and keep your face and businesses, or tear that up, and I'll take everything you have."

"You lying, conniving son of a bitch!!

"Did you forget who you went into business with?" He clams up realising exactly who the I am and what he's now involved in. That's what desperation does for you.

He lets the paper gather in one hand warning me that it isn't over before shoving past Charlie in the doorway to get out, but I call out after him.

"Yeah it is, Dan!" I don't hide the humour in my voice either. I look to Chris and Fred, "Follow him and make sure he leaves without any drama." Fucking idiots thinking they're gonna play me at my own game. People will do anything to get what they want and pay any price to get it.

"That went as expected." Charlie chuckles, coming inside and sitting in the seat Daniel just vacated.

"Always does, fuckin' dickhead."

Silence falls between us for a moment before Charlie speaks again. "You thought anymore about Remi's deal?"

I sigh sharply, glaring at him. "I said to leave it, didn't I? I wish I hadn't told ya."

"I just don't think it's right for her t—"

"I said to fuckin' leave it!"

"Fine!" Charlie bites back, "Bury your fuckin' head, and believe it'll work. But don't be moping like a lost puppy when you ain't seen one another for months and she dumps your grumpy arse! Jimmy certainly ain't gonna stand for it."

Charlie rarely raises his voice, let alone at me, so I do take notice, but I don't acknowledge it because I'm not going to. We will make it work.

"My dad ain't gonna do shit, what I'm doing with my life is gonna be the last thing he needs to think about when he's back. Now shut up and go and get the car!" It's what she wants, and I'm not gonna stop her because ultimately this is the fucking reason she came over here. We've been together a few weeks, I have no right to have a say, but I do get what Charlie's saying because she called me out on it—it's gonna be hard going days and weeks without seeing her, holding her, kissing her, hearing her raspy voice when she wakes up in the morning, making her the strongest black coffee I've ever known anyone to drink... but I'll do it. For her.

Owen: Still wanna go out? You can just come round to mine. We can watch a movie and chill out on the sofa or in bed? No need to get dressed up, or be dressed at all

He would go there, wouldn't he? *Damn you Owen Turner*. I haven't seen him, and it has been torturous. I expected him to turn up at some point, but he said he has been really busy, so I have to respect that. But it was hard, and something I have a feeling I will have to get used to. The thought of abandoning our night out at a club is certainly enticing but Lucy and Riley have been planning it since being at the spa.

Remi: You truly are the embodiment of an asshole aren't you?

Owen: That's not a surprise to you

Remi: Definitely not. Lucy has been telling me this since the first time I met her actually

Owen: Answer my question

Remi: So impatient baby 😊

Owen: Demi...

I pause, intentionally making him wait before deciding to call him. He answers on the second dial tone. "Is 'O' and 'K' too hard to type now?"

I giggle. "You know, and I'd love to do that, believe me, but this is the last night out we can have before Riley and my dad go home."

"I know. I'm gonna be wherever you are, so if you're going to the club then so am I."

Excitement bubbles up in my stomach. I've really missed him. "I'd hope you'd say that. We're on our way to have dinner now, then we're meeting Lucy and Spencer there."

"Okay. Say my name at the door and they'll get you straight in." he commands with the deep and authoritative tone I enjoy so much and counteract it with the sultry voice that affects him just as much.

"I'll see you there, Mr. Turner."

"Remember, Remi, we can't go and fuck just any ol' place when we're there, so behave yourself."

Oh fuck!

"I might... or then again, I might need another lesson."

I hear him suck in a breath. "You're gonna be the death of me woman."

I giggle. "Hopefully not. I kind of like having you around."

"Good." He says revealing the smile on his lips, "I'll see you in a bit. Enjoy your meal."

He ends the call just in time for me to arrive at the restaurant where I am meeting Riley and dad for dinner. Our meal is full of talk from about the memories made whilst they have been here, and it hits me that they're going soon. My dad pays for the bill and the two of us say goodbye to him before going in our own taxi to the club with him going back to the hotel. I'm unable to hide the smile on my face as we get closer, the excitement and eagerness to see him making me restless.

"Oh my God, you are so nauseating." Riley states, rolling her eyes and looking out of the window.

"Why? Because I want to spend time with my boyfriend?"

"No," She scoffs, "because you're so freakin' in love with the guy."

My eyes bug out of my head. "What?! No, I'm not!"

"You so are! You're smiling like a fucking crazy person just sitting there. Don't even get me started about what you look like when you're messaging and talking to him…"

"I like him, a lot, but it's not love, Ri. It's been three weeks!"

"And love has an entry level, does it? *'Love can't happen until…?'* You know it doesn't, Rem." I have absolutely nothing to say and can only stare at her as she cocks an eyebrow at me, hoping the answer will form in my mind any second. It doesn't. Nothing floods my mind other than Owen's face and how he makes me feel. "Look, don't acknowledge it if you don't want to. I'm just calling it how I see it." She shrugs a little and turns to look back out the window of the cab.

I can't deny that I feel for him more than I have felt for any other boyfriend, but this is lust, infatuation, falling for him... right? I can't fall for him. Not yet.

"Hey, forget I said anything. I can see your brain whirring around over there." Riley says, gently placing her hand on mine. "Let's just have a great night, yeah?"

I finally notice that we have pulled up and instantly see the long queue of people lining the street to get in. Time is up for questioning myself over how I feel about him. "Yes, let's have a fantastic night!"

Paying the driver, we make our way over to an extremely tall and broad bouncer with mousey brown hair and strained eyes. I have no idea if this is his usual look, or he has simply narrowed them because we walked immediately up to him—just like Owen told me to. "You need to get in the queue, ladies."

"I'm here with Owen Turner." I confirm confidently, but he laughs out abruptly.

"Ha, that's original. Queue." He points. "Now!"

"No! He said to come her—"

"And *I'm* saying to get in the queue."

"Hey asshole!" Riley steps closer pointing at his head, "Why don't you do your job and use that thing in your ear to check, huh?"

He scowls at her before turning to the side, holding a button on the cable running from the earpiece, "Hey, it's Alex. I've got two girls down here, saying they're with Mr. Turner?" His face turns back quickly looking over his shoulder at us. "Names?"

"Remi and Riley Prentice." I confirm which he repeats, and waits, and I watch in delight as his face goes from obnoxious to horrified in a slow second.

"Well?" Riley asks Alex instantly.

"You can go in."

"Just because you're built like a house, doesn't mean you gotta be as dumb as a brick." He looks bemused as Riley moves in closer, her neck craned all the way back to look up at him. "She's Owen's girlfriend!"

He's taken aback, swapping from looking down at her to me.

"You'd better hope Owen isn't too pissed off that you stopped us going in." I say holding his attention. He clearly knows who Owen is, and right now I'll play on that even if Riley knows nothing.

"I'll apologize to Mr. Turner, don't worry. Have a great night, ladies."

Gathering Riley's hand, she's still locked eyes with him as we enter the thumping space.

"I have to admit, for a jackass, he's pretty hot!"

"Been there, sis." I laugh out loud, casting a look around the place unsure of where to go when I notice Owen scanning the crowd we're in from the balcony above. He hasn't noticed us but my heart beats faster, challenging the bass vibrating through the floor and up my body for power. He must have come straight from work here judging by the dishevelled hair and top two open buttons, but even so, he is still the sexiest man I've ever seen. "And look where it leads you."

Our eyes eventually lock, and his stern features soften instantly to a soft hint of a smile. Butterflies reproduce astronomically fast, flying around in my belly, because he is here. I get to spend time with him at last. He points in the direction of where we need to go, before disappearing in the direction himself leaving me no choice but to guide Riley that way too. Even though my brain didn't, my feet seem to know where to go, and we make it to the base of a dark staircase that has red strip lights running along the edge of each step.

When I look up, Owen is already there to meet me. Captivated by every essence of him, I let go of Riley's hand and begin the walk up the stairs, forgetting everyone around us. The music disappears and my tunnelling eyes end on the man in front of me. I must look like a crazy person, not blinking, just staring at him, but I can't help it. That gravitational pull has never felt stronger, and I have never wanted to be in the arms of another person so much. I want him to kiss me and never let me go.

Once I'm on his level, I throw myself into him, kissing him with a passion I haven't recognized in myself. His arms encircle me securely as my fingers cling to his hair and open my mouth wider to engulf him, pouring my feelings into him because despite how much I have missed him, seeing him I know one hundred percent that Riley is right.

I am falling in love Owen freakin' Turner.

Thirty

Our kiss feels like it goes on for an eternity, and I love every second.

Until Riley opens her mouth, that is. "Are you two going home already, or are you going to start undressing right here? You know, just so I know…"

Owen pulls away first but still focuses all his attention on me. "When's she goin' again?"

"Not soon enough being around you two love birds, believe me!" Riley answers before I can, but doesn't actually answer, so I do, still smiling like a schoolgirl.

"Monday morning."

He puts his arm over my shoulder, turning to walk to our table with Riley walking on the other side of me. "What a shame. I will miss havin' the two of you together." His sarcasm isn't lost on either of us.

"Aww, is the big bad wolf going to miss Little Red Riding Hood?" Riley teases equally as sarcastic.

"Well, if Little Red Riding Hood was as annoyin' as you, I get why the wolf fuckin' ate her!"

I gasp bemused, as Riley rolls her eyes. Owen and I had our own retaliations, but their unique 'friendship' takes it one step further.

"You know you will miss one another really." I add, but neither say anything. I do notice Riley smile a little. Despite her not wanting to, I know she does like him—no matter how small that amount is.

"Yay!" Lucy shrieks, jumping from her seat beside Spencer. "You're here!"

"We got delayed because she was sucking the life source from him," Riley explains as we all take a seat at the collection of tables where Jack and Freddie sit too. "I thought she was going straight home again."

Owen pulls my chair using the base so I'm closer to him, before taking hold of my hand. His eyes smoulder as he seems to take in my whole appearance for the first time. The deep blue, plunging dress, with an asymmetric skirt and long sleeves. He leans in to talk through my hair, his breath tickling my ear. "With you lookin' like that, I wish I had of."

"I'm sure you do baby, but just for tonight we really need to behave. You only have a couple more days and you can have me all to yourself, as much as you like."

His eyebrow raises. "As much as I want, huh? You might live to regret that." He swipes my hair behind my shoulder and whispers in my ear, "especially when your little pussy is sore as hell from me fuckin' you so hard."

I shift nervously in my seat, breathlessly pleading with him. "Baby, stop... please—"

"We could've been at mine, right now, your pussy wrapped around my dick, but you chose to come here." he teasingly drags his finger up the inside of my thigh, "wearin' this delicious fuckin' dress."

My eyes slowly start to close as my body caving and giving into him until the clearing of a man's throat makes them spring back open. His hand doesn't leave its position, stationing it protectively on my skin instead.

"Um, Mr. Turner?"

"Who are you?" Owen asks, taking in the man referred to as a house by my sister, who just happens to notice him too.

"Ewww... it's you. What do you want?"

"Alright firecracker?" Alex smiles, taken in by her despite her clear distaste. "I just came to apologize like I said I would."

Owen looks between Riley and the bouncer, frowning a little as she glares at him and he looks back at her with a curious little glint in his eye. "He do somethin' to you?"

"I was just doin' my job."

"Oh really?" Riley says bitingly.

"Yes, really! D'you know how many little girls rock up here tryin' any excuse to get in? Loads. So sorry, if I thought you were the same."

Owen isn't impressed, narrowing his eyes as he spits back at Alex. "They ain't little girls, mate."

"I can see that." Alex looks to Riley as he speaks but she isn't looking back.

"So, what ya apologizin' for?" Owen asks, still needing an explanation.

"Just to say sorry for the mix up about them gettin' in. It won't happen again."

Owen raises an eyebrow at me, "It got sorted really quick, let it go baby." I rest my hand on his, the grip on my thigh easing his tension.

"What's your name?"

"Alex."

"Well, Alex, she's tellin' me to leave it, so I'm gonna leave it, but don't fuck up again, yeah?"

"Trust me, if I see either of these two ladies again, I won't be making that mistake twice." He continues to look at Riley with the same look as before, and I see her lips raise a little clearly loving the attention she's getting though she won't return or acknowledge it. Taking the hint, he offers the group a friendly nod before disappearing as quietly as he arrived, considering the stature of the dude.

"Well, that was fuckin' weird." Freddie says, breaking the awkwardness before two waitresses arrive at the table to deposit trays of fresh cocktails and shots.

The evening is spent enjoying ourselves; us three girls dancing under the watchful eye of five men.

Needing to use the bathroom, I quickly return to collect my purse off of the table, but Owen's hand grabs mine, stopping me from leaving. "Ready to go?"

"Calm down, Casanova, I'm going to use the bathroom."

Disappointment floods his face. "Don't be long."

"I won't." I insist, playfully blowing him a kiss before walking down the hall to the ladies. It is well prepared for the queues and has enough stalls that I can be in and out quickly after washing my hands and reapplying my lipstick. I take out my phone to check it on my way back and notice that I have a message from my mother. When I open it, I collide with someone, dropping my phone and purse as a result of the impact.

"Oh my Gosh, I'm sorry, I wasn't looking where I was going."

Two hands join mine in gathering my belongings. "I'm sorry, Rem," Jack says, "I didn't notice you there either."

I smile politely, standing up and taking my phone from his open hand. "It's fine. Thank you."

This is the first time we've been alone since the day I informed him about Owen and me, and it's awkward. I drop my head to exit in the direction of my friends, giving him one last hesitant smile, but he finally speaks, "Owen told me about the record deal, congratulations."

"Oh, he did?" *Why is he discussing it with Jack?* "I have a lot to think about, but it's certainly a great opportunity."

"Why ya thinkin' about it? Surely it's a no brainer?" Jack says, his eyes knitting together.

I look down at my hands, pretending to check over the condition of my phone. "Things have changed a little."

"Why?" he exclaims. "Because of Owen?" Jack's words aren't bitter, but they're also not friendly. Has he been pretending that things are okay when they're still clearly not? I'm glad I have kept my distance.

"Among other things, yes."

"You can't throw away your chance for him, Remi."

"I don't exactly see how that is any of your business, Jack!" I take another step, then another, walking away because I am not doing this, but Jack grabs my arm, pulling me back.

"You don't know who you're dealing with. He's not who you think he is."

"Let go of me!" I shake my arm abruptly out of his grip. "Don't ever grab me like that!"

"I'm sorry, but you need to know who he is."

"And who is he Jack?!" I close in on him, holding my shoulders back. I don't care who he is. I was never afraid of Owen, and I'm certainly not afraid of him.

"He's sick, Remi! He switches in a flash, he could hurt you!" Hearing him throw those judgements completely out of context makes my blood boil. "Do you know he's married? He threw his own wife down the stairs and hurt my sister!" *Is he for real?* Clenching my teeth so tightly, I can feel tension protruding from my temples. "He beat me up because I kissed you. You need to get away from him!"

My clenched fist thuds against the side of his jaw. My knuckles begin to throb with a pain I've never experienced before, because I have never punched someone, but I was not going to listen to anymore. *Owen is not that man.* I won't let anyone slander his character or bend the truth.

And Jack got that message loud and clear from the punch I threw, looking back at me shocked.

I take one step closer to him to make sure he hears me loud and clear. "You know NOTHING about him! He has told me everything—"

"What he wants you to know!"

"No, Jack. E-very-thing!" I let each syllable fall slowly off my tongue for impact. "So don't you *dare* stand there and twist the truth to suit yourself. My relationship with Owen is none of your business. You're a sick motherfucker trying to drag him down." Feeling the anger still surging through every molecule of my body, I spit out the rest. "I'm glad he beat you up! Now, leave me AND Owen alone."

I stomp away, leaving him to take in what I said and wipe the droplets of my saliva from his face. I don't care what he thinks of me, but how he could do that to Owen? To someone he grew up with. They were as close as brothers! Is he really that jealous of him?

I can't shake my mood when I get back to the table and Owen notices immediately, standing up to intercept me. "What's happened?"

"I want to go." I avoid eye contact, but he holds my shoulders forcing me to look up at him. "Not until you've told me what's happened."

"I handled it. Please, can we go?"

He nods, not believing me but appeasing me so we can say our goodbyes for the evening. His hand holds protectively onto mine as we descend the staircase and through the crowds out to his car. We sit in silence for most of the drive until he clearly can't cope with the tension any longer, and pulls over, killing the engine.

"This is the only chance I'm givin' you to tell me what's happened, before I head back to ask every fuckin' person in that club."

I shake my head annoyed with him, "Owen, please... I'm trying to protect you."

"I don't need protectin', babe." He laughs unamused, making me turn in my seat to look at him, lifting my hand to stroke his cheek.

"It's not always about who can fight the hardest and shoot the fastest. I don't want you to do something you can't take back."

He takes my hand gently from his face, and places a soft kiss on the inside of my wrist, "I promise to hear you out before doin' anythin' okay?"

I don't want to watch his anger displace the softness in him, but I have no choice but to let him know that Jack is not who he thinks he is. "When I went to the bathroom, Jack collided with me on my way back. I thought it was by accident, but now I don't think it was."

"Did he hurt you?!"

"No. He told me his twisted opinion of you and the truth about Portia and Alice. He thinks he was telling me new information."

His face screws up in disgust, as he gazes down at the steering wheel in front of him. "I'll fuckin' kill him."

Those words coming from anyone else would be an empty threat, but from his mouth, I believe it. The instant he moves to push the button to start the engine, I pounce across to stop him from pressing it. "Listen to me!"

"What did he think he was gonna achieve?" He fights my hand and arm, still determined to turn on the car, ignoring my pleas. "He's fuckin' done it this time! I swear to God, he's a fuckin' dead man!"

"Owen! Stop! I already punched him in the face. It doesn't matter what he tells m—"

The abrupt stop of his actions makes me pause to look up at him. "You punched him?"

"Yes," I confirm, moving back to sit in my seat, "and it hurts like hell, but I just couldn't stop myself. I wanted him to know that nothing he said would change my feelings for you."

He raises an eyebrow at me while an elated smirk grows on his face. "You have feelin's for me?"

"Yes, Odin..." I blush and say, "I have feelings for you. Doesn't mean they're always of the positive kind though."

A deep, delightful chuckle escapes from him as he moves in closer to me, sliding his hand behind my head and pulling me closer to meet his face. "I wouldn't expect nothin' less, *Demi*."

He presses his lips to mine, hard, easily forcing his tongue into my wanting mouth. His hand fists the hair at the nape of my neck. It's unexpected in timing but completely expected from him. *My perfect contradiction.*

Gripping his jacket lapels tightly, I rise from my seat, manoeuvring across the shifter and straddling him in his seat. His hands slide under my skirt and cup my naked ass cheeks, softly moaning., "Looks like those feelin's are good right now…"

"Mmm," I murmur against his lips, "they're getting there. I think you need to make them even better."

His fingers grab handfuls of my skin, evoking a whimper in pain mixed with the pleasure he creates in me. "Be careful what you wish for."

Shifting beneath me, he undoes his pants and frees himself before finding my underwear and freeing my entrance. He holds himself whilst I slide down onto him quickly. I've missed him inside me. The way he fills every part like he was made specifically for me, and only me will never grow old.

I ride him deep, making sure no space is left between us before slowly rising again. I want to feel every millimetre of his dick. His hand pulls my dress apart from the centre, allowing my breasts to become exposed, taking each of my nipples in his mouth in turn, sucking and nibbling on them, making me moan in delight. The way he mixes the soft pleasure with the gorgeous pain, drives me crazy.

"Owen... oh my God..."

"Is that feelin' good?"

"Yes!" I pant, eyes squeezed close with my back arched to keep my breasts close to his lips. He starts thrusting his hips from below, pushing us closer and closer to our highs by holding me down with one arm wrapped around my waist. "I'm gonna come!"

"Wait for me." he commands, getting deeper, using his hands strength to hold me low so he can deepen his tip.

"I can't! Please..."

He keeps going, and without a doubt, people will be able to hear me from outside the car as I scream out with my release. Tightening around him, I slow right down as he pulsates away inside me, unable to stop his own climax, and swearing loudly into my neck.

Once our breathing settles, our eyes lock as I dip down to connect my mouth with his again softly.

I love you.

This enigmatic, *'would kill anyone who hurt me'* man has overtaken my heart without me even registering it and is the last person I ever expected to fall for. He is kind and caring, and a wonderful father. He has a good relationship with his family, many people respect him, and I know he has genuine friendships with the rest of the guys. My mind wonders back to what Jack said, though.

Owen may be some of what he said, but that isn't all he is, and despite the character assassination from Jack many times, he has always tried to fix it and be his friend. Jack should be jealous of him, because right now Owen is the better man out of the two of them without a doubt.

Thirty One

We stumble through the door of my place, our lips managing to separate just long enough to walk from the lift to get through my door.

Though the second we step inside, I pin her against the wall. I've had my appetiser, now I want my main course. I encourage the shoulders of her dress to fall away, watching her shimmy it along the rest of my body. Sliding my fingers down her body, I quickly discover she slid her thong down with it.

"Prepared... good girl."

"I can behave sometimes…" *Yes you can, but I love it when you don't.*

I rapidly undo my trousers and push my boxers out the way to make myself free and ready for her.

Even though we fucked already, I want her again; right here; right now, in the hallway of my flat.

Lifting her naked body, she wraps her arms and legs around me, clinging on so she doesn't fall away. It's quick and rough, sliding in and out with a ferocity I only have with her. I don't allow her the chance to slowly build; I wanna hear her screams. I want to feel her wet pussy right before she comes.

She whimpers into my ear, gripping my neck, pulling my skin. It burns, but I like it. Like the pain she gets when I grip her throat or spank her arse, it makes every nerve ending hyper aroused.

I push my face into her neck, smelling her incredible scent, and I go to town pounding into her. The language and screams pouring out of her drives me on.

"Oh... myyyyy... *GOD*!" She screams out just how I wanted her to, bringing me to my own release. I come powerfully, filling her for a second time tonight, but definitely not for the last.

"Mm-you weren't lying when you said you'd make me sore."

I breathe out a laugh. "You think that's it?"

"There's going to be more?" she asks, withdrawing her touch to look at me.

"So much more…" I confirm, loosening my hold so she can carefully put both feet on the ground. I know our cocktail will be sliding out, and I love that thought.

I take her hand and slowly lead her up to my room, only letting her go when stood beside my bed. I discard my own clothes, only talking when I'm as naked as she is. "Take your shoes off." She bites her lower lip as she slowly slips off each slingback heel, dropping the four inches to the ground with each step down. Her eyes smoulder back at me. "Turn around."

The pleased pout of her lips is barely noticeable, but I see it. I can tell from the secret smile in her eyes that she loves when we're like this. Slowly, she rotates on the spot allowing me the opportunity to roam my hands down along her skin before I step up behind her, pressing my chest to her back holding her in place. My lips skim and tease her body as I guide her to the bathroom. She drops her head onto my chest, placing her soft hands on top of mine.

"You're such a tease, Mr Turner."

"And you ain't complainin', Miss Prentice..."

Her gentle laughter makes my heart flutter. I haven't forgotten about Jack. She's helping me to stay calm, but my anger is still bubbling under the surface. I know that if I am with her, I can avoid leaving to rip his head off, but God help him when I'm not.

I don't let her go until I turn on the shower. It heats up in seconds, and even though four people could easily fit in here, I leave her standing outside while I step under the waterfall, savouring the feeling of it cascading down my face. She attempts to join me, but I stop her with a look. "Did I say you could come in?"

Her eyes glaze over with heat and lust, "I didn't think I had to ask, *Odin*?"

"I'm sure you didn't... *Demi.*" I gave myself an internal smile, gathering a handful of the body wash and begin to lather it all over myself, paying close attention to my dick. When I see her eyes glued to my hand stroking it up and down the shaft, I feel the undeniable surge of blood flood it and the thickness grow under my touch. "Touch yourself."

Catapulted out of her trance, she looks at me wide eyed. "What?!"

"Play with yourself. Just like you did in my car while you watch me."

"But…"

I know she's filthy right now; I've blown my load in her twice, but I don't care. It's sexy watching her pleasure herself. "Fine. Your loss." I'm playing devil's advocate; I know she will.

Closing my eyes, I continue to clean my body before returning my hand to the piece of me she wants. Peaking an eye open, I see her hand slowly playing with her clit. *I knew it.*

"That feel good, baby?"

"Mm-hmm."

"You want some of this?" She nods slowly, looking back at me through her lashes. "Then come and get it." Her hand falls away and she stalks her way into the shower, smiling like she's won first place in a race. "On your knees." She does as she's told, dropping to the grey marble tiles with no questions asked. I step closer to her, positioning my dick right in her face. "Suck it."

Licking her lips, she holds her tongue out, lapping it over the tip, before swallowing me with her voluptuous lips. I watch in adoration as she bobs back and forth, sucking and rolling her tongue around me. The water rolls down her face and body, the small beads of hot water causing her nipples to harden from the difference in temperature. I slide my hand into her hair and force her deeper, wanting her to choke herself again. I want to feel myself down the back of her throat.

She moans in pleasure as I hold her in place for a second before letting her continue, only to repeat. The graze of her teeth against my sensitive skin only enhances the sensation. I ain't going to last much longer.

"Take me deeper." I say, pushing her closer to the base of my dick with my hand. From the beginning, I was curious to whether she could use her mouth for more ways than giving me attitude, and she's proves it every time, taking me unrestricted until I hit her uvula.

I feel my climax brewing when she stops and slips me free from her second-best orifice, using her hand to take over, but I don't want her to stop. Not now. "What are you doin'?"

"Come over me." *Is she serious?* When I gawk at her, she repeats herself, "Come over me, come on my chest." She smirks, running her free hand across each of her tits in turn, "you know you want to." *Fucking too right I do!*

"See, I told you you were naughty." She matches my grin as I take over from her hand, revelling in her being submissive, gazing up at me like some fucking God. When I thought she couldn't consume me anymore, she lets me do this. Watching her head drop back as my cum lands on her gives me a sense of euphoria no climax has done before because although it was me coming, she got just as much pleasure as I did.

Only when I've finished pulsating does she look back at me, collecting some of my cum from her skin and bringing it to her lips, "Mmm… delicious."

I reach down and hoist her from the floor in a second, loving the squeal that she lets out. I don't care that I taste myself as I kiss her. I look past the feeling of my jizz now spreading across my own chest; she is so bloody incredible that I want her to know I'm grateful, and like her, my feelings are growing. She had my back today with someone she could have shied away from, and that, I will never forget.

***

"You're so cute sometimes."

I peck a kiss on her lips, carrying her bridal style from the bedroom to the steaming bath. "Don't tell anyone—not that they'd believe ya anyway." I offer playfully, with a wink.

"I won't."

I lower her down into the water, hearing her wince as the heat hits the tender area between her legs. She sits in the middle, letting me sink in behind her, putting my legs either side and wrapping my arms around her. Laying together with nothing but our breathing and being lost in our thoughts, I don't think I've ever felt so content. I've never done this soppy shit ever, but with her, I can do this and the bossy stuff, and she goes with it; she never questions it. Yes, she can be a stubborn, pain in the arse, but is never judgemental or makes me feel uncomfortable. I am truly myself for the first time with this woman.

"You doin' anythin' Tuesday night?"

"No." Her voice is tired, and I know it's because we've been like rabbits fucking all night.

"Will you come to my dad's meal with me?" I know I told my mum that she was coming already, but I've been nervous to ask her. Even with all the will in the world to keep her out of this shit, I want her with me. I want to hold her hand, touch her and kiss her and announce to everyone that she's mine.

She turns her head to look up at me, and like a slap in the face, I can see the feelings she has for me; the pride and joy that I asked her. "I'd love to."

I can only look at her, mesmerised by the look in her eyes and the feeling travelling through my own body, "Okay then. Will be nice to introduce my girlfriend to my mum and dad."

The happiness clouds over with worry and anxiety as she turns away from me, lifting a hand to play with the surface of the water. "That'll be something to look forward to…"

"What's the problem?"

"Your mom hates me, and apparently your dad is just like you, so he'll probably hate me too."

I force myself not to laugh, I don't want her to feel worse than she does, but she needs to know the truth. "My mum ain't exactly your biggest fan, but I know when my mum hates someone, and trust me, she don't hate you." I feel the tension in her shoulders slowly slip away, "And yeah, me and my old man are alike, but I never hated you either."

She looks back too quickly, glaring at me in disbelief. Okay so I did, but not in the way she thinks. "You thought I was the cleaner!"

"True, but I also thought you were gorgeous."

There's a curious glint in her eye, "oh, you did, huh?"

"Don't act like that news to ya?" I ask curiously, but shocked she didn't know.

"Knowing you thought that from that horrendous initial meeting is absolutely news to me." I snuggle around her more, so content with being here like this. "But if you think your parent's will be okay with me being there, then I would love to join you."

Remi

Owen left after our relaxing bath to do whatever it is he has to do today, and I was grateful to get a couple of hours more sleep before I have to meet my dad.

I have a quick shower to freshen up my hair and drag my tired and sore body to their hotel, knocking on the door of my dad's suite.

"Hey, baby girl." He smiles like he hasn't seen me in days. "Come in."

"Sorry, I'm a little late." I step in and quietly close the door, noticing that Riley is nowhere to be seen. "Is Riley still asleep?"

"You know she is. That girl would sleep forever if you let her."

I chuckle, "I'll go and check on her." I twist on the spot ready to leave.

"Actually," he says quickly and authoritatively, "I'm glad I have you to myself for a moment."

Tentatively, I step back into the room as he sits on one of the deep blue sofas. "Is everything okay?"

"I hope so. I've been watching you and Owen when we've been together, and I can see you're happy—" I smile widely, glad he can see I genuinely am, "—but there's something I can't put my finger on." I hold the smile on my face despite the fact I'm now internally freaking out. Dad analyzes people on a daily basis, why wouldn't he pick up on something?

"Dad, we haven't been together that long, but just trust me that I really am happy."

Whilst Owen has been honest about things, there is still a lot to learn about one another.

"Please, just take your time with this, Remi."

"I will," I lie, "I promise." What do I say? *'You're right to be worried, dad, he runs an illegal firm, and his dad is in prison'.* "Let me go and wake her lazy ass up."

I walk out of his room and let out a deep breath, tapping on the door only to inform her that I'm using my key. The curtains are still drawn so I walk straight over to them and throw them open. Her sleeping body wrapped in the white sheets is unfortunately not the only thing the sunlight reveals to me. The naked back and hairy ass of a huge man fills the side of her bed.

"Well, well, well!" I chuckle, crossing my arms, as they wake with a startle.

"Remi! Close the curtains!" Riley hollas, throwing a pillow over her head, which stays there for approximately half of a second before a deep, sleepy groan makes her reappear. She flips over quickly covering her modesty, but Mr. Sleepover continues to lay on his front still happily exposing himself to me. "Get outta here!"

"Why, don't you want to introduce me to your little friend?"

Her one-nighter turns to look back at me making me gasp. *Mr. Sleepover is Mr. House?!*

"I ain't little, sweetheart." Alex says confidently.

"I'm sure you're not!" *Nothing on him could be little!* "Well, I'ma leave you two to do whatever, I'll let Dad know that you'll meet us later."

"What time is it?"

"11:34."

Her eyes widen, slapping his ass, "Alex! Why are you still here?! I told you that you to leave by 9am!"

Alex stretches and rolls over. I quickly turn around desperately not wanting to see anymore of him, though curious to see if every part of his is as large... "I tried to go at nine, remember, but someone wouldn't let me!"

"Whatever." I can hear in Riley's voice she's trying not to smile. "Tell dad I won't be long."

"Okay," I chuckle, making my way back to the door, "I'll let you know where we are."

Her giggles and squeal sound out as I close the door, making me shake my head, bemused. For someone who doesn't do one-night stands, and I need her to immediately spill the tea on how she ended up in bed with Alex from the club.

***

"Well, look who finally joined us!"

The glow on her skin says it all. She's had a *good* time, and she doesn't hide it sitting down in front of our dad unapologetically.

"I'm sorry, I didn't realize I hadn't set my alarm…"

"As long as you don't do the same tomorrow morning, we'll be fine."

"I won't. I will be the perfect daughter, and get an early night like Remi did last night…"

I recoil, wondering why I'm now being highlighted when there was nothing to highlight, even if she isn't being bitchy. Her cocked eyebrow shows that she needs the details on my night as much as I do hers!

"Do whatever you need to make sure you're awake at 5am to get to the airport on time."

"I will." She nods like a soldier, taking my drink from beside her and sipping some through the straw.

"Hey, do you mind?!"

"Sorry, I'm just really thirsty."

"I'll get your own, Ri, give it back to her."

I wait until he's gone before turning to her with a big smile on my face. "You always know exactly how to get rid of him don't you." She shrugs innocently, but she is far from it. "So, how in the hell did that happen?! You and Alex the House?!"

"Well, it was fun irritating him, so I kept sneaking off. He must have had enough because the last time I went down to annoy him, he kissed me. And oh my God, Rem, it was hot as hell. He offered to make sure I got home safe, and well, as you can see, he didn't leave when we got there." She raises her eyebrows telling me what I had already worked out for myself when I see his naked ass staring at me; they slept together.

"But you won't see him again."

"I know, and he knows that. I didn't want to lead him on. He said he wanted to make my last night out in London a night to remember."

"And did he?"

She puts her hand to her chest dramatically, beaming widely. "Did he? Sis, he made sure my last night, morning, *and* afternoon in London were memorable."

Thirty Two

I haven't seen Remi since the day before last, not since I left her in my bed. She was back at work yesterday because her dad and Riley flew back home in the morning, and I've had a lot to get sorted, especially as my old man is getting out tomorrow. But I'm pussy whipped. Even with everything on my mind, she has been there at the forefront. Those steel eyes calming me, which I need more than ever today because I've gotta deal with a certain Gentleman Jack today. The little pussy was MIA yesterday— conveniently—and when I got a text to say he was catching up on some stuff, I knew he was keeping out my way intentionally.

I don't know how to handle it. I mean, I know how I should handle it, and had I seen him yesterday, I wouldn't have even thought twice about smashing his fucking head against the brick wall repeatedly. But I didn't, and I've had time to think. He's someone I've called my brother, and I know he's pissed at me.

I run my hands down my face, and call the only one that I want to now; my girlfriend.

"Hey baby."

I smile hearing her voice. "What ya doin'?"

She realises from my tone that something is wrong, and instantly comes back with concern. "What's happened?"

I sigh rubbing my temples with my thumb and middle finger. "I dunno what to do about Jack."

"Don't you want to show him you're still the 'Boss'? That you won't take it?"

"Yeah, course I do, but it ain't solvin' anythin' is it? He's just gettin' more vindictive, and I'm gonna end up killin' him."

"You have a right to be angry, though Owen. He's not being a friend to you."

"I know," I sigh, "I know…"

She pauses before answering with an understanding and calming voice, "I can't tell you what to do, Owen, but if you could take your position out of the picture where it's two friends, what would you want to do? Would you walk away or try to fix it?"

I take in her question's in for a moment. I've never thought about putting things into a different perspective. I've never known a different perspective. "Right now? I dunno what to do."

She gives me a moment to think, and I appreciate her more than I did before I called. Her compassion and empathy, even with something so far removed from her life back home, are mind-blowing to me. I genuinely don't know how I'd have handled this without her.

"So, what are ya doin'?" *I know she's not at work.*

I can hear the smile is back on her face. "I'm trying to find something to wear for tomorrow night. It would help if I knew what to wear."

"Wear anythin', you'll still look beautiful."

"That is no help, Owen." She bites back playfully. "Is this a big occasion or a small intimate meal?"

"It's a bit of a big thing. I'm wearing a suit."

She laughs out loud, and I immediately envision the way her head would have lifted, revealing her long, elegant neck that I love to kiss, and the soft wrinkles that appear around her eyes when her smile takes over her beautiful face. "You always wear a suit. How does that help me?"

This makes my own chuckle break through, which is immediately swallowed up by a negative energy as Chris, Freddie and Jack appear in my eye line. "Sorry babe, but you need to speak to Luce for this one. I've gotta go."

"Okay, let me know how it goes."

"I will."

I slip away from my desk and leave the office to join them. Talking to Remi has helped me more than I expected but seeing Jack now and how he's acting like he's innocent, I need to work out my decision pretty sharpish.

"Mate," Freddie starts, and I already know it's going to be some gossip girl shit, "I'm gutted she's gone back so soon."

"She was only ever staying the week. I dunno why you're chattin' like you were in there." Chris informs him, highly amused sitting back in his chair with a foot resting on his other knee. "You were in the friend zone, Fred."

"Shut up! No, I wasn't."

"You do know that Riley went back with the bouncer that night, don't ya?" Jack adds, and I unavoidably narrow my eyes at him.

"For fuck sake!" Freddie says, throwing his arms out dramatically. "Well, now I'm glad she's gone back."

I shake my head as they laugh at him. "Are you all ready to go?"

They snap into work mode and file out to the car, with Jack doing what I said and getting in to drive. I feel Jacks eyes looking at me periodically through the rear-view mirror as he pulls up at the first place where Charlie, Fred and Chris need to go check on shit.

"You not comin' in?" Charlie quizzes, knowing something's going on but not sure what it is.

"Nah, you three go, we need to pop round the corner. I notice Jack's hand tightens around the steering wheel, causing his knuckles to whiten. "We'll be back before you're done."

"Yeah," Freddie agrees, "they take fuckin' ages!"

They all get out and Jack indicates to pull away "Where we goin'?"

"Anywhere. Long as it's quiet."

I hear him quietly whisper '*shit*' before driving for about ten minutes before pulling off the main road and into some underground car park. He finds a space out the way and turns off the engine, deflating in the chair.

"Alright. Just get it over with."

I take the knife I've been playing with since he drove off, putting the tip against his neck in a flash. I'm so close to impaling him, making him disappear forever, but I don't do anything. His head stays statue still while I spit out my feelings.

"Have somethin' you need to say?"

"No." he insists confidently.

The blade is sharp enough that even though the tip is the only part dimpling his ski, his blood seeps onto the metal. "That's not really true, is it?"

Jack takes a nervous breath, lifting his chin in an attempt to narrow his neck. "She told you?"

"Unfortunately for you, yeah, she did."

"Look..." *Here we go.* Rational Jack trying to get me to understand the bollocks behind his actions.

"What you gonna say, eh?" I raise my voice a little. "You 'didn't mean it?'"

"No!" His arse lifts from the seat as I dig the pointed tip in further, "I meant it! I want her to get away from you."

"Why?! You think you can make her happy? She doesn't want you!"

"She ain't had time to want me! I can give her the chance to have it all; the deal, the life, everything. All you're gonna do is drag her down with you!" he calls back and it hits me like a slap in the face, making me lower my knife and sit back in my seat.

"Is that what you think?"

He wipes the blood from his neck, sighing heavily. "Yeah, man. I'm fuckin' fed up of all this shit! The lookin' over your shoulder all the fuckin' time. I can give her a normal life outside of this. She can have her career and not have to worry about anythin' else."

Unblinking, I stare at the stitching edging the camel-coloured leather, thinking about what he's said. He can give her the freedom I can't. At least not yet. "Can you accept it if it's her decision?"

He sighs again, heavier this time, admitting his own defeat and looking back at me in the rear-view mirror. "Does she really know everythin'?"

"She knows all she can about this shit, and she knows everythin' about Portia and Alice."

He runs his hand down his face, gazing out through the windscreen until he finally pivots in the seat to look at me, "I think she's makin' a mistake, but if she knows it all and she's still here then it ain't gonna matter what I say, is it?"

"I'm askin' if you can *accept* that she's here by choice?" I reiterate, needing this answer from him to make my own.

"…yes."

And now the final crux. "And I need to know if we're good, Jack? I told you that you were on your last chance, and I meant it…" He glances down, dropping his head accepting his fate. "But I want my mate back, not attend your funeral."

He quickly looks back at me with a bitterness twisting up his mouth. "Ain't you fuckin' noble!"

"I'm not leaving this car until this shit is sorted or—"

"Do you love her?" His confident question catches me completely off guard.

"Why does that matter?"

"It's a simple enough question, O. You never really loved Portia, yet you married her. Is this another girl you're gonna hijack just for the sake of it?"

My eyebrows knit together. "What the hell are you bringin' her up for?"

"Well, I met her first. The same fuckin' thing happened then. She fell for you instantly and didn't even look twice at me." he starts, making me shake my head. "I've been this close to what you've had every fuckin' step. My dad could of took over, but no, Jimmy got it didn't he. I could have had your life right now... but no! Instead, I get the fuckin' dad who went nuts and abandoned us!"

I let him say what he must, adding more pissy arguments to his list for the sake of it, but I'm fucking raging.

"Are you that fuckin' deluded?! It's my families Firm! You know it don't work like that. Believe it or not, I can't control what people do and don't do! My grandad picked his son and Portia picked me. But hey, you still want her, fuckin' have her. I don't give a shit." I take a quick steadying breath, letting him know that no matter what he wants, and no matter how 'ideal' his warped dream might sound, I am not letting her go. "Remi chose me too. And I ain't gonna do shit to change that."

We sit there, stewing quietly. I need him to prove to me that he still wants this considering what he said about having doubts. It isn't what we do, once you're in this, you don't just walk away. But if he is that desperate then I'll let him take the risks,

"You have two choices." I begin calmly, "You can leave like you said. I won't stop ya, No trouble, no last jobs. You can walk away clean if that's what you want."

"Or?" He asks.

"Accept me and Rem are together. Stop with all this fuckin' bullshit and move on with your life but stay in the firm." He looks down at his hands as my words sink in. "If you turn up tomorrow night, then I'll know your answer."

"That quick?!"

"That quick," I state. "Don't forget how differently this could have ended, Jack."

***

The phone ringing from my discarded clothes slowly wakes me from my sleep. It takes me a second to realise I ain't at home, but Remi's body still pressed against mine, wrapped in the duvet that smells entirely of her, settles me.

Jack's words stayed with me. Even with my dad taking over again tonight, the thought of someone being able to give her an easy life hasn't been eradicated. It's just lessened it.

Remi was working late last night, so I was waiting at Lucy and Spencer's when she got home. I couldn't have another night where we weren't together, and she knew what I needed. We didn't fuck; it was more than that. I showed her how I feel and how my feelings are developing for her—even if it makes me nervous.

I don't wanna move but I've got to. Quickly rummaging for the phone, it's withheld.

"Hello?"

"I better not have just woke you up?" The husky voice I know so well calls me out, making the hairs stand up on the back of my neck.

"Dad? You out already?"

"Yeah. Me and your mum are on the way back now. You meetin' us at the office?"

Same ol' dad: straight back to work. I look back at Rem still asleep on the bed, as beautiful as ever with soft whisps of hair cascading around her features. *I don't want to leave.*

"Yeah, I'll see ya there."

"Good." He ends the call as quickly as he always does because, if there is one thing Jimmy Turner doesn't do, it's having unnecessary conversations.

I place the phone on the bedside table and get back into bed, spooning my body around hers, whispering her name until she stirs, murmuring. "Babe, I've gotta go."

She rolls over and looks at me, rubbing one eye, "Already?"

"Yeah. My old man's out and on his way to the warehouse."

Getting more comfortable on her back, she brushes the hair from her face, "Lucy said he's a long way away."

"He is but I need to go back to mine to get sorted and be there when he gets there."

"Okay." I give her a quick kiss before getting up and chucking on my t-shirt and joggers, feeling her eyes watching every movement. "Are you feeling better now?"

I smile at her, now sitting up against the headboard with her beautiful long hair sitting softly around her naked shoulders. "Yeah." *You make everything feel better.* "We'll just have to see if Jack shows up tonight."

She nods in understanding, though I know she doesn't—not really. "Let me know what time Charlie is coming for me and I'll be ready."

"I will." I walk over to give her another lingering kiss, "see you tonight."

Leaving her, I stop to speak to Lucy quickly, letting her know what mum and dad are on their way and I'm going to meet them there. Showering quick and dressing even quicker, I race over to double check that everything is done.

"I dunno why you're worryin', it's never been better than it is now." Charlie says, interrupting me messaging some suppliers on my phone.

"Even so, it matters to me."

It doesn't seem long until I hear the same husky voice travelling through the place on its way to me, and on the way to the desk he's sat behind since I was five. He comes into view, with my mum always two steps behind him, gazing around the office as I walk up to intercept him, "God, it don't look like I've even been away."

He's here. My dad, the one who made me the man I am and took the fall for me so I could be around for my son. I don't have Brad in my life as much as I want, but there's a light peaking over the horizon. I wouldn't have been allowed to see him at all had I gone down, and I wouldn't have met Remi. I owe it to him; this is the next stage of my life.

We pause for a second before rushing to hug one another. "It's good to see you out that place."

"And it feels good to be out."

"Dad?!" Lucy rushes over, squealing with excitement and tears in her eyes, making us separate so she can cuddle him. She's his princess, and I know he will have missed her. When they pull away, she walks back to take Spencer's hand. "Dad, I need to introduce you to someone."

My dad's demeanour alters as his back straightens as much as his face, and give Spencer his due, he greets him with a strong handshake.

"Nice to meet you properly, Spence. You been lookin' after my daughter like she deserves?"

"Absolutely."

"Good." Dad softens, watching Lucy gaze lovingly at him. "When's the big day again?"

"11th of July." she beams, cuddling up to his arm.

"It's exciting ain't it, darlin'?" Mum joins in with the enthusiasm from her seat in front of the desk.

"Sure is." he says, walking around us all to take a seat in the chair I've maintained in his absence. It felt odd at the time, like I was a fraud; nevertheless, seeing him get reacquainted makes me realise just how seriously I took the task he gave me.

"Does it feel good to be back, dad?" Lucy asks, smiling excitedly.

"Yeah."

"We're going to dinner tonight, all of us. There'll be Bob and Tracey, Tony and Remi—you haven't met her yet, but you'll love her. We've booked out your favourite restaurant."

"Whose Remi?"

I look at my mum who looks desperate to answer but bites her tongue letting me answer proudly. "My girlfriend."

"Girlfriend?!" Dad laughs out, cocking an eyebrow. "Well, shit me. You kept that quiet, didn't ya?"

"It's new," mum offers with an attitude. "Very new."

"Well, then I look forward to meetin' this new girl of yours tonight."

Thirty Three

I thought the nerves I got from performing was something, but nothing compares to how I feel right now. My dress is gorgeous, my hair has been curled and pinned to cascade over one shoulder, and my makeup is airbrushed to perfection. I haven't ever felt this beautiful, though I have never worn a dress like this. Lucy said it was a black-tie occasion, and well, the instant I saw the deep red, one-shoulder, long-sleeve dress, I couldn't take my eyes off of it, and when I tried it on, the hidden slit that reveals my entire leg when I walk added a sexiness I knew Owen would appreciate.

I wait impatiently for Charlie to arrive, walking out to the car when I see him stop outside. His eyes immediately widen and scroll down the length of my body. It doesn't feel strange, and I only hope that Owen has the same rection.

"Bloody hell, Rem, you look amazing."

I blush slightly. "Thank you."

"Well, your chariot awaits, milady." He holds the door open, bowing in the manner his playful role requires, letting me slip inside.

The second we pull up outside the lavish restaurant with navy and gold signage, the windows frosted for privacy, I see him—*my man*—waiting at the top of the four steps leading to the door. He looks incredibly handsome in the most elaborate suit I have seen him wear. The unusual construction of his black lapels, edged with a thin white line, highlights the design.

He notices the car and makes his way to us as Charlie gets out to intercept him. I watch them talking before Charlie opens the door for me, holding out his hand to help me out with the same respect as he collected me with.

The language that comes out of Owen's mouth as I appear makes me blush harder, smiling widely. "You should've warned me a little bit! Fuckin' hell, babe. You look…" He takes my hand and holds it up, letting me spin to reveal the dress in its entirety. "Wow!"

"You like?" I ask, as he pulls me strongly into his body, making me rest my hands on his chest for balance.

"Like?! There's no word to describe it. You're fuckin' stunning!" He kisses me softly as not to disturb my red lipstick.

"Thank you." I trickle my finger down his chest, hearing his sharp intake of breath, "And you look *very* handsome, Mr. Turner…"

"Made better by the ruby on my arm, that's for sure." I chuckle, feeling his hand grip a hold of mine. "Come on. Got people to show you off to."

The nerves erupt once more as we climb the steps and enter the restaurant. The chatter calms a little with every confident step Owen takes, pulling me alongside him, and faces begin to look at us with a profound curiosity. I feel very intimidated and judged. How can I stand on the stage and perform in front of hundreds of people, opening myself up for critique, but walking through a room of strangers who know nothing about me on the arm of my boyfriend makes me want to look at the ground?

A gentleman with a thick, partially graying beard and equally gray buzzed haircut makes a beeline for us and asks, "son?" *This is dad.* "Is this your girl?" Jimmy opens his arms to welcome me into a hug before Owen can confirm, but he is reluctant to let go of my hand, giving me no choice but to embrace Jimmy one-handed.

When we break apart, I smile, properly introducing myself. I can see parts of Owen in him. They share the same eyes and straight face, but his lacks the warmth I see in Owen's, and the two deep lines in between his eyebrows reveal the strain this life has taken upon him. "Pleased to finally meet you, Jimmy."

"You're the American stealing my boy's heart, are you? Gotta say, I can't blame him 'cause you are pretty."

I chuckle lightly. He's intimidating and a little bit of an asshole—just as Owen was, but I dealt with him; I can deal with Jimmy, right?

"I think so." Owen answers on my behalf, though not confirming whether or not I am stealing his heart. I look up to discover he is looking down at me with a look that hints to the possibility that I might be, just as he has mine.

"Well, I'll leave you too it. It was nice to meet you, love."

"And you, Jimmy."

With his departure, we join Lucy, Spencer, and Paula at the bar. Lucy looks equally as beautiful, wearing a figure hugging, floor length, black dress with an elaborate crystal necklace, and hair sleeked back into a ponytail.

"You look stunnin', Lucy greets me with a warm hug, "Mum, you remember Remi?"

"I do." she says, reluctantly, forcing herself to sound authentic. "Nice to see you again."

"You too, Paula. Are you getting excited for the wedding? It must be wonderful having Jimmy back with you all, you know, for the build-up to it."

"Yes, of course. It'll be nice to have him home in general."

"I can imagine," I sympathize, genuinely, because even though she still has a disliking for me, above all, I want to get to know Owen's parents. I wouldn't be here otherwise. I wouldn't put myself through their appraisal. "It must have been really hard."

"Yes, it has been at times."

As silence descends over the group, both Paula and I are grateful when Owen asks if I want a drink and takes me with him.

"You okay?" he asks, wrapping an arm around my waist and confidently touching me despite being in a room full of people.

"Your mom still hates me." I look down, not for long though, as he gently places his hand under my chin, lifting it to look up at him.

"I told you, she don't, she's just a hard nut to crack. Give her time."

The confidence and hope in his eyes make me believe him. "Okay."

We sip our drinks before being told to sit down at the tables. Other guests sit around us, with Jimmy heading the long table in the centre of the room. I'm pleased to discover that I'm between Lucy and Owen, but unfortunately very close to Paula, as Owen and her sit either side of Jimmy.

The food is delicious and as beautifully presented as the environment and people around me. Paula is alive with conversation, as is Jimmy, a content smile on her face the entire time, and the moment each table setting has been emptied of the dessert plates, Jimmy stands clinking his glass with a spoon.

"Alright, well, I got told by Lucy that I've gotta do a speech." Whoops spread around the restaurant, "I just wanna say thanks to you all bein' here tonight. Some of you it's nice to see again. Some of you, I was kinda hopin' you'd have been shot or put away yourselves." Laughter trickles through the guests, though I get the feeling he isn't joking. "But seriously, you wouldn't be here if you hadn't have been there for my family, so thank you." He raises his glass to his guests before looking down at his wife with a warmth I finally see he shares with his son. "Damn, I've missed you. But don't worry darlin', I ain't leavin' you no more."

Jimmy follows a gentle kiss to Paula by turning his attention to Lucy. "Luce, my little princess. I can't believe you're gettin' married! I feel fuckin' old!" We all chuckle along with him. "You're gonna make a beautiful bride, I'm grateful to be here to see it."

"You always would have been, dad, we wouldn't have done it without you."

"Thank you for supporting your mom and your brother while I wasn't here." He smiles, walking around the table to give her a kiss and a hug. When he resumes his position, he looks at Owen. "You've done me proud, son." I smile, looking at Owen. His face is as indifferent as always. "I wasn't quite expectin' you to be sitting here tonight with a new missus beside you, though she's very beautiful and seems to really like you—" Owen looks at me quickly with a subtle smile on his face. I mirror him, hooking an arm around his and leaning into his body. "So, well done."

Jimmy takes a breath, looking quickly at Paula before he raises his head confidently. "Every day I was in there, I knew you'd be taking care of business out here, and that leads me to what I'm about to say next." I feel Owen stiffen against within my hold, "I'm gonna be stepping down indefinitely."

A few gasps can be heard, with a number of guests immediately asking why. I notice Owens eyes widen just a fraction. Anyone else might have missed it; I didn't.

"I ain't sayin' I'm retirin', or any of that bollocks, but I think its doin' pretty fuckin' good without me. I'm happy to let Owen continue…"

I tune out of what he has to say because I haven't been able to take my eyes off Owen. He's looking down at our hands, linked and resting in his lap, slowly rubbing his thumb back and forth. From what he has said to me about being together, it's clear this was something he wasn't planning for, and from his reaction, he didn't know prior to this moment.

Placing a gentle kiss on his cheek, I whisper discreetly in his ear, "are you okay?"

He turns to look at me, telling me he is, but it's difficult to believe him. I offer an understandable nod before looking away, locking eyes with Paula's.

For the first time I don't see the stern, hard-faced woman I usually discover glaring back at me. Her eyes have a softness to them that leaves me momentarily stunned, managing a delicate smile before forcing myself to break away.

By the time my attention returns to Jimmy's voice, Owen's hand is leaving mine and he's moving to embrace his dad in a natural hug. His stance is strong and authoritative as he speaks to the room.

"Cheers, dad." he says, "It'll be nice to have ya back, but if you're wantin' to be a lazy little shit, sittin' on your arse like you have been for the last four years, then make sure you go on a diet."

Laughter rolls through the restaurant again, while Jimmy engages in the light-hearted moment, but I don't laugh. Owen may fool them, but I know the man sitting beside me a moment ago is not the one on show for the world now. Whatever was going through his mind told me this is not what he wanted.

***

The formality disperses quickly from the speeches with people raising out of their seats to begin mingling again. I stay seated at the table with Lucy, my eyes glued to Owen pacing around the room with his dad going to guest after guest to celebrate with them.

Lucy had no idea either, shocked as much as the room was that Jimmy wasn't reascending to his position. How can a man, who I am told works day and night simply come back and hold no control? I find it considerably hard to believe. Then again, maybe being inside allowed him the time to make that conclusion? Either way, the plans that me and Owen had seem further away than they did before I arrived this evening. If I take the contract like I want to, will we really be able to make it work?

"I was hopin' to get you on your own." Paula's presence makes me jump a little.

"Okay?" I ask, as she takes the seat beside me. "What did you want to talk about?"

"You and my son."

I let out an irritated breath. "Look, if you're here to warn me off him, I know, okay? I know all about what he does. Well, not all of it because I'm not allowed to, but I know. I'm not a stupid little kid, Paula, I understand the risks. So, say whatever you have to say, but know I am not breaking up with your son."

I watch her face go from unreadable, almost frowning, to a gentle smile when she reaches out her left hand and places it on my arm. "I'm not askin' you to break up with him."

Say what?

She must see the confusion roll onto my face and chuckles softly. "I've been watchin' you and him together. He's different around you."

"Is that a good thing, or a bad thing?"

"It's a nice thing." she says after a beat. "He's relaxed around you. It's nice to see him being more himself."

I dare the smile that naturally grows to reveal itself. "He's an amazing man." I can't help myself but to look over my shoulder at him. He's still where he was and doesn't see that I'm looking, and I don't care.

"You love him, don't ya?"

I blink rapidly before looking back at her, stumbling in my mind to find the right thing to say, settling on, "why would you ask that?"

"Because I've been there myself, darlin'."

"Well, we're a long way from that type of discussion." I say, glancing down to play with the fabric of my dress.

"Why?" she asks, and all I can do is shrug a shoulder. "Remi, just because it's not been a very long time, doesn't mean it's not genuine. Me and Jimmy got engaged after two months."

"Really?!"

She laughs comfortably, nodding, "yeah. I fell in love with him the moment I saw him, then I couldn't bloody get rid of him—unless he was banged up, but I missed him like crazy when he was."

I smile along with her as she stares off into the distance for a moment.

"How long have you been together?"

"Thirty-two years. We got married four months after getting engaged—" she lets out a single chuckle, "and I had Owen five months later."

We share a look because that was how things were back then. Couples got married before it became apparent that they were expecting.

"That's really sweet."

"Yeah," she says, reminiscing. "He was a nightmare baby though, and exactly why we waited so long before havin' Lucy. She was a dream, thank God!"

I openly laugh, believing her instantly. If I had to guess which one was what, Owen would have never done what he was told. Lucy, however, has the kindest heart.

"Yeah, Lucy's amazing."

"She is. I'm glad she has a friend like you."

I openly stare at her in disbelief. After the way she has spoken to me since I arrived here, I struggle to believe her; I almost don't want to believe her, but I do. The sincerity she bestows can't be denied—even if I feel like I'm in the Twilight Zone.

"Thank you."

"What's goin' on here then?" Owen surprises us both, his arm slipping around my waist and pulling my chair closer to his, and with a seriousness in his tone, he adds, "I hope you're behavin'."

"Me?!" Paula gasps. "I'm being lovely, thank you very much! Keepin' Remi company as you'd abandoned her."

He looks at me to confirm, which I do with a genuine smile. "Your mom was just telling me how wonderful a baby you were."

He groans. "Great."

"But don't worry, I'm done now." She stands, taking the hint that he wants to be alone. "It was nice talkin' to you, Remi. Think about what I said."

"I will. Thanks, Paula."

I thought when she left he would cocoon me in his arms in the way that I love, but his hand stays splayed on the base of my back. He's looking at me, though I don't feel the same connection to him as I did. "Are you honestly okay?"

"Yes," I reiterate, "but are you?"

Thirty Four

By the time we said our goodbyes and gotten into the car, Owen's clearly not as 'fine' as he said he was. His hand is linked in mine as always, and I look at it before moving upward at his undeniably frowning face. My soft sigh earns a look from him.

"What is it?"

"Nothing." I say, ignoring the elephant in the car because I don't want to ruin what has felt like a wonderful night up until we were leaving. Regardless, the tension that descends is unavoidable. "Are you sure you want me to come back to yours tonight?"

"Why you askin' me that?" he asks with a hint of irritation.

"I, uh, I didn't know you wanted to be on your own tonight."

"Why, worried you won't get fucked?!" The irritation excels to a side of him I know but haven't seen for a while.

"Hey! You know our relationship goes beyond sex, so don't speak to me like that!"

His silence floods the car with more tension, and I'm flung in my seat as he pulls into a parking lot abruptly.

Why has he stopped.

He stares at the wheel in front of him, and although I don't want to be away from him, he coped with being alone, and if he needs that again now, then I'm prepared to give it to him; no matter how hard it is to see him conflicted. "Owen, why did what your dad said tonight bother you so much?"

He runs his hand over his face, letting out a big sigh as he rests his forearms over the top of the steering wheel and drops his head forward. "I'm glad he's home; I owe him big time, but I just had tonight built up differently in my head."

I run my hand over his shoulders supportively. "I think you've paid your debt to him, Owen. You stepped up to take control when he wasn't here—"

He looks up at me, his eyes narrowing, and says, "I didn't fuckin' do him a favor, Rem, it ain't a fuckin' loan. I *owe* him; I'll always owe him. That's just how it is."

"But it was his decision, Owen!"

He shrugs my hand free, continuing to gaze out the front of the car. "You don't get it."

"No, I don't, and I probably never will, but baby, please listen to me. You have to respect that it was his decision, one that he made as a father, and one that I'm sure you would make for Bradley if he were in your situation."

He slumps back in his seat, bitterness contorting his face. "I don't want him involved in this shit."

"Isn't that inevitable?" *I mean, surely it has to be, doesn't it?* He said the Firm has gone from generation to generation; why wouldn't he want to continue that legacy?

"Either way, it won't be the same for him." He breathes out humorless, before sitting for what feels like a long time. I wish I knew and understood completely because I want him to let me in. The reality is that I don't, so I have no choice but to be here for him when he lets me. "Maybe you should go back to Lucy's tonight."

"Owen..." I reach out to take his hand, feeling a stab in my chest when he pulls it away from me. I know it was my initial suggestion, now it's the last thing I want to do.

"I ain't gonna be fun to be around right now."

From my small nod of acknowledgement, he starts the car and sets off with nothing but the sound of the radio filling the silence before we eventually pull up outside of Lucy and Spencer's. I must respect that he wants to be alone. Leaning across from my seat, I place a soft, lingering kiss on his cheek, grateful that he let me. "I'm here, okay, for whatever you need." Those three little committing words play on the tip of my tongue so dangerously that I'd be a fool to spill them. The last thing he needs right now is another thing to process.

Owen

Sitting on my sofa in the dim light of the floor lamp, the silence is suffocating. It used to be perfect, exactly what I wanted after the chaos and busyness of my life, but now? It feels like a fucking morgue. Remi brings an energy, life into it, and into me that's only ever here when Brad is.

When I saw that she didn't even wait for me to drive off before going inside, I know she's pissed off. With me or the situation, I don't know, but I don't blame her because I'm fuming.

I can't fucking believe he's not stepping back up!

I was ready for him to come back and take over, satisfied with what I'd done, but he wants to sit in the background and take all the glory while I delete the picture of my future from my mind.

I owe him and this was always going to happen, but fuck, I had plans; plans that now include Remi. *How can I tell her?* She has to give Bruce fucking Wayne her decision on Monday, and I've done nothing but tell her she should take it and that we'll make it work.

The guys won't give a shit, they'll just carry on as normal—that's the best bit about them—though it wasn't lost on me that one of them never arrived tonight.

I try Jack's number only to be instantly greeted by his voicemail. But Alice answers her's just as I'm about to hang up, "What do you want, Owen?"

"What happened to you two? You especially should have been there tonight."

She laughs viciously, "I'm surprised you even noticed! Me and Jack arrived there at the end, sorry to disappoint you."

"Jack knew he had a decision to make, he should've been there from the start. But you! You knew I wanted you to meet Remi tonight."

"I've already met her, you idiot."

"But it's different this time."

"Oh what," she snipes back full of sarcasm, "because she's your girlfriend? Come on, Owen, you know she ain't going to stick around forever. Jack told me all about the record deal, so do yourself a favour and take this for what it is: a bit of fun until she gets what she came here for." *Is she having a laugh?* It's not like that at all, and I tell her as much. "Please! She's using you just like Portia did, and you're so blinded by her pussy that you can't see that you're gonna be right back where you started."

My face screws up. "The fuck did you just say?!"

"You fuckin' heard me! She's gonna take everythin' she can from you but don't expect Jimmy or me to be there to pick up the pieces a second time."

I don't know this person, because she has never held her support against me like I took advantage, nor has she ever made a comment about what my old man did.

"You don't know nothin' about her, Al!"

"I know she can't be satisfying you that good if you're already callin' me and you only left just over an hour ago…" The pleasure in her voice makes my nostrils flare, and I rise to my feet bubbling with rage.

"Oi! Watch your fuckin'mouth!"

"Oh, whatever. Shout at me all you like, we both know I'll be the first one you turn to when the shit hits the fan, just like I always am Owen!" She shouts down the phone vindictively, "But I'm not gonna be there next time! I'm not gonna drag your dirty, drunken arse off the ground this time!"

"Don't fuckin' flatter yourself." I retaliate venomously. "Wanna know why I always call you? Because you do anythin' I want you to, just like you always have, Al. You think I need you?! I don't fuckin' need anyone!"

I cancel the call and throw my phone across the room. *Stupid bitch!* We haven't been anything other than friends for years, even at my lowest, I didn't sleep with her. It didn't even enter my head! She's my friend. Is she really that jealous of Remi? Not that it's difficult to be. She is gorgeous and intelligent, but does Alice think that I care? I don't think of her like that. It's Remi. She's the only woman I want.

I'm a twat, a fucking idiot. I want her; I might not need anyone, but I need her, and all I did was pull away when she wanted to be there for me. I don't want her to be swallowed up and smothered by this, but I know I can't stay away from her. Even though our future is foggy right now, there's no distortion when I'm with her.

I get to Lucy's as quick as I can and knock on the door before using the key to enter. The house is all in darkness and I have no idea if Lucy and Spencer are back yet. I don't care though, I'm not here to see them.

Knocking on her bedroom door, I brace myself for whatever shit I'll get. But there's nothing. I knock a bit harder, calling her name. *Fucking nothing!* I shake my head and open the door slowly, peeking inside. She's in bed, and either asleep or ignoring me. My eyes adjust to see her dress and shoes laying in a pile on the floor.

"Remi?" I say again, slipping off my shoes and sliding into bed behind her still clothed. As I slide my hands around her waist, I feel her body jolt but then pain! Excruciating fucking pain screams through my nose and spreads across my entire face.

"FUCKIN' HELL!" She's awake enough to headbutt me but can't hear me saying her name!

"Owen?!" She asks, twisting around in the bed quickly.

"Who else did you think it'd fuckin' be?!"

She puts the lamp on beside her bed, but I lay there gripping my nose between both hands. "I don't know! Not you that's for sure!"

"No shit!" I manage to get out before groaning again, "Jee-sus Christ!"

"I'm sorry. Are you bleeding?"

My eyes are full of tears, but I can't feel the tell-tale blood at the back of my nose. "No, I don't think so."

She's silent, letting me compose myself, slowly removing my hands and wiping the droplets from the corners of my eyes. Peeking out, she's looking at me from above. Her reddened grey eyes answer the question of her smudged mascara.

"You been cryin'?"

"No." She turns away to rub her index fingers under her eyes. "I didn't take my makeup off before I went to sleep. They're called panda eyes." She's clearly bullshitting. I might be a guy, but I know the difference. "Why are you here?"

"I realised it's pretty lonely at mine."

"Thought you liked being alone?"

Of course she'd remind me of that. I roll onto my side to look up at her. "I do." She only blinks slowly at my honesty. "But I like being with you more."

Holding my stare for a moment, she finally slides down the bed to join my head on the pillows, tucking her arm under her head. "I'm sorry, I shouldn't have said anything. I should hav—"

I kiss her strongly on the lips. Not only to shut her up but because I have to. It doesn't need tongue-dancing and saliva swapping because, as she rightly said, our relationship is more than just sex. I don't know why I ever thought I could be anywhere she wasn't. "Shush. I'm the one who needs to say sorry. I didn't take the news well and was a dickhead."

She laughs softly, "I'm not going to argue with that."

I slide my arms around her bringing her into my chest where she snuggles into me, burying her head into my shirt. Normally I'd be desperate to get inside her, but this right here is perfect; she's perfect. I shouldn't have pushed her away tonight, as being with her calms me more than I want to admit, I just don't know how I'm gonna manage without her.

"Goodnight, Odin."
"Night, Demi."

Jimmy's monumental return was only two days ago, but it's hard to believe it ever happened now. Owen said his dad has returned in every way except to sit behind the desk, which I'm taking to be a good thing considering he didn't want to come back as the boss.

Owen is back to being the man I fell for. He picked me up from the studio yesterday evening, complete with a single, deep red rose, before taking me out for an early dinner so I could eat before my performance.

I finally had the opportunity to discuss the deal Wayne Burton and his team have offered me with Dom, and while he said it sounded amazing, he's glad I have taken this time to think about it. Working with him has been so invigorating that I find myself singing new lyrics or humming new melodies all the time.

Lost in thought, I feel Owen's strong arms snake around my wet body while the last remnant of shampoo flows out of my hair. His hardness presses against my stomach, making me smile and flutter open my eyes.

"Good morning."

"What was that you were singin'?"

"Oh, just something I've been working on with Dom yesterday. Do you like it?"

"Yeah. I didn't know if it was one of those people who make those songs to dance to."

My head falls back as I laugh freely, "you sound so old right now."

"Oi!" His recoil is so dramatic that I laugh again, trying to get away from his grip, but he doesn't budge. "Aren't you bloody hilarious!"

"Have you only just realized?" I ask, still chuckling.

His hands slide down my back and squeeze my ass, making me yelp. I feel the firmness of his dick wedged between us. "No." He attacks my mouth with his tongue before I can even register it or respond. He pushes my back against the cold tiles triggering goosebumps to cover my entire body as they contradict the warmth of the water. His hand finds its way between my legs where fingers toy with my entrance, teasing and taunting before easily sliding inside me.

I gasp out in pleasure, breaking away from his lips but only for a moment. His mouth soon finds its way to my neck as his fingers pump away. "Ah...*fuck.*"

"That feel good?"

"So good baby... keep going."

He smiles against my skin before continuing down to the base of my neck, adding his thumb to stimulate my clit. The way in which he's pleasuring me brings me to my peak quickly, and I pant, waiting for the fireworks to ignite.

But the fireworks never explode because, although the fuse was lit, it's doused the second he removes his fingers. His long, nimble digits may be far from where I want them, but his hand still rests against mine. My body grinds against it, desperate to seek the high he's just held hostage.

"Only good girls get to come, *Demi*." he teases. "You gonna be cheeky to me again?"

Am I? "Yes." I adore when he does this; maybe not the lack of orgasm on my part but the tease is worth it.

He tuts in my ear. "Is that your final answer?"

"Mm-hmm... I want you to punish me, Owen." I *love* it when he punishes me.

"Good." he says with an evil twinkle in his voice. My eyes squeeze together. I expect to be flipped around or pinned by my throat, maybe even given a hard spanking across my ass, but his hand leaves and then so does his presence.

Blinking my eyes open, I look around and he's nowhere to be found. "Are you freakin' kidding me!"

I would have settled for hair pulling, bent over on the hard floor—anything he could do to me but this? No, this is just mean!

423

I shut off the water and storm into the closet where he is sliding on his pants. He zips up the fly and pops the button, completely ignoring me standing there in a puddle.

"What the fuck was that?!"

"You said you wanted to be punished." he replies, casually.

"No. I wanted to fucking come!"

He steps closer to me, using an index finger to trail down the length of my torso, following the gravitational roll of water droplets down my body. He brushes over one of my hardened nipples before continuing down my stomach to my waiting bud, circling to make me whimper. "That's too bad, *Demi.* You're gonna be horny all day, and only if I think you deserve it, will I let you come tonight." I widen my eyes, and not from the stilling of his fingers again. *He cannot be serious.* "You wanted to be punished, Rem, be careful what you wish for." I'm left stunned because this is an actual punishment. Being left sexually charged for the rest of the day—especially when I haven't been for a long time—is as far removed from what should be happening. "And don't even think of getting yourself off, 'cause I'll know."

"That's not fair."

The shade of his eyes darken tenfold and a pleased smirk tugs on his lips. "All's fair in love and war, babe."

If it's a war you want Mr Turner, then it's a war you will get!

"Then bring it on, *Odin*," I reach up on my tippy toes to peck his cheek, intentionally pressing my naked breasts against his chest. He shudders lightly which I feel under my touch. "Bring. It. On."

Thirty Five

"*ring. It. On.*"

"Oi!" My dad's voice disturbs my daydream. "Are you fuckin' listenin' to me?"

"No." *Am I fuck! I'm thinking of this morning.* If the banter and shit between us is anything to go by, she is seriously gonna play me at my own game. And honestly? I can't fucking wait.

"It's nice to see you've got your head in the game still now that I'm back." His sarcasm is nothing new—he'd just managed to keep it at bay until yesterday, when the sarcy comments returned. Today, though, he's back one hundred percent.

"The fuck is up with you?" I snap back. If he's not going to sit back in this seat, then he needs to shut up acting and behaving like he is..

He looks around at the guys sitting among us. "You lot, fuck off." Charlie, Fred, Chris, Spencer, and Jack all raise up and leave the office, just as if I had asked them; their loyalty split between the two of us. "You're getting soft."

"Am I?" *Trust me, I am nowhere near fucking soft right now.*

"Yeah. You are."

I sit back in the chair that has slowly moulded to my body over the years I've graced it, "Maybe I just run things differently to how you did."

He mirrors my movement, sitting back and pressing his index finger to his lips. "Nah, You're just like me. You punch first, ask later. Always have been." *Where's this going?* "What's goin' with you and Jack? You ain't said one word to him."

"He had a bit of a tantrum."

"He did, or you?"

"I didn't have shit, mate!" I scoff.

"I ain't your fuckin' *mate*, boy!" He spits out annoyed, glaring with the desire for an explanation.

"He was runnin' his mouth, so I leathered him. He recovered and was still chattin' shit, so I gave him a choice—walk away, no problems, or stay and change his attitude. He chose to stay, but from what I can see, he hasn't changed his attitude much."

"Walk away, no fuckin' issues!?" His screwed-up face spits out. "You'd have been happy, would ya, to get all the shit fall on your doorstep for letting him walk? Have you forgot all the bullshit I had to deal with when his old man walked away? 'Ey? He pissed off nearly every bloody firm in the whole country! I had to fight or make connections with every one of them to stop him getting shot, stabbed, or killed! Have you paid attention to anything?! No one walks away with no fuckin' issues!"

"Well, he's still here, ain't he? I don't need the fuckin' lecture."

"Then be grateful that he is."

I know I need to talk to Jack, and he has tried to talk to me, but I've brushed him off. Mainly because I'm still pissed off with Alice, and clearly they're riling one another up; they're their father's kids that's for fucking sure.

"So, what's the deal with this new restaurant thing you're doin'?" he asks flipping 180 to focus on the business side.

I rattle off the ins and outs to him, and I'm glad when he looks genuinely pleased—which is good 'cause I'm not pulling out of it now. I worked Carmen for months for the information I needed on her dad. It might not be what he would've done, but it's not his decision to make anymore.

Remi

"Thank you for coming with me." Arms linked with Roberto, we walk to a lingerie store Lucy recommended before begging me not to wear at her house. She said it's weird hearing me and Owen. And, well, I can't exactly hold back…

"That's alright! It's not my normal forte, as you know babe, but I'll happily advise you on what looks smoking and what doesn't."

"Good, because I'm gonna need you to dig deep and find your inner-straight guy for this. I need to blow his mind, Bobby!"

He cackles a long with me. "Then I'm going to have to dig fucking deep!"

The store clerk is immediately at our sides, introducing herself and informing us to ask if we need anything, before letting us casually look through the racks.

"Owen's favorite color is red so try to focus on that." I say, noticing he is looking at everything.

"Sweets, I don't think he's going to care if it's vomit color as long as it has as little material as this thing." He holds out what looks like ribbons attached to one another. My eyebrows pull together. The first thing I can think of is a rolled-up piece of meat held together with twine.

"What is that? Like, how do you even put it on?"

"Not a bloody clue but think of all the wedgies you'll get!"

"… front and back."

He puts it back and I continue to trawl through, looking for the perfect thing to make him regret starting this.

"Oooh… look at this!" He pulls out a black, translucent two-piece bra and thong, with a black satin trim. It leaves little to the imagination and would be perfect.

"It's not red."

"Clearly, but it's fuckin' hot. And—" he says, quickly before returning it to the rail and pulling two more hangers out. "—it comes with suspenders and a negligée!"

Thoughts cloud my mind, predicting what Owen would say when he sees me in it. Is this enough to make him eat his words? "It's perfect."

***

Lucy was at home when I got back, apologizing again for not being able to come with us. It felt weird showing her what I purchased, but at the same time, I wanted to show her to get her reaction. She said

Spencer would have a heart attack if she wore it, so I knew I was onto a winner.

Getting ready for my performance was more challenging than usual. Normally, I wear pants or a short dress, but with the stockings and suspenders, I had to wear a black pencil skirt that was long enough to keep them under wraps, and I settled on a black satin shirt that would coordinate with what lays beneath.

The Rose is bustling when we get there, though our usual table is not as full as I was hoping with Charlie, Owen, and Jack nowhere to be seen. He swore he would be here tonight. Getting anything out of Freddie and Chris was like getting blood from a stone; they only spilled that Owen and Jack were in his office talking when they left.

I'm midway through my penultimate song when I lock eyes with him and savor the feeling of warmth that flows from my head to my toes. His eyes roam down my body, no doubt a little confused by my attire, because it is so different from what I've worn before. I wink at him, earning a curious eyebrow raise in return.

"Okay everyone, thank you for once again coming out to see me. This is my last song for this evening, I hope you enjoy it."

I signal to Lewis to press play on the backing track and listen as Love On The Brain by Rihanna starts. It is nothing like what I usually sing and picked it solely to begin my pay back on Owen.

Every syllable, word, and letter I sing is for him, and he sits there, statue-still the entire time. Consumed but not yet knowing exactly what I'm doing. The lyrics say what I need him to hear, with one line earning a smirk when I growl out the word '*fucks*'.

When the song comes to an abrupt stop, the generous applause of the audience is drowned out by him. He isn't standing there clapping the loudest, no, he's the only one still sitting with a damnable smile on his delicious face.

I walk over to the table only for Freddie to break the silence as I stand lingering beside Lucy.

"So that last one… was a bit different weren't it?"

"Was it?" I bluff.

"Yeah!" he scoffs, but not before Lucy helps me out.

"I thought it was a perfect way to end the show."

"Thanks, babe."

An unapologetic clearing of a throat draws me to look at Owen. I purposely didn't go to him and he isn't happy about it. "What you standin' there for?"

"Am I not allowed to stand? Is that another thing I'm not allowed to do?"

No one else has a clue what I'm talking about, but from the barely-there smirk that tugs on one side of his lips, Owen knows. He doesn't answer back, and I take his silence as my cue to sit down beside Lucy. But as the conversation flows, along with the drinks, I zone out of everyone around us, innocently looking up through my lashes across the table at him. His eyes meet mine every time. I shouldn't have sat here; my body is screaming to be touched, and the material that fits around my skin is slowly getting uncomfortable with the desire I feel for him.

I stand and slowly move in front of him, cocking my head to the side. "Are you ready to go, or did you want to stay?" Thinking I have this in the bag is blown to pieces when he says he wants to stay.

"Afterall, I ain't been here long, think we should enjoy ourselves a bit longer."

"Sure." I refuse to show my disappointment, so smile politely and sit down beside him this time. He puts one arm around my shoulders and rests his other hand on my thigh. I'm trying to focus on the conversations happening around me but his hand creeps ever slowly toward the lip of my skirt, pulling it backwards. I quickly press my hand on his, stopping him.

"What's wrong?" His voice is flat, to all sense and purpose, uninterested, but his face is full of mischief.

"You may want to stop there." I nod in the direction of my leg. Curiosity gets the better of him and he pushes both of our hands up far enough to expose the lace that sits around the top of my thong along with the belt that clips onto it.

His eyes widen before he moves our hands away, holding my gaze but informing everyone else. "We're goin'."

"But I thought you just said you were stayin'?" Lucy reminds him, teasingly.

"Don't give a fuck. We're going. Now."

This time, he's telling me.

Back at his place, the fervor is gone, and he is as calm and collected as I know him to be. He takes my hand and attempts to lead me through to his bedroom, but I put the brakes on at the island. "What? Aren't you going to offer me a drink?"

"Rem..." he warns against my tease.

"Just a small glass of water." I flutter my lashes. "Please?" He scowls but appeases me, releasing my hand. "Thank you, baby. I'll go and make myself comfortable. See you in a moment."

I calmly walk the rest of the way until I'm out of his view, then speed up to run up the staircase whilst pulling my shirt free from my skirt, undoing the buttons down it, and undoing the zipper on the side of my skirt. I don't know if I'm going to be able to pull this off, but hell, am I going to try! I'm usually submissive, happy to let him do whatever he wants to me, but I'm going to have to fight that instinct. If I'm going to win, I must be strong.

I pull the black satin negligee from my bag along with some extra things I brought from the store and sit perched on the edge of the bed, ready for him to appear at the door. An eyebrow raises as he takes me in, one leg crossed over the other and my arms resting on top of them.

He steps closer, scrolling down my body as he does. "Here ya go."
I join him on both feet, taking the glass from his outstretched hand. "Thank you." I take a sip and place it on the bedside table when his hands move around my waist to pull my back to his body, but I turn swiftly and push him away. "Ah, ah, ah, ah, I didn't say you could touch me, Mr. Turner." He cocks his head at me, bemused. "You need to get naked."

"Do I now?"

"Yes, but please, take your time. I can wait."

"Really?" he asks, not buying it for a second.

"Oh, yes," I stress, "I've been waiting all day remember."

He stares me in the eye as he undresses, watching from any cracks in my presentation as he peels each layer of his attire so painfully slowly, I'm salivating by the time he's gloriously naked and standing to attention.

"This what you wanted?"

"Yes," I say before nodding in the direction of the chair behind him. "Take a seat."

He looks at it, and then at me, playing the game and going to sit in it casually. I stand at the base of the bed before him, taking the straps of my garment and prepare to undo them, "No touching until I say so, Mr. Turner."

"Yeah," he says, with a tight unimpressed smile as he shakes his head. "I don't think so."

I pause. "Then you stay there for the entire night, and I have all the fun."

"Fine." he admits, his nostrils flaring a little.

Pleased that I have him exactly where I want him, I slowly pull the gown apart, letting it slide effortlessly down my arms and pool on the floor. His jaw drops while his eyes darken, looking up and down my entire body. His dick was hard before, but damn, it bucks under the new surge of blood.

"You wear *that* and tell me I can't touch you?! Are you havin' a fuckin' laugh?"

"All's fair in love and war, *babe*..."

Thirty Six

She leaves me so hard it fucking hurts, having to look at her arse in that thong and suspenders as she crawls onto the bed, reaching under a pillow to pull out something I only half believed she owned. *How fucking wrong was I!*

"What you gonna do with that?"

Rolling on to her back she positions herself in the centre of the bed to show me right between her legs. *Is she fucking serious?!* I can't... I can't even process what she is going to do. I thought it would be fun to tease her, but as she runs the dildo across her tongue and down that delicious valley between her tits, I can barely breathe. I thought she'd play about and what she did at the bar was expected, even the sexy shit she's wearing. But this!? No way.

"I'm going to use my little friend here to entertain myself."

"What makes you think I'll let you come? Especially like this?"

She pulls her thong to the side and starts playing with her clit, showing me the glistening entrance to her pussy. *Fuck me... she's winning.*

"Because you want to be in control, *Odin*, and that is the only part I'm giving you." She continues rubbing herself whilst she turns on the pink toy and begins to run it along her nipples. "I'm going to control which spot I hit, where I touch my body, and how fast I fuck myself. Only then will I listen to your command."

I swallow. "And what if I say no?"

She moves it quickly to replace where her fingers were, moaning out from the new sensation. "Then you lose."

This is possibly the sexiest and most frustrating thing a woman has ever done to me. And I fucking love it as much as I hate it. Watching her is like taking the hit from a drug you didn't ingest. It creates all the feelings without the act. *She's my addiction.*

She runs it between her folds, using her wetness to lubricate it. I'm glued to her hand, watching it effortlessly slide inside her as she drops her head back, moaning out in pleasure. I want to move. I want to jump right onto that bed and kiss her. I want my lips on hers so bad, but I'm also transfixed by what she's doing. I want her to do this for herself and for me. *Damn, I want to see this!*

She speeds up, fondling her covered breast with her free hand as mine finds its way to begin stroking myself. I don't wanna come, not until I'm allowed inside her, but shit me, this is the best porn I've ever seen.

"That feel good?"

"Sooooo good."

Listening to the wetness inside her as she pushes it back and forth, penetrating deep, I feel the moisture coat my hand from my tip. "Is it better than me?"

"Nothing's as good as you." *Right fucking answer!* She looks back at me, her eyes hooded and sexy. "Did I say you could touch yourself?"

"Did I ask your permission?"

She shakes her head slowly, glaring at me despite the pleasure she's inflicting upon herself. "If you want to touch me at all tonight, then stop or you'll be a spectator, not a participant." Under the weight of her knowing glare, I withdraw my hand and grip tightly to the arm of the chair. "Good boy…"

Shit me.

Her hand continues slipping it in and out, making my knuckles whiten as my fingers dig in harder to the fabric. "What would you want me to do to you?"

"I'd want you to do your worst." she moans. "To show me just how naughty I am being." *Hell yeah!*

She drives herself on, making sure every inch on offer disappears inside her and hitting as deep as I do.

"Watch. Watch as you fuck yourself. Only when you're screamin' am I gonna let you come." It's torturous, but amazing.

"Ahhh-mmmm... Oh my God! Owen..."

"Harder. Imagine it's me fuckin' you."

She can't stifle the moans by biting on her lip any longer. She pants and moans loudly, and I know she's close when she pleads. "Owen..."

"What d'you want, Remi?"

Her eyes pleading with me. I want her words to beg though. "Have I been a good enough girl to come yet?"

Fucking hell! I need this shit over with. I need to be inside her right now!

"Come." The single command is all it takes to watch her unfold. She convulses, her legs stiffening as she finally gets what she's wanted all day.

When she's come down enough to look back at me, her face is smiling seductively. "Happy now?" I ask, making my way over to stand towering over her.

"For now." She slides the toy out of her, and it's laced with her milky white release.

"Suck it off."

The seductive, temptress switches to a nervous girl in a second. "What?"

"Clean that—" I nod at the dildo still in her hand, "—with your mouth." The surprise doesn't last for long as she smirks placing it into her mouth and sucking it off like it's a fucking lollipop. I swallow hard. *I really hate this sexy, beautiful, stubborn woman...*

"Mmm," she moans. "I can see why you like eating me out."

I snatch it out of her hand and throw it away. She giggles, but I grip her ankles and pull her back toward me fast. "My turn."

I kneel quickly to place my face between her thighs, soaking up the remnants of her orgasm before making my way up higher. Her consuming moans make it so hard to continue eating her out that I peel myself away and join her on the bed, lying flat beside her. "Sit on my face."

She bites on her lip, clearly excited, positioning herself to straddle my head. I grip her arse with my hands, sliding my tongue straight through the folds inside her whilst her voluptuous lips slipped over the tip of my head, finally giving me the penetration I crave. I move my hands to grip the heels of her shoes, anchoring her to me as she massages my balls with her slender fingers, while we both of us pleasure each other with our mouths. I wanna tell her I'm going to come, but she moans as my tongue pushes deep inside her, her hips rocking her against my face. She sucks, deep throating me like I make her, until I shoot my load right down her throat.

I wait a second before encouraging her to move, letting me slide out from underneath her. Turning quickly to kneel behind her, she looks back over her shoulder, fire burning in her eyes. Though I've come, I'm still hard. But thinking of her tonight, I'll be hard for a week!

I push effortlessly into her, gripping her hips tightly. "Holy shit, you're so wet!"

"Fuck me hard like you told me to, baby. Show me how to do it!"

Revelling with her body finally wrapped around mine, and with her thong still wedged in the crease of her thigh, I watch myself disappear repeatedly into her. The sight and the sensations simultaneously gives me another hit of the drug only she holds. *How am I going to survive without this every day?*

"You feel so fuckin' good." Gripping a fist full of her hair to bring her head back, I slam into her hard, pausing for a second to hold myself deep inside her. She whimpers out. "The war done?"

She stutters, "Y-Yes."

"Good." I drag my hips back and pound back into her, lifting my foot up to hit at another angle. With my hand still wrapped around her hair, each gentle tug elicits a loud sensual moan.

"Ah, just like that," she screams. "Don't stop!"

I feel her pulsating around me, pushing back to meet me. "Shit..." I hiss through my teeth. I don't want to come again yet, but when she grips me like a vice, I barely hold back from joining her.

As soon as she's done, I slide out of her, commanding her to stand up. She rises gingerly onto unsteady heels, letting me hold her like I always will. I slide my hands down to her waist, gripping hold of the tiny thong. "You ain't gonna need this anymore."

Before she can answer, in one quick pull, it's gone. I toss it to the floor and place my lips on hers, pulling her body flush with mine as I fondle to unclasp her bra. She lets me remove it before her hands trail down my back, brushing over my ass. She pulls my hips closer to her, and thanks to the heels, her pussy reaches a little higher, almost in line with my semi.

I lift her up before sitting down on the edge of the bed. Her knees cage me in place perfectly, and she reaches to grip a hold of my hair, pulling my head back to kiss me hard, rotating her hips against me. My hand travels up her chest and grips gently around her throat. I feel her swallow excitedly, whimpering my name. *She's bloody perfect, she really is.*

Breaking away, I take one of her erect nips in my mouth, licking and sucking, grazing my teeth around it. She thrusts her chest forward. I don't stop the smile on my lips as I bite down on it enough to cause her beautiful pain but not hurt her more than I want to.

"Mmm." she moans, her throat vibrating under my hold. "That feels so good."

Taking the lead, she slides down, swallowing me and making me fully erect as she slides up and down. I'm sensitive, but her elixir eases it.

"Owen..." She takes my hand away, pushing me down to lay on the bed. She's gentle, moving slowly whilst rotating her hips, and I can't peel my eyes off her, loving watching her ride me. Her hands rest just above my hips, but she hasn't sped up at all. "Enjoyin' yourself?"

"Always."

I lift my hands to caress her tits, palming and rubbing my thumb over them. She arches her back, making sure I get a proper handful of them, moaning in only the way she can. "Do you wanna come again?"

"You know I do."

She digs her nails into my chest, making me wince in pain, bouncing on top of me, like she hasn't just screamed out in pleasure three times already.

"Shit..." I pant out. "Rem, don't stop."

"That feel good baby?"

"So fuckin' good!"

"I'm gonna come! Owen... Fuck!"

I thrust my hips up from below, trying to get there to go at the same time, but she gets there first, throwing her head back as she stills on my body. I try to continue bucking my hips but her entire weight rests on them.

"Remi! Don't fuckin' stop!"

The second her eyes drop back to mine, her fucking smirk tells me everything! *She ain't letting me come!*

She jumps off me quickly, standing at the side of the bed, innocently holding her hand to her mouth, acting like she's in some straight to DVD film. "Oooopsy. Did someone not get off?"

I sit up quickly, my balls fucking throbbing ready to explode. "Remi, I swear to God, you are not fuckin' leaving me like this!"

"Hmmmm… I'm going to go and have a shower," she teases, stepping out of her shoes. But I'm frozen. Absolutely gobsmacked that she played me. Turning back away from me, she reaches down to undo the belt still around her waist, unclipping it from her stockings before letting that add to the pile. She bends down, sliding one stocking off her leg, flashing me her bare arse, looking over her shoulder, before bending down to remove the last shred of material she has on.

I stand and quickly hold onto her waist, stopping her from leaving. "You're not goin' anywhere."

She turns in my arms, bringing her hands around my neck and letting me kiss her soft and passionately. I've been rough with her enough, and she's shown she's a force to be reckoned with clearly, but I'm the lucky cunt who gets to call her mine.

"Well played, *Demi*, well played." I admit, earning a delectable chuckle from her. "You finished now?"

She takes my hand and pulls me in the direction of the bathroom. "I am, but you're not."

Thirty Seven

Waking up with my limbs contorted around his, I don't even remember falling asleep last night, only that we were awake and then we weren't. But with a night like that, how could I remember any of the specifics. Everything was incredible and we were both insatiable. Owen drives me insane in the best way, and I become someone I don't even recognize around him; nothing I do is too much, and nothing he does is too far. He is the last person I ever expected to fall for, yet the last one I ever want to.

I tried to tell him how I feel; I wanted to scream it from the rooftops when he made love to me for the last time before we collapsed with exhaustion, but I couldn't. I know what his mom said, but he's not there. I can see the conflict in his eyes. But it was enough to know that he showed me in his own way how he feels. He's letting me into his heart slowly, and I know that in time it will be right.

I break myself away from him and use the bathroom, wincing in the process, before soothing my aching body in the shower. When I go back into the bedroom, he's still asleep. I watch for a moment, loving the way the scowl he wears daily disappears, and he is just a man. No secrets, no pressures—just Owen.

I know I need to leave here soon, but I need to kiss him just once more. Leaning over him to press a kiss to his lips, I squeal as he grips his arms around me quickly, rolling me onto my back.

He holds himself over me, his hair dishevelled. "Thought you'd left without sayin' goodbye, again."

"Was last night not enough hellos and goodbyes to last you a lifetime?"

"Last night was—" he brushes the hair out of my face, tucking it behind my ear, "—
amazing."

We look into each other's eyes. Little clips of memories flash through my mind, my heart beating fast from how I feel about him.

Say it.

Don't say it.

But neither of us declare anything before I reach up to kiss him, pulling him down by his neck with my arms. I would stay in this moment for eternity, I really would, but I have my meeting with Wayne this morning. "Baby, I have to go."

He pulls back reluctantly, looking down at his chest before returning to me with the scowl back in place. "I know, I'll take ya home."

***

The nerves build on the journey until my leg is shaking on its own accord as I sit waiting to be called in by Wayne's assistant.

I've been down this road once already; I know the process, but I hope that what he's offering isn't too good to be true. I check my phone one last time, wanting to message Owen but unsure what to say. He's excited to be collecting Bradley this afternoon, and he has been nothing but positive and enthusiastic, even reassuring me as he kissed me goodbye.

"Miss. Prentice?"

I blink up, noticing the stunningly beautiful redhead looking down at me smiling patiently.

"Oh, I'm sorry." I rush to put the phone back in my purse and follow her to an office rather than a meeting room. Wayne stands the second I enter, coming to greet me with a kiss on each cheek, and just as before, encourages me to sit.

"I'm so pleased to see you again."

I smile, silently thanking the assistant who showed me into his office before sitting down in a seat opposite him, "Thank you for the time to think about things."

"Well, I think it's important. You're making a life changing decision at the end of the day." *Way to help the nerves!* "Can I ask what conclusion you have come to?"

I glance down, fiddling with zipper on my purse, before shaking the hair out of my face and looking back at him confidently. *This is it.* "I'm ready to do this."

"Great," he says enthusiastically, nodding his head. "Then you should have a look at this." He hands over a bonded booklet of papers.

"Is this it?"

"The first draft, yes."

"Thank you."

"I'll give you a few minutes to look through it. Can I get you a drink?"

After accepting a strong, black coffee, I begin reading through it. I make notes on my phone of the areas I need to check with my dad because I want to check that all is legitimate, but all of it looks to say exactly what they promised in the first meeting, as well as a lot of long, legally sounding words.

I'm almost finished scanning the last page when he re-enters with a different woman carrying a small tray with two coffee cups on saucers behind him.

She places it down in front of me, letting me thank her before disappearing back through the door.

I close the booklet and look back at him.

"So?" he asks, confidently.

"It all looks pretty accurate to what you said. I have to get my father to look at it, you know for the legal side of it."

"Of course," He takes a sip of his coffee, letting me steal the chance to have one of my own. "That is yours to take with you. Once we're all happy then we can make it official."

"How soon will you want me to come back to you?"

"As soon as possible."

It will take a couple of days due to the time changes and with us going away for the weekend, so we mutually agree that I will return on Monday morning.

"But I have to know," he adds, "what's the deal with you and the Turners?"

My smile drops a little, not expecting that question in the slightest. "What do you mean, 'deal'?"

"Well, how *close* are you?"

"I'm very close to them. Owen and I are dating, and I've been friends with Lucy for a while now. I'm living with her and her fiancé, and as you saw, I play in their bar."

He places his index finger above his lips, resting his head on his thumb as he leans against the arm of his chair. I'm not sure what he's getting at with this, and I can't tell from his expression what he's thinking. "We may have to review that situation."

My eyebrows draw together. "Review what situation exactly?"

"The relationships."

I recoil, shaking my head. "I'm sorry, I'm confused as to how my relationships affect anything? If it wasn't for them, I wouldn't even be here. You wouldn't have seen me perform."

"And I'm aware of that, but having a connection to them may not be, how can I say this, beneficial to your career." I open my mouth to argue but he talks over me. "I know what I'm talking about here, and I've seen it happen before. I only have your best interests at heart, Remi."

"And I appreciate that, but what I do behind the music is down to me. Who I'm dating does not impact my ability to sing or do an interview. I can still do that irrespective of who I am with."

"Of course, but I'm thinking of your career, and the Turners aren't exactly people you want to be around involved. Their name is associated with a lot of areas you don't want the press getting wind of."

He's treading so carefully that I'm sure he's aware of their lives and what they do but it makes no difference to me.

"What are you asking of me? Do you want me to cut them out of my life for my career?"

"I'm not saying cut them out completely." He lies because the forced smile that sweeps across his face tells me that is exactly what he means.

"It's what it sounds like!"

Called out, he leans to rest both elbows on the desk, clasping his hands in front of him. "Okay, I am," he says it bluntly, losing all the façade and subtlety that he used before. "I advise you to reconsider your relationships, particularly with him, if you want to be the biggest star you can be with the least amount of drama."

"And what if I choose not to take your advice?"

"Then we may have to rescind our offer."

I stare at him, utterly speechless. Well, now it's me who's a liar because I really want to shout as this asshole! How do I choose that? *Why* should I choose that?

"I can see you need some time to think about this." He pulls me out of my thoughts, "Think about what I've said, speak to your dad and I'll see you again on Monday."

I run my hands over the file before slowly picking it up. It holds everything I wanted inside, but my childhood dream never factored in Owen freakin' Turner, and the thought of him not being included leaves a bitter taste in my mouth.

"I'll see you Monday."

Walking out of there, I'm in a daze. I didn't expect this. Ever.

Last time I lost my chance because of a guy who couldn't commit to me, and now I could lose it because I want to commit to a guy—a guy I'm in love with.

Owen

I was clock watching all day, not only to hear back from Remi, but to leave in plenty of time to get Brad. Though the more time I stayed with them the less I wanted to. Charlie pecked my head as soon as I got in. He hasn't let it drop that I'm pushing her to take this record deal, and this time he was in ear shot of my old man, who fucking loved quizzing me about it. Shockingly, though, he commended me on encouraging her to pursue it, so now I've gotta ride the storm.

Pulling up outside Portia's, I see Brad's little face waiting at the window, waving at me before running away from it. The door flies open, and he stands there jumping on the spot as I walk down the driveway to him.

"Alright dude?" My face matches his, as he runs towards me and jumps into my arms. I swallow him up, squeezing him tightly. *God, I've missed him.*

"How ya doin'? You been good for ya mum?" I don't care if he hasn't been, but I do care that he is polite and respectful.

"You're early." *Talk of the devil.*

"Traffic weren't too bad." That and I left in plenty of time so she couldn't moan I was late. "All his stuff ready?"

"Yes." She holds the Nike duffel bag out, still standing at the door. I put Brad down, and take his little hand to get the bag from her.

"Daddy, mummy said I'm going to be a big brother."

I glance at him frowning. "What?" Looking back at her she laughs nervously and moves the bag away, revealing a little bump that definitely weren't there last time. Wonder who the poor son of a bitch is that's knocked her up?

"I'm four months so though it was time to tell him."

"Well," I say, snatching the bag from her, "good for you." I ain't being her best fucking friend 'cause she wants to be today. "We'll be back Sunday."

I turn and walk away, but she stops me, reaching out to catch my arm and saying my name. "Can I have a quick word?"

"Can it wait?"

She looks at Brad. "Not really."

Sighing, I take him to the car, get him settled in and put the bag in the boot before reluctantly heading back to stand in the doorway.

"Well?"

"I just wanted you to know that the baby's dad is movin' in this weekend. That's why we wanted you to have Brad so he wouldn't be in the way."

I glare at her. "In the way of your new life?"

"No!" She insists. "In the way of boxes and moving stuff!"

"Has he met this dude?"

"Yes. I've slowly been introducing him… but it's been sooner than I had hoped. We hadn't exactly been together long when I fell with this little one." She rubs her belly, but I roll my eyes. I can't stand being around her for any second longer than I need to but I wanna know who the fuck is moving in with my kid and the house I still pay for.

"How did Brad take it?"

"He's fine, was excited about the baby, but he seems to get on alright with Dan." When I cock my head curiously at his name, she offers the answer. "I'm seeing Danny Fitzpatrick."

I actually laugh out loud. I've known Danny since we we're at school. He wanted to get in with Jack and me, but he's not got the stomach for it, should I say. "You and Danny? Fuckin' hell. I thought you stooped low before with Scott."

"You don't need to bring all that up again Owen! It's not the same as when I was with you."

"Well, it's nice to know you only cheated on your husband!"

"I can't change it, Owen." *No, but you didn't stop it.* She looks down to the floor with a hint of shame. I'm done with dragging up the past, especially now my dad's out of the nick.

"Look, as long as Brad's happy, I can't do shit about it. He comes first to me, end of." She nods in agreement and that's my chance to get away from her. I start to walk out of the door when she says my name once more. That doesn't stop me; the next part certainly does.

"I'll sign the papers."

Slowly turning around, I point at her. "Don't fuckin' play with me!"

"I'm not!" she claims sincerely, "I'm not... I will. But you can't fight for custody."

I knew there would be a clause.

"Not a chance. You've stopped me from seeing him for two thirds of his life! You don't get to ask me to do shit!" I twist on the gravel and take another step away from her.

"You know why I did it!"

"Oh really?!" I call back uninterested.

"Yes! You know I still loved you, and I hoped we could one day go back to how we were. How happy we were when Brad first came along." She calls out to me, "I didn't blame you for me falling down the stairs. It was Jack who twisted all of that, but I just thought because you never did anything to me meant you must still love me too."

That sneaky little cunt! He seriously hates me don't he!

I march back up to her, getting right in her face without putting even a strand of bleach blonde hair out of place. She needs to hear this once and for all, the fucking psycho!

"If you weren't his mother, and now with a kid, I'd snap your fuckin' neck, do you hear me? I hate you." I snarl, "I would sit and let your body rot in a box quite happily for what you did to me and my old man. I never loved you. I *could* never love you. You're only breathing because I love my kid; don't get it confused, sweetheart." Tears fill her eyes, but I couldn't give a fuck. I mean every single word, and I would give anything to rip her throat out right now. "Sign the papers, Portia, and let me get on with my life, but you either give me as much access as I want, or I'll see you in court."

I turn away from her, quickly replacing my scowl with a smile to make sure Brad isn't concerned. He jumps with excitement as I get in my seat, looking back at him in the rearview mirror.

"Is mummy okay?"

"Yes, mate, she just told me Danny's movin' in. But guess what? That means we get to see each other more!"

Thirty Eight

Getting into the mindset to perform is hard. I'm here and getting my make up ready, though my head is everywhere but where it should be. I used the copier in Lucy's office to send it to my dad. Though as each page went through, it felt tainted.

I had it in the bag, I knew what I wanted and was ready to take that chance, but this ultimatum? This is not what I envisaged. It isn't what *we* planned. And it's not just my relationship with Owen, it's with Lucy, Spencer, Freddie, all of them.

I don't want to do this.

Tears prick my eyes, stopping me for a moment while the emotion subsides, but the last thing I need happens when Lucy gently taps on the door before entering with a big smile on her perfectly made-up face.

"Hey, babe, you alright?"

I put the brush down and look back at her in the reflection forcing a natural smile, "Yeah, are you?"

"Yeah, how'd it go?"

I nod, trying to figure out what to say. "Yeah… he gave me the contract and from what I could see, it's everything they discussed with me and my dad. I sent it over to him, so I have to see what he says. I'm going back on Monday to finalize things."

She squeaks with excitement, and I imitate her but all the while feeling the complete opposite.

"Babe, I'm so happy for you! What did Owen say?"

"I spoke to him quickly, but he had Bradley with him, so I couldn't talk too much. We'll see one another tomorrow though. We're going to the beach!"

"Well, I'm sure he'll be happy for you." I laugh nervously, looking down to pick at my nails, which blots her enthusiasm quickly. "Are you sure you're okay?"

"Mm-hmm. Just getting my head around how much my life is going to change."

"Yeah. Make the most of the anonymity while you've got it, babe!" she says chuckling and I follow suit. "Right, well I'd better let you get on."

"Thanks, Lucy," I say solemnly, turning back to the mirror.

This is the toughest decision I have ever been faced with, and I have to face it alone.

**

Being up on stage, losing myself in the music made me realize singing is such a massive part of my life. If I choose to keep them in my life, could I be content with this? Performing a few nights a week? Potentially letting go of my dream for my heart? Would I end up resenting Owen? And what if we don't last? I will have nothing all over again.

Lucy caught me staring off into space and didn't give me a chance to argue before insisting that we go home. I get into the back, and instead of sitting beside Spencer, she opens the opposite door and gets in the back with me.

She lets us drive a few minutes in silence before she turns in her seat to face me. "Right, you gonna tell me what is goin' on? Because you don't look like someone who has been given everything you ever wanted."

I bite the inside of my lip, letting out a deep breath as lights and people blur beside the car until we stop for a red light. "Wayne wants me to break up with Owen."

Her eyes widen. "What?! Why?!"

"Because he thinks it won't be good for my career."

"How!?" she asks, forcing me to look at her. "Okay, fine. That's fair, but how does he know about it?"

"How the hell would I know! He didn't specify any thing, but he said your family name is connected to things I may not want to be. What if I didn't know, Luce, what would I have said?"

She shrugs, "I don't know. I guess we'd have had to tell you then." *How noble of them!* "So, are you going to do it?" I can't look up at her because I still don't know. "Remi? Are you?"

"I don't want to." I admit, returning to watch the lights rush past the window.

"But you're thinkin' about it?" She's irritated, which I expected, and is why I thought I wouldn't be able to discuss this with her. But she's my friend, and between her and my family, she's the only one I'm able to.

"I came here for a chance, Luce! One you offered to me. Do you think I wouldn't consider it? I've been with Owen like a month, and it is wonderful, but I've wanted this my entire life!"

"Then why are you even considerin' it?" She spits out with a tone I haven't heard directed at me before. "It sounds like you've made your mind up."

My words come out weak, but I know this is the only answer I can give. "Because I have feelings for him."

I don't want to let anyone down, but I have to speak my truth. The density of her gaze weighs heavy, until she finally turns away. "I dunno what you want me to say."

I don't either, but I do have one thing to ask. "What would you do?"

"I don't know Rem, but I know nothin' would come above Spencer."

***

After a night of little sleep, I throw my bag together in time for Owen and Bradley to arrive. I have no idea where we're going, only that we're going to the beach.

Now, it is not hot, not even close, and I am used to going to the beach in my bikini, but shorts and t-shirt with a sweatshirt will do.

Grateful to have missed Lucy this morning after our tense conversation, the second I see Owen step out of his car with a larger than normal smile on his handsome face, I know exactly what she meant. A month or a year, it doesn't matter because I know what I feel for him is like nothing else; only that it's the love I always hoped to find.

Bradley giggles excitedly as he runs into my legs. His arms clinging to my hips is the best feeling, and I instantly drop to my knees to hug him properly, noticing his jumper for the first time. "Hey Superman. How are you?!

"I'm going to be a big brother!" Bradley blurts out enthusiastically. The shock must be evident on both of my face as Owen comes closers to explain.

"Yep. That's one of the things I found out yesterday, and part of what I needed to tell you. And she's finally agreed to the divorce."

I blink at him in shock. "Really?!" He nods, but let's me acknowledge Bradley. "That's pretty cool! I think you're going to be the best big brother in the whole world."

Owen takes my bag to put in the trunk, and as soon as the door is closed, he pulls me into an embrace. I melt instantly, gripping the back of his casual jacket like I haven't held him for a month, not a day. Tears sting my eyes as I listen to his heartbeat, and in that second, I know without a doubt that whatever the repercussions, I can't let him go.

When we break apart, he locks eyes with me, frowning a little as he asks. "You okay?"

"Mm-hmm," I nod, "I am now."

His face doesn't change but he leans in to give me a quick kiss.

"Are you daddy's girlfriend?" We smile down at Brad as he looks up at us quizzically.

"Would you like Remi to be my girlfriend?"

"Yes." He answers seriously.

"Then I'm your daddy's girlfriend."

His smile widens to show his tiny little teeth. "Are you having a baby like mummy?"

I laugh nervously, looking at Owen curiously.

"No, dude," Owen answers, ruffling Bradleys long hair. "That's just your mum. You ready?"

We drive for over an hour and a half with Bradley quizzing Owen repeatedly about where we're headed, and his amusement is contagious. I wonder if this is the first time he has taken Bradley away?

"Is that the sea?!" Bradley squeals, hands splayed on the window as we drive alongside the water. "Are we going to the beach?"

"No." Owen teases. "Did you want to go to the beach?"

"Yes!"

Owen's park up at a lot close to the beach. Carrying a blanket under one arm and a bag over his shoulder, our hands link together as we stroll behind a very excited Bradley.

Owen's eyes watch his son intently as he skips and runs around, picking up shells and stones, making sure he never loses sight of him—not even for a second. The love he has for his child permeates the energy between us, and my heart beats harder for him. I had him all wrong when I came here. He's still an asshole; he does bad things, but with me and his son, he's the best version of himself, and I'm grateful I get to see it.

"He's having the best time, isn't he?" I say, smiling softly as we both watch Bradley making sandcastles.

"Yeah. You can never get bored at the beach."

I chuckle. "No, I guess not." I allow the ambience to filter between us before I muster the chance to talk again. "Owen, I know it's not ideal right now, but I really need to speak to you about something that Wayne mentioned yesterday."

His head turns to me quickly. "What is it?"

"He sai—"

"Daddy! Can we get an ice cream?" Bradley's innocent little voice stops me, and Owen looks back and forth between us unsure of who to listen to.

"It's okay," I insist, "we can talk later."

"You sure?" He asks, unconvinced.

"Of course. And hell, someone just suggested getting some ice cream, that definitely can't wait."

The rest of our day is filled with more sandcastle making after we ate the biggest ice creams Bradley could find and paddling in the sea—which is pretty disgusting—with fish and chips for lunch before brushing off the sand and taking a walk to the fairground. Bradley grabs Owen's hand and pulls him towards one of the rides he wants to go on, and I stand, watching them with glee as Owen laughs like I've never seen him laugh. He dreamed of taking his son to Disneyland; well, today is as close to that as he is going to get, and I take photos on my phone so he can have more than just the memories of this time. It doesn't matter that I couldn't tell Owen what Wayne said to me, because I know I've made the right decision for me—regardless of the consequences. I will never not pick Owen, and I wouldn't want to be anywhere else in the world right now.

***

Unsurprisingly, when we get back to Owen's, Bradley is exhausted even though he had a little sleep in the car on the way back. He orders us takeout, and we cuddle up on the sofa watching a Disney movie until a big yawn from a restless little body calls time on the night, with Owen telling Bradley to say goodnight.

"Let me put him to bed, then we can chill together."

I offer a content smile. "Okay. I need to call my dad anyway."

As they disappear out of view through the kitchen door, I dial my dad's number, waiting for him to answer.

"I was just about to call you, are you having a good time?"

"Dad, we've had the best day. We went to the beach, and to the casino things they have here, we ate fish and chips on the sand and then went to the fairground. Bradley has just gone to bed because he is so exhausted."

"That sounds amazing."

"It really was." I smile softly, moving onto why I called. "Did you look through the contract?"

"Yeah. It all looks above board. It's the same usual jargon as I would expect, and it doesn't appear that they're trying to screw you over. You will own the rights to the songs you write regardless of whether you record them or not, and you will get a percentage of the sales of the ones you release. If you sell any songs, then the pay-out for that is pretty good, too."

I nod to myself, absorbing it all. "Okay."

"You don't sound very excited."

"I am…" I lie. *I need to tell him.* "But I don't know if it's going to work out."

"Why?" He's confused, and I don't blame him.

I release a lung emptying sigh, resting my head in my hand, "He wants me to break up with Owen."

"What?" he says back shocked. "Why?!"

I can't tell him the truth, but I can be honest to a degree. "Being in a relationship won't be ideal right now. He doesn't think it will be good for my *image*."

"That's horseshit, and you know it." I murmur in agreement as he continues. "Remi, I know this is all you've dreamed about, but this is one offer. If you want to be with Owen, then be with him. You'll get spotted again."

"I know what I want, dad. I guess we'll just have to see what he does with the information. If it's over before it even started, then so be it. It was never meant to happen in the first place."

"Exactly. And if I'm being honest, I didn't like the guy when I met him, but I didn't want to sway your decision."

I chuckle in surprise, hearing him laughing to himself. "I knew you didn't like him!"

"When do you need to tell Wayne your decision?"

"Monday. He won't let me leave it any longer."

"Okay baby girl, I'll let you enjoy the rest of your time together. Say hi to Owen for me."

"I will. Love you."

"Love you too. Bye."

I feel better after speaking with him. He validated my feelings and reassured me that if they rescind the offer, then it was never meant to happen because I refuse to let Owen go. Time slowly ticks by with no reappearance from Owen. Maybe Bradley needs more time to settle than I thought? I scroll through my phone before my impatience gets the better of me. I walk into Bradley's little room and see the two of them curled up in his bed, fast asleep.

Owen's arms wrap around Bradley's waist as he spoons him from behind. I know they always share Owen's bed when he stays, I bet he couldn't get to sleep without his dad with him. I creep closer to give them both a kiss goodnight.

This is enough for me. Anything else is a bonus.

Thirty Nine

I slowly stir awake, discovering I'm still alone in bed. Checking the time, it's later than I was expecting. Opening the door, I can hear the TV singing some children's songs. *Why did he let me sleep in?*

I use the bathroom, put on my robe, and make my way down to the kitchen. Bradley is playing with some miniature cars and action figures while Owen stands by the island and types away on his phone.

"Good morning!"

Bradley smiles and says it back before returning to his imaginary world, but Owen only manages to glance up from the screen for a second with a tight smile. I move to where he stands, wrapping an arm around his waist and placing my other hand on his arm. But he doesn't stop, doesn't look, and doesn't let me kiss anything other than the arm I'm holding.

"Are you okay?" I ask innocently.

"Yeah, just some shit to sort out as always." he says with a hint of irritation followed by a big sigh.

"Can you tell me about it?"

"Nope."

My arms slowly slide away as he snaps back the single word. Whatever it is can't be good. "Okay. What time are we taking Bradley back?"

He finally looks away from the phone to me, but the warmth in them is missing. He's tired, and the small lines creasing between his eyebrows tell me that, in time, he will have more similarities to his dad. "I'm taking him back in a bit." *I'm?* "I'll have time to take you home, don't worry."

"Oh, sure. I'll go and get dressed then…"

When I'm ready, coming back to them in the kitchen, Owen is almost his usual self, and when we get into the car, he holds my hand like usual, even though his mind is still busy and distant.

"Sorry I have to take you back first. I need to get to work and it works out better 'cause he's closer…"

"It's fine, you don't have to explain, I understand." I try to be upbeat, hoping that it will ease whatever stress he's under. "Can I see you tonight? I still need to talk to you; before tomorrow."

He shifts in his seat, confirming that he will with a quick, "yep."

The rest of the journey is silent except for the radio, and when we pull up outside Lucy's, Owen lets Bradley free from his seat so I can give him a big hug goodbye as he retrieves my bag.

"I'll see you soon, okay?" I say, stroking his fair hair as his hands grip tightly around my neck.

"Yeah. Daddy said he is going to see me more, which means I can see you more."

I smile at Owen, who doesn't reciprocate. Has he told Bradley that because he's trying to make it easier on him? Or is he hopeful that will happen now Portia's agreed to sign the divorce papers? It's hard to tell, but I'm praying it's the latter.

"Alright, dude, go and get back in the car. I'll be there in a minute."

Obeying his dad's request, Bradley lets me go so I can gently place his feet on the floor, watching him climb back into the car before I walk to the door with Owen fast behind me. He drops the bag in the open doorway, letting me have a moment alone with him at last.

"Babe…" I take his hand, pulling us closer together so I can put my arms around his neck. He automatically places his hands on the base of my back, but not quite on my ass. "I know you can't tell me, but I'm here, okay. You don't have to go through everything on your own."

He releases a sharp single breath. "I wish that were true."

"Can your dad not help?"

"No," he says, shaking his head. "He's helped already. The rest is up to me now."

"Oh," I offer a sympathetic smile, "I'm sorry."

He holds my gaze for the longest he has all morning. "It's okay."

I run a hand down the side of his face, watching his eyes slowly close from the tenderness. *I love you.* I keep the words from escaping but reach up to kiss him.

His arms hold me tightly. He can't tell me what's wrong, but he can show me through our connection that this is what he needs. The way he kisses me deeply and hungrily leaves me breathless and yearning for more when he pulls away.

His arms fall away from my body, and my lips, still tingling from his touch, manage to muster, "I'll see you tonight."

***

Flexing my fingers, I play a soft unplanned melody on the piano keys to get myself ready. Ready for what? I have no idea. Dom is busy this afternoon, which is fine, because. I don't know if anything I write today will be worth the time it'll take, but I had to get out of the house.

Lucy is doing wedding things with her mom, and Owen will be doing what he does all day, so I'm in the only place I want to be.

The hours pass in a blur, and I check the time to see that it's late and I still haven't eaten. I pass a sandwich bar on the way to the bus stop and slowly eat it while I wait for the bus to arrive. It's dark when I get home. Owen's car is ready and waiting, but the stillness tells me he isn't inside. Using my key, I find him waiting in the kitchen. His arm rests on the table top impatiently; his energy is worse than it was this morning.

"Hey…" I muster cautiously.

"Where ya been?"

His attitude is like a slap in the face. I glance around, checking that it is indeed me he's talking to before answering. "At the studio. Then I got some food, why?"

"You said to get you and you weren't here."

"I know but we never settled on a time. Why didn't you call me? You could have picked me up from there."

His eyes finally lift from watching his finger running along the ledge of the wood. "Do you think I've got fuckin' time to check where you are? Drive all around the place lookin' for you?"

My brows knit together as I recoil back. "I wasn't asking you to! Why? Is it only when your secret is revealed that I'm worth it? And not because you're in a relationship with me?!" I cock an eyebrow, crossing my arms, but he doesn't respond. He doesn't say anything, and I'm left waiting, watching his jaw rock from side to side before he says, "this ain't gonna work."

My heartrate spikes. Shaking my head rapidly, I take a seat beside him.

"What's not going to work?" I try to take the hand resting there but he snatches it away.

"Us." He stands and begins to move back to the front door, leaving me stunned and still staring at the place he left.

When were we not working? It didn't feel like we weren't working yesterday or this morning when he kissed me goodbye. My heart doesn't feel like this isn't working.

I catch him as he leaves through the door. "Hey! Don't walk away from me! You can't just say that and then leave!"

"I do whatever the fuck I want," he calls back, taking step after step toward his car.

I run to catch up to him, pushing him to stop with my hands. "No! You're not doing this!" I fight the tightness in my throat and ignore the stinging in my eyes. "Don't run away like you always do!"

"I ain't doin' anythin' you weren't about to do anyway."

"What?!" I say, trying to figure out what he means.

"I heard ya. Last night, on the phone with your dad, so don't stand there and lie to me. I've had enough fuckin' women lie to me," he bites back, pushing my arms away.

"I'm not lying!" As he steps aside, I position myself in the way once more. "That's what I was going to talk to you about!"

His face twists into someone I don't recognize, cutting me up instantly. "I tell ya what, don't waste ya breath. You don't need to worry about bein' in a relationship no longer."

I feel like I've been punched in the gut. This is not the Owen I know. This is Owen '*King of the fucking Assholes*' and the reality is the biggest slap in the face causing the tears to blur my vision. "You're seriously breaking up with me? Just like that? You're not going to let me explain?"

"You and me were never gonna work. It was a fuckin' fantasy, so take the deal," he spits out, making sure to get right in my face, "and fuck off."

"Owen..." I plead, feeling the tears fall onto my skin. "Don't do this. You've got it wrong!" My words are pointless and all he does is walk away like I mean nothing. "I don't want the damn deal, I want you. I *choose* you!"

He doesn't offer me even one look before he gets into the car, leaving me standing under the light of the porch, my tears flowing from my eyes in utter dismay.

He got it wrong. Why won't he let me explain? The lights come on as the engine starts up, and I don't even register it, running up to the passenger side and banging on the glass. "Listen to me! Owen, please fucking listen to me!" The passenger window drops down an inch though he simply stares ahead. "Please don't do this..." I sob, "I love you."

He blinks to look me dead in the eye, holding no life in them but shining bright enough so there is no doubt in my mind that the man I love is gone. "Then it's a shame I don't love you, ain't it."

***

I don't know how long I've been sitting here since he drove away leaving me standing there before I fell to the ground. My tears have dried, and I don't register how cold the night is until I make my way into the house and the shaking of my entire body begins.

It's over.

He's gone.

Like a zombie, I walk up the staircase and into my room, gathering the fluffiest blanket and wrapping it around myself. But the comfort and warmth I need never comes.

How could he just do that? Like we were nothing? Like I was nothing?

I pull out my phone and click on FaceTime, dialling and not caring what the time is back home. I need my mom.

Seeing her face appear in an instance forces another wave of emotion to surface. I cover my face with my hands, still wrapped up in the blanket as the tidal wave escapes.

"Remi, what's wrong?" Her voice full of concern makes the tears flow faster.

"Owen and I broke up," I sob, feeling like a fool for ever letting him in. I should have stayed away, ignored the pull towards him, and heeded his warning that he would hurt me, because he has—more than I thought possible.

"Oh sweetheart, what happened?"

I tell her as much as I can, wiping the tears away as I do. The pain in my chest is like nothing I've felt before. "Mom, I love him so much. It hurts so bad." I drop the phone into the bed and sob into my hands. I want her here; I need her here. *I wish I had never left her.*

My mom's voice is laced with sympathy and thick with emotion. "I knew you did. I'm so sorry, I wish I was there with you."

"I want a hug from you so badly."

"I know, sweetheart, and I want to be there with you too. Remember what I've always told you? You are a strong, beautiful woman. It's not your fault. If he didn't let you explain, then that's on him. He's the one who will regret this, because there is no way he couldn't know you and not fall in love with you."

Hearing her say that twists the knife he stabbed in my chest because I wish he did, more than anything but there is no way he could look at me or say those words if he loved me too.

"I shouldn't have come here."

"You're hurting right now, but I know you don't mean that. You got everything you went there for. And I can't wait to see my daughter selling out stadiums and being played on the radio, because that is your dream, Remi. And you did it."

Drying each tear feels like sandpaper across my skin, but I sob from the realization that I did. Irrespective of what he can do or say to me, he can't take away what I worked so hard to achieve.

"As long as you're there beside me, I can do it, mom."

"Good, because that's exactly where I'll be."

Forty

I never thought I would be sitting here as confident as I am. I have barely slept, and Max Factor is my best friend today, but I spoke to Lucy this morning and she helped me to get ready. Though she is furious with Owen, she supports my decision to be here, and swore to me that she would do as I said and not get involved with Owen and I. The last thing I want to do is get in the middle of their relationship. They're family and that is important.

"Remi, glad to see you." Wayne gestures for me to take a seat, and I choose the one I sat in last time with my shoulders back and my head held high.

Thanking Wayne, I'm offered the usual beverage, but I decline, wanting nothing more than to get this done. "Did you get to speak with your dad?"

"I did. He agreed with me that it was just as you promised."

He smirks, "I don't make empty promises."

I sit up straighter in the chair, looking him in the eye. "So, I'm in." Just as I expected, he leans forward in the chair, smiling and satisfied. "But I'd like to counteroffer."

"Okay." He twists his head a little. "What would you like to put forward?"

"I want the best deal you can give me. Three albums minimum. I want the chance to have World tours, if I make it. I had that offered to me last time."

He raises an eyebrow at me, clearly surprised by my shift. "Did you now?"

"Yes." I state confidently.

"Well, I think we can certainly take it into consideration, if the opportunity is there."

"I also want to record back home—in America. I already have a song writer that I worked with before, he was the one who helped co-write the ones you've heard from me. I would like you to consider bringing him on board."

"Again, we can look in to this further. But I have to ask, about the situation we discussed last time?"

My confidence takes a hit when I'm forced to think of the man who broke my heart only a handful of hours ago. "Owen Turner is no longer an issue, but Lucy is not up for discussion. She stays in my life, or I leave here right now and you miss out on your next platinum selling artist."

His barely-there smirk gives me the strength to hold my back straighter. I know the true reason why I crossed paths with Lucy, and it was not to find the love of my life. It was for this moment, this opportunity— my opportunity.

"All right," he says, standing and reaching over his white desk with an outstretched hand. "Then Remi, I guess all that's left to say is welcome to WB Records."

To be
continued

Cutting Ties concludes in

Part Two ~ Family Ties

Coming soon

CUTTING TIES

Special Thanks

First and foremost, to my husband and children, who for the last couple of years have had to put up with me being consumed with writing. Thank you for your patience and unrelenting support. I love you.

To my family and friends who, at times, have felt like I disappeared off the face of the planet, thank you for your understanding when I finally told you what I was up to.

To my beloved Nan. Though you never lived to see me create these, my name is in dedication to you because you were my biggest cheerleader, and I was always your Princess. I miss you.

To the Chapters readers, without you, I wouldn't have written more than a handful of chapters on my first project. Though I have a love/hate relationship the app, I appreciate you all more than I can ever express. You will never know your worth to us all.

To my new friends, especially Kayla, Danielle, Becky, Alex, Kerri, and Kirsty. Creating friendships with fellow writers is something I never expected when I began, but it has been incredible. Thank you for letting me pick your brains, answering my endless questions, and supporting me along my journey.

And finally, to Rian aka *Rianne Boden Kemp* aka the ying to my yang! Not only did you achieve the impossible of making me cry when reading, but you have become much more than an 'author friend'. Whether this would be here now without your support, we will never know, but I can't thank you enough for your unwavering friendship—including the virtual slaps when I've needed them.

Annie Jo Hawner

Follow me

Annie Jo Hawner

on Facebook, Instagram, and TikTok

Contact me at

anniejo.author@yahoo.com

Annie Jo Hawner

Printed in Great Britain
by Amazon

23040717R00280